PRA

Chasing Justice

"With *Chasing Justice*, accomplished historical novelist G.J. Berger makes an impressive debut in the conspiracy thriller genre. In a league with the best of Grisham and Baldacci."

—Dan Pollock,
author of *Lair of the Fox* and *Duel of Assassins*

"A brilliant legal thriller, well-crafted characters, and the abuse of governmental power results in a riveting, tension-filled tale. *Chasing Justice* is a must-read. Expect a rollercoaster ride as decency and goodness struggle to triumph over morally corrupt brokers of evil."

—Laura Taylor,
6-Time Romantic Times Award Winner

"G.J. makes his characters real people you will cheer on as they fight to make good come out of a nasty criminal conspiracy with national implications."

—p.d.r. lindsay,
author of *Tizzie, Bittersweet, Jacob's Justice*

OTHER BOOKS BY

G.J. Berger

Four Nails—
History's Greatest Elephant and
His Extraordinary Trainer

South of Burnt Rocks—
West of The Moon

PRAISE FOR

Four Nails

"[R]ichly imagined . . . much to savor here."

—Publishers Weekly 2/13/2019

"*Four Nails* is a satisfying historical . . . a big book packed with history and adventure."

—One of four novels recommended in "Pack-Your-Suitcase Reads," Huffington Post, April 2016

"Berger's epic historical fiction . . . A highly entertaining, sophisticated look . . . through the eyes of an unlikely hero."

—Kirkus Reviews

"The result is a fast-paced and richly entertaining . . . The fact that the author not only manages to work in a love story . . . but also makes it feel natural rather than forced is just an added bonus. Recommended."

—Historical Novel Society Review, August 1, 2016.

PRAISE FOR

South of Burnt Rocks

"[W]ell researched and engrossing novel . . . considerably enlivened by Berger's outstanding talent for stirring set pieces and gripping action sequences."

—Historical Novel Society Review, Aug. 1, 2015

"In Berger's captivating debut historical fiction, a young Iberian-Celtic she-warrior makes a stand against the invading Roman army . . . A wonderfully crafted balance of Roman-era drama and the fierceness of battle."

—Kirkus Reviews

CHASING JUSTICE

A LEGAL THRILLER

by

G.J. BERGER

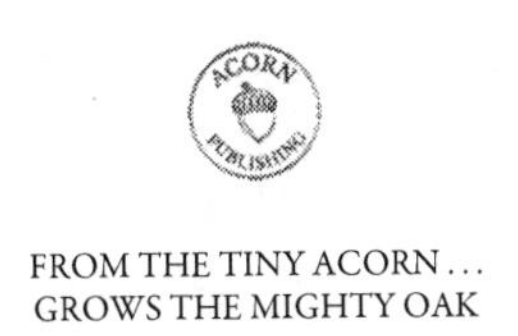

FROM THE TINY ACORN . . .
GROWS THE MIGHTY OAK

www.AcornPublishingLLC.com

For information, address:
Acorn Publishing, LLC
3943 Irvine Blvd. Ste. 218
Irvine, CA 92602

Chasing Justice

Edited by Laura Taylor
Cover design by Damonza
Interior design and formatting by Debra Cranfield Kennedy

Printed in the United States of America

ISBN-13: 979-8-88528-025-9 (hardcover)
ISBN-13: 979-8-88528-024-2 (paperback)
LCCN #: 2022912095

To Michael Cowett,

A lawyer's lawyer and a great friend.

"[I]T'S AN UNJUST WORLD,
AND VIRTUE IS TRIUMPHANT
ONLY IN THEATRICAL PERFORMANCES."

—W. S. Gilbert, *The Mikado*

Chapter One

Angela 1986

My roommate mumbled, "Can't. You go. Must sleep." So, before daylight I made one of those no-big-deal-at-the-time decisions. I ran alone in the backcountry.

At an unpainted wooden three-mile sign, a thin trail of dirt and pine needles veered off the fire road and rose around a forest bend. The familiar sounds of leaves shushing, the fast tap-tap of a woodpecker and other birds welcomed in the day. I looked around once, twice, and took the narrower path up the mountain.

The cool night air still dozing in the lodgepole pines gave way to a meadow flanked by gray rocks under a fast-rising sun. Out in the open where the path leveled, I raced wind gusts and then looped up to a remote chair lift base and back down to Aspen. Nine miles and all of it above eight thousand feet, nothing else felt this good and cleared my mind this well.

In the village on the nearly empty sidewalk, I eased into a walk and let the sun warm me.

"Hello, young lady." I must have jerked a bit, hadn't noticed him until he spoke. "Mercy, I did not mean to startle you."

The stranger sat upright on a bench in the shade behind a low wrought-iron fence in front of Aspen's courthouse, which was closed on this Sunday. Dressed in a gray suit with a black tie, maybe he had once been a lawyer and now, in the fog of his late years, couldn't stay away. That possibility tugged at me for an instant until I noticed his deep-set eyes. The power in those eyes made me want to look away, to leave, but held me too. His hair, neatly trimmed and parted on the left side, was full and white, and the ends of his white mustache curved up into handlebars. His voice was level and younger than that white hair, than the rest of him.

I said, "That's okay. I just didn't expect anyone here, not today, this early."

He turned and pointed over his shoulder at the tall statue of chrome above the main entrance of the courthouse building. "Do you know her?"

"Yes. That's Lady Justice." Some afternoons before my shift at Elk Burgers, I had passed under her on my way to the largest courtroom and the quiet tension of a murder trial, a trial still going.

"Do you see what is wrong with her?"

I searched fast for any flaw. Under her robe, she had long lines with small firm breasts, but strong, athletic enough to fight any man. The raised left arm held scales to compare the weight of the evidence—guilty and not—in each opposing pan. The right hand clasped the hilt of a long sword out of its scabbard. As soon as guilt had been proven, justice must be swift. I knew that much about the statue's message. "Nothing wrong with her. She looks great."

"Well, where's the blindfold?"

The old man was right. This Lady Justice looked straight ahead out of eyes wide open. No blindfold cord tied down her thick curly hair.

"A master sculptor in Germany fashioned this one and a twin statue at a courthouse down south. By the time someone over here noticed, it was too late to make corrections." He paused, then said, "Lady Justice ought to peek at the accused and the accuser, and sometimes ought to decide before that arduous ritual of weighing evidence, don't you think?"

Nothing had prepared me for this, not for him or his questions. I pulled something out of some college course a while back. "Juries get it right most times . . . don't they?"

"Ah, perhaps. But only if all the evidence makes its way onto those scales, only if the blindfold comes off."

I chuckled at my next thought. "Juries don't have blindfolds. They do see everything."

"That's an interesting observation. Well, I must be going now." He extended his hands, palms up, as if saying with those hands, whatever will be will be. "So long, until we meet again, talk again." His eyes clicked off, lost their power to hold me.

I didn't stay one second longer, didn't look back. His strangeness got to me, so out of place in this town of hard young bodies, tourists, and residents with their massive second or third homes strewn over the hillsides.

EARLY ON MONDAY, THE BENCH WAS GONE with no marks from its legs on the evenly mown grass. Had yesterday's run jumbled my brain? Had someone slipped something into my water bottle? *Lady Justice stands there all right, no blindfold. I didn't make that up. Or did I?* Her face of chrome and the big sword brought up paintings of a warrior readying for hand-to-hand combat. *That's me if I curled my hair and owned a long sword.* I laughed out loud. *Don't think so, not where I'm heading—not as a One L at Stanford.*

Late that Thursday, the jury in the murder trial returned a not-guilty verdict for the beer-fueled bar fight ending with one dead. The verdict jolted me. The defendant had bashed the now dead man with a bar stool when the victim was on his way down. Maybe the jurors didn't care as much as I did, maybe some key evidence didn't get onto the scales.

Over the rest of that summer, I saw no more signs of the old man or his bench. Some late afternoons when the sky grayed up and a chill wind blew from the north, his final words crept in, *until we meet again, talk again.* Somehow, I knew we would meet again, talk again. And that chilled me even more.

Chapter Two

Angela, August 2010

In the big courtroom across the back hall from my chambers, more than fifty lawyers stirred like stockyard cattle. They checked the wall clock, their watches and smartphones. A few quietly asked the bailiff if the judge was here, when she might appear.

I was their judge. A long black robe gave me the power to settle them, listen to their earnest comments and probe a bit. Then I'd rule and send them off happy or dreading that next call with their clients—but not without Mora. Only she, my court reporter, could put on-the-record the words uttered by anyone. Mora had phoned and said she'd be ten minutes late. That was forty minutes ago.

High time to go out there and say something. I slipped into my robe, zipped it nearly all the way up, and headed out.

Mora opened the hallway door an instant before me and scurried over to her little desk in her little office just off our shared waiting area. While talking fast, she shed her purse, iPhone with its cord and ear piece, a paperback novel and water bottle. "Sorry, Judge. Trolley troubles, on Friday morning again. On top of that, cops are keeping everyone away from the criminal courts and my shortcut. Had to go all the way around."

"Good morning. It's all right. We'll manage."

"Oh, thanks, Judge. Thanks for understanding." Mora grabbed her transcription machine and looked at me, the tilt of her head signaling, *I'm ready, let's go.*

I followed five beats behind and then waited in the open doorway at the back of my courtroom. My bailiff's strong low voice rang out, "All rise. In the presence of the flags of the United States of America and the State of California, Department 63 of the San Diego Superior Court, the Honorable Judge Angela B. Cornwell presiding, is now in session. Please be seated and come to order."

After six years, that opening call and all that came with it still got to me—everyone standing up at once, the sounds of clothes shifting, the spring-loaded seats flipping up, the quieting while my bailiff spoke, and the many faces looking hard at me. For each ruling in every case I tried to get it right, to be the *Honorable Judge*, to show even the whining, broken, substance-abusing lawyers some respect.

I stepped in fast, up the three steps and into my chair on the raised platform. "Good morning."

A chorus of lusty, "Good morning, Your Honor," answered, as if each lawyer wanted to be sure I picked out that one voice.

The papers, along with fat casebooks tagged by me with colored flags, for the first batch of this morning's twenty-three hearings, sat fort-like in three stacks to my left and right. If needed, I worked better flipping back and forth through real law books, not pages on a computer screen.

I looked over the gallery, every seat taken, even jury box seats. "Sorry for being late. Next time, this Court will cut a little slack when any of you is late. It will be this Court's first ever I-Owe-You. We'll keep today's list of appearances until we've given each of you one make-up."

Rolling laughter and "thank yous" responded. *How funny and kind this robe makes me.*

I leaned over to my clerk, Ms. Patterson, sitting down to my right, and mouthed, "Number eleven, thirty minutes each side, hmm?" Earlier this morning, Ms. Patterson had taken down how long the lawyers on every case wanted to talk to me, to "argue" in legal jargon, and noted the times on today's case list. I said into my mic, "Number eleven, Hollenbeck versus All-American Insurance Company. I've read the papers. Five minutes per side."

Seven lawyers sidled through the half gate in the low barrier separating the gallery from the counsel tables, the jury box, and my podium. A lectern separated Susan Hollenbeck's solo lawyer standing at his table from the opposing six standing around their table. That many lawyers with their helpers and client rep appearing for the insurance company didn't surprise me. This case could turn ugly in front of a jury.

In the legal papers for today, Susan's lawyer had painted her as a mother of three, dying too young of uterine cancer while All-American refused to pay six hundred thousand dollars in medical bills. The lawsuit claimed that her bought-and-paid-for insurance coverage should have allowed her to stay in the family home and protect her meager savings, all used up before she qualified for state-sponsored poor-person coverage. Her lawyer claimed, if All-American had honored its obligations from the start, Susan might not now be terminal.

The insurance company papers asked me to dismiss that lawsuit today and months before any live witnesses could testify and a jury could decide. The contract of insurance plainly did exclude coverage for any condition known by Susan and not disclosed in her application. All-American claimed Susan said nothing about her alarming symptoms in that application.

It would be too easy to send All-American packing today and let a jury decide later. But what if Susan had not applied for this policy until too late and had kept quiet about her symptoms? I had to keep my Lady Justice blinders on and do what the law commanded, and the law said—

Odd movements from my bailiff, usually just sitting quietly, shoved their way into view. He was out of his chair, held his radio phone against his ear and whispered at it, whispered some more, looking up at me the whole time.

I said to the seven lawyers standing at attention, "Here's what I'd like to do first—"

My bailiff holstered his phone, quickly moved up closer and stared at me with a shrug that said he didn't want to interrupt but had to. A second uniformed bailiff entered through the main double doors. Loud—too loud—crowd noises came in with him from the wide public hallway outside. This one, legs spread and hand on his holstered pistol, stood with his back to the door. No one would try to get past him, in or out. My bailiff hovered over Ms. Patterson and mumbled something I didn't hear.

I stalled. "We only need at counsel table the lawyers who'll argue this morning. Why don't you gentlemen—"

Ms. Patterson came part way up my three steps and, a cupped hand by her mouth, said, "May our bailiff speak with you, Judge?"

I said loudly, "We're off the record. Excuse us." I got out of my chair and descended the steps.

My bailiff said with quiet urgency, "We're ordered to clear this courtroom, Your Honor. Have to get IDs of everyone here."

"Someone forget a big briefcase?"

"No briefcase, Your Honor. We must clear the floor, the whole building."

"What's going on?"

"We'll take care of it, Your Honor. We'll release them one by one and get proper IDs. You'll have to clear the floor, too, and Mora and Ms. Patterson."

He had ignored my question. He never did that. "Why are you, we, doing this?"

"I'm not sure how much I can say, Your Honor. It's still an active situation."

"Give me something I can tell these folks."

He glanced down and breathed once, deeply. "Ah . . . Judge Brookfeld is dead, dead in his chambers. It's messy down there, bad crime scene, maybe—"

Melvin Brookfeld, mother of Jesus. I felt blood rise into my ears and cheeks, questions piling in. *Dear Melvin, supposed to be on vacation.* I interrupted. "He's a friend, and I know he's out of town. You sure?"

"Your Honor, it's him. More than one of us bailiffs had eyes on his body. We're pretty sure it's safe in the main hallways, elevators, escalators, and out to the street."

"You're only *pretty sure* it's safe?"

"Got the main halls and exits covered. San Diego P.D. is helping. I . . . I . . . I'm not saying . . . but whoever did this . . . could be in one of the back hallways, maybe mixing in." He glanced around at the faces locked on us. "Ah . . . if Judge Brookfeld did it to himself, we need to get all witness statements anyway."

"Okay then. You and your helper better get to the exit and do this fast."

Back on my bench, I grabbed the top of my big leather chair and remained standing, knees flexed—double trouble if I passed out. Had to sound confident, unruffled. "Ladies and Gentlemen," my first words came out okay, "there's a public safety issue with a courtroom." *Bit of a mess down there . . . pretty sure safe . . .* "Purely as a precaution, we must clear this floor. My calendar clerk will contact you about a new hearing date, and we'll send you a notice. As you leave, please check with one of these bailiffs. They'll want to see your Bar card or driver's license and match you with our attendance sheets you signed. Let's start with the back row and then the next row and so on."

The bailiffs posted themselves on both sides of the main door, and the exiting began.

Melvin. Not Melvin. He's on vacation . . . brilliant, strong Melvin.

Chapter Three

Frank, July 1977

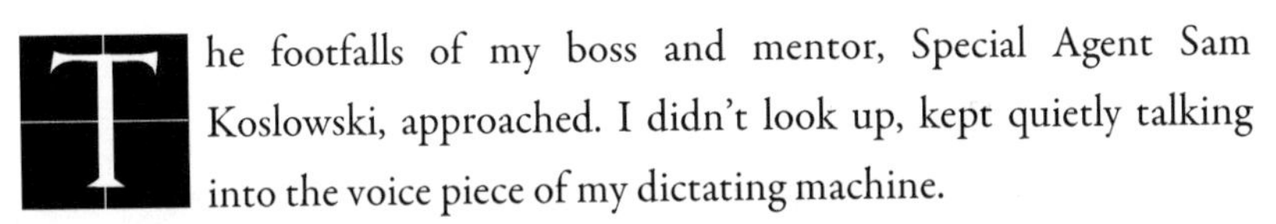

The footfalls of my boss and mentor, Special Agent Sam Koslowski, approached. I didn't look up, kept quietly talking into the voice piece of my dictating machine.

"Hey, FNG, need your help."

FNG—Fucking New Guy—was my real-life job title. The newer FBI recruits were all FNG's. Old timers hated dumb-ass questions and rookie mistakes and too often acted like they couldn't be bothered with us new guys.

Sam dropped a piece of paper onto the open transcript I had been summarizing when interrupted. The paper had a hand-printed name followed by a phone number. "I'd go with you, but DNR is all over it already. They think it might be our jurisdiction 'cause it likely crossed state lines. Ever seen a floater?"

"No, sir, I have not."

"Only a skel now, female skel, and the DNR doesn't have any missing female file that matches. That makes them think it crossed state lines and gives us jurisdiction. Call that number. Then get out there and see what they want. If we can help with forensics or our MP files, great. If not, don't crowd them. Their ME will be in charge, so do whatever he wants. Never know when we might need them to help us. Got it?"

"Yes, sir."

I didn't know what DNR stood for, but I'd find out soon enough. I dialed the number. In the fifteen-minute call, I learned DNR stood for Maryland's Department of Natural Resources, with its own police force for its waterways. A detective, a medical examiner and uniforms were on site and wouldn't move for a while. On my way out the door, I stopped by our equipment clerk for a camera and six rolls of film.

THE LAST SIGN ON THE WAY SAID, JUG BAY Wetlands. The sign, green and white with metal gray from bullet holes, sat just a bit higher than the vegetation. Would have been easy to miss if the DNR person on the phone had not told me where to look for it. A few miles in from that sign, the dirt road stopped, but someone had cut a path for vehicles to go farther in. I followed the tracks in the grass and rolled down my window to hear if anyone tried to hail me.

No more than twenty miles from Baltimore or Annapolis as the crow flies, but it felt like a full day's drive from any city. Sky-gray water meandered away through grasses and trees. The warm wet air made the far shore look like something out of an old movie. Duck noises joined a van engine's hum down closer to the water's edge. Smaller birds flitted through and peeped all around me.

Two uniforms parked in their cruiser gave me a thumbs up. They had to be "crowd control" in case locals got wind of this scene. My gray Chevy and blue jacket gave me away. More people and vehicles came into view. I parked and walked toward them.

A diver in a full wetsuit and air tanks came out of the water carrying a box. A cord tied to the box ran to the shore. The diver set the box on the water's surface, and a woman on the shore pulled the box in. She searched through the box, tossed rocks and pebbles away and placed everything else onto a large black plastic sheet. When the box was empty again, the diver pulled it back out to deeper water by a cord on his side of the box.

A human skull with ribs and big arm and leg bones lay out on the sheet. A man standing near the woman noticed me about the same time I saw him. "You must be Agent Maier. I'm Detective Walsh." The detective had on overall waders and gloves. "This is lab tech Barb. Couldn't do without her," he said with a sincere smile.

After one quick glance my way, Barb ignored me.

"Good to meet you both. Call me Frank. Let me know how I—ah, we—can help. Anything useful yet?"

"Not yet. No wallet, purse. Nothing close to an ID. Your Bureau's got the best MP files in these parts, so here you are, Frank."

"Brought a camera, just in case there's something to take back and check against our files."

Walsh turned his head toward the trailer. "We've got all kinds of cameras and film in there—but, hey, whatever you think." He turned away and said a bit louder in the direction of the trailer, "Hey, Stu, Agent Maier here wants to maybe take some shots to check against Bureau MP files. Can Barb point him to a couple things?"

An older man stepped out of the open trailer door and walked over to us. "Thanks for coming so fast." I shook hands with the ME. "Technically, it's Dr. George Stuart, but call me Stu."

"Pleased to meet you, Stu. My senior agent said it was a floater?" I handed out my card as we talked.

Walsh answered. "Two fishermen up from Baltimore snagged a hook two days ago." He shook his head. "Told them not to leave these parts, and that must have scared the daylights out of them. But it wasn't them. To answer your question, technically not a floater. Under her, we found gravel that's not from around here. Whoever saw her alive last wrapped her up with maybe a sack of gravel. Metal weights or chains would stay put a lot longer than gravel, might be easier to trace. Knew what they were doing."

"Any teeth come up with it?"

"Sure did. Barb will set them up for you."

"Anything we can do? Anything you want me to report back?"

ME Stuart answered. "Here's what we know. Female, taller than average. Right index knuckle bone broken, crack over left eye. Might be what killed her, knocked her out anyway, but can't know that, not without lab work and a bit of luck. Whatever they wrapped her up in broke apart. She was dumped here naked is my guess."

Barb held the skull and detached jawbone so I could shoot a good set. She laid the separated teeth out on the black plastic while I kept shooting. Two loose teeth had tiny gold fillings. Ah, the beauty of gold, I thought, expands and contracts with heat and cold and doesn't break down.

When done, I dared one more question of Detective Walsh. "Did they dump her here?"

"Right here. Takes a hurricane to lift her and the gravel. Tides won't do that. Hazel in fifty-four was our last and could have moved her. It'd be twenty years, more, if she'd been dumped back then. The bones would have been buried under too much silt for a fish hook to snag 'em, would have decomposed long before now. These bones sat down there a year, two, maybe three at most. Longer than that, and they'd be gone."

"Locals come here to fish a lot?"

"Not many. The better fishing's in deeper water downstream. The guys who found her threw a couple lines out late in the day on their way out, and the skull came up pretty easy."

"They need a license to fish here?"

"Fresh water license in these parts. That's where I'd start looking—if we can date these bones."

When it seemed right and I couldn't think of more and they left me alone, I said good-bye. As I tromped through the hazy heat to my car, more details than I could sort out quickly piled up. I knew a lot about the killers already.

Probably more than one asshole hauled the limp body and gravel out here in a boat and dumped all of it rolled up tight to keep the gravel and body together. They knew their way around these wetlands, knew the seclusion of this spot. Wasn't much of a place for catching fish, no beach, no rocks, no boat landing or ramp, no decent road nearby. Whoever had done this guided the boat to a spot where only someone hiding out in the tall grass or dense trees could see them dumping. Whoever had done this owned a pickup or station wagon plus a trailer, a boat with a cover tarp, and was real patient.

Now to get my film developed and find a file clerk to search our MP files for a match—long shot.

⚖

WHEN I GOT IN THE NEXT DAY, THREE sets sat on my desk. I'd have one set couriered to Walsh, give another to our file clerk to try to find a match in the MP files.

As I walked to the file room, new thoughts crashed in. *No. It could not be. It could not be her. Not that one.* Young woman, tall, missing for two years, good teeth. How many others would match that? The missing females in our active and recent files were kids or old ladies who had lost their minds. A few were drugged-up hookers, and they had bad teeth. This skel matched none of those. Only one file I knew about deserved a first look.

A couple years back, Agent Sam had put me on it to do his FNG grunt work. We hadn't added anything to the file since then. No new leads. It was the first serious file I worked on. She was tall, stunning, wore a lemon sherbet summer dress and had probably gotten soaked in a sudden downpour on her way home the day she went missing. She, in that whole-body wet T-shirt look, was just the thing to catch the eye of some beasts.

There wasn't much we could pull together back then—the 302s of interviews with her co-workers and husband, a bad copy of her fingerprints taken for her job, the intake form on a possible kidnapping, husband's polygraph charts and notes, news clippings about the weather and altercations in the area, my own notes from calls to emergency rooms, and her dental X-rays.

I remembered her name, so the clerk fetched it right up and watched me hold the dental films to the ceiling light then down next to my photos, then back up again and down, only had to do it twice. The two gold fillings—bright white on the X-ray films—and their teeth exactly matched the teeth in the shots I had taken out at Jug Bay.

I thanked the clerk, grabbed the whole file. "I'll bring it right back." Should have signed this file out in my name, but I couldn't wait.

I trotted up to my squad room. Sam was on the phone and hung up when he saw me bearing down on him.

"Sir, that Maryland DPR case you sent me out on yesterday? We've got a match, an ID in our own MP files."

"Well?"

"It's that one, the one who worked at State, married to that lawyer."

"Holy shit. You sure?"

"Sure as I'm standing here. It's one Madeline Brookfeld."

"Slow down, Frank. Start me at the beginning and tell me the whole thing, every fucking gnat's-ass detail."

Chapter Four

Angela 2010

After clearing the courtroom, my bailiff led Mora, Ms. Patterson and me across the back hallway. He searched my chambers, its closet and the little bathroom before letting us back there, then stood at my door while I shed my robe, and we collected our purses and things.

Down on the street, the crowd must have thinned from the time Mora arrived earlier today. Police shouted out, "Move along. Nothing here to see. Keep the sidewalks clear. Move along."

Three local news vans and camera guys hung around. I half expected the courthouse entrances to be crossed by yellow police tape and was relieved they were not. Crime tape over the front doors to our house of justice would have sickened me even more.

I didn't know where to go, what to do other than head home. I wondered about Melvin, his staff, his family, though I knew really nothing about his family. The news on my car radio didn't have anything more yet.

That little house, in the too-expensive-for-us neighborhood, we called home was empty and quiet. Our twin girls were at their morning summer camp. Peter might have been here but wasn't. Involuntarily, I scanned the kitchen counters for newly-bought green bottles that he'd intended to put away before the girls and I spotted them. The kitchen surfaces were clear. I wasn't going to snoop in the cabinets and fridge. He—we—weren't that low yet.

Lately, it seemed Peter's favorites came in green: Heineken, Camarena,

Dos Equis XX, Stella Artois, Beck's, Tanqueray. Our evening glass of wine had changed to a glass of wine for me and beers, gin or tequila for him. Our end-of-the-day sitting close had slid into winding down in separate rooms with each of us fiddling at our own computers until we went to bed at different times.

"Downsized" from his job at Sony this last January, his hollowed-out spaces nagged at him, at me. I didn't know how to help, fretted that any suggestion, any light-sounding comment about his status or job leads, any comforting gesture by me would sting. So, I—we—avoided talking about things that mattered.

He returned late morning from a run and walk on the beach, he said. I filled him in. He listened but said nothing, showered, then left to pick up the girls. I went to my laptop in my little home-office on the wide staircase landing. Peter didn't say whether he'd heard about it on the news, didn't act surprised, didn't ask how I felt, didn't offer to have me come with him. As he walked out the door, I shuddered at my morning, at the cold reaction from the father of my children.

That evening after the girls were down for the night, the local station led off with its usual Breaking News blast and then, "Chaos in the downtown courts was quickly quelled. The police are investigating one dead but will provide no further details until next of kin are notified. Anonymous sources confirm the decedent was sitting judge and that he died in his chambers."

I silently thanked the news crews, the writers and editors for not hounding the police into releasing more details about the death scene, whatever the hell the scene looked like, for not speculating about the life and death of the smartest, wisest man I'd ever known.

SIX YEARS BEFORE, ON THE DAY I HAD ARRIVED in my court office—it never felt comfortable to call my modest office, "chambers"—and set up my personal law books, computer, hung my certificates and family pictures,

Judge Brookfeld stood in the doorway. I didn't notice him until he cleared his throat.

"Hi, I'm Melvin, last name Brookfeld, but call me Mel."

"Hello Judge, I mean Mel. I'm Angela Cornwell—ah, Angela."

He reached out his hand and clasped mine firmly, but not one of those crushers some men like to use. He peered at me over half-glasses. "You and I are going to be neighbors, at least until you get the hang of criminal cases, and then they'll move you to more civilized disputes."

New judges always went where the Presiding Judge sent them. I had never worked on a criminal case and had to learn fast. The *more civilized* civil cases—disputes about business deals gone bad, accidents, and complaints by fired employees—fit what I had been doing for private clients.

"If you need anything, poke your head in."

"Oh. Thank you."

"Until you get your own research clerk, feel free to use mine. He works just down the hall door and knows criminal law and procedure about as well as anyone—even I. He's hunting for a file in the clerk's office right now. Sandy, Sandy Shields. He said he might join us at your swearing in."

"Thanks for that, too. I'll need him. I hope I'm up to it."

He eased back a bit and looked as if checking me out. "I'm sure you're fully ready. You'll come to love it and will wonder why you deserve the best job in our time on this wonderful planet."

"I hope so. But that short training course our state gives us in judge school is not the real thing."

"Ah, yes, it is all real here, and every case brings something new to ponder, to learn, to remember. That's why I look forward to every case they send me and am ever reminded that," he paused, "a mind stretched by new experience can never go back to its old dimensions."

I mouthed, *A mind stretched by new experience can never go back to its old dimensions.* "That's good. May I steal it?"

He jutted out his lower lip as if caught in a fib. "It's not mine, though I wish it were. Oliver Junior said that."

"Oliver Junior . . . Not Justice Oliver Wendell Holmes, Junior?"

He responded with the enthusiasm of a fan who had just found another fan. "Yes, indeed, that one, my favorite Justice. As a young man he bolted out of Harvard to help in the war against those who enslaved black people. On the High Court, he was the only one who befriended the first Jewish Justice when others shunned him."

"Louis Brandeis?"

"It was. You're up to it, and you will make a fine, a very fine judge, Ms. Angela."

We both laughed; I with embarrassment, he with delight.

"Rumor has it your first trial comes into your court on Monday."

"What kind of case? I've got to log into the system and learn what's up."

Melvin grinned. "See you a bit later at the swearing in."

"Yes, at the swearing in, *my* swearing in. It will be nice. I hope . . ." I stopped before blurting out that I hoped my little speech would not ring of false modesty. Other judges in this courthouse, court staff, partners and associates and office workers from my old firm would all form their first impression of me as a judge, and I had only one chance to make that first impression.

Judge Brookfeld's eyes sparkled with a warmth that touched me and always would. "You'll do splendidly." And then he left.

I had not seen him before that day. But I had heard of this Judge Brookfeld, of his presiding over the nastiest death penalty cases. With Judge Brookfeld controlling all parts, those monster cases unfolded as the law said they should, and the State never had to do them twice. Older lawyers, in my firm and elsewhere, said Judge Brookfeld was the smartest of all the seventy-something judges in the county's courts. They couldn't understand why he never moved up to a higher court.

⚖

Over the weekend after Melvin died, I kept the courthouse administrators' e-mail site open, but nothing landed until Sunday evening. It said we'd open as usual, and my Monday through Thursday trial would start up again. Nothing was posted about what we ought to say to lawyers and juries if questions came up. Business as usual, though it was not.

What I'd tell people on Monday was easy to deal with, but not that creature gnawing inside me. I didn't know enough about that creature, couldn't see its shape. I did know Melvin did not, could not have taken his own life, not like that, not in that hallowed place where he worked at *the best job in our time on this wonderful planet*. Someone had waltzed right in, murdered a sitting judge in his own chambers, and waltzed right out again.

Chapter Five

Frank

Aristotle is supposed to have said, "Give me a child until he is seven and I will show you the man." By the time I applied to the Bureau, I knew Aristotle was right, knew I'd lost any soft edges very early. How my mom died, Uncle Yuri and Hilde and Muriel, farm work and hockey had done that. Or maybe I had just been born hard and gnarly and looked for ways to let that out. Happenings that bent others out of shape were no big deal to me.

I learned how I came into this world in Ashland, Wisconsin, hard by Lake Superior, from sideways glances and sentences unfinished.

"Bottom first, and then the head . . ."

"Poor girl, that damned blizzard . . ."

"Johanna, so young and so beautiful."

People in town glanced at me and Father and mumbled to each other. After we passed, they talked louder, didn't mind us hearing from behind our backs. "Ludwig knew her before, don't you suppose?"

"Had to be."

"My woman says Ludwig . . . unfaithful to Johanna when she was with that child."

"The big German hussy, to marry him and move in so soon."

One day when I was five years old, I put it together, though not piece by piece like a jigsaw puzzle. In a solitary instant, I saw all of it. My mother,

Johanna, died on the kitchen table birthing me in the blizzard of forty-nine. The big hussy—I didn't know the meanings of *hussy* or *unfaithful* back then—married my father, Ludwig Maier, and moved in with us less than a year after my mother died.

The new wife's name was Hildegard Oberbaum, but most called her Hilde. I never thought to call her "mother" or "mom". Those labels remained taken.

At bedtime Hilde tickled me and laughed in her German accent. I've wondered if a person could laugh with an accent, but Hilde's laugh sure sounded German. I hated her tickling games and hated worse that I couldn't help laughing with her. Some nights her fingers touched places that made me curl into a ball against the wall next to my bed. Not long after starting school, I squirreled up enough courage to say, the last words yelled, "No, don't do that. I don't like that. I'll tell Father if you don't stop right now."

She did stop, but weeks later tried again until I yelled again, and then she stopped doing that for good. I sensed that everyone would believe my tattling about her a thousand times more than they'd believe that she had done nothing bad to little boy Frank.

Hilde'd slap my face if I dallied coming into the house after she called or if I said a bad word. She called them an *Ohr Feige,* ear fig in German, and she'd say, "Do that again, and you'll get a good spanking." I didn't remember any of her spankings but knew what they were. She must have wailed on me good before my memory set in. All the kids I knew got spanked and slapped, hit with belts or switches, so I couldn't protest that.

When I was in second grade, Hilde and Father made their own child, Beatrice. I wasn't much interested in Biddie. That's how I pronounced her name, and it became her nickname.

Hilde had me collect eggs from the barn coop. I talked to the hens, fed them seeds out of my palm so they'd let me lift them off their nests, their breasts heaving, maybe from fear that this was the day of the cooking pot.

When a hen stopped laying eggs, Father cut off its head with a hatchet. The legs kept moving, kicking fast. One time, Father set the headless body on its feet. It ran upright for what felt like a long time, blood spurting out of the open neck. Later I wondered why the legs of grown men shot clean in the head didn't run.

Some weekends my grandparents picked me up in their burgundy Ford.

Black and white photos of me and my real mom sat on their fireplace mantle. Images of my mother always come to me in black and white, her big eyes in a quiet face that locked onto me from any angle no matter where I sat.

Grandma Ida said, "Your mother was the kindest, smartest girl everyone around here ever knew. She turned down a full scholarship to the University of Wisconsin's Teachers College. To marry your father, no less."

"What's a full scholarship?"

"That's where the school lets you take classes without it costing, not even for room and board."

Back then I guessed at what *room and board* meant. I wanted to ask more about my mother but never did, what with Grandma's eyes downcast and voice low and slow from sadness beyond my ability to comfort.

"We lost Johanna too young but have you now. The Good Lord thinks that's blessing enough. So it must be."

I knew the rest of that story after the first telling, but Grandma or Grandpa needed to tell me again and again.

"Your father should have taken Johanna into town and stayed at the hotel up the street from the clinic. To him there was no hurry until her water broke. He protested he couldn't afford a couple nights in the rooming house. Darn him. We're not that poor. I suppose he meant well. He had managed all right through all kinds of storms."

About here Grandma always choked up. "I told him we'd pay for the rooming house, and Yuri would watch the farm. But your father wouldn't have it. Johanna said let it alone. She'd be fine. She . . . loved carrying you . . . inside her."

Grandpa Yuri took over the telling in his Russian accent. "Couldn't see da road, couldn't hardly see hand in front of face outside. Ida and neighbor lady Maria have nothing but towels to stop blood. Your father get young doctor from clinic . . . dear Johanna is cold."

Yuri's accent was stronger than Hilde's. Over time I picked up that Yuri fled Russia as a young man, had to kill another man on his way out. If Yuri had to do it, then the dead man had it coming. On that trek, priests gave Last Rites to most all the babies that starved or froze to death. But Yuri's eyes were always kind, his voice always calm. He taught me chunks of Russian. *Perdet* was the word for fart, and *govno* meant shit.

I got the best grades in my class and decided my smarts came from my real mom, though I didn't miss her. In time, I understood it was not my nature to miss dead people, to regret the past. Maybe like Grandpa Yuri, most everyday things didn't matter for long, and you'd better not look back.

⚖

GUYS SAY THEY REMEMBER THE GIRL THEY first kissed. In the fall of sixth grade at junior high school, I met Muriel. *Met* doesn't do it. We never dated, never touched, never talked. But she was the first girl I'd remember.

One day a week, we had a study hall period, where we'd stay in our home room or study in the library. I liked the library with all its books waiting until I finished my homework. Older kids came to the library, and they seemed to know who I was, probably from hockey. Talking was forbidden, but I could tell by the way they looked at me, the way the girls moved near me, kept turning my way. By then, Coach and the local paper said I was the best hockey player in my age group in Ashland County, maybe in the state.

Muriel sat alone in those study hall periods one table over from my favorite place. She wore crooked and scratched up reading glasses and let her long hair hang over the sides of her face. She had to be in eighth grade but seemed older than other eighth grade girls. Her expression was part sad, part afraid, with her eyes shut too often for too long while hunched over a book but not reading. She never turned a page in that book with its brown grocery bag cover.

The kids I knew didn't have much. We worked in kitchens or fields or shops from the first day we could help, and our school books often had paper bag or newsprint covers, but we were happy, never sat still for long and laughed a lot. Not Muriel.

She was pretty, but no other kid ever sat at the same table with her. Once or twice her tattered hand-me-down skirt rode up over her knees. One time she caught me looking, pulled it down quickly and then kept staring at the open book in front of her until her eyes closed again.

Over the weeks and months, she didn't have much of a change of clothes, and her hair looked clean only on Mondays. She wore the same brown shoes, one of the toes with gray tape to hold the sole on a while longer. One time, she broke her yellow school-issued pencil with a loud snap and left it there on the table.

After that pencil-breaking afternoon, I didn't see her for a couple weeks. When she came back, an old bruise covered her cheek, and bad bruises marked the backs of her calves. None showed scrapes as if from a fall on a playground. It looked like a person had done that to her. My hockey and farm work taught me about bruises, what kind of blows—sharp and skin-splitting or blunt but hard—caused them, how they colored up at first and then toned down as they healed.

I wanted to ask what had happened, but I chickened out. I didn't see her around school except in the library at study hall. Our lunch periods did not mesh. Classes and hockey practices and chores at home left me no time to hunt for her.

Years later, I realized that wasn't it. I didn't do anything to help her, not because she was hard to find but because I didn't know what to do. I felt helpless and too young, thought grownups would take care of anything that needed taking care of. Later I learned most grownups avoid the tough problems of others. To this day, I wish I had waited for Muriel outside the library and talked to her, made her tell me what was wrong, had helped her.

After our Christmas break, Muriel didn't come back. I forgot about her until one day in late winter when the whole school talked about it, and it was all over our local paper and TV station. Muriel Theissen, eighth grader at Ashland Junior High School, had been found dead in the basement of a relative's farm house. He'd confessed. The news didn't say how they found her, but I figured grownups must have known what was going on. Had to have known or they never would have found her until years later or never. Even I sort of knew too, knew that Muriel was in real trouble and I hadn't done a damn thing.

I went back to the library one last time during my study hall period. I stayed only long enough to break a pencil and leave it on the table where she always sat. I wanted to break other things, to shout at the librarian and Muriel's teachers for not seeing, for seeing what I saw and doing not a damn thing. In time, I came to understand Muriel made me try to fix bad things that others wouldn't straighten out.

Chapter Six

Angela

Mora and I both arrived back at court early on Monday morning after Melvin's death. She quickly left—no doubt to find courthouse friends she had not talked to over the weekend. Our court clerks, bailiffs, janitors and reporters had the best seats. In hushed voices, relatives of victims spoke to court workers about things not shared with another soul. Needy lawyers told court staff secrets that could get them disbarred. Maybe last Friday morning, a sleepy security guard or janitor had heard an argument, a gunshot, caught a license number on a car leaving too fast. If so, soon every court staff person would know it.

As Mora came back from wherever she had been and set up her machine, I let out a sad sigh and said, "Good morning. Can't get my head around this one."

"Yes, Judge, sure agree."

"Mora, mind if I ask what you hear? What are they saying out there? Admin hasn't told us a thing besides what's on the news."

Mora let go of her transcription machine, swiveled her chair around, and looked at me now sitting on the old leather sofa against the wall in the little foyer between our two offices. "Well, I don't know if I should say."

I waited. It's a rare person who reveals any morbid truth without a little build up. And it's a rarer person who keeps a morbid truth to herself. Mora had an open face, no guile in that face.

Mora looked over at the clock on the wall and back at me. "I guess I can say this much. Sandy found the body, and, after he, well, he got a hold of himself, Sandy hustled out of there to find the nearest bailiff. On his way, Sandy told Natasha to not go in, to not do a thing, to just sit there. But Natasha couldn't help it.

"And, well, Natasha has been telling anyone who asks, and everyone's been asking her. Natasha is best buds with Fay, and Fay clued me into this job opening with you. Anyway . . ." From her seated position, Mora kicked the door to the hallway shut. "Not to tell even the police if they come around to ask. Can I trust you, Judge?"

I suppressed a laugh at this good question. I was bound to not obstruct the investigation, to tell what I knew if asked by the police. "Tell me what everyone's talking about, what you'd tell anyone if asked. Melvin was . . . my best friend here . . . and one of our lawyers or jurors might ask. Can't freak them out by saying anything that's not right."

Mora frowned and pursed her lips. "Yeah, I kinda knew you and he were kinda like father and daughter. Well then. There was a gun on the floor down by his chair, him slumped over to one side in the big chair, big mess . . . and a whole lot of blood. They'll never get all that blood off the floor and everything, never get the stink out of there. No judge is gonna want those chambers. I mean never. Natasha didn't stay in there for long. Judge, are you following what I'm saying?"

Mora's question sounded as if from far away, too many images of the body slumped over, of blood and an exit wound, and how on this earth it had all happened. "Yes, I follow."

"If anyone asks, you can sure, well, like it's all over the news he committed suicide." Mora paused, and I waited for Mora to say more. Mora's face said she knew more. Mora shook her head. "Didn't need to lock this whole complex down. Nice to get off without them docking our pay. That's a rarity these days. Shouldn't say more, 'cause if you're asked you'll be duty bound to tell them I told you, and I could lose my best friend around here. That's all I better say."

⚖

MORA'S LITTLE PERFORMANCE REMINDED ME of another Melvin observation. My first trials had been over lesser crimes. Back then I'd ask Melvin about some of the lawyers on those criminal cases, if I could trust the law they cited. "Will this lawyer toss any old spaghetti up at me hoping it sticks? Must I read every case in his papers?"

"No, no, not young Edwin Jones. I've seen him a fair number of times." Judge Brookfeld never forgot any lawyer or lawyer's name who appeared in his courtroom, any argument made to him. "You can trust him—plain-spoken and honest, night law school. As Oliver told us, simple people are very quick to see the live facts going on about them. The big firm lawyers first mislead themselves, then mislead their clients, and then try to mislead us with a complex elegance, an elegance that's often wrong. They waste bushels of time shoveling smoke." Melvin had grinned. "That bit about shoveling smoke was his, too. Oliver's. Most people say blowing smoke, but shoveling smoke works better, seems to me. One can move more smoke waving a big shovel than you could ever blow it."

⚖

NO SHOVELED SMOKE FROM MORA ABOUT what Natasha had seen. "Thanks, Mora. That's a relief, I guess—not having to watch out for a psycho running around our halls."

Yet Mora's downcast eyes and pauses betrayed that she—and all the court staff—didn't feel safe. The court staff sized it up the same way I had. Judge Brookfeld, of all people, would not foul his chambers with his own blood and body tissue and bone splinters. He knew the carnage one fatal self-inflicted bullet would inflict far past its intended target. *And if dear*

Melvin did not do that to himself, oh shit, what now, what then?

I tried to not let Mora see or smell my own fear. "The demons that man must have faced, and who knew? I didn't. Whatever it was, he hid it. Thanks. That's more than enough to know for now if someone asks. Back to the People's work."

⚖

"HOW WAS YOUR DAY?" PETER SAID WHEN I got home. He didn't kiss me, as he would have after a big day down at court, just stood in front of me, close enough that I caught a clean soap smell from him, a good smell.

I wondered if he masked that other smell and hated that I wondered. "Just okay, until right now. Now it's good." I smiled at Peter from the inside out and thought of earlier times and warmer greetings.

Before I could say more or reach for him, he turned to the side and yelled, "Mommy's home." No answer from our twins. "Must be the climax of Alice In Wonderland. Anyway, they're fed and our dinner's in the oven. And I left the paper open to what you might like to read first."

That calmed me a bit. "Thanks, thanks a lot. Fireworks in trial today, and lots of homework for rulings first thing before the jury comes in tomorrow." I wanted more from Peter, wanted a signal that he still wanted me as much as I yearned for him, that he knew my whole being was there for him. He walked away as if all he wanted was to collect our girls for their supper.

On the front page of its Local section, the morning's *Tribune* read, "A police spokesperson said all indications are that Judge Brookfeld died of a self-inflicted gunshot, but further details will not be released out of respect for the next of kin. They have asked for privacy and understanding."

Melvin had never said much about next of kin, never talked about the photos of people on shelves in his chambers. Once, twice, Melvin talked to me about Madeline.

⚖

THE DAY I CAME BACK TO WORK AFTER MY honeymoon with Peter, Melvin said, "You know your eyes are sparkling."

I put my hands up to my cheeks, felt my face turning hot and could not suppress a laugh. "Sorry, didn't mean to be so obvious."

"Ah, not at all, but you bring back memories—of when it's right between a man and a woman."

"Oh . . ." I caught his sadness and cut off what more I might have said. I wished I knew more, knew enough to say the one right thing or keep quiet.

He broke the awkward silence. "I first saw Madeline in the dusky evening light of the main library. I loved her from that first glance. You would have liked her. She would have liked you."

The ache in Mel's voice, his staring off to the side made me hate that I had made him remember. I eked out, more to myself, "I'm sure I would have liked her."

He let it go, swiveled away from me and back to the papers and computer on his desk. "Enough of me and things that happened long ago. We can only influence tomorrow."

A year or so later, Melvin and I, with me looking over his shoulder, together read a copy of a California Supreme Court opinion that had come down that morning. It affirmed another death penalty sentence Judge Brookfeld had imposed after the jury recommended death. As he read, he said, "Every time Madeline and I studied together, the room grew very quiet, and yet we seemed to converse the whole time. That's how it was with us. Ah, Angela, you do bring back those memories. They get easier with time. I have not forgiven myself, though I did the best I knew how then."

He turned a page in the court's decision and followed the text with his fingers, his signal that he did not want to say more.

We reached the end of the decision, and I stood up to leave.

He said, "She departed from this life too soon, and for that I am always sad and sad for what I might have done differently. It doesn't help me to dwell or for others to know more. Except this: Madeline inspires me every day to do what I do and do it as well as I am able."

⚖

NOW, AT HOME WITH PETER ROUNDING UP the girls and me getting into jeans and a loose top, I kept thinking, figuring. Someone must know more about Madeline and the rest of Melvin's family. Maybe now we'll learn what happened back then and last Friday and everything in between. Maybe Mel's sadness or guilt or whatever got bigger than any of us knew.

In the middle of our quiet dinner, I said, "Peter, Love, thanks for this article. Would you keep an eye on the obit pages the next couple of days? Friends from back east or family will have a service, take care of the body after the coroner releases it. I sure hope so, anyway."

He nodded a small nod.

The next morning, a "Confidential" memo from the Presiding Judge landed in my In Box. "The family of our dear departed Judge Brookfeld asks any donations be made to the American Jewish World Services (address and web site below) and advises that private services will be held for family members only. I propose we have our own celebration of his life and invite all our judges and staff. I will circulate suggested dates and times."

I was relieved that Melvin had a "family" somewhere, doing something.

Sandy Shields, the one Mora said discovered his body, had not come back on that next Monday. He didn't show up on Tuesday, or the whole week. He had helped me before I hired my own research attorney. Sandy, of all people, was entitled to recover, and I could not imagine that Sandy took the week off for reasons other than cold shock.

More would come out, had to. New security procedures would surely take effect around the courthouse, procedures to stop and catch a killer, a killer with a gun, who left the gun behind, who came and left without anyone noticing. This suicide talk was, well, just talk maybe to throw off the killer. Had to be. Or was it all bound up with whatever happened to Madeline long ago?

Chapter Seven

Frank

fter I debriefed Agent Sam, wrote up my full report, and Sam compared the skel's photos against the dental X-rays, he asked for a meeting with the Region Assistant Special Agent in Charge and me.

"If Region approves, I'll keep you on this one," said Sam.

Sam's boss said, "Think you are up to it, that you won't fuck up?"

"Thank you, sir. Really appreciate it. I'll check with you every step."

"Okay, then. To-do list. Got to notify her husband and next of kin, get a report from forensics on any fractures, any threads of cloth, anything. The local coroner shouldn't give us any trouble. When we're done, release the bones to the family. I hate those meetings. You check with his secretary and get a meeting set up, but don't say why on the phone. Then let's both tell him. Wouldn't be right to just show up at his work and spring it on him. "

I had tagged along with Sam on bad news meetings, and it was about the hardest thing I had to do—though Sam did all the talking. Most missing person cases that turned into a kidnapping didn't end well, the stakes for getting caught too high. Great FBI work was seldom good enough to change one particular reality. A dead victim can't ID the subject.

Sam continued. "Interview all the old witnesses—again."

"Yes, sir. Should we check tackle shops for anyone who took out a freshwater license about that time?"

"Yea, no harm in that. But it's a long shot. Go for it." Sam paused. "We'll split up the old witness phone numbers to set up the meetings. I'll get you a copy of my calendar, so you don't go committing to something I can't do. And . . . if you think we ought to just show up without calling first, let me know."

"Yes, sir." Good leads pop out easier if witnesses make up their story on the fly, if they can't call their lawyer ahead of us. Bad witnesses will be gone if they know you're coming. The ones who don't vanish but have something to hide won't say a damn thing if they're ready for us.

"Check weather and news records again. You might find something missed the first time through."

"Yes, sir."

The weather and her last work-day movements had been easy to reconstruct—up to the point she went missing. Madeline had left at the normal time that day, had not said anything about any plans. She didn't act like she was in a hurry. On good weather days, she liked to walk home, a solid twenty-minute walk, longer when a bookstore or bakery display delayed her. Melvin rarely got home early, and she'd have dinner ready whenever he arrived home from work or a hoops game. He'd always call her if he'd be home extra late.

Her co-workers had seen her leave. Some left the building in the same few minutes after five p.m., remembered her from that day and other times, her beauty mixed with a seriousness, and her friendly wave. Their memories were consistent. She had worn a light-yellow summer dress and walking shoes, not much protection from a dousing shower. No one remembered that she took an umbrella home that day.

Parts of Washington weren't safe for most people at most times after dark. But it was summer, light until late evening, and many people would have been out—to shop, to visit with neighbors, and to walk home from work.

No one had called about a young woman in a yellow dress and in trouble. No one had reported any screams or struggle, but a downpour would muffle most sounds. On that late afternoon, the weather had turned bad, one of those steaming summer days that grew heavy clouds fast. Drenching thunder showers hit. She might have stopped in a shop to wait out a cloud burst or on the street to catch the bus or hail a cab—if she could find an open one.

Back then Melvin Brookfeld had agreed to take and easily passed the polygraph test.

ON THIS DAY TWO YEARS AFTER MADELINE vanished, Melvin greeted us in the lobby area of his floor. He wore a suit jacket over his white shirt with bow tie. He took us back through the maze of cubicles and open offices with their sounds of clanking typewriters and ringing phones. After he closed the door to his little office, he said slowly, deliberately. "Gentlemen, I expect you have bad news. You would have given me good tidings on the phone." He sat down behind his desk and motioned us to sit in the two visitor chairs.

Agent Sam said, "Sorry to say you're right. Sorry to report we now know Mrs. Brookfeld has passed."

Melvin stared at Sam from across his desk, then at me for a long time. A short stack of legal papers sat on his desk with pens, a legal pad, and a photo in a frame with its back to us. I didn't dare snoop to look at it. He put both hands up to his face and sighed deeply. "You may tell me whatever details you care to. I can handle it."

Sam said, "We don't need to make this any harder, don't need to get into the forensics."

Melvin said quietly, thoughtfully, "As unlikely as it seems, one or another detail in the forensics may tie to something useful that I recall.

Nothing can be worse than the outcomes I've imagined. I will tell you when I've had enough of the forensics."

Sam said, "All right then. You can't tell anyone, can't talk about any of it unless you've got something for Frank here or for me?"

"We know how to keep confidences."

"And let us know right away if anyone asks about why we were here, would you?"

"Certainly, not likely though. We on this floor often deal with FBI, CIA and other security types. You'll not draw any interest by coming to see me once every two years—other than my own. My secretary is professional."

"Well then," said Agent Sam, "two fishermen found her remains in tidal water not far from here."

"Oh . . . no . . ." Through tears and slight trembling in his voice, he said, "Did Madeline drown?"

"Not likely. Seems whoever did it dumped the body, weighed it down," said Sam.

Melvin clasped his cheeks, closed his eyes, breathed deeply, nearly sobbing, shaking his head back and forth. He set his hands flat on his desk and slowly said. "Did she suffer . . . a long time?"

"Not likely, Mr. Brookfeld. From all the signs, she passed quickly, and whoever did it left the body far away from where she died." Sam waited, letting the implications settle. Sam was good at this, matter of fact but comforting in his simplicity, willing to wait and allow the relative to indicate when ready to hear more.

Melvin shook his head. "I take it the remains you mentioned . . . are just bones . . . after all this time in tidal water?"

Through the blizzard of his hard thoughts and memories, Melvin picked up on every clue and where each led, instantly figured out that a body in tidal water for years will not yield much, and that whoever had done this had long ago ditched her purse and whatever else would not decompose.

"Special Agent Maier was down there at the recovery site," said Sam, giving me permission to speak.

"That's right, sir. I watched them pull the bones out. Whoever did this had weighed the body down. Nothing came to the surface. It's blind luck anyone found her. A couple fishermen snagging their lines."

Melvin said, "How deep?"

I said, "I'd guess four to ten feet in a normal tide, maybe a little deeper. A diver in full gear pulled up what he could, but not far from the shore."

"So, the perpetrator had help, might have been more than one."

Agent Sam said, "What makes you think that, Mr. Brookfeld?"

"I imagine she was hard to transport, weighed down with whatever they used, from wherever they had her, then to a car or truck, then to a boat, then off the boat in out-of-the way tidal water. Would take a strong and big man to do all that alone. What did they use to weigh her down?"

"They found gravel under her remains," I said. "There's no gravel out there."

"My dear Madeline."

Agent Sam said, "What makes you think it was a boat?"

Melvin said freely, not at all as if he thought Sam wanted to ensnare him. "Had to be. No one would wade around at the edges of tidal water carrying her weighted down to get into deep enough water. Too hard. Too risky. Takes too long. Even at four feet, the water's too deep for a man on foot. He—they—could be spotted too easily lugging and dumping something so large, would leave big footprints on the land, in the grasses. Too obvious."

Sam said, "I know this is hard, Mr. Brookfeld, but if you remember anything that might connect someone to any activity, any place like that, anyone you know who owns a boat, a truck and trailer, tell us."

"Of course."

Sam said, "As before, sorry to go over old ground or irrelevant stuff, but have you ever done any fishing, ever owned a boat, or a pickup and boat trailer?"

Melvin stood up and came around the desk. "No, no, and no. And, as before, I understand you must ask. I never went fishing, don't have the patience for it. Basketball and a bit of chess and reading are my avocations—but you know all that."

I suddenly saw a different Melvin than what I had remembered—not a total intellectual, the big hands, the long arms and lean waist.

Melvin said, "And right now . . . I can't think of any of our friends who were into fishing either." He had suddenly flipped from grief to all business. "Well then, unless there's something you need from me, when you release Madeline's remains, her bones, let me know. I won't tell anyone else a single detail of the circumstances, the terrain, unless I clear it with you first. Whatever you need from me, call or stop by again, any time."

"Sure. Thank you. So sorry we did not have better news," said Sam.

Melvin looked at us over his reading glasses that he had just put on. "Thanks, but after all this time . . ." He shrugged.

"And if you leave the area for more than a couple days, make sure someone here can get hold of you. We'll be interviewing all her contacts and others again. If any of them should call you, let us know right away."

A cold hardness took hold of Melvin's face, his jawline and mouth, his eyes. He led us out his door, saying, "I understand. If I get a call from someone with whom you've just talked, I'll listen. And . . . if he lets out something only you and I know, I'll be ready."

We left.

"What do you think?" said Sam as we headed back to our squad room.

"I think he's leaving something out, something important."

"Now what makes you think that?"

"He was too ready for us, and too quick to get rid of us. He switched from distraught husband to all business faster than a light switching on. He didn't ask about any new leads, who we'd talk to next, what we'd be looking for that we hadn't known back then. Heck, if Madeline had been my wife, I'd have wanted to talk to us all day long, would want to ride along with us on all our interviews and see right now whatever turned up. He knows, he knows more he's not saying."

"Don't put that in your 302, Frank. I get where you're coming from, but a jolt like that makes people act strange, twists them to talk and act different than when everything's normal. And, remember, he passed the polygraph real easy."

"Thanks for keeping me on this one—and for not thinking I'm nuts about Melvin holding out on us."

⚖

WE STARTED CALLING, GETTING NEW TELEPHONE numbers where the old numbers had gone dead, meeting with any potential witnesses within a reasonable drive.

Those who had moved far away took more time to round up and interview. We needed to get the local FBI office in the new locations to open a file and send someone to interview them again. Some of the tackle shops kept copies of the annual fresh-water permits from three seasons back. Some did not. No peculiar names or addresses close to the Brookfeld apartment, close to any of their friends, or any of their co-workers showed up on any of the available permits issued the year she disappeared.

After five weeks of calling and interviewing, we had nothing new except from forensics—a bad right index finger break, skull had received a hard blow, cracked open and no signs of healing. A smaller unhealed crack showed up on the back of the skull. She had been hit hard from the front and fell back onto something hard, was my guess. Had Melvin done that to her? I couldn't believe that, but it wouldn't let me go either. A pissed-off goon might have done that to Madeline. All reports were that Melvin never even spoke loudly to Madeline, not to anyone, for that matter; he was a gentle and kind man except on the basketball court or in court.

Chapter Eight

Angela

Melvin's death crowded out any impulse to give. I hadn't given enough to Alice and Abigail, to Peter, to all my cases, to me. I hadn't cajoled the girls into a walk or a board game, hadn't made breakfast for my family since that Friday. My darling girls each suffered in silence and didn't interrupt me in my tiny home office. They did say *thank you* and *please* more often than most times. I'd get through it, hoped I'd get through it—as soon as my need to learn more, do more about Melvin left me, a need that, as far as I knew, no one else shared.

On this Monday morning, a week and three days after that death-dealing Friday, I left home not long after sunrise. I arrived at the courthouse earlier than anyone except the night-shift security, got there at a time when maybe the killer stalked the hallways, and maybe something would come to me. Soon after I arrived, I tried Sandy Shield's courthouse phone extension. It was all I could think to do. If he came in at all, he wouldn't be in yet, and I could leave him a message, give him a while to think about how much to tell me.

"Hello, this is Sandy Shields."

The same demons must have brought him into work early too. "Hello, Sandy. Angela Cornwell. I . . . we . . . Can we meet for lunch perhaps? I'm open tomorrow or the next day."

"Yes, certainly, Judge. I could meet really any time. I'm not doing much, haven't been reassigned yet."

"Good, in a way. I'm here too already." *That was stupid—he can tell I'm here already. Breathe.*

"I could meet you now, Judge. Shall I come over?"

"Wonderful. But let me come to your area. I'll be right there."

I needed to go there, get closer to the scene, learn what I didn't know, anything. Security personnel manned the courthouse doors on the street level and inside the criminal court wing. The hallways on my way to visit with Sandy breathed an uneasy quiet. Air hummed through the vents. Traffic noises down on the street joined the faint cries of angry men up early in the jail section with no place to go while awaiting their trials in one of the courtrooms. No one had made bail for them, or they had done such repulsive things the judge set no bail.

Did Mel's killer notice the same sounds? Or was he so cocky, so angry, so focused that he heard none of this? Or had he come up here at night after closing time, snuck into Melvin's chambers, maybe slept in his chair, and waited for his early morning arrival?

Judge Brookfeld's office area remained sealed with yellow tape. A short way down the hall, Sandy Shields's office door was wide open. He shared that office with other research clerks but was alone this early. He sat at his desk-top computer and monitor and looked up, eyes tired, skin pasty as if he had not been outside in the last nine days and had not slept. He always struck me as studious, serious about his work but ready with a funny line or pun. Now all cheeriness had left him. Our prior chats had been so easy, mostly about a point of law and the sources I asked him to find in law books—a task called *legal research* by the more pretentious.

"Sandy, thanks for letting me come right over. I'm sorry, sorry for us all."

Sandy stood and offered a handshake. I pulled him into a hug. Releasing, I said, "Your judge and I, well, I'll miss him."

"Yes, me too, Your Honor. He was the best." Sandy talked with an eagerness that surprised me, as if he had not spoken to anyone in the last nine days and now needed to catch up. "Heck, he didn't need me. All I ever did for him was get books with the cases he already knew by heart, and I'd check the citations and quotes he rattled out of his computer keys." Mimicking, Sandy sat down and poked fast at his keyboard with the index finger of each hand. "A copy editor is all he needed to polish up his rulings and longer decisions." He stopped and stared at the monitor as if he had typed something legible.

I said haltingly as I fought tears, "Amazing man, our Melvin. We say too often after someone passes, they broke the mold. With him, they did."

Sandy removed his glasses and cleaned them with a tissue out of a box on his desk, set them down, and wiped his eyes with the backs of his hands. "Me, too. I still can't get my head around what happened to him—or what he did. Excuse me, but you should know. Judge Brookfeld mentioned you and things you said and did and how you ran your courtroom. Even after you moved over to civil, he talked about you more than any of the other judges in this courthouse, said you kept your sense of humor at serious times."

I smiled a "thank you" smile. *Nice. Maybe I ought to leave it there, good place to end this meeting, but no, can't. Go easily, softly.* "They say you found him."

Sandy looked out the door over to that other room. "Yes, Judge. I found him."

"Sandy, whatever you can tell me, I'd appreciate it very much. But if now is not a good time, that's all right."

Sandy calmed himself. "Sure. Can't sleep and when I get to sleep, I dream about it—wish it were just dreams. I was bringing to his chamber copies of filings for our Monday and the casebooks open to the pages he'd want to look at first. He still likes the books and to flip back and forth—I mean, he liked to do it that way."

"Helps us a lot—to have all the books out at one time—why on Friday?"

"Judge Brookfeld wasn't due back until Monday, but after vacation he usually came in on the weekend. We had a new felony for Monday and some motions. His door was closed but not latched—I pushed it open. Funny, I remember being kind of glad it wasn't latched, wasn't locked so I didn't fiddle with the key or put down the pile of books I was carrying. I was gonna arrange my stuff on his desk in the order he needed for each of the motions. My brain didn't register for a couple seconds. Then it froze. Like, Holy Christ . . . I looked up, walked around his desk, and smelled . . . don't remember what I did with the books I was carrying. Later I found the books on my desk and figured I had to have done that some time before his place was shut down. I shelved them before they made us all go home. I know I did that."

Sandy looked down and shook his head. "Man, was I glad I knew where the waste basket was and lined with a plastic bag. I ran downstairs to the bailiffs at the main entrance. That's it. That's what I know."

"Sandy, don't answer, not now if you don't want to. But do you remember what you saw?"

"Sure. If you . . . I can tell you."

"Please."

"He sat in his chair, slumped over to his left." Sandy did the same in his smaller desk chair and then straightened. "Eyes were closed or nearly closed, thank God for that. I couldn't look but for a second. Blood across his cheek, down his mouth and chin, white shirt, his bow tie, over his chest and shirt and down to a big pool on a plastic sheet that his chair rolled on, and off to the rug. I stepped around to where I could see his right arm and hand hanging over the armrest on his right side. It was like his finger pointed at the gun on the floor. I'm no gun guy. It was not a long barrel thing. This is hard. The left side of his face and head were a worse mess. Then the smells . . . and that's when I lost my breakfast and got out of there. Sorry, too much information."

"Sandy, I'm sorry, not too much information. Hear anything, the shot, a stranger on your floor? It's quiet in these halls now."

"No, no shot, no footsteps, no talking. For all I know this could have happened late in the night after the cleaning crew came through. With his door closed, there'd be no one to look in until I did."

"Anyone could hear a shot like that all the way down the escalators to the bailiffs on the front door."

Sandy shook his head. "I didn't hear any shot, any talking, any noise out of place, didn't see anyone. I would have caught anything like that." Sandy sat up straight, looked directly at me. "My judge would never do that to himself, to us, to this place . . . in this place. And . . . that's all anyone has come up with."

I had been standing. Sandy stood and bowed, silently confirming he had told me all he remembered. We shook hands. "Thank you, Sandy, so much. Judge Brookfeld go back East on his last vacation?"

"Sure. Said he always had good and useful things to do there. That was his phrase, good and useful. He had friends back there still. His family has a beach house on the shore outside of D.C. somewhere."

Still holding Sandy's hand, I said, "I owe you that lunch. The main cop who questioned you, I bet he gave you his card?"

Sandy reached down into the narrow center drawer of his desk. "Yes, they did question me, couple times. Here it is. Detective John Pitts, wants to be called Johnny Pitts."

I held the card long enough to remember the name and the direct line telephone number. I could do that, even on mornings like this. "Sandy, would you let me know if they tell you anything new, if they come around again for more?"

"Sure, Judge, happy to." Sandy looked down at the floor. "Glad someone else cares. Thanks for that."

"Sandy, I'm going to ask you a favor." Sandy's expression urged me to continue. "If Detective Pitts, or our presiding judge, or another staff, or anyone tells you what happened over there in Judge Brookfeld's chambers, call me or send me an email right away. I can't stand not knowing why our judge did this. I can't stand the explanation everyone's coming up with."

"Me neither . . . I'll let you know right away, Your Honor."

"If someone—someone else—did this to him, I can't get my head around that one, either."

"Judge, I'm not sure I want to think about that either. But that would be better, wouldn't it?"

"Sandy, you've been around enough cases . . . once in a while, some evidence comes kicking and screaming through the courtroom door at the last minute that paints everything white that we were sure was black. I hope this is one of those times. Until then . . ."

"Your Honor, if you need help, I'm not assigned to another judge yet. I mustn't get laid off in budget cuts or whatever. I would very much like to work for you."

"Sandy, I will look for the chance to work with you. Right at the moment, I have all that kind of help the court gives me. But, there will be things that only you can do."

Sandy's eyes opened wider.

"Now, I must go. Full calendar this morning. Last question."

"Sure."

"Judge Brookfeld had his own laptop. Was it with him?'

"Ah, yes. He took it on his vacation . . . but . . . I don't remember whether I saw it that morning, just don't remember . . ."

"Okay. Thanks very much. Let me know if I can help you land more assignments." We hugged again, and I left.

As I made my way back to my courtroom, my insides told me Sandy Shields would not last thirty minutes in Johnny Pitts' interrogation if he had seen or heard a stranger but did not tell—or if he, Sandy, was involved somehow, showing off a new toy until a cruel accident, or something like that. If that had happened, he would have a lawyer, and they would have taken him in, and there'd be no talk of suicide. Sandy had not shoveled a wisp of smoke at me this morning.

But Sandy had seen more before his guts took over. What file lay open on Judge Brookfeld's desk, and why did Melvin not have his laptop with him that morning, or did he but someone had made off with it?

Sandy had told me nothing about Melvin's court reporter, Natasha, about telling her to stay put and not go in. When did Sandy run into her, and where was she at that moment? He had said, *I . . . didn't see anyone.* Maybe he meant he didn't see anyone right around Melvin's chambers, maybe Mora had fibbed. Maybe Natasha arrived just before the police shut everything down but after Sandy had run out of there. Maybe Sandy ran into Natasha on his way downstairs. Maybe Natasha had shoveled smoke at Fay. *God, help me, help me to stay out of this, but I can't. It's all too wrong.*

I had to come back to Sandy, and maybe to Mora or Natasha. But maybe not. Others were already doing that. Maybe just one more thing to do and I could get closure: I had to learn what Detective Johnny Pitts would tell me.

Chapter Nine

Frank

Every week in the winter of senior year at Ashland High, another batch of full scholarship offers landed in our mail box. My grades, test scores and hockey did that, mostly hockey. I'd fall asleep giddy and excited about this country, about my good luck. The letters said things like, "you are a special young man . . . honored to have you join the class of 1973 . . . please call on my home line with any questions . . . great privilege to offer . . ."

Father let me pick, and I picked that school in the Finger Lakes of New York—for its world-class hockey teams and reputation for agriculture and Russian. Perfect combination for what I thought I wanted back then.

It seemed crazy at the time, but I was the only freshman I knew who brought a small set of tools to campus from home but no car. After I left Ashland, I never felt one pang of homesickness, missed only the work on machines, tearing out and replacing rotten sections of our barn and house, pounding stuff with a hammer. Tools took to me as if I were born with them. By third grade, I pounded nails fast and straight, ran beads of caulking neat and clean. Hand tools became my friends. They calmed me.

The women on campus broke my surprise meter. Thousands right here on this campus looked out of fresh faces, eyes ahead, chins leading. They walked fast, talked way more than the guys. That confidence mixed with smarts tugged at me more powerfully than any farm girl I had ever been around. Here no parent called to come inside or made them be home for supper.

Classes were easy, the homework not as bad as everyone warned. Hockey try-outs couldn't start until October 15, but conditioning drills weekday afternoons and operating the big dishwashing machines five evenings a week kept me plenty busy. Hockey covered my meal plan, and washing dishes gave me decent pocket money.

She stood in front of me, both of us waiting to check books out of the main library, and we started talking. Rebekkah from New York City, three years older than me and a senior, lived in a sorority house on the other side of campus. She wore glasses most times, and they made her look even smarter than she was.

Freshman dorm rules said, "four feet on the floor", and sleeping-room doors had to stay open while entertaining a guest. Her sorority house—radio and record player music pouring out of open doors, sounds of hard-heeled shoes on wood floors, curious looks—was no place to seriously entertain young men.

On a Friday evening in early October, Rebekkah said, "Let's go to a special place this evening. I've made a reservation."

I had taken the lead for pizza dinners and moonlight walks, then hot groping and kisses in dark places. I didn't have enough money for more.

She said, "Not to worry. My treat."

"Wow, thanks. Do I need a jacket? Yeah, I guess we should talk." And I meant it, wondered how far, how fast, how long she and I would go, but didn't ask more about the reservation. I trusted her on that one. No other choice.

She shook her head, took my hand, and tugged me along—all the way to the new Holiday Inn down on the Commons. It did have a nice place to eat, but for parents and visiting faculty.

"Wait here," she said and made me sit at the end of the lobby across from the registration desk but not far enough away that I couldn't see and hear most everything. She filled out the white registration card, slowly, proudly. I saw her select the room's location from a paper mat on the desk, watched her pay with cash. The registration clerk, a middle-aged man, never looked up or out, never glanced my way. He must have done this sort of thing before—many times.

When she slid the key into the room lock, she laughed. "What do you think of this place for dinner?"

I shook my head. That's all I could do, surprised, crazy for what was to come, and a tiny bit guilty, a tiny bit afraid, but as amped-up and horny as a stud stallion.

As she opened the door, she said, "I got you covered the whole night, and we can eat off the room service menu if we want." She caressed my hair. "Get in here. Real women pay their own way." She grabbed my collar and pulled me into the room darkened by heavy closed curtains that remained closed until morning. She tumbled back onto the bed, pulling me on top of her.

That first Friday became a bit of a ritual, if not on Friday, then Thursday unless one of us had a big exam the next day. After I got over the newness of real sex, I noticed we weren't the only couple checking in and languishing out the next morning. In time, I thought I recognized some repeat couples but no one from the hockey team or any of my classes. Would have been fun if I had.

When naked and alone with me, Rebekkah let down her soft black hair. It extended to below her waist. Sometimes she made it fall over her shoulders toward the front and between her perfect breasts, the end strands lying against her white skin and pointing to where her smooth and strong thighs came together. I'd stare at her as she stood like that, and then she would slowly walk toward me. When we were apart, that image stayed with me, made me study until I understood all my course materials, motivated me to play hockey as well as I knew how. Great women did that to their men.

IN JANUARY OF 1970 AFTER THE CHRISTMAS break, snow lay waist-high on the campus, wind-blown drifts and shoveled-out sides deeper than I was tall. But the walkways and roads had been cleared. Rebekkah nuzzled my face in the cold. The clouds of her breath smelled of gum and perfume. She rested her head against my shoulder. She looked and sounded different than before the Christmas break, her eyes too red. The bubbly part of her talk, of her soul, had left. All could not have been right in the Tannenbaum New York City household over the holidays.

"Missed you."

"Me, too," she said without looking up, held me tighter.

We found an empty sofa away from the windows in the farthest, emptiest corner of the lounge in my dorm.

"What's wrong?" I said.

"Nothing. Why?"

"I can tell . . ."

She let out a long breath. "When did you become a mind reader . . . but you're right."

"Family, huh?"

"Sure, family, but not mine."

"Tell me, if you want."

"I can't, not anyone."

"Must be bad."

"Horrible."

"If you're hurting, I'm hurting." It was nice to be sitting next to her, listening to her, her nearness warming me again, making me see past her bulky sweater, her jeans, her boots. I leaned into her tighter and waited.

"I'll tell you if you swear to never ever repeat any of it." She looked up, locked her eyes on mine. "Not one word."

"Sure. I'll swear."

"It's my roommate, Sarah, crazy Sarah. You think my eyes are red. She can't come out of our room—not our house, anyway—can't go to class, can't let her teachers see, can't let her parents know, her eyes are too red and black and green and getting worse."

I reached for Rebekkah's hand. I knew Sarah, smaller than Rebekkah but cute in her own way. Friendly. The first time I met Sarah, she sort of leered at Rebekkah and winked at me, and the three of us laughed. "Wow, I'm glad you're okay. So . . . what kind of fight did Sarah get into?"

"A townie, damned fucking townie."

I had never seen Rebekkah flash anger and tucked away to never get her that angry. I said, "Yeah, Buford, wasn't it?"

"We all told her not to, so low class, so crass. Well, she told him she can't see him anymore, that they're done. He beat the shit out of poor Sarah, then tried to fucking kill her . . . throw her off the bridge but couldn't get a good enough grip on her bulky clothes before she bit him hard in the face and made him let go."

"God. My God." I probed the obvious. "Sarah should go to the cops. They won't want this to get out and give this town a bad name. They're probably used to it, have seen it many times. They'll take care of old Buford, I bet."

"And they'll call her parents or someone on campus—and Sarah will just die, die . . ."

"Nah, she won't. She's not the first babe who got tangled up with a bad guy and broke it off, and he didn't let it be. She's old enough that they won't call her parents."

"Oh, Frank, sometimes you can be so naïve, so young . . . But I guess that's why I fell for you."

That hurt. I sat up and moved back a bit. I was young and new to these boy-girl fights, but I was getting it, the rest of what happened to Sarah. "Bekkah, I think . . ." She turned away and leaned forward as if to get up, as if to end this talk. I said, "Let me guess. The asshole got Sarah knocked up too, and she's got a bigger problem that she can't talk to the cops or her parents about."

Rebekkah let out a solitary squeal like a faraway bird on Lake Michigan in winter. She stared at me with that intense anger, head forward, her perfect full lips two lines. "Frank, you big dummy . . . how did you know?"

"That's the only thing short of her dying that fit, that would make you so . . . crazy, would make old Buford so fucked up, that would stop Sarah from going straight to the cops or her parents. What's Sarah going to do?"

Rebekkah choked up, blinked, stared at me. "Sarah's already done half the hard part. That's what took Buford over the edge."

I mentally crossed myself for Rebekkah being on the pill. "Oh, I'm sorry. What's left except to heal up, maybe go home for the semester? This school will let her finish."

Rebekkah shook her head. "Her family can't know. Trouble is Buford knows—and he knows where she lives, where she walks, where her parents live." She looked up and around to make sure no one listened in. "He knows how to fuck up her whole life for all fucking eternity—and he will. He's pissed enough at losing her and losing both his future bride and his baby to do anything."

A plan was forming, distant lights on the shore that I, rowing hard, had to reach in the night, but with each question and its answer the lights got clearer, closer. "Where does old Buford hang out?"

Her eyes got wide. I had not done that very well. "Frank, why? This is not your problem, nothing you can do."

I lied. "I didn't mean it that way. Maybe he'll cool off, find another honey."

"That scumbag will never find another Sarah, and he knows it. Grease monkey, high-school dropout."

I knew mechanics, had hung around them for lots of hours. They were mostly solid as the day is long, knew their way around cars and trucks, tractors and any gear attached to a motor. "Good mechanics are mostly good men, the ones I know, anyway. Everyone needs a good one. There's money in fixing cars and machinery."

"Hah, not this one. His old man runs the biggest used car lot—that's how Sarah met him when she was looking for a cheap car at the start of our last year here. All Buford does is wash them, change the fluids and set the odometer back—says Sarah. He's no real mechanic."

I had enough now, just one more thing to check. "You know I've seen a lot of black eyes and busted mouths from when I was a little kid until right now. Do you think Sarah would let me have a look at her? I might know something to help her heal up faster."

⚖

REBEKKAH AND SARAH, MOTHER HEN AND little limping chick, one sad pair, but the wounds were all true. Sarah's right eye was a nasty puss-crusted slit along the closed eye that looked like a peach left to ripen and rot. Her left arm hung down, her hand so big and sore Sarah could not get a mitten on it. Sarah held her right hand over her mouth as she talked slowly. Her mouth must have looked like an old hockey defenseman's. And Buford had been calling the sorority house a couple times a day, sometimes calm and nice, sometimes yelling.

I told them to alternate hot and cold compresses, and no aspirin for a few days. Near as I could figure, the left arm was broken and had not set itself. "Need to get that X-rayed, set and splinted, or you'll be messed up for life. Guess you can tell your dentist you slipped hard on the ice. That much should work."

Sarah looked at me as if she already figured all that out.

"That arm, if you don't get it right, they'll break it again later or your muscles and feeling could be gone for good."

Sarah winced and caught her breath.

Our team's trainer was a square guy. He knew the best bone and muscle doctors and knew to not tell parents or anyone without a damned good need to know. "Let me check with someone. He might help. Does it all the time. I'll talk to him later today, won't mention any names or even that you're a girl unless he says he'll help."

Rebekkah and Sarah both said, "Thanks. Thanks a lot."

⚖

THE DEEP SNOW AND COLD OF JANUARY winter gave me great cover. No one would look twice at a guy in a ski mask with only the mouth and eyes showing. Between hockey practices, games on Friday evenings, school work, and dishwashing duties, my timing was tricky. But most late afternoons, I did have about an hour of free time.

My fourth time checking out Mason's Best Pre-Owned Cars seemed perfect. The overhead door to the dark repair bay next to the office was closed, I'd seen only one person around, and I had my favorite hammer in my deep pocket.

I entered. He looked up from a chair behind the counter while I pretended to want something from the shelves, maybe a can of oil or antifreeze. Windex, wiper blades, fan belts, tire chains, and other car items covered shelves near the front. He stopped looking my way. I tested the door's bolt lock. It slipped into position easily and clicked shut without making any sound. My back to him as if looking out the windows, I turned the sign to "Closed". He didn't seem to care, too busy with his day's-end paperwork. I turned the front window shutters a tiny bit, so no one outside could look in. I grabbed a can of Mobil 40-weight motor oil and moved to the little counter and desk area as if to pay.

His head down made my task easy—the stack of *Playboys*, a full centerfold open in front of him alongside what looked like invoices and a ledger book. "Hey, got the December double issue there? Best of the year, if you ask me."

He looked up and smirked. The smirk changed to a puzzled pout, a James Dean look, as I moved around the counter fast and stood over him. "You're Buford, right?"

Buford closed the *Playboy*. "Sure, be right with . . ."

I swung my two-sided hammer down hard and fast. The grip fit my hand just right, the balance of the thing was great. The flat end of the head caught Buford's right hand as it patted down the magazines, caught it right above the knuckles and below the wrist. It made a sound like a wild dog crunching down on chicken bones inside a plump thigh. The opposite side of the high-quality forged metal head, the side pointing up now, was wedge-shaped and pointed straight up at Buford's mouth wide open and starting to scream or yell.

Only a half yell made it out, and Buford managed to rise out of his chair only halfway. I had moved around behind Buford and with my left hand stuffed a cold oily rag into his face. I hit Buford on the back of the head with the flat middle part of the hammer head. I had calculated right. The blow buckled Buford's knees, made him sit again, but not lose consciousness, not fall over or miss the chair. Flat blows to the head with a hard object did that—knocked the legs out and jiggled around the soft brain mass in the hard skull but showed hardly a scratch on the outside.

I pressed the rag in tighter, snuffing his screams. This would be easy. Buford was almost as tall as me, but thick through the middle and chest, a thickness brought on by fat, not much fight in this body. "Easy, big boy. If you don't want to get hurt worse, stay there. Sit tight and keep quiet." The tension in Buford's jaw, the shoulders, lessened. "Sit on your hands. Do it now."

Buford obeyed, but slowly and only with the left hand. He shook his head. "Can't," he croaked through the rag.

"Hand back on the table and flat where I can see it. Keep your left hand under you." I held the hammer high toward the front of Buford's face, and he obeyed again. Through eyes wide from pain and surprise, despite the dark rag still in his mouth, Buford was no mechanic. His fingernails were clean, his upper body not bulked out, his black hair wavy. Chicks could go for him, I guessed. "I'll take this rag out of your mouth, but only if you keep still. Got it?"

Buford nodded, breathed hard and fast, closed his eyes over tears.

I clamped the rag onto his broken right hand lying on the desk and put my face six inches from his. "Listen to me like you've never listened to anyone. Your former girlfriend does not want to see you, talk to you, get a call from you ever again. Do you understand?"

"Yes, but . . ."

I tapped Buford on the head, hard enough to hurt but not knock him over in his sitting position. "No buts allowed." I sensed a protest rising in the body connected to the broken hand, but then the protest died. "Guys who beat women don't get any buts. If anything happens to Sarah, to her friends, to her family, I will finish this. I. Will. Kill. You. Got it?"

Buford bobbed his head as best he could and mumbled, "Got it."

"She did not send me." Then I lied, but a good lie. "She does not know me, never laid eyes on me. Think of me as the almighty fucking guardian angel protecting good people against bad people like you. Got it?" Another hammer tap, this one on top, on the wavy hair.

"Got it."

"Promise?"

"I promise."

"Head down on the desk and eyes closed. Do it, and I won't hit you again."

I pulled two cords out of my other deep pocket and quickly looped the end of one around the wrist of the broken hand, pulled that hand back and tied both of Buford's hands together behind his back.

"If anyone asks, tell them it was a robbery at gunpoint, but they must not have found much, what with the cash register already emptied out for the day. I saw you do that too. Tell them you got lucky, that everything seems to be here."

I tied Buford's feet together with the second cord. "I'll turn the lights off on my way out. Count to a hundred before you move. Got it?"

Head still down on the desk, eyes still closed, Buford groaned, "Got it."

My ski mask was starting to itch, to get hot, and I was glad this had gone so well, so quickly. One last look around, and this was the first time I noticed the padded Band-Aid on Buford's cheek on the side that had faced away from me, where Sarah must have bitten him. I wiped the can of Mobil oil clean of any fingerprints, put it on its spot on the shelf, backed out, turned off the light and exited into the cold darkness.

Chapter Ten

Angela

Six weeks after that cut-off court session, I again started with the *Hollenbeck* case—to finish what had been so grotesquely interrupted. The lawyers had the right to talk to me, and I had some questions, for one side anyway. The insurance company's entourage had shrunk down to its main lawyer, Mr. Pierce Montague, and two helpers.

In another full courtroom on this Friday morning, I asked Mr. Montague, "Ms. Hollenbeck's application for insurance did not list any health issues, and she had indeed spotted abnormally before the date she signed that application for insurance under penalty of perjury. Do I have it?"

Montague cleared his throat. "Rightly so, Your Honor. That's the crux of our position."

I detested that expression from lawyers—*our position*. A courtroom lawyer's purpose is to tell the true facts, present the controlling law, not to *position*. "And you assert that she was obligated to tell All-American Insurance about her spotting. Do I have that?"

"Yes, Your Honor, right again. The application for coverage, signed under penalty of perjury, requires no less, and without any disclosure my client properly, under all law, had the right to not cover the sequelae of that abnormal spotting, whatever they might turn out to be," Mr. Montague bowed his head, "however unfortunate."

"But your client knew of the pelvic exam and the spotting, didn't it? Knew before the date of the policy? Do I have that?"

"No, Your Honor. I believe the court misapprehends. There's nothing in her application for coverage about any of that, not a hint."

"Ah, Mr. Montague, what about the email in your client's files with her medical records attached, that said, 'On pelvic exam, patient complains of spotting.' Do you dispute that e-mail and the records on which it was based?"

"Our position is that the email is not properly before the court. There is no proof of authenticity. Your Honor, anyone could have written that, put any date on it. The applicant has a duty to disclose on her application. And my client has the right to rely on the application."

"Mr. Montague, if Ms. Hollenbeck had not somehow in some way, perhaps by giving your client permission to obtain her medical records, or in a phone call told your client of that exam, of that spotting, then who did? Or did your client hack into and download Ms. Hollenbeck's med records without permission? You're not saying that, are you?"

Mr. Montague snorted, opened his mouth but nothing emerged for several beats, then, "With all due respect, Your Honor, that string of supposition is hardly admissible evidence, and besides any such disclosure by her came too late."

"Are you, Mr. Montague, telling the court that this email is dated after your client issued the policy, but someone within your client company forged an earlier date onto it?" That one brought laughter from the gallery. Not to my liking, but my question did sting.

"Your Honor, the dates on the emails are not best evidence. They could have been easily backdated. And, more to the point, the dates on the emails do not prove when my client received them or sent them."

"Mr. Montague, that's what trials are for. I have no doubt you'll help us sort all that out at trial, will help us get to the bottom of any improper emails, on whether Ms. Hollenbeck knew enough to be concerned when she applied for your client's coverage. Motion to dismiss Ms. Hollenbeck's case denied. I'll send out a written ruling."

Mr. Montague knew when to close his briefcase and leave. Young Mr. Lucas, Ms. Hollenbeck's lawyer, had already packed up and turned halfway to go. I said, "The court appreciates your good papers on both sides. Makes the court's job easier."

Both lawyers thanked me back.

At the morning break, Ms. Patterson handed up a note with a phone number. "A Detective Johnny Pitts called. Said he's returning your call. You can reach him on his cell any time this morning or next week, he said."

I stepped down halfway and said softly, "Ms. Patterson, please ask him if I can call him right after we're done here. If he asks what about, tell him a mutual friend and that I should not say more, that I'm in session. Thanks."

I never called Mrs. Patterson by her first name. At the beginning, the age difference and newness made informality uncomfortable. Later, I sensed she appreciated the tiny sign of respect. Respect flowed both ways in all court business.

"Yes, Judge, will do so right away."

PITTS SUGGESTED WE MEET BEFORE THE dinner and take-out crowd started to pile into Ortega's Mexican Food three miles from the courthouse. He said he knew the owners from way back and they'd put us in a corner around from the supply room where we'd be alone.

If court staff saw me talking to a strange San Diego Police detective on anything other than an application for a warrant, questions would start. No detective would ask me for a warrant, now that I sat in a courtroom that handled only civil disputes. Prosecuting lawyers needing warrants went to their favorite judges in the criminal wing of the courthouse. Judges had no business talking to a witness except in open court in front of lawyers on both sides, and judges were not supposed to have personal reasons for meeting with detectives. If any judge who knew Judge Brookfeld started her own little investigations, rumors would bubble up to the Presiding Judge, and my off-record probes would get shut down. I could not let that happen, not yet.

The real Johnny Pitts didn't match his snappy name. Red-faced, gut that long ago prevented his jacket from buttoning up, I guessed he now drew the easier investigations on the way to retirement. But his eyes were alert, curious about what a sitting judge wanted from him off the record. Old school, no laptop for Johnny, he readied pencil and notepad.

"What can I do for you, Judge? Only one mutual friend comes to mind." He looked up from his diet coke and got ready to write. The can sat next to his glass. This place had no soda fountain, but it did have great prices for good food.

"Judge Brookfeld was my mentor. For three years we had adjacent courtrooms." I waited. Most times, waiting made the other one talk, but Pitts must have known that trick, and the silence lasted for what seemed like five minutes.

Finally, he said, "And you asked to meet here to tell me that because . . . ?"

"He . . . he couldn't have, not that way, not ever in the place he loved so much. I asked to meet with you to tell you that."

"And why is that?"

Later I thought that I must have sounded foolish or rude, maybe both, the way I said too much and too fast, too emotionally. "No one's said anything about suspects, persons of interest, leads to a killer, motive—only suicide. The papers and TV wouldn't go there without someone official putting that out to them. But that's crap, stinks. Someone's laughing that Judge Brookfeld killed himself up on the third floor of the courthouse swarming with bailiffs, judges and court clerks, and within spitting distance of the holding jail. Ain't that dope, someone's saying."

Pitts ran his tongue around the inside of his mouth as if he had been eating peanut butter. "Judge, you read some of that right. But we can't tell the papers and TV hounds all we know."

So, someone did stalk the hall that Friday morning. "I get it, Detective Pitts. Makes me feel better, makes more sense now. You want the perp to think no one's onto him, or her?"

Pitts shook his head. "For you, Judge, and his family, I wish that was it."

"What am I missing?"

Pitts looked down that broad red nose at me. "You're a nice lady, and I wish I could tell you. But my report is not final, not approved. As you know, when finished only immediate family can have it, unless the news hounds and their lawyers make us release it to them, and that won't happen until after it's done and approved all the way around."

So that was it. Pitts wasn't going to tell me anything more. "He was like family. And I'm imagining a nut job killer lurking in our hallways. I want to stop looking over my shoulder. I want to stop worrying. We in the courthouse hear so many bad things done by bad people, and that makes us more leery than most. I knew him maybe better than any other judge—and he'd never do what you all say he did."

His eyes scrunched but not shut, calculating, thinking. "I need to interview you anyway, you being all that close to him. You tell me what you've heard, what you think you know, and maybe I can straighten some of it out."

Clever. Detective Pitts really did want to tell me what he knew, at least enough of it and might tell me where I had it right or wrong. "Sure. Here goes. Everyone in the courthouse says a gun lay next to him, and his head had a big gun wound."

"Well, Judge, I've got no reason to ask you about what folks say about that unless you saw it yourself."

"No. But I sure never knew Judge Brookfeld owned a gun, any gun. He'd sure never bring it to court if he had one."

Pitts pulled his head back a bit as if to signal he already knew a lot more. "Tell me, Judge, what makes you so sure he didn't own a gun? Did you ever go to his home? Did he ever talk about that?"

Pitts was a good one, after all. "No, I never went to his home. He said he lived in a condo with an ocean view over in PB. He never talked about owning a gun."

"He ever say he didn't?"

"What? What are you saying? That was his gun?"

"Can't say, but I'm not telling you anything you don't know. We can trace most newer guns to the original sale, to the dealer. Let's just say we've done our job, and it all checks out—the gun ownership. And we know how to check the splatter, the trajectory, the heat burns, the body position, and put all that together. If there's any blood where the shot wouldn't send it. You know we know how to do that, Judge. The prints on him and on the gun dealer paperwork, the FSC, comparing his real signature and the signature on the gun app, and the checking with family. We know how to do that, too."

From presiding over a gun sale gone bad case in my first year as a judge, it all snapped in tight. FSC stood for the California Firearm Safety Certificate required for every handgun purchase. *It was his gun, he bought it, even got trained in gun safety some time back, and bought the ammo and brought it in and killed himself.*

I wanted to say, *I'm done with you. A killer too clever for you is out there.* I said, "Oh, my ever-loving God." If I weren't a sitting judge, I might have let out a string of curse words. "It was his gun, owned by him, bought by him. But someone could have known he kept it and used it on him?"

Pitts shrugged in a way that said, in theory maybe, but not in reality, not possible. "Judge, I can't say, but I can say you have a great reputation."

He paused at his own BS ladled my way. "Some of the assistant DAs still talk about your first cases down in the criminal wing, all deserved. One more thing, Judge."

"Sure, go ahead. I've got nothing more."

"We know how to check the whole scene—for a struggle, for strange prints, for any knickknack out of place, for footprints on the rug. We did that, too. Your PJ McGee has been all over us to do this right. The Judicial Council, too."

"What about killers Judge Brookfeld sentenced, their lawyers, their families?"

"Sure, they had motive, but not . . . opportunity."

I mouthed *opportunity* with him. "But anyone with a California Bar card goes through the no-metal-detector entryway, and up they come to the floor, find one open door into one courtroom or to the employee area, and bingo, right to his chambers."

"No disrespect, Judge, but we follow the evidence. It's about as open and shut as it can get. Besides, we know how to call all the lawyers on all his big trials of say the last five years, of all the lawyers on his capital murder cases. We know how to trace the kin of everyone he ever put away and how to check their alibis. We check for release dates of those our judges sent away for a long time and who might have just gotten out. There's not many Judge Brookfeld put away that's been released that we need to check on. There's not that many he put away. The kinds of trials he presided over lasted for months. He only got a few every year. And he was no hangin' judge. Always fair, always giving a break where a break might help. But you know all that. Judge, you know of anyone who's got it in for him?"

I had nothing more. "No, no one." I grasped the whole event, the entire investigation, the leads chased down, all of them pointing to one set of closing notes and conclusions in the police file. *Downright happy ending—my dear Melvin Brookfeld, sitting in his chair early on that Friday morning, blew out the most precious part of him, the seat of his wonderful mind.*

I stared at Pitts while he talked and saw that he believed what he said. Then, again, cops always made the best liars. "And I expect you've traced the telephone numbers he called in the days and weeks before, checked everyone he called around here."

For the first time, Pitts smiled, the kind of smile that let me know he saw right through my little trap. "Let's say it's easy for us to get his phone records for whoever he called—both around here and any friends or family back East. He was back East just before."

Only one more card to play, one fact to challenge all the others. "Detective, none of the staff, bailiffs, heard anything? I'm not a gun person, but a pistol with that kind of wallop makes a big noise. Someone had to hear it, run up there and see something way before Friday morning."

"Yea, we've been down there a time or two. You know, people hear gunshots all the time and pass them off as a car backfire, as kids with firecrackers, as crack whores squabbling, and the squabbling gets out of hand and them shooting at each other. Someone probably did hear it, but figured it came from somewhere else. Or someone got a firecracker into one of the holding cells next door. Bad things go down not far from where you preside, Your Honor."

Nothing more came to me, to say, to ask—or maybe one thing.

"Detective, any gun dealer will have great security cameras. I suppose you matched the digital images, the date of gun purchase by our good judge."

For the first time, Pitts hesitated in a way that told me he might have missed something. His eyes flickered. He looked away for an instant. "Ah, let's just say for now we know how to do that, too."

I bet you do, but did you, you all-knowing jerk? You didn't check the cameras at the gunshop, did you? "Detective, I'm feeling a need to reach out, to let them know someone cares, to hug someone. Can you get me contact info for the family?"

Pitts took a last sip out of his glass but got only ice. As he chewed that, he said, "If it's okay with them, it's okay with me. I'll email you or call. Sorry, got to go, but if you think of anything, by all means let me know. Damn shame—and I wish it were otherwise. Look for our report. Won't be too long. Good meeting you, Your Honor."

He got up, shook my hand, dropped two singles on the little plastic table, and did not wait for me to leave with him.

I sat until a waiter took the money, the glass, the can, and asked if I wanted anything, then slowly made my way to my Camry.

Images of Melvin streamed in, of earlier times.

WHEN I RETURNED TO WORK AFTER THE TWINS were born, Melvin helped me lift some boxes of filings in "heavy" cases. We worked with sometimes massive paper filings in our cases back then, some so massive they arrived in boxes and were brought to us on dollies or wheeled file tables. Our court's conversion to electronic briefs and other filings came later.

He lifted those boxes like a much younger man, more agile and trim than his age, though I never checked how old he was. When I finished putting the boxes where I wanted them, I had said, "Wow, this is hard."

He looked at me, frowning with a tilt of the head.

I laughed. "No, not moving these files around. Giving birth and nursing them and then having to leave them, even for a few hours. I've left the better part of me back home. Their precious lives have just begun, and I must be there for them, for their every breath. Judges are not supposed to cry, but Mel, I've been tearing-up since I left them this morning."

I sensed he wanted to come closer, but workplace rectitude stopped him, allowed him to just look at me, my eyes, my nearly flat belly, my heavy breasts that my blouse could not hide. "The real religion of the world comes from women much more than from men—from mothers most of all, who carry the key of our souls in their bosoms."

"I bet Oliver Jr. said that."

"Yes, he did."

I set a box of papers on an open corner of my desk and just looked at him, at what he had just said about women and their place.

He talked on. "At bottom what we do—set the rules, tell the police to lock him up, tell the marshal to collect the debt—we do that for all mothers and their babies out there, so they may sing their little ones to sleep and not concern themselves about strange noises outside the window. You know, Judge Angela, new mother of twins, there are times I wish I were young again. Today, looking at you and at all you and your little ones have in front of you, is one of those days. But . . . then Oliver reminds me, to be seventy years young is sometimes far more cheerful and hopeful than to be forty years old. I shall carry on cheerfully, most especially with people such as you for company."

Chapter Eleven

Frank, May 1970

Freshman year turned out better than I'd expected—by a mile. I'd competed against the smart, loud kids up from the Big Apple, kids from Exeter and Andover, the best junior hockey players, and I beat them more often than they beat me—nothing lower than a B+ in the classroom, most valuable freshman hockey player. Now, I had a summer job as a crew boss in fruit orchards a short ride north of campus on the number eleven bus. On top of that, no one had come around asking me about Buford, not campus security, not the local cops, no townie friend of that asshole. Bekkah never mentioned him. She would have if Buford hadn't left Sarah alone. And Sarah healed up really well.

"Then when will we see you again?" Father said in our weekly call.

"I don't know. You know how it is with crops and farm hands. I might get some time off after Labor Day, might not. And classes start right up. Might keep working and making money until all the crops are in and hockey starts up."

"Your little sister misses you, and I could use your help. Times are tight around here."

"Father, I could send a little something home until school starts up again. My bunk is free, and they feed us well at the worker mess, and I'll get jobs fixing sheds and barns and other stuff."

"No, that's okay, son. We'll manage. Hilde works a part time job in town now. That helps. Maybe we can come and visit you after all my crops are in—if the prices don't drop more."

"That would be great, great to see you and Biddie. You'll be amazed at this place."

⚖

THE SUNDAY AFTER I CLEARED OUT OF MY dorm, Rebekkah's mother and father came to pick her up in their green Buick Skylark station wagon. Rebekkah had asked me to help carry her stuff. And she had a lot of stuff: boxes of clothes, books, and class notes, big speakers and her Grundig radio, shoes and suitcases filled with girlie things. All my dorm stuff fit into one duffle bag after I turned in my used books.

I saw right away that Rebekkah's parents were not the type to lug heavy stuff down three flights of stairs and across a stretch of grass to the car, the skin on their arms too sagging, their waists too round and soft.

Rebekkah had not asked me to sit with her at any of the graduation ceremonies, and that told me I'd never see her again after this day. I hoped my roommate, Hubie, had it right. "Women are like buses. Miss the one you want, and another one will be along in ten minutes." But on this day, I wasn't sure the next bus would be as good or as soul-satisfying.

"Mom, Dad, this is one of my friends, Frank Maier. He offered to help load me up."

"Nice to meet you," said Rebekkah's mother. Then, "You must be the one who called last winter. I remember now." Her father blew out the smoke from the last puff on his cigarette stub.

I had called. A maid must have answered, but I didn't have a number where I could get calls coming in.

"Are you going home soon, too?" said the mother. Most of the underclass men and women had cleared out the week before. The graduates left last.

"No, ma'am, staying round here and working over the summer."

"Oh, you live far away?"

"Not sure if it's that far, ma'am. Wisconsin."

"Of course. I should have known by your accent."

Until that moment, I did not think I had an accent. The kids from the City and Rebekkah's parents had accents.

"You got a job on campus for the summer?"

"No, ma'am, but not far from here."

After I stuffed the last large box in back, Rebekkah walked away from the car and the sorority house. She motioned for me to follow. Around the corner of the sorority house where no one near her parents' car could see us, Rebekkah took my arm and pulled herself into me. She took my head—sweaty and dust-streaked—into her hands and kissed me, softly and long.

"Thanks for a great senior year. Call me some time when you get down to the City. You're a great guy. I'll remember you for a long time, the fun we had, what you did for me, for taking care of Sarah."

I searched Rebekkah's eyes. "I didn't do anything. Our trainer took care of her, got her to the right people to fix that arm and keep quiet about it."

"Oh, Frank, you're so, so young . . ." She said it like a teacher about to reveal the answer to a tough problem. "We women have a way of knowing things men don't."

"Okay, and what does that mean?"

"It means you are easy to figure out." She kissed me again and made me wait. "Our whole sorority watched for Buford, asked our townie friends about him, after what he did to Sarah. It got back to us how badly beat up he was, how he couldn't work for months, his hand in casts after more than one operation."

"You never told me about his hand and all. Hope Sarah did that to him." Damn. I hadn't said that right. I had a hard time faking surprise, faking anything.

Rebekkah put a finger on my lips. "It's okay, what you did. Buford's dad made the police come around and ask a lot of questions. Luckily, by then Sarah's face looked almost normal, and the cops seemed to accept that she fell on ice and broke her arm. All of us kept our story straight. But . . . it got out what someone had done to that scumbag. He couldn't hide his smashed hand. Strangest robbery when nothing is missing, just some guy about as big as you in a ski mask, a guy who told that asshole to stay away from Sarah."

"Wow. You're not thinking I did anything like that?"

"Frank, only one person in the whole world fits the description, has the chutzpah, is enough of a mensch, to have done that. The police said whoever did it might not be from around here, that he talked like someone from not around here, talked like someone from maybe Chicago."

The thrill of it, of her knowing, all of them knowing what I had done brought up goose bumps. No tentacle of guilt on this one, just feeling good about it all over again. I crossed my hands on my grubby white T-shirt. "Lots of guys could have done that to an asshole like him."

"Trouble is, Bubele, the only guy fitting the description in the whole world who also knew what he had done to Sarah, who would warn him to stay away from Sarah is . . . you."

"What? What are you talking . . .?" I couldn't finish, didn't want to finish. It was right that they knew it all turned out as it should have. It was better they knew I had done it, better than no one ever knowing and wanting to know.

Rebekkah took my hands in hers and kissed them. "Mom and Dad will be looking for me."

As we walked back around to the front of the sorority house and car, Rebekkah moved away, strode ahead of me. Today she wore jeans that fit her just right and sandals with low heels. I couldn't not see the swivel in her walk, athletic and easy but all female. It made me sigh. She waved and yelled, "Mom, Dad, we were looking for you. I'm starving. Let's get out of here and get something to eat on the way."

She looked back at me. "Want to come—your favorite pastrami place? They won't mind—just no touching, no kissing in front of them. I couldn't stand the questions all the way home."

"Nah, you go on."

Her parents were close now, staring, quiet, brooding as their senses might be telling them about things their daughter had not told them. I reached out my hand to Rebekkah. "Well, good luck. Good to know you."

She brushed her fingers up over her forehead through her long black hair, as she had done so often when we were alone. I had loved her doing that, had told her so. "Yeah, and thanks for helping. You're the best." She turned to her parents. "Mom, can I sit up front so I can direct Daddy to the deli for this one last time?" Then, "Frank, you sure you don't want to come?"

"Sure. You go," then to her parents, "Nice to meet you."

Her father moved over to me, reached out his right hand balled up in a fist. "Thanks for helping our Bekkah, son."

I sensed it might be a dollar bill, maybe a Lincoln. "Happy to. You have a cool daughter." I ignored the older man's clenched hand.

"Well then, good luck to you." He turned away.

Rebekkah looked down at her feet. I caught a new feeling in how she didn't move, didn't want to move, wanted to say, then started to say something but caught herself—regret, wishing things were different in our lives, in hers, wishing we might meet again. "So long then, Frank."

I watched them drive into the bright spring day until the Buick turned the corner and its engine noise faded. Another family that was not mine.

Over the summer, I didn't try to contact her, too awkward to inject any of the truth, too complicated and wrong. I, three years behind her in college, almost four years younger in age, as un-Jewish as they come, had mated with her every chance we got. But our talk, what there was of it, evaded how it would end, knowing it would end, and knowing the ending could be hard on one or both of us. I didn't think of her as my first love, maybe my first woman friend and lust reliever rolled into one. I had no idea what love meant, what it felt like or was supposed to feel like. No angel choirs sang when I thought of her, no heart broke when she was far away. But I knew she had made me better, and I tried harder in all ways. She brought me peace whenever I was with her, and she would have for the rest of my days if we had stayed together.

For months I had known this day was coming, but hadn't planned anything, had not bought a little thing that might remind her of me. I didn't know whether to fight for her, to make her want to see me over the summer and after that, to follow her, to ask her to follow me, to wait for our separate lives to unfold, maybe together. Much later, I understood I wasn't sure of anything about me, where I was headed, what I wanted. And without knowing who I was, where I was going, it wasn't right to ask her for more, to ask her to jump into the rowboat of life with me. And I was sure she wouldn't anyway.

I loved Rebekkah's freedom, loved that she had picked me from among the thousands, loved her making love to me as hungrily as I made love to her. If she had asked me to stay in her life, I probably would have. But in the end, she was not free to walk away from her family, her inheritance, or whatever, to make a life with me, and I had no right to make her change that.

I had said to Hubert, "I thought I was using her. Now I know I got it all wrong. Women rule. Damn, they rule."

"Hey, FM buddy, I'll have you know you're the envy of everyone I know."

After Rebekkah's Buick pulled out of sight and sound, I headed for the bus that traveled north along the lake and the towns opening for summer tourists. I had settled into the field house with my clothes, my tools, a couple books and a bicycle one of the seniors sold me for five bucks. Staring out the bus window but not seeing, I whispered into the window pane, "I can do this, I can, I will."

FATHER AND BIDDIE, WITH OR WITHOUT HILDE, never made it to the university campus. In the fall of sophomore year my father said through the phone lines, "Son, I can't come to visit."

I caught the *I* instead of *we* and wondered. "Sorry, Father. I thought the money I sent would help, some maybe."

"Thanks, son. What you send helps out. There's more. Hard to tell you over the phone. Wish you were here."

"What's that? Tell me. Whatever it is, I can handle it."

"The women's movement, they call it, I guess." Silence for a long time then my father cleared his throat, "Hilde left me. Took Biddie with her, and the judge said it was all right for her to do that. If I want to see my daughter, I need to go to the big city, to Milwaukee city. Hilde's got a city job, and some strange lady comes around to the place she's renting to check on Biddie after school before Hilde gets home. I went down there once but can't get away from here until all the crops are in. Right now, all my neighbors are busier than a hive with a new queen."

"Sorry, Father." I did feel sorry. It must have hurt to lose Johanna, and hurt worse because it was my father's fault, and now Hilde up and left him, no loss there though. But Biddie. Father was crazy about Biddie. I couldn't say all I wanted to say, not on the pay phone, not unless face to face.

"Son, I can't send you pocket money, not for a while. Hope you can get on without my help. In fact, if you had a little extra from odd jobs or whatever, I could sure use more. Peach prices aren't so good, and I must give Hilde something every month for Biddie. The judge said I didn't owe alimony, he said, on account she's got her own job, making a steady wage."

I pushed two more quarters down the slot for another three minutes, clang, clang. "Sorry for that too, Father. Don't worry about me. I'll get by.

Most of the kids here are rich and don't want the odd jobs, plenty of them. I can work as much as I want."

"Great, son. Wish I could see you, talk to you about all the things that have been happening to me for a long time, for, well, you know . . . since your mother left us, the day you came into the world."

"Me, too, Pops." I had never called my father by that name, and the realization made me stop talking. Many of the kids around me, especially the men, referred to their dads as Pops, or Dad, and not one of them as Father.

"How's Grandma and Grandpa, anyway?" I had last seen them the Christmas before. They had looked at me constantly, hugged me hard, asked me all the questions I expected them to ask. I felt sad each time I left their house over that last Christmas. Grandma had tears in her eyes, too.

"No change there. The money from the sale of their farm land and Social Security should hold out. They're not the same since that sale, though they managed to keep the house. Last time I visited, Grandpa wouldn't look at me, and Grandma cried until we started talking about you. You're their bright light, their only light, you know. Frank. I wish you were around, but I'm glad you're not, glad you got out of here when you did."

"Thanks, Pops. Got to go now, no more quarters. I'll call again Friday. Maybe by then peach prices will pick up."

Father scoffed. "No chance of that, but thanks, Son. Talk to you next week."

Chapter Twelve

Angela

On Wednesday before the Labor Day holiday, Detective Pitts called me at home. He called late, after our girls were down.

"Judge Brookfeld's next of kin would be glad to talk with you. One of them said Judge Brookfeld talked about you a time or two. He told his kinfolk . . . hang on, I wrote it down, it was so good . . . here it is. Brookfeld told them that you confirmed the equality of women in all things and their superiority in some." Pitts' voice held a hint of disbelief. "His oldest sister, Naomi—Romberg is the last name—start with her. She's the center of the family and East Coast friends. I'll email you her address and phone number."

"Thanks. Thanks a lot."

"Judge, one caution, though."

"What's that?" In a strange way I hoped Pitts would frighten me, warn me to walk the courthouse and its private parking lot only with others around because a killer might be looking for another judge.

Pitts said, "Don't let Ms. Romberg talk your ear off. Old people, you know, go on and on. But she's still sharp."

"Thanks for that warning, for everything you've done."

"You're welcome, Judge. I sent Ms. Romberg a copy of my report, signed off by the higher ups. Judge, unless something or someone new comes up, it's final. We've checked and double-checked every lead. Funny, some of them."

"How's that?"

"No anger in any of the families of the ones he put away. Families are the first to know when they're living with a serious nut job. Some of those family members of perps he put away had seen the news of his death and seemed kind of sorry. Quite a guy, this one, mostly a real good man. Too bad. Like I said, your PJ and the Judicial Council have been all over us to get it right, to follow every rumor. And we've got it right, no doubt about that."

I whispered to myself, "He was more than that—hope the report can be reopened, hope you're wrong," and I realized I had spoken out loud. I wanted to ask what the hell Pitts meant by *mostly a real good man*, wondered if I had misheard—and was too frazzled to ask.

"No statute of limitations on murder, but you know that, Judge. Have a good evening and a good Labor Day weekend."

That was it then. Final. Except maybe for that last comment about no statute of limitations on murder. The smartest man I had known, able to quote from judicial decisions written before he was born—and then from memory state the volume and page number of the case books where the language he quoted sat—ended his life in the neediest, the most desperate way. It was all official. Final. Today or the next, news outlets might briefly mention that the police had closed the file with a self-inflicted gunshot as the sole cause. Done.

Did anyone else care? Did anyone else see it? Sandy had found another judge to give him work and had to keep his head in his new job. Mora and Ms. Patterson said how sad that Melvin had done that, though early in the mornings and late in the day they each always found a buddy to walk with them from or to their cars, from or to the trolley stop down Broadway. Deep down, they didn't believe suicide either, not fully.

And why should I care, care enough to follow blind paths? Because no one else gave a damn, because Lady Justice might as well be made of straw if someone does not care, because one of the last things Melvin said that came from Oliver Jr. went something like, *a man may fulfill the object of his existence by attempting a task he cannot achieve.* Oh, hell, Oliver Wendell Holmes, Jr. was deader than Mel, and neither of them had twin daughters who needed them. Oliver had never had any children, and Mel had hinted he never had any either.

Oliver. Something nudged me every time Melvin mentioned Oliver. That first time Melvin talked about the great Supreme Court Justice, I felt I knew him maybe as well as Melvin did, though I couldn't quote all his sayings. In law books and other places, I had seen his black and white photographs.

Early the next day, Thursday, before the Labor Day holiday, my Peter snored, and our twins dreamed of things five-year-olds dream about. Day's light had not yet pressed through the shutters, but my first pot of coffee had already cooled. I didn't need it. My fingers tapped on the counter, driven by thoughts, none related to any cases rolling out in my courtroom.

Pitts must have done one more thing, and it brought me back. He must have whispered to lawyers in the criminal defense bar or to local prosecutors that his report was done, and that no credible theories or leads were left to chase down. A group of them organized a celebration down at the Hilton on the bay. The event was this evening, the day before the Friday when everyone hustled out of town for the long weekend. All judges and some court staff were invited.

I had asked Peter if he wanted to come, for only an hour maybe. I said we could leave the girls with Nadine, who owed us more than one evening of kid-swapping.

He said, "Do we have to RSVP?"

"No, not at all. Guests can come and go any time between four and eight, the usual open bar with two drink tickets and heavy finger food. No worry about dinner except for the girls, all very informal."

"Hmm, interesting. Let me think about it. I'll check with Nadine. I know you want to go. Melvin Brookfeld was your best friend down at court, I got that."

Like a tide creeping closer, Peter's agony had started to show a bit more. I hadn't seen it at the beginning. He had taken his new job as house husband with the enthusiasm of a teen jumping into his first car. In the early days of his job change, he would never have deflected my plea. He would have said, "Sure, Hon. I'll come, too. Your sister judges lust for me, you know." And we would have laughed, though I knew he meant it. Some of the other women judges and court staff had left their jaws open looking at him, winked at me and then made big eyes at him. In earlier times, he would have said, "We'll find someone to cover the girls, even if Nadine can't. Heck, if worse comes to worst, I'll take them and hang out by the bay while you mix and mingle." He would have wrapped his arms around me and squeezed hard enough to let his energy flow into me and let his strength say all he needed to say about commitment.

Yesterday evening and last night, he hadn't done any of that, and I was sure he had not checked with Nadine.

I had seen it in victims and the accused, in the down-and-out who asked me for mercy or for some other person to pay for life's accumulated unfairness. Self-pity eats away until no more flesh is left. I didn't know how to help Peter, stop his descent, his pulling away, how to find a job for him that excited him. And that, most of all, kept me from sleeping and made me whisper, "Dare I spend one more minute chasing after Melvin's death?"

⚖

THE GUESTS GIVING THEIR LAST RESPECTS TO Judge Brookfeld laughed and acted giddy. Did any of them worry about security in this pleasant place? What if . . . from one moment to the next I wanted to jolly-up in one of the clusters but then run to another floor, find the ladies room and puke. The guests were all too happy—or was I crazy?

I didn't see Sandy, but that did not surprise me. Shy thinkers tend to avoid group things, and surely Sandy did not want to answer one more question from anyone.

The older women judges clustered in their usual grouping. In these social gatherings, we all gravitate to those who became judges around the same time. Now, the one who had served the longest, Judge Susan Greer, held a glass with a clear drink and olive in one hand and napkin topped by a toothpick-stuck piece of uncooked fish in the other hand. "Angela dear, good you could come. How are Peter and the girls?" She beamed and continued, "We hoped you could bring him."

"Great, they're great. Thanks. Hard to find a sitter on a long weekend."

"So sorry about Melvin." Susan held the *so* and the *sorry* longer than needed. That and her gaze readied me for the follow-up. "You and he were so close, what on earth do you think possessed the man to do that, always cheerful and healthy? At least he seemed to be, never missed a day." Judge Greer did not wait for an answer. "And so smart. Just proves again that smarts is overrated. The smartest do the dumbest things." She tilted her head to the side. "What do you know that you're not saying?"

The others all looked at me as they nodded along with Judge Greer's observations about human nature, about what more I knew. I thought, *anyone who thinks Melvin did this to himself has rocks for brains—and, no, we were not close in the way you insinuate.* "Maybe we'll know someday. Until then, it's just sad."

Judge Greer turned away to another conversation before I finished, didn't try to hide the rudeness, the I've-got-better-things-to-do-than-talk-to-you message.

I drifted over to a modest photo collage of Mel at a lectern along with a few newspaper headlines of big cases he had presided over. He had been a private man, and all his family had stayed away from this courthouse while he lived—and from this event now. I wasn't interested in talking to lawyers who might soon want something from me.

At the height of the evening when the room seemed the most crowded, Presiding Judge Michael McGee tapped his glass for attention. The clusters of conversation and laughter quieted.

"Good evening. First, on behalf of the court personnel as well as active and retired judges, a heartfelt thank-you to the criminal defense bars in our county and prosecutors for hosting this remembrance of our dear colleague and friend, Melvin Brookfeld."

Soft applause rose up.

"Second, I prepared some remarks, but that was before I read a letter from Naomi Romberg, Melvin's oldest sister. She sends regrets at not being able to fly cross-country, says her creaking body complains too much about airplane seats and all the security fuss."

After the expressions of agreement faded, Judge McGee went on. "I called her and thanked her this morning. I asked if I had her permission to read her letter to all of you. At first, she didn't want me to broadcast it, but then said I could so long as I also told you that Melvin never wanted any accolades, that he always said there's more to do before any compliments rain down."

Judge McGee pulled folded sheets out of his inner jacket pocket and placed reading glasses onto his nose. "Here then, from Naomi Romberg, are all the remarks needed,

Dear Judge McGee,

The recent past has fallen harder on me than anything in my eighty-seven years.

Deep in the night when I am the most morose about the last minutes of Melvin's time with us, I imagine that his spirit speaks to me. He tells me to think of him in his times of laughter. Melvin laughed often right through our last visit this summer. When he was a toddler, I, the oldest sister, had to watch for him, chase him out of the street that ran in front of our brownstone. He'd look back and laugh at me trying to catch him.

As he grew into his boyhood, his mind and body raced one against the other, not to beat anyone else, but to see how much he could accomplish and how soon. He lettered nine times in high school—and graduated a year early as the valedictorian.

We were too poor to send him to an Ivy League school. So, he rode his bike to Brooklyn College. Then it was known as City College of New York. Graduated number one there too, though he said that was far easier than today. The law school at Yale University took him on a full scholarship. It must sound monotonous, but he graduated number one there too.

Had he wanted it, he might have obtained a clerkship on the Supreme Court. The second man in his law school class did get a clerkship there. But he and Madeline both took jobs down in Washington. We hoped he would stay around these parts and perhaps follow in the footsteps of Justice Brandeis.

After Madeline was gone, Melvin took off for your West Coast. He rode the Greyhound for three days and two nights. It was half the cost of train or airfare.

We often asked him to come back. He'd shake his head and explain that the work he found with you made him useful. He said he had a good perch in the Grand Central Station of life, down on the train platforms and in the grime of the tunnels where he could do some real good. I think he meant that his trial work affected people far more than decisions from higher courts. And after what happened to Madeline, that's how he wanted to spend his time.

Melvin's chambers displayed no photo of anyone who might have been Madeline. Perhaps he had decided now was the right time to rejoin his darling Madeline? No, no, I answered back to myself, *that* he would have done long ago and in a far different way.

Judge McGee stopped, pulled a second page from beneath the first and put the second on top. He took off his glasses and looked out. "Some of you may not know. Naomi allowed me to tell you that Madeline and our Judge Melvin were married for too short a time. Naomi said Madeline was taken from him in a most frightful way. That, perhaps more than anything, brought him to us and made him ask to be assigned our most serious criminal cases. It was not my place to probe, and that's all Naomi said. And now she concludes her letter.

"He talked of you and your court. He said the weather is always the same, and he rather liked that. He said it kept him young to not be reminded of each season changing to the next. He often expressed his thanks for the wonderful, important cases you allowed him to manage, though he hated to impose any sentence of death but sometimes had no choice."

Judge McGee paused again. "Judge Brookfeld never had a single one of his cases overturned for any judicial error, not a one in more than two decades." Sounds of awe and amazement rose in the room. Death penalty cases received the closest scrutiny from the higher courts.

"Here, then, Naomi again.

"Most of all, he loved the people he worked with, his research attorney, Sandy Shields, his courtroom clerk, Francis Clarkson, and every one of the bailiffs assigned to his high-profile courtroom. He said often that he never met a better group of hardworking people, whose elbows were never sharp, whose cleverness never hurt, who would walk through walls for him and, most of all, who did all they did with a quiet grace.

"We who knew him here where he grew up, who loved him more than I can put onto paper, are mystified by how he left us. I hope those who are younger than I and care about him learn why he left us as he did.

"I will ever remember his laughter that I hear still, and I will remember with awe his wonderful mind that has helped bring some closure to many suffering hearts.

"Thank you, Judge McGee, and please thank others for holding your gathering to remember our Melvin Zachariah Brookfeld. Though I cannot be there with you, I appreciate it so much.

"Sincerely,

"Naomi Romberg"

Judge McGee folded the letter, slid it back into his coat pocket. "That's it. I've circulated a card of thanks to Ms. Romberg. Hope most of you sign it. Start an extra sheet if you run out of space. Leave it on that table over there, and I'll make sure she gets it with the photo displays."

In the quiet of that moment, I marveled at the control, the things unsaid by Naomi, and I knew I had to find her. Maybe that letter got to some of the others in this room, some of the heavy hitters in legal circles, heavy enough to start yelling at the District Attorney and the police chief. The room had turned very quiet, each of the lawyers and judges pondering Naomi's letter and maybe pondering the what and why of it.

I turned to tell Peter, but he was not there. I had forgotten. If he had been next to me, he might have seen and heard what I had to do, even to make him help in this.

I stopped by Presiding Judge McGee after the holiday weekend, asked him to let me take three days off for a "family situation back East." Judge McGee was new to the job of shepherding seventy-some other judges, and I didn't know how he would take it.

He said, "The disposition of your caseload is and has been as efficient as any of our I/C judges. You've earned a break. Hope everything back there works out."

That, and him not asking for more details, made me slot him into the good-guy column.

Chapter Thirteen

Angela

The house presided over a large lawn off a country road. I had landed at Kennedy the night before and let my mind wander on the two-hour drive to a place that felt like another country.

Naomi Romberg sat in a wicker chair on the front porch. She stood and called out, "Well, Ms. Cornwell, right on time. So glad." She moved to the top of the steps. "Come, come, come on up and visit with this old lady for a spell."

Naomi had the same laughing eyes, the same firm but friendly voice, the same solid handshake as Melvin. "Good to meet you at last, so good that you came."

She opened the screen door. "If you're wondering what a Brooklyn girl is doing out here, half this town and most of my neighbors have moved up from the city. After my Daniel and I retired, we thought country life would be just the ticket. It has been for me but not so much for him. The quiet made him restless every waking minute until he lay down for good. But enough of that. You didn't come all the way out here for that."

No easy response came to me, just more wondering about what I was doing here. My neglected cases now gummed up the system a bit more, and Peter sat alone with the twins all day and night.

I glanced down onto the chair where Naomi had been and glimpsed the cover of a novel. The author's name was three times bigger than the title.

For an instant, I mused how nice to sit on a porch and just read. Birds chirped high up in the two matching trees on the front lawn, one on each side of the driveway. A brook babbled on the other side of the road behind my rental car. *What great country to go for long runs. Glad I brought my shoes, maybe later . . .*

Naomi said, "Powder room is right down the hall, while I get us something to drink. I'll meet you in the parlor over there."

"Thanks. I'll check in at home."

I pulled out my cell-phone and worked through the presets. Peter answered.

"Hi, hon. I'm here. Wish you and the girls could have come . . ."

"That's good."

"The trees are so green they blind me. Here and there patches of red and gold, haven't seen trees like this in a long time."

"Where are you exactly?"

"In a lovely old house in the Hudson Valley, nearest town sign said Milton. Naomi is coming back, and I should go. Love you. I'll call tonight."

"Sure. Have a productive visit," said Peter, but no "love you" back as he used to, no "hurry home" as he would have in earlier times, no "I can't wait for your next call." I had listened hard for Peter slurring his words, though it was nine in the morning for him. No sound of slurring, a small thing, but relief washed over me.

I turned into the room that must have been the parlor and to a high-backed sofa guarding a coffee table. Next to the table sat a box with Mayflower labeling, open to reveal tabbed files. A lone manila folder sat on the dark table.

Naomi came back, carrying a silver tray topped by two containers filled with apple cider and grape juice, two glasses with ice, and a plate of crumbly cake squares. "Please . . . help yourself, all made right here in this valley."

The cold sweet drinks—I took some of each—brought other thoughts crashing in. Why wasn't I home getting breakfast for my family? What crazy notion made me find Naomi, leave Peter and Alice and Abigail behind after Peter said all four of us could not afford the trip? We shared all bank accounts, credit cards and our one checkbook. We could have paid for this quick family trip without borrowing. But I didn't protest, thanked him for letting me go, and Peter had said, "Sure, do what you think."

Naomi took me to the here and now. We talked of family and kids, this valley, this old house too drafty in the winter, and I lost a bit of my guilt for coming here.

She, sitting next to me, looked at the closed file in front of us and pointed and stared at me. "Angela, I so wanted to see you face to face, to talk to you before I sent you any of this stuff. It is so good of you to do this. We don't know what to make of it, but this I know, we all know. I can't, I won't believe it to my dying day. Then . . . the talk of Melvin's thumbprint on the application makes me wonder."

"Application?"

Naomi picked up and opened the file. It held a stapled batch of pages typed on a form—the City of San Diego police report. Naomi flipped the pages to nearly the last. "Here, look."

I read to myself where Naomi pointed, typed words in part of a long addendum. The body of the printed form did not allow enough space for all that had to be typed into the separate lined blank space.

> Partial right thumbprint on pistol grip is a match for right thumbprint of deceased. Deceased's right thumbprint is a match for print taken by gun dealer on the application. Signature of deceased on application matches other sig. samples. Dealer kept application and deceased's test on file as per stats. Proper sales procedures followed.

The dealer had taken the application in January and sold the gun in February. The start of the long paragraph gave the dealer's name and address in a town called El Cajon just east of San Diego. I knew El Cajon all right. Everyone in San Diego knew that town of red necks and pickup trucks.

I had the outlines of the drill from my first years judging criminal cases, the mandatory waiting period for the gun buyer and background check by the gun dealer, the required thumbprint and the written firearm safety test taken by the purchaser. They all matched up. Melvin bought the gun and used it that Friday morning. After a long time, cold questions no longer born of denial or panic, sensible ones, surfaced.

Why would Melvin trundle all the way out to El Cajon for his weapon? He lived at the opposite end of the San Diego metro area, close to the beach. Other gun dealers must have been nearer to him. Maybe he didn't want to run into a neighbor, someone he knew? A sitting judge in a gunshop buying for his own use could come across as strange, worrisome. If a high-powered judge, who dealt with big crimes every day, needed the protection of his own handgun, we were all in trouble.

I said, "Naomi, did Melvin own a gun growing up, did your father?"

Naomi scoffed. "Heavens, no. The Italians in Bensonhurst had guns and some of the Irish, but not our people in our neighborhood. Melvin was never, ever afraid enough to buy a gun, even after what happened to Madeline, never, never afraid enough to bring a gun into the house. I dare say he wouldn't be caught dead owning a gun. Oh, dear, that was bad, wasn't it?"

We both laughed a laugh of people frightened by leaves suddenly rustling on the other side of the open window. I, still holding onto the report, stood to check on squirrels playing in the season's first fallen leaves.

What then had happened in January to make Melvin buy a gun, a lot of trouble for a proud and confident man who had never been a gun guy?

I flipped forward in the report to the Conclusion and Recommendation at the end of the form. *Self-inflicted gun-shot.*

Hunger poked, reminded I had not eaten this morning. I drank some more juice and took one of the crumbly-looking cakes, custard-filled and good, then another.

I pointed at the gun dealer's location. "Naomi, this is out of his way. If Melvin had bought it, he didn't want any neighbors or people who had seen him come and go in his neighborhood to know what he was doing."

"Melvin didn't care what people thought as long as he did what was right. If he went out there, if this is his print, he might have been bargain hunting. That's all I can come up with."

Nor would he spend twenty bucks on gas and a couple extra hours driving around to save money on a gun. He had trundled out to the gunshop for other reasons I had no clue about. And if someone else ran that errand for him, not possible either, not with his thumbprint and signature on the gun application. And if Melvin hadn't done it? Had someone forced him to shoot himself? Never. Nothing would make Melvin take his own life in his place of work. But the police had locked it down. Was I that tired, that distracted, or a little crazy that I didn't allow myself to see the obvious? I gestured at the box. "Stuff from his chambers?"

"I don't think so. These files came from his home office down on the shore."

I looked up. "His clerk said something about that."

"Bear with me a minute. Our family has had a place since we were little. Uncle Edgar's actually. He paid cash for it from his first big real estate sale. The beach house is roomy enough that Melvin had his own room up on the third floor under the roof. The beach house suited him and Madeline. They used it for their honeymoon, and he'd try to go down there every time he visited, to sit by the warm Atlantic waters surging up our coast all the way from Africa, as he'd say. Warm up on the top floor, but it always has a breeze."

I made a mental note to come back to that.

"We, his family, went through many, many boxes from there and what they sent us from California. We've divided up or tossed a lot of his papers and other things. But this box has files that we didn't know what to do with. Some came from a big lock box at the little local bank down at the shore. None of us knew Melvin had secrets. His Will gave me whatever was in the bank box—as long as I was alive and functioning, ah, of sound mind and body, it said." Naomi laughed. "Oh, mercy me, here I was expecting nice jewelry or gold coins and just got these old papers," Naomi pointed at one of the files. "And one surprise."

I said, "Easy to scan all that on his computer for anyone to copy, to see."

"That Pitts fellow said there's nothing worthwhile on his computers except case notes, and they'll soon send us his laptop too if we want to pay for the shipping. I swear . . ."

"Yep, budget constraints everywhere. "

"I so hope you can give us a clue or tell us they are nothing . . . that helps us, lets us give it a rest. One file . . . you'll see. It might be something, though I hope not."

I thought out loud. "Why me? Your family or Detective Pitts should go through these things, maybe his research clerk, Sandy Shields."

"Angela—a couple things I don't want to talk to anyone without you looking at them first."

"And why me?"

Naomi sat up straight, reminding me of my mother readying to launch into a lecture. "Our Melvin talked of you often, spoke of you as the daughter he never had." Naomi tapped her right temple with her forefinger. "He said you were the only one as smart as he was, at least the only woman. And we know that's mighty smart." Naomi sat back and nodded a nod of one who has found and spoken a deep truth. "The last time I saw him this summer, he said you were his kind of judge, the kind who didn't stop until you got to the bottom of the thing. Take a look. If nothing bothers you, if you can explain it all or think it's nothing more than old criminal files or evidence from old cases, we'll be done with it. Your coming here is enough, will give me, will give those he left behind, some comfort."

I let go of the police report and reached over to the file tabs, some written by hand, the ink faded, others with typed tags, all in apparent alphabetical order. Some of the files were so thin they might not hold a single sheet. One file bulged with tightly packed papers. I got the same little gut clench as from a big new case file, the clench that said lots of work lay ahead to find the keys, to try the keys in all the slots, make sure I missed nothing. At least on this one, I'd be able to dig and think and dig some more without lawyers screaming at me that the other lawyer had it all wrong.

I tugged at a bulky file near the front, labeled, "Bank Checks", and said, "May I?"

"Certainly, they are all yours."

A tall clock against the wall across from us chimed twelve times.

As the last chime's echo died off the old house walls, Naomi said, "Ah, that's our cue for lunch. We said twelve fifteen at the diner on 9-W."

That was the main two-lane highway up this way.

The page I tugged up out of its file folder made me want to skip lunch. It was a copy of a piece of paper that looked like a check, then another and more behind that one. They weren't checks, but old copies of cashier's checks. The copies had been made from the pink or blue pressure copies of the originals and others from poor microfiche copies. They were issued by banks and made payable to cash or blank to be filled in later. The amounts ranged from $100 to $4000, all round amounts, not much now but a lot at the times of the dates on the checks—1961 to 1970.

Naomi cut in, "We must go now. I hope you'll drive. We can talk on the way."

"Maybe we can find a place where I can have some of these copied?"

"We didn't want to overwhelm you with a whole box full to take back, but we have an extra set of everything. Take whatever you like, or we can send the whole box."

I puzzled over who she meant by *we.*

Naomi stood and led the way out. "Maybe we should have made two sets."

"One will do. I can make more if I need them when I get home. Do you have the originals of these?"

"Some and some better copies. Just in case they—well, in case they give us clues to Melvin's murder—mostly, we kept the best set and any originals down in the family vault. We should have made another set for the man who called me the day before yesterday."

"Oh, who was that?"

"Said he was from the FBI, following up on our tragedy. Didn't want to tell him anything until I talked to you."

"Naomi, how did he leave it?"

"He was very nice, very low key, as if this were routine. Said he might send someone to interview me, the other family members around here, in person and check the papers our Melvin had left back here. I told him about that box. His low key got higher when I told him about Melvin's papers."

Suddenly, though I could not find it right away—too many other things to think about, the keyless key for my strange rental car, unlocking the door on the passenger side, releasing the parking brake, backing out without wiping out the mailbox—my insides told me this FBI chap had shoveled smoke at Naomi.

Pitts didn't have a clue or decided to write a false report. No FBI agent would be snooping around Melvin's death and papers with Naomi of all people. If a corrupt judge did himself in, Naomi and whatever she had collected up would not change a thing. And no corrupt judge would leave an evidence trail with Naomi. Never. Something else was at work here.

"Did he give you a name?"

"Sure did. I'll never forget that name—it means bacon fat in our Yiddish, the stuff we spread on rye bread when the cupboard's bare. We've done that for a long, long time. He said his name was Harlan Smaltz.

Suddenly I knew to send myself all the documents via FedEx, to my own chambers would be best.

⚖

AT THE MILTON DINER, AN OLD MAN BELLOWED out from the far corner, over the long counter and tables filled with lunch patrons. "Here they come, sister Naomi and the judge."

Naomi said under her breath, "Uncle Edgar, my Daniel's brother. He's all bark with a heart of gold."

Ten people sat around two tables shoved together. All were middle-aged to elderly, and all peered at me. I spotted more than one cane. Nine of the ten stood up. The one who must have been Uncle Edgar remained seated in his wheelchair.

Every one of them reached for my hand. Some leaned into me and pulled me into gentle hugs. Through the hand clasps and hugs, I felt their hope that I might ease the agony, the constant burden left behind by one of their own. Melvin was the family star, a man who made them all feel good from sharing just one loop of his DNA. The police had told these ten around this table and all their offspring that the star of the family had blown out his brains in a most peculiar place for no good reason. The act would now become their legacy. The date of it would mark the date for all other big family events. *Remember that was a year after Melvin died . . . . it was the month before Melvin . . . three summers before,* they would say around tables like this one. Some of them here and those who came after would at dark times wonder if they too tended to suicide. That kind of impulse does tend to run in families.

Edgar motioned me to sit next to him with Naomi on his other side, in the only two empty chairs.

After their many questions about my cases, about Peter and the girls, where I had matriculated, how long I had worked in law firms and as a judge, and after telling me how much younger I looked than my age, after they told me in a chorus that Melvin could not have killed himself and begged me to keep pushing the authorities until the truth came out, and after they had ordered from the big menu, their food had come and they all quieted down, I leaned over to Edgar. "Did you get a call from someone official about Melvin?"

Edgar set his spoon on his empty plate. "Sure did. How did you know?"

"Naomi said she got one too."

"Ah, yes." Edgar pointed around the table. "He called most of us. Very thorough, that FBI."

"Did you get his name?"

"Yes, yes, I did. Harlan Smaltz, retired but on assignment now, for this case, he said."

"Anything strike you about that call?"

"No, not the call. But for the life of me, none of us has the slightest idea about why he would call us, want to talk to us. Melvin never gave us a clue about anything troubling him, his health, his workload, anything. Everything bad happened to him a long, long time ago. That's why we put all the files—the originals—in the vault. Too many people are interested in nephew Melvin's files. That's why we were so glad you could come see us, help us sort this out."

The FBI had opened a case, was calling all family members—despite the local police conclusion of self-inflicted death. *Oh my, no routine suicide in this FBI case. I'm not going crazy, not crazy to be here, but what can I do?*

Chapter Fourteen

Angela

Naomi pointed at the open police report. "Now you know our family a bit. None of us saw anything that would make him do this, not now, not ever. If there were, he would have ended his life a long time ago."

I had not dared scratch off the scabs while Melvin was alive. But now . . . maybe something had reminded him of Madeline, of that life ended, of their lives together lost, and he decided to be with Madeline at last. Maybe his insides died a long time before he ended what was left on the outside. I had to ask about her, though I knew it would hurt Naomi, would hurt me. "Tell me about Madeline . . . if it's all right."

Naomi looked off to the tall window, the afternoon light sprinkling in through the laced curtains. "Yes, you ought to know." She blinked away tears as she talked. "Oh, God of all life, of all love, theirs was a union made in heaven.

"At their wedding, we danced until the morning song birds joined in—we danced better than they danced in Fiddler." Naomi tapped her fingers on her knees. "Such a wedding. Our neighborhood, some we had not invited, hardly knew, danced in the street with us. They met in his last year at Yale Law. She was a senior undergrad. Two bright beautiful people in a country free of the boots that have been on our necks since before Moses. Oh, their children would have been loved, surely loved. And it all ended before their third anniversary."

Naomi paused, but didn't want to stop, too much to tell me, too much pent up. I sensed that among her family she had been the strong one, had held it all together, had done the thinking for all of them.

"In our time growing up, Brooklyn was a neighborhood. We knew everyone, looked out for every one of our youngsters. When women came home after dark, as soon as they stepped off the elevated everyone knew them, looked out for them. Washington was not like that. There were riots down there after Dr. King's assassination. For years they called our nation's capital Murder City, USA. Melvin and his bride couldn't afford much of a place but wanted to stay close in so they wouldn't need two cars. He started as a G-9 lawyer. She worked on the staff of the Secretary of State—the great Henry Kissinger himself—got the job right away. Both together on the path to a wonderful life. Until that night when she didn't come home."

Naomi put a hand to her mouth, bit on the side of her finger and shut her eyes. "Two years after that night . . . the police found her. They studied what they found for a long time, then gave us what they found, just bones and teeth, nothing more . . . no DNA back then, no national database of fingerprints. Never found anyone who used her credit card, never found her purse or any clothes. They never found who did it, how it happened. If the FBI ever told Melvin any of it, he didn't tell us. He never talked about what he knew. We didn't ask, wouldn't have helped him or us."

Naomi stopped, had to, had to let the tears flow and let her elegant wrinkled face scrunch up. She turned away and didn't try to fight the sobs. "Old people aren't supposed to cry . . . sorry. I got over Madeline . . . but not yet Melvin . . ."

I slid closer to Naomi, hugged her gently and waited.

Naomi recovered a bit. "Melvin died back then with her. We all did. He holed up in the beach house on weekends and holidays. After they released her bones to us, he came out of that room but hardly talked to us, to anyone—as if he had been struck dumb. He packed what he could carry and took off for California. I expect his judging the big criminal cases helped him make amends for not picking her up from work that evening, for not looking for her, for not moving to a safer neighborhood.

"One of the folders in that box has her name on the tag—but it's empty. If Melvin ever put anything in that file, in her file, it was only in his head and is gone with him."

Naomi stopped but was not done. She peered at me, into my eyes with the look of a beggar who could not survive another night on the street in winter's cold. She took my hands into hers. "You're a judge. You know how these things work. You knew him. Keep after them, please. I—we—beg you to keep after them until they find the one who did this, so our family can have some peace for how he died."

"I'll do what I can . . ." I wanted to add, *no promises, though.* I had to get into the box of files. Melvin kept them all for a reason, and all the reasons might have drawn a killer to him. I had to dive in, had to for Melvin, for his Madeline, for these lovely people.

I ticked my thumb nail along all the tabs of all the folders in the box—maybe twenty something folders. "The checks are all copies, but the file folders look old, like the real file folders he set up before computers."

"Oh, yes. Some of the folders and papers have little markings that wouldn't copy at all. We thought you should have the real folders and the best copies. Our other set has the copies of the file folders as best as we could get."

"Well, I can start looking now."

Naomi patted my arm. "Excellent. I'll leave you alone. Spread out on the dining room table. Sorry none of these rooms is set up as an office. One of the last things Daniel made us do is get a decent Internet connection. So, we can look up anything that's out there . . ." She laughed softly. "We have the weakest Internet password in the universe. It's password, spelled out."

"That table will do fine. I'll get my laptop. It's in the car."

As we walked out the front door, Naomi pointed at her book on the porch chair. "I must finish that, been slogging through it for our book group. I don't get these writers puffing like peacocks, roiling around as if every character needs therapy from the day she was born. Real people don't think what modern writers cram into their heads." Naomi's eyebrows raised in a new thought. "We'd never get a thing done if we stopped every second to analyze what everyone around us just said, how they glanced our way, what mommy did to us when we were five. Takes this writer two pages to get the damn olive from the plate into the mouth, what with all the analysis of all the looks exchanged across the dining room table.

"Winter is supposed to come early. Won't be able to sit or nap out here too many more days. Holler if you need anything. Oh, and talk to me before you open up that envelope in the P. J. file."

I spotted the file tag with "P. J." handwritten on it and started with a deeper look into the copies of checks. More than a hundred cashier's checks, not including extra copies, the earliest was December 10, 1961, and the most recent September 3, 1976. The largest amount, $4000; the smallest, $100. Some of the checks had tiny hand notations scratched on them, mostly tiny numbers which didn't seem to correlate with anything. Some checks were copied multiple times.

All the checks totaled $340,500. They were written by different banks, seven in all. The total amount from each of the banks ranged between $30,500 and $52,000. Maybe that's the going price for something back then, a price with no name, not the name of the one who bought the cashier's checks, not the name of the one who got the checks. *Unless every recipient was named Johnny Cash*, I thought. Likely none of the checks was deposited into an account, more likely each turned into large green bills very fast.

I Googled the value of constant dollars. In 1962, twenty thousand dollars bought ten new cars, or a decent house. The jab of recognition poked me, an uncomfortable jab. The total dollars added up to far more than walking around money for a young lawyer on a government salary, even one with a working wife.

The next thought flashed in—the person who got the money would not hold receipt copies of the checks. The copies belonged to the ones who paid, the ones who bought the original cashier's checks at the bank. And young lawyer Melvin did not buy blank cashier's checks and then pay seven or more people over $300,000. He had no way to get his hands on that kind of money, not even from Uncle Edgar. But someone had given Melvin the receipt copies, or he, with whatever legal force he could muster, made the banks give him the copies. Or maybe the people who bought the cashier's checks, who received the pressure receipt copies, gave them to Melvin.

Patterns seeped up to the surface. Mega banks—Bank of America, Bankers Trust, Citicorp, Chase, Chemical New York, First Chicago, JP Morgan, Manufacturer's Hanover—issued all the checks. Big people doing big business used these big banks, people who wanted branches in many places, foreign branches, people who wanted large sums for individuals but the amounts routine, even small, in the money flows of these mega banks. And maybe the people ordering the cashier's checks wanted the traces buried under so much paper activity every day that no one would ever find them. And not one check had an amount that by itself would attract attention or need to be listed on daily large-transaction bank reports.

I turned to the rest of the files. Twenty-five of the twenty-eight file folder tags had names in alphabetical order, from A. D. Burdick, down to S. Yerkes. Most of the files were empty.

Admiral Douglass Burdick's file held a copy of his newspaper obituary in 1984. An Annapolis graduate, he rose fast in the Pacific naval battles against Japan, served again in support of the Korean War, and finished up in Washington as someone in a "clandestine" service that sounded a lot like the CIA. He, like many Admirals, retired to Coronado in San Diego

County. He drowned on his morning swim in a rougher than normal sea; the paper said too rough for an eighty-two-year-old man. The first hundred or so Google threads brought up nothing more on the dead admiral, no suspect who might have helped him drown, no court case files, no autopsy.

S. Yerkes stood for Senator Yerkes. Google did better on him, handsome and vibrant junior Senator from Texas, served only one term from 1970-76, and decided to not run for a second term, wanted more time for his family, for "his lovely wife and five young children all still at home." Senator Robert D. Yerkes died of natural causes at age seventy-three in 1988.

Some of the other files in between these two collected up no information on lesser people. Except for a name on the tab, they were empty. M. Brown, according to Google, might have been a civilian engineer who had published some papers on the most effective metals for bullets of different types—those meant to tumble on impact, or expand fast, or penetrate in a straight line and keep moving.

P. Davenport might have been the Congressman from Indiana. He sat for two terms, lobbied hard for farm subsidies—and then by all accounts faded away.

Niles Garland collected old rifles. Maybe Melvin had been a gun guy after all.

And Henry Grant might have been a Navy seal.

C. W. Thomas Googled into a State Department employee possibly posted to Mexico or Cuba. His boss might have been C. Orloff.

"JE Memo" on the file tab had nothing in the folder.

More patterns. All the people I could find anything about connected to Washington in the nineteen-sixties and seventies, all men located close to the center of power, of big decisions. All but Admiral Burdick and Senator Yerkes lived small enough lives that their passing, if they had already passed, didn't generate enough Google hits to land on the first five pages of threads under their names. All but the Admiral and Senator Yerkes seemed to come from the quiet side of humanity.

As the afternoon shadows lengthened and the dining room light softened, I got to the "P. J." file. I checked inside the few files past this one and then came back to it. Inside the folder sat an unsealed manila envelope. Both the edge-curled folder and the envelope had lost their sheen and crispness from age and humidity. To me, PJ was short for "Presiding Justice", the judge in charge of the local courthouse or of the branch of a higher court. What the hell did PJ mean? Back then, maybe President Johnson, and I chortled at my stretch of a guess.

I found Naomi asleep; her novel sat pages down in her lap. I nudged her shoulder. "It's me, need to ask you. May I look in this P. J. envelope, open it?"

"Sure, Angela, do open it and let's talk. That's really the one that made me beg you to come see us. I have not shared that one with any of the family and made its copies myself. But we better go inside. We must look at that one in the house."

I wondered what made Naomi say that last, and I studied the front yard grass, the driveway out to the road, listened for the sounds of birds. They now chirped and sang louder than earlier, readying for their night perches. Nothing out there to set the birds off into warning screeches or to make them go quiet. Yet Naomi closed and bolted the front door behind us.

Back at the big table, I said, "Are all these hand-written initials on the tabs in Melvin's writing?"

"Yes, yes."

I pulled four glossy eight-by-ten black-and-white photos from the envelope. It held nothing else. Not three inches out of the envelope, the top photo made me stop, look at Naomi, and pull it all the way out.

Taken from above as from a ceiling, the first photo showed the two dark-skinned men, bare-chested, lying on floor bedding, arms and legs thrown over and around each other. The sheets wound a tangle of torsos and limbs. Black pools of blood joined contorted faces and stained large swaths of bedding in black streaks and odd shapes. Exit wounds had blown out the sides of each face, the good sides frozen in twisted mouths and eyes wide open. I found it hard to look, but harder not to—and imagined the final expression on dear Melvin's face.

The next caught a young mustachioed American-looking man in the company of two dark-skinned men, all three in loud shirts and plain shorts, strolling on the sidewalk of a busy street, next to buildings crowded on each other, glaring signs in Spanish, and nighttime street lights. The two dark-skinned might have been brothers. Cars and people, intermixed, extended down the middle of the road. The three smiled broadly, as if laughing at a joke. Slim, handsome, the three faced the camera unaware. They were not posing.

The third photo showed the same young white man and another man about his age, balding, both sitting in an open-top Mustang at a beach parking lot full of American cars. Again, both men unknowingly faced the camera.

The fourth and last showed the same Mustang in the driveway of a little bungalow and a small front lawn. Police tape cordoned off the entire scene.

"My ever loving . . . Help us now." I pointed to the one photo. "Melvin must have wondered if this could happen to him. Maybe that's why he got the gun . . ."

For a long time, Naomi stared in silence from the other side of the dining room table, her hands clasped to form an A. "Maybe it's all nothing. Probably from an old case file, some unsolved murders Melvin was on before he left for California, probably nothing. But . . ." She said more quietly, "If it is something and your local police call his death a suicide . . . well, I didn't want even the police to know." She stood up and laughed. "I've seen too much TV, but you never know, do you?" She laughed, more a snort than a laugh. "Maybe Detective Pitts knows a whole lot more. Maybe this—" She pointed at the police report folder off to the side, "is one great big whitewash. I didn't ask Detective Pitts to send along whatever photos he had of Melvin. He must have scores of them, but they're not part of the report. Makes me wonder. Well, that's the worst of the strange files in the box, for sure."

"Naomi, let's sit a minute. I'll go through the rest of them, not that many, after the shock of these leaves me."

"And I'll get a little supper organized." Naomi left the room.

As the evening breeze pressed through leaks in the window frames and into other openings of the old house, I flipped at some of the files lying out on the table, read the name tags again. One of the file folders held the only hand-written sheet. Its tag said, "DK. TF." The sheet listed sets of capital letters, three in each set. They might have been initials of something or someone. Seven of the sets had check marks next to them. I recognized the handwriting—Melvin's—but nothing more clicked in.

These mostly empty files fit what I expected. Melvin never needed to make notes, never needed to write down a published case name or its citation. His mind filled these file folders and added what he needed to the copies of checks, the newspaper article on Admiral Burdick, the scant notations on some of the tags, and the list of letters with check marks next to seven. But he had kept hard copies of some items, photos and papers, all items that might one day turn into real evidence in my kind of courtroom.

I pulled my sweater tighter, hugged myself and shivered from the cool air, and from the bits of larger stories in this box. Or perhaps I shivered from the truth in these papers—someone had killed dear Melvin for what he knew, for pieces of evidence he had collected, for having found out something worth murdering a sitting judge. No hopped-up junkie or a hard scrabble youth needing to bust a cap for his initiation into the gang in his hood had killed Melvin. Someone able to saunter in and out of my courthouse, into the back chambers and leave without anyone noticing had done this to Melvin, had done it for reasons explained by the items in this box.

Chapter Fifteen

Angela

The dry evening air cooled fast, perfect for running. Naomi sent me to this track around the football field down behind the high school. Others trotted or walked, singly or in pairs. Once into my easy lope, I noticed them only when I passed them, too many things to sort out, to work through, to let go of or grab onto harder.

Peter, Alice and Abigail. I hadn't seen my girls in two days, hadn't talked to them yet this evening, had to call them before they went to bed.

As always on my long hard runs, thoughts went where they pleased—to mom with Parkinson's, to a father I had never known, to my cases with no one else shepherding them through the system. The state of California paid me a decent enough salary, set me up in good working conditions, provided me and mine a great health plan, and... gave me the power to change other people's lives. Yet here I was. *I'm a judge, a judge, no investigator, no cop, no prosecutor. What am I doing?* My feet ticking on the new rubberized track asked, over and over, *Why did I come here?*

Ego, or ambition? Take my pick. Did I miss life as a hot-shot junior partner at a hot-shot firm? Did I miss helping wealthy clients get wealthier by bashing their adversaries. Did I miss it so much that I needed this snooping after a dead man—and who knows how many other dead people with their heads a bloody mess? Not ambition. Boredom, that was closer. Judging bored me, made me chase Melvin's past? Ego, ambition, boredom, why else? Maybe it was that other Ambition, the one with a capital "A", the need to prove I was as good as the rest, to show them I was as smart as Melvin, smarter than Detective Pitts, that I could run to ground whatever Melvin and Pitts had let get away?

That was closer, wasn't it? The wisest, smartest man I had ever known hit a hard wall and killed himself, or let someone outsmart him, get to him, and I had to finish up what he could not. *Dear God, help me*, said my feet, said my thoughts, over and over.

Why did I take to running, anyway? I was a runner before I remembered, was always good at it. Is that why I did it, or to prove I could beat the boys in my class, to make them look at me with respect, instead of just as another *girl*, and later to prove I could beat men, too? *I sure as hell hope that's not it, that's not what makes me do this.* To tamp down longings for a real dad?

The day's last light over the hills changed from pale blue to rose then gray, and floodlights clicked onto the field and onto the track around it. I upped my pace and started to sweat. *Justice . . . justice . . . justice . . . finding the one right thing . . . finding the truth.* That was better, that had to be why I did this. No one else lifted a fat finger to find the truth. And if that wasn't it, then a slow madness had set into me.

What about that FBI fellow snooping around now? Should I let Smaltz take over, let him run this to ground? Maybe. But that didn't feel right. The FBI had no jurisdiction over a local suicide, even a local murder—unless it knew who did it and whoever did it had crossed state lines. Damn.

A couple of men—high school teachers, maybe—said something as I raced past them, said it in a tone of surprise at a babe with a ponytail racing past them, then giving them a good view of her long legs and great butt covered by her full-length running tights. I looked good in this outfit, younger.

Peter and I had met like this, me blowing by him on a hard run, and him kicking back not letting me pass him, not until I passed him for keeps, and him laughing through his hard breathing as I pulled away. His laughter, kind and strong, had made me stop at the end of that 10k race and look for him. I spotted him but acted as though he was not my target, that someone else was.

Then and even now he was lanky but not scrawny, not a long-distance runner but an athlete with good shoulders and a great torso but not one that came from ten thousand crunches and heavy weights. He looked as if he had been born into his body.

He spoke first. "Hey, you're the one who kicked my butt. Nice run." He laughed softly at me, at himself. "You're the only girl who passed me, must have come in first for the women, huh?"

I pretended to have just caught on, to have just figured out who he was. "Oh, oh, yes. I guess I remember you. Nah, I didn't win. There's always a couple D-One runners in these things, and they start up in front of the pack... and I'm way past my prime, can't catch them if they start out ahead."

He laughed again and shook his head, a head of good dark hair even sweat-soaked. "Yeah, I know the type. Once they take the lead, no catching them." And he laughed a laugh that said he did not mean that last, but sort of did.

And I was smitten.

Now, on this night, in four more laps I passed the two men again. This time they stopped talking when I came up on them and then passed them.

I kicked up the tempo and lengthened my strides. Old Joe Ward of my firm said every busy lawyer needed something to cleanse the mind, and in six decades Joe said he found only two mind cleansers—alcohol and long-distance running.

The cleansing began. Again. The harder I ran, the farther everything receded until only the tick, tick of my feet, my heavy breathing and strong pulse remained. All I felt was the running, the flying in that instant when both feet were off the ground, my kick into the next stride. So good, so needed. By the end, the all-over thoughts always lined up neatly and waited for my commands of what to do first and next and after that, what could wait until my next run, and what to toss aside.

Drained, breathing past my limit with a heart rate higher than ideal, I slowed and eased around to the side of the bleachers that said "Home" in large green letters across and above the last row. I headed back to the front of the school and the parking lot. Trouble was, after this run I still didn't know what to do next—other than to call Peter and the girls and get out of here tomorrow and onto that flight back home.

"Hello, there."

The voice from the shadows where no floodlight reached made me jump, not from surprise but more because I knew that voice.

He stood this time, leaning against the cold concrete of the side wall, the same white hair, the same mustache, maybe even the same suit. "Again, I did not mean to startle you."

"Shit," I both said and thought. I closed my eyes so that his eyes could not take hold as they had the last time.

This hard running really messes me up. I'm too old for this.

"I won't take more than a minute. Give me that. No Lady Justice statue lessons this time."

I looked around, back to the track, out to where I was headed. No one else was near, no one else noticed. I slapped my face hard enough to feel the sting.

The old man seemed to smile at that.

"What the h . . ." I caught the rest of the word. What if there were a hell and this thing came from there? "Okay, what is it?"

The old man raised his hand for me to listen. "Hope you did not hurt yourself with that slap. You have grown a lot since the last time, have grown well, taken on a lot and that is good. Far too many people die with the music still in them."

I had recovered enough to breathe normally, to know I might soon feel the cold air. That last thing he said made me say, "I've got . . . too much music in me, I think. Others need me . . ." I could not get out more, talking to a ghost or with a figment my jumbled brain had conjured up, the same figment as that other time in the mountains. His eyes peered at me just as hard, eyes that did not blink or fade in nearly total darkness.

"They'll get by. And in the end admire you more, love you far more for the doing of it than if you do not. In the end when we are done, the pain that comes from doing nothing is the far greater pain."

I waited and backed up, but the old man did not fade. He moved along with me, a normal gait, his shoes on the pavement making normal sounds. At last I said, "I . . . think I know that, and that makes it so . . . hard."

"That is as it should be."

"But . . . I don't know what to do. I can't do this alone . . ."

"Everything worth doing starts with a solitary idea in a solitary living thing acting all alone. Help will come, even from places you don't expect, as long as you press on with everything you have."

I heard our voices echoing a bit off the big concrete wall that held up the bleachers, his voice just as real as my own. I thought and said all at once, "I don't know where to start."

The old man smiled, his good teeth visible. "If you knew, it would be easy. If it were easy, Melvin would have closed this off and would be in your world still."

How did he know about Melvin? How did he know why I was here? I didn't dare ask about things that in the end did not matter. He knew about Melvin and knew I was here. I had to stay with things that mattered. ". . . I don't know, and I'm afraid too, afraid of finding nothing more, afraid of that other answer, afraid that Melvin is not the man we all thought, and more afraid of finding that he found something that made another man shoot his brains out."

The old gent paused and held up his hand, as if waiting for just the right words to come to him. "You know, your inner self knows this: all there is is to bore into it as hard as you can."

"Oh, God . . . sorry, that's not right. I don't think you're that God, the one with the capital G. Whoever you are, I don't know that I'm up to it."

"Go then. Do the best you can. A life fulfilled is a life of grappling with things that we don't know we can bring to ground. That's all that is asked of any of us, of you. Go, I won't hold you any longer."

I turned to leave but repeatedly looked back until I could see him no longer. The old man waved. I waved back. And then he was gone.

Groping in the little pack for the rental car's smart key, walking out and around the school to the parking lot, feeling the cold night air reach into my spent body, it hit me, the connections to Melvin, old photos from books, books about the history of the laws that are meant to guide us, check our dark impulses and encourage the better behaviors. That old chap was surely *him*.

I conjured up his photo, maybe wearing that same tie. There was only one head of hair, one white mustache, one set of deep boring-in eyes like that. *Melvin . . . dear Melvin, did you send him? No, you couldn't have. He came to me that first time long before I knew you. Did he send me to work with you? In the same courthouse you and I, practically roommates for my first years? Did he know what would happen, know that I'd be the last one to care? Spirit of Melvin, spirit of Justice Oliver W. Holmes, Jr., help me now, help me make sense of this, and after I've made sense of it, help me get through this.*

Heading out to the parking lot, my mind spun back to the hardest trial I'd handled as a lawyer before I became a judge. At the start I had only a mousy old woman, sitting across the conference table where I first met her, with a halting, soft-voiced story of life-long abuse by two older brothers about to send her to an old-age home and steal her one-third share of a family fortune. I hadn't known where to start but knew that nothing would get done unless I did it. By the time we got close to trial, all manner of help blew on our sails—old family friends who had seen it but had been afraid to do anything, the family's long-time financial advisor, the family doctor, people from her church. Her case taught me like nothing before it that one committed soul will cause heads to turn and will fetch help from unexpected places.

I laughed out loud, told myself that I've got to stop running. *No, as long as my knees will let me, I can't stop that, but . . . this is ridiculous. Maybe a tumor's growing in my brain . . . maybe I wound myself too tight. I know, tightly is more correct grammar. Dear Melvin or Oliver, give me a sign that I'm not going mad, that I can keep going, that I can do all that must be done.*

⚖

"WELL, HOW WAS IT?" NAOMI GREETED ME from the porch.

"Thanks, great track, great run. Just what I needed. Lots of people shedding the troubles of the day down there."

"Well, the best stuffed cabbages and mashed potatoes in this valley await us."

"Ah, yes, I can smell them. Wonderful. Must call my girls and get cleaned up. Won't take long."

Peter picked up the phone. I started, "Hi, Love. Nice to hear your voice."

"Remind me when your flight gets in."

I didn't know why he said that of all the things he could have said. He had my flight info. Damn, this was getting harder. I told him the time and that I'd go straight from the airport to court, grab my car parked there, and hurry home.

He said, "All right. I'll put the girls on. They are asking about their mommy."

His speech and voice sounded okay, just flat, hollow.

But our girls were happy and bubbly and excited to tell me about their day, the cut-outs they had made while daddy fixed dinner, their running in the park that afternoon. Peter was still their great dad. That had to be enough for now.

Over supper Naomi made small talk about this area, the high property taxes which allowed the school district to turn lights on the track at night , how the seasons changed and this land changed with them, the quiet at night. But Naomi's look had not changed. Silently, through the evening meal, the cleanup and dishes, Naomi begged me to keep going on the path that brought me to her.

Naomi seemed to exhale in relief when I said, "Who other than Melvin has gone through these files?"

Elbows propped up on the table with her hands under her chin, she said, "Probably me more than anyone. The others in our clan no longer have the patience to study difficult things, and the younger ones of us, the smart ones who might figure something out, are too busy tweeting, Facebooking when not texting, and playing video games. Not one of the young ones gives a hoot about old Uncle Melvin. And besides, they're scattered all over, move all the time." Naomi laughed. "You know how it is. Why am I telling you?"

"Naomi, I don't know where this is heading, but I've got what I'm going to be doing in my spare time."

"Oh?"

"What all the kids are doing—Facebooking, and stuff like that. But do me a favor."

"Certainly."

"If anyone—your family or a stranger, or that Smaltz guy—asks about that judge lady from California, tell them I couldn't help, didn't have time, and that I left here telling you all that the authorities have it well in hand."

Chapter Sixteen

Frank, October 1977

Something jolted me out of my usual deep sleep, made me sit straight up in my single bed. The alarm dial said 3:10 a.m. "Holy shit." While I had slept, my insides tried to tell me something, and I just got it. I dropped to the floor for push-ups until my head cleared. The oxygen-deprivation in my upper arms said this was real, no dream.

The guy I interviewed yesterday, Russian Yegor Kaminev, had done that. And what was it about him? I had it now, all worked out while I slept. The pauses before Yegor answered weren't right, some too long, and other answers came too fast. It wasn't an English-as-a-second-language problem. Yegor spoke English very well. If you didn't know his name, didn't catch the rounding of a vowel here and there, the "ch" sound too far back and high up in the mouth, Yegor could pass for a Brit. Yesterday, Yegor's face and hands were calm, professional as any high-level advisor to a Russian diplomat stationed in D.C.

Average liars can control their faces. Good liars can control their hands, and how they breathe when they make up their stories, can even control their blood pressure and keep all redness out of their noses, their ears. But it takes a great liar to control all that plus the off-screen parts of the body. And this chap was no great liar. Under the table between us, Yegor's feet moved, scuffed the rug at moments that didn't call for restless feet unless something I asked, said or hadn't said, made Yegor's feet want to run the hell out of there.

What question had set Yegor's feet to moving? I paced in my small bedroom, two steps in one direction, hard turn, two steps in the other.

Yegor Kaminev, then and now liaison to the US State Department, the same Department where Madeline worked, had insisted on his special restaurant for the interview. "Let's meet at my favorite restaurant. I can get a good quiet table where we can talk," Yegor had said.

Meet him where he said, or we'd get no meeting, nothing. Sam said, "We'd better meet him there. But check out the owners. I bet they're Ruskies and have installed whatever listening devices they want, whatever transmitters they want." Our meeting did take place in a Russian restaurant recently owned and refurbished by Russians.

Agent Sam also said, "What you want to bet this Yegor chap has to show off and pay for lunch—has to put it on his tab. Then I bet he goes back and writes a report to the Mister Resident that he's working on recruiting us."

The Resident, short for the head KGB at the Russian Embassy, was probably listed for State Department and customs records as one of the Soviet Embassy's cooks or waiters.

Yegor had said, "How you say, my treat? You guys buy next time. They know me here, and I can—how do you say—run a tab." That offer and the idiom pleased Yegor enough that he spread his arms wide.

Agent Sam looked at me and waved Yegor off. "Can't do that, my friend," and smiling back, "fill out too many forms if we do that. As we say, we'll go Dutch."

And now deep in the night, I sensed Yegor's nerves caused the grand gesture over a petty-cash lunch tab. The fear of getting caught, the shame of having to confront his tough bosses, the dread of a good capitalistic life unraveling had betrayed him.

None of it was evidence usable in a courtroom. Shuffling feet, pauses at the wrong times, blinking too much or too little. Acting like a big shot over nothing could never become real evidence. None of it showed what Yegor might have done in Mrs. Brookfeld's vanishing and death.

There was that other thing, too. Solid smoking-gun evidence could never get Yegor into a courtroom. Under diplomatic immunity, mere personal crimes by official embassy staff were off limits from prosecution. If we could haul their embassy staff into our courts, the Soviets could do the same to our embassy staff for any reason or no reason at all. And so, both countries gave the other immunity for anything done by the official list of embassy idiots.

"Yes, as I told you the last time, I remember her well." He had said, smiling. "What man would not remember? Beautiful girl—even if she was a Jew. On a hot summer's day, she in that dress, you know. American women have no shame." He shrugged, no doubt thinking of lemon sherbet melting in a warm summer rain, of that lemon skirt clinging in a wet wind to her long legs.

Bastard. Arrogant Commie Bastard. I knew this much—this Yegor chap, whose last name translated to "of stone," would pay for his drooling.

After a permission-granting nod of the head from Sam, I had said, "Sorry to go over old ground. Do we have it right that you stopped by State that day?"

"Yes, of course. That's how I know what she was wearing—but then I always notice what all the young American women are wearing. Part of my job to know."

Yegor could not lie about having seen Madeline the day she disappeared. At every visit he had to sign in, had to note the time he arrived and left, had to write down the name of anyone he came to see, and had to wear a visitor badge with a number. And on that day, Yegor had come to see Madeline's boss.

I had responded, as dryly as I could and with a man-to-man inflection, "Yeah, you know it's part of our job, too, checking out what the honeys are wearing, whether they might be trolling for a hot date. But I'm single."

Yegor didn't skip a beat. "Hah, in my country married men are expected to keep a mistress. Makes us interesting. And, I must tell you, that yellow number was my favorite. She didn't have many outfits, not too many to keep track of. I always looked for her when I went over there. How you say, flirted with her. Never know when a guy gets lucky, yes?"

I took a long shot. "Say, Mr. Kaminev, and when you do get lucky, where do you take them, so your lovely family and coworkers won't find out?"

Yegor laughed. "A thousand places, a thousand, I tell you. You guys know our apartments all over this city, but maybe not all of them. My country wants us to get close to the natives. But you know that already, yes?"

From Yegor's file, I knew this, but the candor, the laughter over everything—not only the nervous laughter, but another more in-your-face laughter—confounded me. What more did he know, what had he done on that hot and rain-soaked evening?

Yegor had been an arrogant hot shot since his pre-teens, a wrestler hand-picked by the Soviet athlete machine. He had medaled in many big meets, won a bronze as a middleweight Greco-Roman wrestler in the Rome Olympics of 1960. I wondered where the medals and trophies sat, maybe in some big cold room in a big cold building in the Motherland. Yegor's handshake was one of few that matched mine when he wanted to show off.

I wondered if I could take him. I had youth and conditioning, but this old Bolshevik no doubt knew holds inside of holds, holds that crushed like the jaws of a bulldog. In yesterday's interview, I had asked, "Ever do any rowing or water sports? Any hockey?" No doubt Yegor had a file on me.

"Nah, no time. Too boring, no challenge there, you know. Why do you ask anyways, what's this got to do with that Mrs. Lemon Dress, what's her name?"

"Aw, it's nothing. I played some puck in my day, I'm still on the Bureau team. And . . . you guys are the best."

Yegor nodded, then scratched his prominent chin. "Yes, we are good at lot of things. Now I must stop talking about her . . . unless you're going to arrest me?" He threw his head back, exposed his thick neck and let out a laugh that said he knew we could never arrest him even if he had done terrible things to Madeline. He leaned up and signaled for the checks. "Ah, so sorry. And . . . good luck with finding more about her in her wet dress, even after all these years. Maybe you'll find she ran off with a real man, another Russian maybe?" And Yegor laughed some more.

Damn. I had to figure this out. Chances like this don't come along often. And then it hit me—the thing that woke me up, the secret screaming from the part of the mind that never falls asleep. Pioneer Point. Fucking Pioneer Point. That's what screamed like my alarm clock a little while ago. Seven years back the Soviets had bought an old estate on leased land right on the water at Pioneer Point, not close to Jug Bay but no big deal in a covered skiff. Besides, they would have been crazy to bury the body near their little resort. They figured that place and water nearby were watched round the clock—even if they weren't. And someday someone would find a body buried near them, and all hell would break loose.

Another truth piled in. The Soviet regular diplomats probably had no clue, would not have allowed it, the scandal too big, the fallout too painful. This was all done by a closed group, by specialists every bit as secretive as CIA black ops hit men.

Now, on this very early morning, no other thing brought on these feelings, so good, so strong, so empowering. Time to start the day. Time to start this game, time to find out why someone took Madeline off the streets, why Melvin shut us down and kicked us out too soon, why Yegor's feet shuffled like a deer on slick ice at some of our questions.

I didn't tell Sam any of my musings about Yegor. I'd be laughed at. An FNG's feelings were the opposite of evidence, of anything useful.

On my days off, on evenings when I didn't toil in the squad room, I hung out around the Russian embassy. Not close, down a couple blocks but close enough that I saw cars coming and going through the gate and, with my opera binoculars, made out the faces of the drivers unless their side windows were dark. A camera would catch me some of the time. But I didn't care. A Russian techie might look at the film or the monitor, might notice me, run to his supervisor, might try to ID me or my car, and then what? A new grunt FBI agent watching the Russian embassy, nothing new in that, happened all the time. Sam need never know.

My waiting and watching paid off. I caught Kaminev leaving in his car, a clean black Mercedes with red leather interior. Son of a bitch. That fit. Better yet, Kaminev didn't much care who followed him all the way home. His home address must have been listed on the Russian Embassy employee roster given to our State Department, but I had no access to that list. And on a Tuesday afternoon, I got lucky.

Yegor pulled into his driveway and stopped his Mercedes and, still in his car, turned to me sitting down the block on the opposite side of the street and waved.

Cocky son of a bitch, might as well make the most of it.

I got out and waved back. We shook hands hard, each silent, each looking hard, each smiling, each not wanting to talk first. At last I said, "I just had to ask you a couple more questions. Hope you don't mind. That Madeline girl and her husband keep me up. And it struck me you might have been the last person to see her alive. That log-in sheet showed you and she left right around the same time."

Yegor lifted the handle of his garage door in the apartment complex. "Got to get me one of those machines to open this by remote, yes? What more can I tell you, Agent Frank? So, she's dead, not run off with the building super, aye?"

Damn. I had let down my guard—and been caught. In the Russian restaurant, neither I nor Sam had said that she was dead—or that Yegor might have been the last one to see her alive. And I had just blown it. I tried to wiggle out. "After all this time, it's a good bet. Don't you think?"

Yegor turned to get back into his car and drive into the garage but stopped. "Maybe, maybe not. Your American women have become so—how you say it—so liberated. I been thinking that maybe she take off to California with the building super and is too embarrassed to tell anyone?"

I shrugged as if half agreeing, but Yegor had said that last too fast, had slipped into grammar mistakes. Something was bothering him. I had only one question really but couldn't come right out with it, not yet. I stalled. "Seriously, look, you guys know a lot that we don't. She worked for State. You and her boss had a lot of dealings. Did you guys hear anything, see anything, anything we missed, any clue what happened to her?"

Yegor raised his finger, signaling wait a minute. He got into his car, still running, and eased it into the garage, the garage half given over to bikes, tools, and junk. I followed. I hadn't seen a woman or kids over the weeks I'd swung by here. Yegor's wife and kids were supposed to still be here, still living with him in this very building.

No second car here, no boat, no pickup, no sacks of gravel, no rope of the kind that would tie up a body . . . and then I saw it. There it sat above the work table strewn with tools, scrap wood pieces, nails and paint cans. It hung there, protected under glass and edged by a brushed-gold metal frame with a small border matte of deep maroon. The navigator's map of the central part of Chesapeake Bay was big enough to cast its yellow hue outward in the late afternoon light. The Jug Bay Wetlands sat right there inside the left border of the map.

Shit, best not stare, best not let on. Shit, what to ask him now, you son of a fucking bitch. I tried to take a close look without Yegor noticing, wanted to walk up to it, touch it, run to get a camera and take a roll of film of it and its surroundings, check if it had a mark where the two fishermen found her bones. But I couldn't do any of that, had to pretend I'd not seen a damn thing, had to turn back to Yegor now getting out of his car and continue our friendly chat about nothing except who did better at this or that. He didn't know we had found her bones or where. In Yegor's cocky head, this chart could tie Yegor in only if Madeline Brookfeld's bones made it out of Jug Bay. This Yegor chap never expected that to happen, not in his worst dreams. Even so, best to turn around, as if the work bench and chart above it meant nothing.

The engine turned off, the Mercedes door opened and slammed shut, footsteps came at me, and Yegor's challenge interrupted my thoughts, even though I had been looking right at him. "Why should we know anything, Agent Frank?"

Suddenly I wondered if Yegor Kaminev got a little thrill in his lower gut every time he went into this garage and glanced at the navigation chart, wondered if Yegor and his buddies downed their vodka shots and came out here to admire the chart, if they ever wanted to put a little gold hammer and sickle on the spot where they dumped the body. But I'd better answer. "Aw, I don't know, just wondering. You guys probably learn things about our guys and gals, follow them here and there where we don't. You might have had a tail on her tail."

Yegor pulled down the sides of his mouth and shook his head. "Mr. Agent Maier, please get off my property." He grinned. "Or I'll call the police. How you say it? That would be a pisser."

I had to try one more, a little test, a tiny loaded question. "You like to go boating, I see."

"Actually, no. We don't have a boat. But, as you know, some of the guys at the embassy like to go fishing. Some fish every moment they can out and around our camp. It calms the busy mind, you know. And these charts are so, how you say, so cool? One of the guys gave it to me, said a new one was out. So . . . I took it and hung it out here."

I wanted to act all FBI, wanted to ask who that guy was who gave Yegor the chart, but that would lead nowhere. "Thanks. I guess that's all then. Appreciate it. Have a good weekend." I left without looking back.

Chapter Seventeen

Angela

From the place behind the mind, from inside the insides, I felt more and more that the task which brought me to this country house and took me around a strange high school track three thousand miles from home was a task I could never achieve, but the trying of it honored Melvin—and honored my existence on this planet.

I hopped around the Internet, searching for clues on why I had to do this, could do this—all in the normal range of human behavior, I hoped. Only daughter of a GM assembly line worker when GM had a big assembly line in Van Nuys, California—until he died far too soon. Helping my secretary mother, track and boys and getting top grades in whatever courses consumed me. Until law school, I had paid no attention to courts, to justices. Until the day I became a judge, I hadn't cared much about strangers dying too soon. Now dead people ate me up, threatened to ruin my marriage and my career. The Internet told me nothing about these kinds of obsessions. I pressed on, vowed to stop soon if nothing else came up, to leave it to the FBI that seemed to be on it, or was it?

Finding real information about names in Melvin's files turned out to be easy. I found them or their kids or grandkids, pictures of them, their families, their real friends and Facebook friends, Twitter followers and followees, phone numbers and addresses in People Finders sites. *Get our basic search free and, for as little as $12.95, get our full and comprehensive* *report sent to your e-mail inbox instantly.*

My next step loomed a bit tougher.

Hi there. You don't know me. I'm Judge Cornwell of the California Superior Court down in San Diego. A couple months back, my dear friend Melvin blew his brains out, they all say. I think someone else did it to him, and your (here insert "dad" or "granddad" or "mom" or whatever) might have a lead to a treacherous killer. Help me out here, would you? What's that? You get into trouble . . . Ah, I don't think so, but, if what I'm thinking might have happened to him, actually did happen to him, there might indeed be big trouble comin' down if you talk to me, if I talk to you . . .

I laughed into my pillow in the downstairs guest bedroom of Naomi's house until I choked, until I worried I might wake her out of a good sleep. No, that would not do, had to come on them unannounced with a piece of paper, like a subpoena for old records, something that gave me clout. I had to talk to them face to face in a place where they couldn't run, couldn't hang up. No doubt Melvin had thought of that, maybe done all of that, and look what it got him. And who the hell would give me a subpoena on what I knew?

This was too much, too complicated, too hard. It needed too many hours to even begin. Maybe Judge McGee would give me more time off. Judges checked out and neglected their cases for all kinds of reasons. One, a while back, went to the Del Mar track some afternoons during race season. Some, who could afford it, did take months off, but my family could not. Not one judge in the history of my courthouse had ever checked out to hunt down a killer.

Why the hurry? There's no time limit on prosecutions for murder. But there was a hurry. Whoever killed Melvin must have left traces. The killer must have traveled around San Diego, maybe stayed for a while, must have been seen by someone, rented a car, used a credit or ATM card. Time wipes away the traces. And time wouldn't warm up the traces in Melvin's old files, wouldn't make them any clearer, any easier to track down. Maybe Pitts would get on it some more now, after what I had to tell him, after what I had to show him. Maybe?

Another picture eased in from the last time I saw and heard Melvin. We hadn't seen much of each other in his last months, separated as we were by long hallways and many doors. And by then we each presided over cases that never overlapped. That last time, we were both on the sidewalk outside the main building of the courthouse complex heading in, Melvin a few paces ahead of me.

I caught up to Melvin. His face was angled down and away, a cell phone pressed up against his right ear. We nodded at each other. My entrance to the courthouse complex was a block before his door to the other wing. His phone—where was it now, who had it, what calls had he made, received? Pitts said he tracked that, easy to do if you knew the cell carrier, easier if you had the phone. I had to talk to Pitts first thing, had to give him my list of numbers and contacts snatched out of the ether from the leads in Melvin's box of files. Pitts didn't have what was in Naomi's box, and Pitts wouldn't have known to run Melvin's recent calls against telephone numbers I pulled up from leads in that box.

More questions piled in, snipping any buds of sleep. Why didn't Melvin go to the cops a long time ago? Then again, maybe Melvin had only traces and dead bodies in far off countries. He must have known enough, far more than I knew. He surely had enough to go to the cops or the FBI? Maybe Melvin had begun to tell others what he knew, and that had gotten him killed? Maybe even old Detective Johnny Pitts knew way more than what's in his report?

Maybe Supervising Judge McGee knows more, or Sandy or Natasha. Maybe dear Naomi and her files are no safer than her dead brother? Or maybe nothing's covered up, just not fully checked out, and because it has not been checked out no one is excited about whatever might be there?

And the next truth piled in. I couldn't go crashing around in the underbrush, couldn't draw attention, couldn't let anyone know what I had, what I thought, not yet, maybe not ever unless I wanted to end up like dear Melvin and those men in the photos. Suddenly I felt like a deer in tall grass, ears up and rotating for the sounds of lions. But there were two things I could do and do them without drawing bad people close to me, without risk to me or my little family.

The next morning, while packing and loading up the rental car, I said to Naomi, "Listen, if that Smaltz calls you or comes out here, can you telephone me—maybe on a phone that's not yours?"

Naomi looked away and pondered. "You think my phone's bugged."

"No, probably not. But it's easy for anyone in law enforcement to get a list of all the numbers you call."

"Oh, yes . . . I see. Land sakes, this is serious, isn't it? I'm glad you think so, too, Angela." Naomi said as if to herself, "Let me dig around. My Daniel had his own cell phone. I don't think we ever canceled it, just kept paying that little monthly bill. Might come in handy now."

Good thought. "They won't ask for the list of calls by a dead man. And when we talk, go outside. Tiny mikes and transmitters pick up people talking anywhere."

"Oh, my heavens. This is indeed serious, isn't it?"

"I must go now."

"Yes, yes, go now. Never know about traffic between here and JFK."

We hugged. Naomi said with her eyes and squeeze of her hands, *Help us if you can . . . and thank you, thank you for coming, thank you for trying to find out what really happened to our dear Melvin.*

I called Detective Pitts over the noon recess on my first day back in court. I called him to probe deeper, not about what was in his report, but what wasn't, what he knew that he wouldn't tell me.

"Hello, Detective . . . Thanks for taking my call. Just wanted to let you know I've visited with Naomi and some others of Melvin's family."

"You went all the way to them?"

"Yes, yes, I did."

"Hope you don't mind wasting your time, Judge."

"Ah . . . but I'm glad I went and met other family members, nice folks."

"Well, Judge, that's good, glad you did. Hope you didn't say we had anything to reopen the file."

Stay in role now. "No, not at all. Not after Naomi let me read your report."

"Then, Judge, may I ask why you're calling me?"

"Because, Detective, they all asked me to, asked me to tell them of any new leads, asked me to be sure you and your helpers tracked every lead. Not one of them believes he killed himself, even after your thorough report."

"Judge, would you mind meeting again, not long?"

We met in the same Mexican restaurant about the same time of day as our first meeting back last summer. He was waiting at the same table and again stood up to greet me. But there was one difference from the last time. This time he was the one who asked to meet face to face.

I forced myself into my safest role—puzzled and horrified and so terribly sad that Judge Melvin had taken his own life, wanting to know why, still wanting to be sure that any loose ends had been tied off.

"Well, Detective, thank you again for meeting me. Naomi. Great old gal, just like her brother."

I wasn't sure if it was his routine detective stare, or if he wanted to take in how I talked, how my hands and head moved, how I breathed—to figure out if I was shoveling smoke at him. There must have been a reason he wanted to meet with me, but I hadn't yet seen it.

He started. "They have my report. You said you got a look at it?"

"Thumbprint match on the gun. Signature match on the application. Melvin bought it at a gunshop out in El Cajon. Pretty tight. They all wonder what made him do that, go out there when he lived at the other end of our city. Me, too."

"Yeah, we did, but not for long."

"Can you tell me why's that?"

"Judge, I know this is bugging you and hard on his next of kin, but . . . we have all we need to put this one in cold storage for all time. We know why he bought that gun, why he used it. I can't go into specifics, and it's best not talked about on a work phone. That's why I asked to meet."

"I'll bite. Why did he buy himself a gun, what more have you got?"

"You know Judge Brookfeld had his own laptop plus that court desk top."

"Yes, most of us have our own laptops."

"His was on and open that morning, right there in front of him. You know, our crime lab is nothing compared to the FBI or a couple of the big cities, but our tech guys have all the tools to find anything on a simple laptop. They didn't worm far into his. We cleaned it out and will send it on to Naomi any day now." Pitts looked off to the side at the counter and kitchen behind it when he said, *cleaned it out*.

Damn it. It can't be that. "Detective, only three things on Melvin's laptop could make you close your file real tight and clean out his laptop before sending it on to folks. And one of those you'd put all over your report and would let family know. Hell, one of those things his family would tell you about. So that leaves only two things on his little laptop that could close this up for you and make you scrub off his computer before you sent it to Naomi."

Pitts nodded this time. "Judge, you are following me real good."

"If our dear Melvin had a serious, grinding health issue, if he was in pain and near the end, you would have put that into your report. And he, of all people, would have left detailed instructions, and . . . would have told Naomi. Hell, Melvin was back there earlier this summer. She would have known, would have seen if Melvin was that kind of sick and dying."

Pitts shook his head. "His medicine cabinet was cleaner than mine. Yeah, we would have put that in the report. Gives the living some comfort that he had his own maybe good reasons for taking charge of how his life ended. We can't make that up, won't hide that."

I looked away out the window and to the street, better to think without having to see the big rosy face, a face too sure of everything. They wouldn't hide a health disaster. Would the San Diego Police Department hide something else, to protect his reputation, the court's reputation, protect the family? "I guess Melvin could have had a big-time gambling problem, could have taken bribes from lawyers."

Pitts furrowed his wide brow. "Maybe. It's happened before in your very courthouse, ending with three of our best judges trundling off to jail. But you know all that."

I did know about that, everyone around the San Diego courts did. "But those were civil cases, and the bribes came from one hot-shot contingent-fee lawyer. And . . . Melvin had no money problems, no money ambitions. Hell, he needed maybe one third of his salary to live on. He played a bit of chess, at a high level. And that's a cheap hobby. Vacations on the East Coast were his only vice. Only one thing left . . . and he couldn't face it, couldn't stand it . . . the one other thing you couldn't put into your report. No need to, with him gone."

Pitts pulled a last noisy sip up through his straw from the bottom of his glass. "Judge, you got the picture real fast."

I was not that sure I had the picture, not clearly anyway, but what Pitts said next gave it to me in high definition.

"Judge, you'd be surprised how many men of all ages, all ranks, all family set-ups have that problem. Once law enforcement links them up with the provider, they can't run, they can't hide. The images sent to them can never be erased. They can double delete in their computer, but the sender still has their computer address and the images the man downloaded. And if the law has the sender and the sender's computer files, it's game over."

This is such bull shit, such madness. No one who lived and loved as Melvin would download any images of that kind. Anyone could have sent images of youngsters to Melvin's computer and then killed him. This killer could have downloaded those images in a minute or two after killing him—or even before from a remote location with good hacking software. Stay in role, stay in role.

I put my hand up to my mouth, swallowed. "Detective, I never saw that coming, never had a hint . . . and . . . Melvin . . . This is just too much."

Pitts stood up, again dropped two one-dollar bills on the table. "No need to put anything like that in our report, no need for you to speculate with family."

"Thanks for telling me, I guess. You told me this because . . . ?"

"Yeah, I wasn't sure about your need to know. But then when you told me how far you had gone to visit Naomi and the family, how much that little trip must have cost in dollars and time away from your cases and all you have going on out here. Well, I didn't want you to keep wondering and guessing and traipsing all over. I didn't want you to give them false hope."

"Yes, thanks. I won't be giving them any false hope."

"It's a closed file, Judge. And you can now rest easy about some killer running around your halls."

I stood up. "Thank you, Detective. You have wrapped it up for me, but I can't stand it either. Part of me doesn't believe it . . . but pictures don't lie . . . I guess." *Stay in role, damn it.* "Thank you very much for your time and candor. For helping me get back to the People's business without distractions. I'll call Naomi and tell her nothing's new."

"Chalk it up to the devil in each of us, and may he rest in peace. Can I walk you to your car? Almost dark now."

"Sure, thanks."

As we walked, I pondered some more that an FBI type had called Naomi and her family. No need for them to start out checking with family if a customer of child porn purveyors had killed himself over that. Naomi sure wasn't the type to be receiving or sending child porn.

Hell, this Pitts chump walking next to me has closed nothing, doesn't know the half of it. Pitts hadn't said anything about when the imagined child porn had been loaded onto Melvin's computer, how close to the time of death. Pitts and his tech hands hadn't checked that, didn't bother. No need, no time to challenge Pitts with any of this, not yet.

Chapter Eighteen

Frank

United States Deputy Attorney Dennis Rasmussen listened for the better part of an hour. Here and there, he moved his right hand as if reeling in a fishing line, his signal for me and maybe Agent Sam Koslowski to keep talking, that his notetaking and thinking had caught up with us. Once, he raised his hand to stop us and changed the tape in the portable recorder. A couple other times, he flipped through Madeline's file lying on the desk, flipped through the photos and compared them to the dental X-rays.

Rasmussen listened as if he cared, head forward, shoulders hunched, eyes flitting at who was doing the talking and then away so that he might absorb and evaluate. Each time he looked up, he shook his head, not so much in disbelief as in sadness.

Finally, he asked, "Anything else?"

Sam and I said, "Nope," at the same instant.

Rasmussen looked like a lifer, a once brilliant law student who opted for "government service" at the tail end of World War II, instead of trying to become rich at a high-powered private firm and now, maybe thirty years later, would be doing the same thing every day until that good retirement. Heck, Rasmussen could probably retire now on eighty percent pay. Rasmussen knew what he was doing, knew the law, and whether what we had was enough to take a case to a judge and jury or needed lots more. No excitement came from this old codger. He had been down this road evaluating evidence collected by others many times.

Rasmussen put down his pen. "You've got nothing, and likely that's not news to you?"

Sam glanced at me and smirked, pointed his thumb at me. "I know that, but it's good for our hot-shot FNG to get it straight. He won't take it from me."

"Shit," I said. I had sort of expected any prosecutor to laugh at me, at what I had, what I said I could get. The worst disappointments are the ones that come riding in hard on your own guilt for not having prepared enough, for not seeing the traps, for seeing them but ignoring them, for not being smart enough—or just too damned stubborn.

Rasmussen waved his hand as if to brush away my guilt. "If your potential subject had no immunity, there's plenty enough here for our favorite judge to give us warrants, search his apartments, vehicles, for wherever this Kaminev hangs out after work, and maybe something useful would turn up. And you could pull him and his buddies in and talk to them until they invoked their Miranda rights, and then you'd know you were on a useful track. But we can't get more than what you have already from any properly listed embassy worker—and he is listed."

"Oh, shit," I said again, couldn't hold it in, though I knew my little outbursts once again marked me a newbie, a guy who didn't know what he was doing.

Rasmussen tossed me a life ring. "Maybe we can quietly pass along what we know to the bosses and can get Kaminev and his buddies shipped back to where they came from. But that's it, that's all we can do. His bosses likely know everything, so that's not much of a lever."

Sam said, "Let's not do that. I'd rather have him stay here where we can at least watch him and his asshole comrades." Sam didn't say that maybe Kaminev would run into a telephone pole if he stayed around long enough, didn't need to.

I begged, "That Kaminev asshole is all over this one. I know he picked her up, maybe waited for her to leave. I know he offered her a ride in the rain, got some of his boys over and had a fucking damned good time that went way too far. Or he knows who did. Shit, shit, shit, the way he called her a Jew. You—we can't just let it go—there's got . . ." Hard to remain calm, calculating, no sense getting tagged with a bad point on my Internal Analysis form for acting "unprofessional."

Rasmussen said, "You know, there is one interesting aspect in what you've told me. It's a bit unusual for them to be so forthcoming, to meet with you so willingly, though he didn't tell you much. That does happen, but not without the higher ups in on it, giving them permission—and usually more clandestinely, not openly. He met with you back then and again now, twice, and didn't tell you, Frank, to get lost. I wonder what that's all about. I wonder if that presents an opportunity."

Sam said, "I've been thinkin' about that too, maybe he wants to tell us something. Maybe he's already told us and," turning to me, "we missed it."

Rasmussen said, "Yes, of course. Maybe he wants to come over to us and not get sent back to the ice-hole Russia. Or he wants some leverage of his own with his bosses, something he can trot out when they threaten to send him, his wife, and two little ones to Angola."

I said, "I got none of those vibes, nothing that made me think he was afraid his time here would get cut short. He was all macho and hard and cocky both times."

Sam said, "That's their nature. Even if he wants to come over, he'll act like he's doing us a fucking favor. He's feeling you out maybe, maybe deciding if he can trust you."

I calmed down a bit. "I guess. So . . . if he did it and wants to come over, wouldn't he have signaled something in the last two years? There's something else going on with him."

Sam said, "Good call. He's not wanting to come over. Hah, maybe just showing off—at what he can do, can get away with. Or just wants to swap info that we can't get, swap for what he can't get."

Rasmussen flipped the pad into his open briefcase and stood. "Well, it's been interesting. I have no problem, Frank, if you want to develop this a bit, see if he'll meet again." He looked at Agent Sam. "There's not a single listed Russian embassy worker who isn't encouraged to develop friendships with us. Getting tight with an up-and-coming FBI man might fit right into Kaminev's portfolio, especially an FBI man conversant in Russian. But know this: every move he makes is approved in advance by his boss and someone in Moscow. And know this, too, he was not in on anything bad that happened to Madeline."

Rasmussen waited for that last to register, looked hard at me to make sure I got it. Then, "The listed Russian Embassy workers are all afraid of their own shadows. If they are careless, or greedy, drink too much, or get into legal trouble, they get sent home—and might face a firing squad. Has happened more often than we know, and we know of several. If a Soviet was involved in her kidnapping or murder, he'd never be listed as Embassy staff. He'd be rogue, and we probably have nothing on him, no file of any kind to link him up, might not even know he's been in D.C.

"Gentlemen, I'll be on my way. If you learn a US citizen was in on it, call me. Interesting situation." He pointed at me. "Mr. Maier, never forget he'll be working you every bit as much as you're working him. There's no doubt he spotted you lurking around his apartment, around the embassy, was expecting your little meeting in his garage."

"Yes, thanks."

No classroom work, no physical tests, no stories from old timers, no study of cases in the law books on the rights of criminals had prepared me for this dead end. And Sam rubbed salt into the open wound, letting me get caught in my own trap, set by my excitement, my ego. Damn. It'd be a long time before Rasmussen would trust me to develop a case with real witnesses, real documents, real tape recordings. Maybe next time I'd draw another deputy US attorney. *Hope that dick Kaminev would see me some more, must figure out how to get him, . . .*

⚖

YEGOR SAID, "SO NICE TO SEE YOU AGAIN," as if he meant it, and gave me a good crushing handshake. When we were seated at the counter on swivel stools, Yegor started talking, too fast and too much, still nervous about something. "You know, I looked you up, asked around about you. You were good at puck. Your old goalie did it to us in the Olympics. Why didn't you tell me you spoke Russian? I like that. You said you want to talk some more. Any other thing, other than her. You want to talk about her, and you get nothing from me." Yegor laughed that laugh, the one which made his neck bulge.

"No, just some follow-up."

"I'll talk about her all you like. Besides, it's good to cooperate with you guys, I think. We help you, you help us maybe someday." Yegor slapped me on the shoulder as if to seal the deal.

The deli was stuffed with the lunch crowd, no table or booth available. Good choice. Even if I were wired, it would take the best filters to sift what we said out of all the other loud talking, dishes clattering, waiters yelling at customers, then at the cooks in front of them, and the cooks yelling back, "Comin' up . . . anything else? Enjoy."

And I wasn't wired.

What was it Yegor wanted in exchange, and for what? Had to be something, or he wouldn't have agreed to meet so easily and so soon. Only one way to find out. After we ordered, I said, "Yeah, the girl in the yellow dress, we found her, what was left of her."

"No shit, as you guys say? That's why you guys wanted to talk to me again after all that time. Well?"

"Well, what?"

"What you going to tell me about what you find?"

Yegor's talk sped up, and he left out his "to be" verb. Russian has no "to be" verb. His fast talk exposed him again. *Shit, this guy was in on it and is all nerves, and I'm here talking bullshit and can't do a fucking thing. Might as well set the hook, yank hard and see what happens.* I leaned over like a kid telling his best friend a secret. "Just bones, all nicely together. And the old cloth or rope or whatever they were wrapped in gave us some good leads."

"No shit. When, where? Oh, sorry." He actually looked sorry, looked down at the little paper place setting.

"We found her at a spot on that chart in your garage." I spoke slowly, trying to growl out the words. I didn't tell him that whatever she had been wrapped in was gone, decomposed, flushed out with the tide. "But I'd bet the farm you know exactly where we found her."

Yegor snapped upright. "Why you say that? Why you accuse me like that? What chart? You are a fucking crazy man. It's not true, what you think."

This was getting good. This thug was not prepped for this. They don't train them how to handle the aftermath of any up-close killing in the good old USA. Wonder how much his bosses really knew. "Just evidence, Yegor. We follow the evidence where it leads us. You saw her that day, waited for her to leave in a downpour. You waited in a no-parking zone right on the curb where she'd come out. Only you guys can park there. When you saw her leave right on time, you thought you might get lucky if everything broke just right. Things went bad for you and your boys, and you're the one who knows about Jug Bay. You with some help took her body out on a boat from your kiddie camp in Pioneer Point—far enough away that no one would connect her remains to your camp. How's that stacking up? How am I doing?"

Yegor slowly shook his head, but I caught a tinge of fear in the long pause, in him running through what to say next. "Let's talk puck."

So that was it. No denial, no outrage, no you-got-it-all-wrong. Not even an attempt at an alibi. I was not about to switch to hockey talk. "Tell me, Yegor, what do you think would happen to you and your lovely wife and kids if we passed what we know on to your embassy, maybe spiced it up a bit? Will your Elena and little Lisa and Nikolas go back to your shit-ice home?"

Yegor rubbed his chin. "Don't do that. It not work, anyway. My bosses know it all and more. They are not going to send me home, not over this."

But he was worried, got his verb tenses wrong again.

"You know what we tell your higher ups might leave some things out, might be just enough to get them pissed off—at you. What we got from forensics on that lovely lady would disgust even a Cossack, and it would be way different than whatever bullshit you told your bosses. If your bosses don't believe you, as we say, you'd be toast."

The waitress plunked down our big platters of sandwiches and coleslaw sides, pulled a fresh bottle of catsup out of her pocket, set it down and took the old nearly-empty one. "Enjoy, fellas, and holler if you need anything else."

Yegor said, "Well, your forensics are bullshit. It's not what you think, nothing like that."

"I'm all ears."

Yegor took a bite of his pastrami and kraut on rye. His mouth kept opening wider until he got the whole of the corner in. He chewed a bit, but not all, and started talking with his mouth half full. "It not what you think. No one I know pick her up for a good time, but I can't say more."

Time to play the last card, the only real card I held. "Ah, you or someone with you did pick her up? What the hell for? You know we can't touch you, not for illegal parking, not for this. We just want the truth. Her family deserves it."

Kaminev finished chewing. "Ask that fucking smart husband of hers what happened. He knows. I can't stop him from telling you—but he'd better look out if he does, if he tells you too much." Kaminev was back in full control, made my head want to scream now. Putting it on poor Melvin had done that.

"What? Melvin had something to do with her disappearance, her death? You've got to be fucking to the tenth power kidding me. On your mother's grave, wherever the hell it is, you lie, you fucking Cossack lying son of bitch. You can't put this on him." Once again, I spoke softly, smiling all the while. No sense drawing any other diner patrons into this, but it was hard to hear anything.

No part of his body showed nerves, and then in slow perfect English, he said, "Agent Frank Maier, let me tell you this. Go ask her husband but pray he doesn't tell you too much. You will regret it if he does."

Yegor reached into his pants back pocket, pulled out a wallet and flipped a five-dollar bill onto the counter, and, still chewing, said, "No, he didn't do it, had nothing to do with it, but he knows more than he tells you. He, husband Melvin, caused it all, what happened to her. And what happened to her was not us." Yegor stood up. "We must go Dutch, as you say." He looked right down at me, the big green eyes boring in, the wrestler chin set hard. "It was your own guys. Gotta go now. Can't say more. Sorry. Good luck, my friend, but don't ever find out too much."

I left right after Yegor, followed him as best I could without being obvious for a couple blocks in the direction of the Soviet Embassy building and lost him. I didn't try that hard to keep up with Yegor, too much to think about. *It was your own guys.* Where the hell did that come from? *Your guys? What the hell had Melvin not told us, that we must not learn too much about?*

Chapter Nineteen

Angela

The distractions never stopped. When I bathed Alice and Abigail, when I again, finally, made love with Peter, images of Melvin and dark-skinned men lying in their own blood jabbed their way in.

And the other way, too. On early mornings when I had a bit of time and quiet to tug at the files in Naomi's box, to think, to tease out more patterns, the day's demands crowded out my ability to think, to focus on what lay before me. And I gave less to everything and everyone around me.

Thoughts of guns and bullets became constant companions. One well-placed bullet ended Melvin's life and the lives of those dark-skinned men. One of the men in Melvin's files spent his adult life studying bullets, how different metals and metal combinations made them behave on impact. And there was that mention by Melvin of bullets that hit Oliver, Jr. It seemed random then, not sinister, rather historical and interesting. But now . . . did that say more about Melvin, about his away-from-court fascinations, his away-from-court life?

ON APRIL 9 OF MY FIRST YEAR ON THE BENCH, Judge Brookfeld stuck his head into my doorway. In those days, he and I ran criminal cases in side-by-side courtrooms, often ate lunch together, and talked of evidence and the lawyers and their clients in hard circumstances.

"Do you know what today is? That's not a fair question. Do you know what happened on this date some time ago?"

He did this sort of thing and, it seemed, always at the right time to give me a break when I needed one. His question for a moment took me away from a summary memo by my new shared research clerk on yet another motion in one of the cases in my line of cases. "Sorry, Mel, I don't know what happened on this date some time ago. By your look, I should?"

"General Lee surrendered at Appomattox, the best we can do to peg a date the Civil War ended. We don't celebrate that one. Ought to, I expect. Our race relations might be better if we celebrated that one."

"Wow, I didn't know. We must do more with April 9. But the Southern states won't let us. Too many consider themselves to be occupied territory still." I smirked at that, and Melvin did too.

"You know, Oliver took three lead bullets in that war. The surgeons dug them out of his chest when he was barely twenty. It's a miracle we did not lose him then and there, not so much from lead balls as from the cutting into him, the germs and festering. That would have been a loss. Two of those round lead balls sat very quietly in his personal safe until after he passed away."

⚖

MY GOOGLE SEARCH CONFIRMED ALL THAT Melvin had told me. Maybe Melvin had a sense a bullet would end his life, maybe guns and bullets were his secret hobby—and maybe he did buy that gun and used it on himself? Maybe all those old names and check copies and dead bodies tied into big-time porn rings, bribes and pay-offs among the D.C. crowd?

A Thursday evening call in late November from Naomi wiped away every one of my lingering doubts about Melvin. Peter took the call to not interrupt my bedtime story to the twins, but Naomi insisted enough that Peter handed me the phone.

"Angela, sorry to bother at what must be your dinner hour. I'm calling on that other phone . . . works fine after getting it charged . . ."

"Yes, what is it? No bother at all."

"The FBI fellow, Smaltz, called again, insisted on coming by and looking at all of Melvin's papers. I felt I had no choice, but I made Edgar's oldest be here with me when he came."

"Good. Now maybe someone will get on what happened to Melvin."

"I'm not sure, Angela."

"Because?"

"I kept asking him if he had any leads on Melvin, on what happened. He didn't hear me. All he wanted was Melvin's files, kept asking if there was more, and then some more, made me do something terrible." Naomi said that last with a girlish glee.

"What bad thing did you do?"

"That came out wrong. He didn't make me do anything. I gave him Melvin's old school notebooks, his magazines, his letters, and copies of stuff from his cases, even old photo albums and bank statements, the books we haven't given to charity . . . and the last six years of Melvin's tax returns. But . . . I just couldn't give him that box, the one you have. A little inner voice told me not to."

"Now you've got me curious."

"He wasn't interested one bit in what happened to Melvin. Brushed it off. He said, 'Old men are prone to do that more than most people know.' I had no clue what he meant and didn't ask. He said the investigation on why and how Melvin passed is closed shut tight."

"But he was after Melvin's files like a bloodhound after a corpse? Did you get his name and badge number?"

"He left his card with all his information. The same bacon fat chap who called before you came here. I suppose I should call his office, make sure he's really who he says."

I waited, needed to think. Holding back ugly documents from an ongoing investigation is a crime in any jurisdiction. But Naomi wouldn't care about that, not at her age. She'd let them bring her up on obstruction of justice charges and then enjoy the ride. If that FBI man would not help find Melvin's killer, Naomi could hold back. Any jailhouse crowd would enjoy her, get a kick out of her, and she might straighten some of them out, too.

What to do, what to tell her? If I told Naomi to not turn the nasty files over, I, a sitting judge, could get into very hot water. If that FBI agent was who he said he was, he was entitled to look at all of Melvin's files. "Naomi, how old would you say this Smaltz is?"

"Hmm? Younger than I, but not that much. I'd say close to retirement. Sixty something."

From my years presiding over criminal cases and more years trying to help wealthy clients out of serious trouble, I knew the FBI was not likely to send an old man chasing for documents of a dead judge. Youngsters did those things. FBI agents retired before they became old men. The law made them retire at fifty-something except for the most special cases and then not hang on past sixty. Besides, the benefits were too generous, the market for them to take an easy double-dipping job too strong. This Smaltz fellow was either retired and brought in on special assignment, high up in the decision chain, or not an FBI agent at all.

"Naomi, I need to think some. How late will you be up?"

"Oh, I'm up all hours these days and nights. A little bit of excitement, and I have trouble sleeping at night."

"I'll call this number in a while, and if not, then tomorrow."

"Angela, thanks for staying on this, for at least hearing me out."

"Sure, you're welcome. Must go now."

"One more thing, maybe it means the most."

"Sure."

"Smaltz asked about you by name, Judge Cornwell. He didn't get that from me. Asked how your visit with me went. He didn't get that from me, either. But I made light of it, though I had to tell him you wanted to meet me and the family, that you and Melvin were good friends."

"Thanks. I'll be ready for his call, I guess."

What to do now. How did he know to ask? How did he know my name? Oh, dear . . . Peter, Peter. That Smaltz FBI man, or whoever he was, could call or stop by when Peter was alone. I had better include him, talk to him about this if he would listen, if he might help. Melvin's spirit or Oliver's spirit—or whatever—had given me courage to keep going a while longer, but Peter had to come with me from now on.

Abigail gave me the opening. "Mommy, that call before was from the lady in New York, wasn't it?"

"Yes, why do you ask, you nosy little lady?"

"'Cause when you came back you forgot you were telling us a story. That lady made you upset, didn't she?"

"No, not really. She's a lovely lady."

"Mommy, tell us again why you had to go to New York."

I pulled the comforter up to my daughter's chin. "Court business, judge business."

"Does that mean you can't talk about it?"

I felt Peter standing next to me, felt Alice's gaze from the bed against the other wall. All three wanted an answer—and it better be a good one. The only good answer was the right answer. "No, Abby, I can talk about it . . . but if I tell you, then you can't talk to your friends or teacher about it."

"Oh, I won't tell."

"You, too, Alice."

Alice mouthed okay.

"Some time back a good friend died. He was a judge, and he was my first judge teacher. No one seems to know why he died, and no one wants to find out why. I think I'm the only one who wants to know why he died, besides his sister and some other family of his far away. I had to go back to New York to talk to them. That's all, really."

"Okay," said Abigail.

I bent over and kissed Abigail on the cheek. As always, the same pure breath of that young body soothed me and made me wish all good things for my girls in their life journeys. "Good night now. Sleep tight."

Abigail whispered back, "Is he the one who killed himself?"

That jarred. How did Abby know? Why did she care? "That, Abby dear, is what no one knows for sure."

"Hope you find out soon, Mommy."

"Thanks, Abby. Good night."

"If a bad man killed him, I hope you get the bad man and that he doesn't get away, Mommy."

"Good night."

I reached for Peter's hand as we crept out of the girls' room. I feared he'd pull away, but he didn't. He took mine as if he didn't want to let go, like all the times before his real job ended.

He said, "That call earlier."

I nodded.

"What's going on?"

"I don't know . . . I don't dare talk here. Let's go outside."

I hated how I felt, the creeping fear, the not knowing what to do, the not knowing what had happened to Melvin, and others on the hunt for secrets in Melvin's old files, others tracking Naomi, and now tracking me.

Until deep into the night I told Peter everything, silently showed him my copy of the box of files, told him of my Google searches, my visits with Detective Pitts, told him of my many exchanges with Melvin over the years, about how he could not have taken his own life, about the still frightened court staff, and I told him that a stranger searching for Melvin's old files had asked Naomi about me. The only things I left out were those crazy visits by

Melvin's favorite Supreme Court Justice.

At the end Peter enfolded me in his arms, held me for a long time, said nothing. He smelled so good with not a trace that might have come out of green bottles. Then he said, "Well, I'm with you. Unless we're missing something, Melvin's no pedophile and did not kill himself—someone terribly evil hacked into his computer. Easy to download images into someone's hard drive once you have their computer open. Also easy to kill someone sitting at a computer."

Peter meant it. My worry had wormed its way into him a little. He wanted to help, to share whatever troubled me, wherever it led.

Peter said, "I guess Melvin could have felt the way I do now."

"And what's that?"

"Wanting to get a gun, never knowing who might come knocking on the door. When you're at work next and the girls at school, do you mind if I snoop around these files some, Google some more?"

My turn to hug Peter, pull his head gently down against my face. "Thank you, darling. Thank you for not thinking I'm crazy."

Peter looked into my eyes. "Dear Angela, you are the least crazy person I have ever known." He waited, but I could tell he wanted to say more. He put a finger to my lips, ran it along my cheek and up to my ear, as he used to when we first fell in love. "Sorry for having been such a prick these last months. My great job search is not yielding the results I expected." He laughed a little laugh. "Not unless I leave you and our girls and go work in . . . say, North Dakota."

"Love, as long as you and I are together that will work its way out. Our alarm will go off too soon. And I must not call in sick after the extra time away."

"I'll get the kids off and make us breakfast and wake you at the last minute," said Peter. "Tomorrow evening, we'll have our glass of wine again."

For a few hours, I slept better than I had in months.

Chapter Twenty

Frank

After I lost Yegor, I tucked into a pay phone. Had to check with Sam, see if he'd let me set up another meeting with Melvin. Sam didn't answer, but Melvin surprised me by taking my call and saying I could come right over, that whatever I wanted to see him about was his number one priority. I said I had to check with my boss and would call him back.

When I found Sam, he said, "Good work. Sure, see what Melvin says and let me know and write it up ASAP." Sam laughed. "That Ruskie buddy of yours is sure full of shit. If they did it, putting it on us is what they'd do." Sam's tone said he expected nothing much to come of anything Melvin knew. "Hey, Frank, the bottom line's not moved. Whoever killed Mrs. Brookfeld will never see any formal charges, and it sure wasn't your Ruskie buddy—and not Melvin, either."

When I called back, Melvin must have sensed that something had changed in what we knew, what we had. "Let's get out to the Mall by the Lincoln Memorial, the steps. Good to get out of the office," he said. "I'll bring an umbrella."

For early fall it was steamy, a hot wind filled with moisture blowing up from the south. Thunderstorms could hit any time, like on the day Madeline left work for the last time.

Melvin looked tired, worn, open collar with no bow tie.

"Well, Agent Maier, what news have you for me this time?"

We walked along the reflecting pool, its surface trembling in the wind. I told him of the pieces, most of them, of Jug Bay, the FBI forensic report, Yegor Kaminev's behavior and the navigation chart in Yegor's garage. Then, "He said a couple times it's not what I think. No one picked up your wife for a good time, he said. Wouldn't tell me more, anything really. Said I should ask you."

Melvin stopped, looked out over the water, then again started walking along the straight edge, his head turned toward the other side. Then, "How much do I value my life, now that Madeline is gone? How much do I value the lives of my kin? How much can I tell you before what happened to her happens to me, to others close to me? Can you answer those questions, Agent Maier?"

"I'm sorry, Mr. Brookfeld. I have no idea what you're talking about."

"You are not in on it?"

"Never heard of it, and I'm not in on anything. I'm just an FNG—that's fucking new guy. The agents call me that. I'm just trying to learn my job, do what I'm asked, and maybe get lucky and do what's right."

"How can I be sure? But then one of the great impossibilities is proving a negative, isn't it? How do you prove to me that you are not part of it? How to prove not one tiger runs loose in Manhattan's subways is very, very hard."

"You've got me there, sir. I have no idea what you're talking about."

"Here's the next question, Agent Maier. What if I tell you too much? What if I tell you too much, you follow up, and they come after you?"

"Pardon me, sir. I have no idea—but ol' Yegor kind of said the same thing."

"Do you have a family, Agent Maier?"

"Yes, sir. Yes. A sister, a dad, grandparents. My mother's gone."

"Do you want them in this world for a while longer?"

"Sure do." *Damn, what's all this? Holy shit! He looks like he means it.*

Melvin Brookfeld waited a long time, then turned around to look across the water. "You see that guy over there? Won't point, but he's at about two o'clock from me with a big lens pointed at us. He's been paralleling us for a few minutes. Maybe a random tourist ambling along at the same pace we are and taking pictures in our direction."

I saw him and whistled softly, realizing why Melvin had kept his voice low and his back to the water.

"I'm not souvenir material. You aren't either, Agent Maier. What's he taking? Is he with you, or is he tracking me? Is that a photo lens he's aiming at us, or is it a sound parabola?"

"He's not with me, of that I assure you."

"Let's get out of here. Too easy for a parabolic antenna to pick up what we are saying. This water surface is not a good sound absorber. Let's walk fast."

After a half mile of silent fast walking and quick street crossings against yellow lights and many sudden turns, Melvin said, "The night Madeline didn't come home, I got a call. I'll take that call to my grave. The caller said, 'If you want to ever see her again, stop what you are doing. It's bigger than you, bigger than her, bigger than you know. And don't ever go there again. We know how to find everyone else you love—and we will.'"

I lost any connection to where we were, to others on the street, to car noises. I had to look at Melvin to make sure Melvin had said that. I recovered a bit and started guessing, but couldn't reel it in, whatever was that big, whatever Melvin might have been doing that he had to stop doing. "What the hell was that you were on, that big, that dangerous to them who called you?"

"You don't know, do you, Agent Maier?"

"Not a clue." After a pause to think, "And why didn't you tell us two years ago, when we might have had a chance . . . ?"

"Forgive me, but I thought she was alive back then. And she was far more important to me than what I was doing. I read that call as a promise that if I stopped, shut it down completely, they'd let her go, that I'd get back the only one I've ever truly loved."

"And you shut down what you were working on. But that did not save her. You know that now. Can you tell me, tell us, if you like, sir, this thing you were working on?'

"Best not, not yet, Mr. Maier. Telling you will not bring her back and could bring harm to us both. I don't care about me or about you particularly. But we both have families. They are as innocent of this as these strangers on the street. Their lives must not end because of my work. And that's just part of it, maybe the easy part."

"I'll bite, sir. What's the other part?"

"That caller was right. If I had gotten where I was going, all of this—this city, its memorials, its government—would have been covered in a slimy filth from which this country and its people would take a very long time to recover. And . . ." Melvin glanced sideways at me. "I'm not sure broadcasting the truth of what I was working on is worth that, not any longer. And I suggest you not put any of this conversation in your 302, not tell anyone, not for a while at least. Once they think you know too much, you, Mr. Frank Maier, and any relatives to whom you may be close, are no safer than Madeline."

Large warm rain drops started to pelt us, the sidewalk, the car tops. Melvin stopped under cover of an office building entrance awning, into a set-back away from the sidewalk and people.

Out of respect for Melvin, for his suffering, for his real and imagined burdens, I turned to face into the building. I watched the main entry door revolving with people, heard the door's swishing sounds through the rain getting louder. I thought of Biddie, of my father and grandparents, and I tried to figure out what Melvin had stopped hunting down that had killed his Madeline. I searched to say something that showed respect and patience and might begin to give me answers. And I wondered how much of this to tell Agent Sam.

When I turned back, Melvin was gone.

I TOLD AGENT SAM HALF OF IT, THE PART about the call Melvin had received. "I wonder what Melvin was working on, what he got close to. He sure as hell didn't tell me anything about that."

Sam said, "Ah, you know those State guys. They're all hush-hush from us. We're beneath them, good enough for common crimes, but not the big stuff they work on. Maybe Melvin was getting goodies from an informant, some big money laundering thing, or bribery thing, or double agent thing, and the Kaminev crowd couldn't stand the heat." Sam laughed and coughed. "Hell, maybe someone from our side in bed with the Russians called Melvin off."

Melvin's warnings had taken. I dared only, "Not likely it was anything authorized and official that Melvin was working on. Easy enough for his boss at State to just put him on other cases and take that one away from him. My guess is that Melvin was on his own, moonlighting."

Sam stared at me in silence for a long time. I had never been around Sam at a moment like this, at behavior like this. Sam's broad nose breathed out hard several times. "You know, Maier, for a fucking new guy, you think good. Wonder what the hell Melvin was working on. Let's find out. I'll go with you this time. You set it up, but don't tell him I'm coming. Sometimes takes me eight, ah, nine visits before I can shake out the truth from a weirdo like Melvin."

"Sure, sir. Just give me times that work for you."

Sam was good at interviews, had a ton of experience. If there was anything there, he'd pull it out. And if Melvin was making it all up, was running a diversion, Sam would sniff that out too. If it was all crazy and imagined by me, having Sam along would be good protection for me.

"Remember, Maier, how this case came in? I see it now. That smart-ass prick lawyer was holding out on us all along."

I did remember. "Sure. Melvin didn't pull us into this. His boss over at State got a call from Madeline's boss at State, how she had not come in to work and how Melvin wouldn't tell anyone anything. So, his boss called over here to open a file and get on it."

⚖

MELVIN INSISTED WE COME TO HIS OFFICE, to the place that might be bugged, where all phone conversations might be recorded, where others might overhear. I knew right away that Melvin would give us nothing new, no matter how sly Sam might be, or how open and honest and sincere I tried to be, no matter how many times Sam interviewed Melvin.

This meeting started off with Melvin asking if we wanted a coffee or a Coke, took us to a conference room, one with a glass wall facing the interior where many people could see us, maybe even hear us.

Sam jumped right in. "Agent Maier has brought me up to speed, and I'm sorry I must get official. Like it or not, we are investigating a kidnapping and murder, and now know you've been holding information, holding it since back then when it might have made a difference. I don't need to tell you, Mr. Brookfeld, that you have been and are impeding an ongoing investigation. I don't need to tell you the possible consequences."

Melvin looked at Sam without fear or wanting to befriend, with a look that said, *I know so much more than you do, not telling you any of it, and don't care what you do about it.* He said, "Am I under arrest?" then paused, "I know my rights and waive them."

For all of Koslowski's experience, he hesitated. His wheels didn't turn that fast, and he was no lawyer. "Ah, no. You are not under arrest . . . but keep it up and we'll see . . ."

"Agent Koslowski and Agent Maier, I'm sorry to say this. Over the past two-plus years I've tormented myself far more than you, your judges, your federal prisons could ever torment me. I have told you or Agent Maier here everything I will tell anyone. I have stopped the project I was working on. If I go back to it, no one will know until I'm ready to tell them. Now, either arrest me or excuse me." Melvin stood up.

Koslowski stayed seated, as if by not getting up he could squeeze something, anything, useful out of Melvin.

But Melvin was ahead of him. "This little conference room is reserved the whole afternoon. You are welcome to use it. It has no bugs and is used for our top-secret meetings. Good day to you both. If you have something new for me, dial zero on that phone over there and ask for me. The operator will put you right through."

After Melvin had left, had closed the door, Koslowski let down the shades on the window wall, and said, "Let's talk this through, as good a place and time as any, and we know it's secure."

I had trouble figuring out what to talk through.

"What the fuck was that, him telling us to fuck off? I've already talked to our SAIC. I talked to the head lawyer here at State, and he claims to have no fucking clue what Brookfeld was working on that was so hot, which got his wife kidnapped and killed, or what he's hiding. Any thoughts, Maier?"

Slowly, I spun out some thoughts. "Brookfeld's not talking, but he has to have some documents related to what he's working on . . . someone had to know what those docs showed or could lead to. We could subpoena his work files."

"Yeah, that's what I've been thinking, but you know it'd be a screwball application for a warrant. Something like . . . Dear Judge, please sign this here search warrant of Brookfeld's house and office and files in storage that might contain any docs or other records related to the kidnapping and murder of his wife."

I said—and meant it, "Let me try putting something together for you to look at and run by Rasmussen."

"Thanks, Maier, do that."

We left this conference room for the last time.

Over the next weeks, I didn't sleep much, the pursuit too thrilling, needing to remain patient too hard. The application for search warrants was a bit tricky. Hard to get sufficiently specific about what we wanted and why we had the probable cause to search for those things when I had no idea what to ask for.

The larger task was learning everything I could about what Melvin had been working on more than two years ago, the something that had gotten his beautiful lady dumped naked into Jug Bay and, if revealed, would cover this land in slimy filth.

Only one thing could do that and make a very smart man paranoid. I pulled a copy of The Warren Report with all the exhibits I could get from the FBI Library. I studied it every spare moment, studied it like I had not studied anything since the first course in Russian at Cornell. Then I searched the microfiche library of the New York Times and Washington Post for more. A fuzzy picture of what Melvin had been working on—and others made him stop—started to form.

Chapter Twenty-One

Angela

A late evening doorbell ring, then a loud knuckle rap on the front door broke into our evening routine. Peter opened the door's small window. It was too late in the day for door-to-door hawkers, and this was no neighbor needing a cup of sugar.

Peter came into the girls' room. "Hon, are you in for Special Agent Smaltz? Says he can't tell me what it's about." Then in a softer voice, "As if we didn't know."

"No harm, I guess." *Damn, that was fast. But maybe that's good.*

I opened the solid front door but left the chain fastened. I first noticed the hat, then the dark suit and proper tie. Not many men wore hats these days, not even to court, and most FBI agents I had been around went out in sport coats, not suits and never a hat. He took off the hat and put on a friendly expression, eyes wide open with sincerity, mouth and chin relaxed, all more than they should have been for an unannounced call this late at night at my home. Close-cropped hair nearly all white.

"Judge Cornwell, I presume," he said, his voice low and steady with no friendliness.

"Yes. What can I do for you?"

"Hello, Judge. Thanks for not shutting the door on me. As I told Mr. Cornwell, I'm retired Special Agent Harlan Smaltz, s.m.a.l.t.z. Lots of folks get it wrong." He handed me a card through the door opening. "Sorry to come around without calling first. If I'm disturbing you, I can come back later after the twins are down or first thing in the morning before you start court."

I pretended to look at the card but saw none of what it said. He knew about my court schedule, knew we had twins we were putting to bed, knew where we lived. Other faces, other times crowded in, faces of those who stood in front of me at that moment before Ms. Patterson cleared her throat, paused, and then let the latest jury verdict spill out. Those feelings of a verdict being read to the court combatants swarmed into me now, moved at me and around me, bad forces maneuvering into position to swallow me up. And I had no choice but to listen, to stand there, to perhaps let him in, but not wanting to, and powerless to do anything about what came at me after that. Whatever this verdict soon to be read, I said a silent prayer that it was no life-changer.

The connection to Melvin's box of files had come to me soon after that last call from Naomi. Harlan H. Smaltz. HHS. His initials, in Melvin's handwriting, sat on that sheet of ten sets of letters in Melvin's file marked, "DK.TF." on the tag. No check mark sat next to the HHS initials. Had this Harlan Smaltz also visited Melvin the evening before that Friday morning when Melvin's body lay slumped in his chair? What did the check marks mean? What did no check mark mean?

His coming around without warning said he wanted to catch me off guard, to test my defenses, my alertness, openness, the truth of what I might say. His eyes, unblinking, reminded of a lion prowling. If I slammed the door in his face, the lion might just slink off into the bush but finish the hunt when least expected. Hell, I had paused long enough, too long, and that gave away too much.

"Yes, what can I do for you, Agent Smaltz? What's the emergency? As you must know, I can't sign warrants for Federal courts."

He laughed a little, but it came out more like a soft growl. "No, no, not a warrant. Just covering all the bases on your colleague's untimely death. We're making sure no stone is left unturned. I won't take much time but would like to interview you—and as soon as possible. This is time sensitive."

Is that the line you used on Melvin, on Naomi? Did you bow slightly the same way with them? Or maybe you are chasing the killer, hope so. "Ah sure, the best time and place might be after court in the next few days. Our girls need to be put to bed, and I've got lots to get ready for trial in the morning. You're welcome to my office, ah, my chambers, or wherever works for you."

"How about if I wait in your courtroom tomorrow, and we chat after you let everyone out at the end of the day?"

"See you then. Hope you can help get to the bottom of what happened to him. But I don't know much." *Dang, I'm talking too fast, saying too much. That's a dead giveaway that I'm nervous. Slow down, turn this at him.* "Are you from the local Bureau office. You need directions to my courthouse, my courtroom?"

"I'm from back east, the D.C. region actually, but they let me use the San Diego region office whenever I want." He laughed that soft low laugh again. "Old enough for mandatory R, but they let me hang out, give me odd jobs. I know how to find you tomorrow."

I fiddled with the door chain, still attached, as if to open the door. Another test question flashed in. "Agent Smaltz, one more thing."

"Sure, what's that?"

"Have you interviewed others closer to the scene, closer to him, Judge Brookfeld's clerk or court reporter?"

"We're working through everything, I assure you, Judge."

"Detective Pitts?"

"Judge, for anyone else I'd have no comment," a tired breath, "but I can tell a sitting judge. I've not yet met with the San Diego PD but have the report."

Damn. Smaltz hadn't talked to Sandy Shields or Mora or Mora's friend,

Natasha, who had worked for Melvin. Any of them would have come running to me with that news. Hadn't even talked to Pitts. No, this Smaltz Agent, or phony agent, wanted to talk to me before checking in with anyone closer to the scene. Smaltz didn't want to know why or how Melvin died. He was interested in other things, and I knew about those other things, was learning more about those other things. "All right then, Agent Smaltz, I'll see you tomorrow afternoon."

Peter hugged me as soon as we heard the visitor's car leave our block. "Let's get the girls to sleep."

Later I continued thinking out loud. "And now he's after me and what I've got way more than he cares about those who saw Melvin's body. Heck, he might have just been checking if we're home. Want to take us and the girls to a motel?"

Peter shook his head, but no surprise showed on his face, no expression that said I was crazy. After a long moment, he said, "Let's make sure all our doors are bolted and windows locked tonight. And let's make copies of everything Naomi gave you. This guy will want that. Let's upload those copies and send them to ourselves."

I mentally flipped through the files in Naomi's box. "We'll give him everything. Can't obstruct a proper investigation, if that's what this is. Can't lose my black robe over this. And let's use our scanner, slow as it is, on the four photos and the DK TF list. Let's send those into the ether and back to us here and to my court computer."

I hugged Peter and pulled him close to the kitchen sink, turned on the water and whispered, "Harlan Smaltz doesn't give a care about an old man's porn, about an old man's suicide. He wants whatever Naomi gave me, whatever she told me."

Peter mouthed, "And we don't know why . . . why Melvin collected this stuff."

"We'd better figure it out fast, figure it out and tell others before it's too late, before there's nothing and no one left who cares."

⚖

HARLAN SMALTZ HAD SOME MANNERS. HE entered my courtroom after the witnesses and lawyers, their clients, and the jury had cleared for the day. Different suit, same hat but different tie, all low key, all business. *One of those old guys who knows how to read people, how to disarm them with that weary face and the power of age.* His kind were the most dangerous, the professional liars, the big-time cops or cons who instinctively found the "yes" buttons on their targets.

Easy to let my guard down, too easy. But here in my own domain, I could handle him, handle myself, better than at home. I got out of my robe, hung it over my chair, took the three steps down off my perch and headed straight at him through the swinging little gate to the courtroom gallery area. "Agent Smaltz, so nice to see you again. Sorry I was crowded for time last night."

I had not noticed his tan in the light of late evening. This one didn't spend all his time behind a desk, still a bit of a field man. Damn. Field men kept up on their marksmanship, their surveillance devices, kept in touch with their informants and street thugs.

"It is indeed nice to see you, Your Honor. And thank you for seeing me now." He reached out a hand and properly shook mine.

I gestured at the empty visitor seats in the gallery half of the courtroom. "Should we talk here?"

He glanced in the direction of Mora folding up the metal legs under her reporter machine, over at Ms. Patterson, head down making notes on some files, and at the bailiff clearing off his own little desk area. He said very softly so only I could hear, "May interview the staff later. Should talk where no one can eavesdrop."

My chambers didn't seem right, too private—and Melvin had been slaughtered in his chambers. Besides, I had asked my bailiff, Mora and Ms. Patterson to not leave right away, to wait for my signal or for Agent Smaltz to finish and leave. "I understand. Let's duck into this room."

Smaltz and I each took a wooden chair in the small attorney-witness room. My good manners overrode my fear, and I closed the door.

"Well, Agent Smaltz, fire away." I put on my ready-to-answer face.

Rock-still gray eyes, jaw muscles flexed, his hands flat on the desk slowly clenched into fists, he said. "Judge, I'll get to the point. We know how your friend died, but need to know why, why now."

"Yes."

"Judge, why do you think, why now?"

"You should talk to Detective Pitts, really should. I've talked to him. They've done a very thorough job. I'm sure the City police collected up everything belonging to Melvin—his computer, his case files, anything, very thorough really. And they've closed that file and seem confident they've got it. If anyone knows why now, they do. Last evening you said you're just covering all the bases. Seems to me they've already been well-covered." Damn, I had said too much, said it too fast, let my nerves, my fears show.

The unblinking lion's stare came back. The jaw muscles flexed again. "Yes, and you cared enough to meet with Naomi, other family, with Mr. Pitts and learn all you've summarized so nicely. But . . . you have a good memory, and I must have been a bit too flip last evening. There is more to this one. Please, Judge, trust that I know what I'm doing, that we know what we are doing. Right now, I need to know what you know." Smaltz reached down into the briefcase I had not noticed until now and pulled out a yellow pad and black pen. He wrote the date and my name at the top. "I may ask for a recorded statement or declaration later, but for now I'll just take down the high points. All right?"

This guy was all business under the courteous behavior. I looked at my watch.

"If you have a big load this evening, I can come back here later."

"No, please. Fire away."

"I'll get to the main point. We understand Judge Brookfeld had some files in a vault at the family summer home. His sister gathered them up and had copies made." He waited.

Had Naomi said too much, shown him more than she told me?

Smaltz answered my silent question. "Only one copy service in Naomi's town. Most folks have copiers at home, but his sister didn't or had the service make copies. We have reason to believe she gave some of the judge's important papers to you. Did she give you some of her brother's files, Judge Cornwell?"

The choices crashed in, all of them, and I had to pick the best one fast. Leave this little room, this meeting right now. Leave and tell him he'd hear from my lawyer. Stay and act ignorant, play the fool. Stay and make up a story—obstruct an investigation. Let him pull it out of me, one timid response and then the next until he had it all. *Take control*, my insides yelled at me. Oliver came in again, *All there is is to bore into it as hard as you can.* Time to bore into this slick, dangerous Smaltz chap right now and build my thorn-covered high fence to keep him off me. This might work better than anything else—for now.

"Well, then, that's easy, Agent Smaltz. Where shall I send what Naomi gave me, to the address on the card?" I smiled my knowing smile. "No need to follow me home."

"How about if I stop by at . . ." He looked at his watch. " . . . at six sharp, give you time to get home and round everything up." He didn't say that this would not allow time to copy what he came to collect. Another lion stare, and he reached for his hat.

I tried to match him, take back some of the control. "Before you leave, Agent Smaltz, what makes you think I have any of Melvin's old stuff, any of his papers?"

The face relaxed. "Judge, I'd never tell most folks, but I can trust you. I met with Naomi at some length, and other family members. She brought me every doggone thing she still had of Melvin's. There was a whole lot. I asked her for any copies too, asked real nicely. You see, I had already stopped by Milton Copies and Graphics and asked them about copy jobs. They had it all on computer, sorted by customer and date and number of pages copied. His sister had them make lots of copies, and she wouldn't do that for just junk—tax returns, old letters. She had those copies made for another purpose. The arithmetic on the number of pages run by the copy service and what Melvin's sister gave me didn't add up. So . . ."

I started nodding.

" . . . either his sister kept the copies and refused to turn them over to me or . . . she gave them to you. Fifty-fifty shot."

"And why me to whom—?"

He cut me off. "Seems only you and Naomi want to dig up the judge's past, really don't believe he did it to himself. No one else cares, but I do. The people I work with care a whole lot."

I exhaled loudly in the small room and put on my most professional happy face. "I'm so glad, so relieved. Keep me up to speed. I care about our dear Judge Melvin."

Smaltz grabbed his briefcase. "Whatever we know, whatever we learn. It's disclosed only on a NTK basis, all top secret. Sorry. You'll all be fine, just don't give it another thought. See you at six."

And he left.

I dialed Sandy Shield's courthouse number. "He's gone. I don't think he's bugged this phone, and he didn't follow me back here. What have you learned?"

"Judge, Agent Harlan H. Smaltz seems to be totally legit. He's in the D.C. Region. He's retired, but they keep bringing him back on special assignments—under contract. I did a little check, and mandatory retirement is fifty-seven, and not one day more. For very special cases, an agent can stay up to three years extra. But they gave out no hint about what he was up to. They told me to try him tomorrow, that he's out in the field today, out in the field a lot, even gave me his number and it matched his card. That was a bit unusual, giving me his number. But when I explained where I worked, they opened up a bit, might even have known he was on his way here."

"Any luck with the other?"

"Oh, yes, Your Honor. That was a great thought. The Milton copy service does not keep or save its downloads after a copy job is picked up and approved. Would take too much server capacity, and they don't want the headache of being everyone's cloud for every document they copy. Someone could dig into its servers and maybe pull old orders out, but that would take a lot of time and, I'm guessing, a subpoena. Once a copy job is delivered and approved by the customer, they delete their back up, and after seven days their system deletes it automatically. But they do log every copy job with a page count and customer name."

"Thanks, Sandy, thanks. Have a good evening. Good to know the big boys are finally on it."

"If he comes around here, I'll come clean and tell him that I checked up on him, I suppose."

"Only if he asks. I hope he does. Maybe Melvin's file is not closed, maybe they're looking for a killer. That would be a relief—at last."

I had fibbed. No relief at all. Whatever this was, whatever had killed Melvin was so much worse if the FBI knew about it, was in on it, and could not or did not save him from it.

Had to hurry home, get there before he did. Harlan Smaltz had calculated just right. I had enough time to get home, round everything up for him, but no extra time to make copies of more than maybe ten pages on any home copier. Thank God Peter had copied everything in Naomi's box deep into last night. That's the only thorn fence protection I had against lions out there for now. Had to find why Smaltz was here, what he was after, and had to find it fast.

⚖

SMALTZ PULLED UP IN WHAT COULD HAVE BEEN a Bureau-issued Chevy a couple minutes early and waited until six on the dot.

I didn't want him in my home, didn't want the twins to see him. I came to the door.

Agent Smaltz got out but left his hat on the car seat.

I didn't let him leave the area around his car. Peter, carrying the box, and I came out to where Smaltz had parked. "Here you go, everything as I got it from Naomi." And it was all of that, the whole box of files exactly as I had taken from Naomi, put into and shipped to me in this very FedEx box.

Smaltz opened the trunk. "Thank you. That was easy."

I said, "Sure, happy to help. I've got my copy of the FedEx bill. Mind signing it, so I have a record."

"Sure. Set it down here, and I'll write 'received from', date it and sign it." Smaltz got a pen out of his shirt pocket.

Peter set the box on the back fender. I placed the bill on the box, and Smaltz hunkered over it, writing, signing under the streetlamp. Not great light but good enough. Peter pulled his cell phone from his pants pocket, lined it up on Smaltz writing and signing. Two flashes and then one more proved that the camera feature worked.

At the first flash, Smaltz's head jerked, but he didn't look up, didn't comment. Done, he stood up, put the pen away, slid the box into his car trunk. "You didn't need to do that, did you?"

I was ready. "Agent Smaltz," and with a false cheer, "you really got to me with how important this is, whatever it is. Someday, someone may come around again and question me again and ask for these files again. Must have a first-rate evidence chain of custody on these docs. If you like, I'll email you these snapshots—of you picking up these files."

His long silence, his thinking told me I had gotten to him. "Nah, no need to bother. I know I have them now."

As Smaltz talked, Peter took one more of the two of us talking, at least that's what it looked like. I knew Peter forwarded the snapshots to both our home and my chambers computers, building thorn barriers against this lion. I said, "Great. Hope you get whoever did this."

"What makes you think someone did this to him?" The lion stare again.

"Anyone who knew our wonderful Judge Brookfeld would know he could never have taken his own life and not in his hallowed ground, in the place where he worked." I touched Smaltz's forearm. Most men are suckers for a woman's touch on the elbow. "Whatever happens, get the person or people who did this—and let me know. Will you?"

Uncertainty flitted across the face, no hard jaw, no rock-still eyes for a flicker of time, but then they all came back. "I'll let you know what I can. And, Ms. Cornwell, Judge, if you think of anything else, find anything else, call me. Don't try to do this yourself. Stay out of it. It's much bigger than you imagine, much bigger than you, your Peter, your twins." He waved his right hand as if throwing a Frisbee out into the night air. "Much bigger than all of this, all of us."

"I understand—even if I don't. Maybe someday you can fill me in."

"We'll see."

I couldn't let that go. "Ah, when you're done with them, can I have these files back? I've got nothing else left from my favorite judge."

Smaltz looked at me, uncertain again. "Ah, we'll see. We'll see." He slammed the trunk shut, got into his car, and left.

Chapter Twenty-Two

Frank, Winter 1978

I had written up the 302 Witness Report on our last meeting with Melvin back in October. Rasmussen's favorite judge had issued the warrants to search Melvin's office and home for any documents related to the project that got his Madeline murdered. She and Melvin lived in a small apartment not far north from the Watergate apartment complex, but miles from it in luxury and rental fees.

A long day of simultaneously searching both Melvin's home and office area, with multiple agents in each place, yielded nothing about Melvin's troubled project, nothing more than copies of tax returns, household papers, checks, check-stub books, magazines, dry cleaner receipts, letters among family members, honors and awards for Melvin and Madeline, and legal research memos on State Department legal questions. The searchers collected up all the legal papers for later study, but their studying yielded nothing on secret, deadly projects.

Sam had given me a little oral report. "Hey, I got a call from one of the guys that searched Melvin's office. They asked him for notes, asked where he kept them. He told them he hardly made notes of any kind. Told them his research, the case citations and case quotes stayed in his head until he needed to pull them up for a legal brief or argument. Making notes, he told them, was 'make work'. I hadn't heard that expression before. Must have pissed our guys off."

"Did our guys believe him?"

"At first they though he was fucking crazy or lying or sent his notes down the apartment incinerator. He dared them to strap him up again, call his section boss, told them everyone at State Legal knows how he works. They did call over there and learned he walks on water. No one could believe it when Melvin started working there, but it was all true, and from the steno pool up to the top, they were in awe. Said he was by far the smartest lawyer anyone had ever been around. And they get a lot of young Ivy League hot shots."

I believed it. "Anything from his apartment?"

"Just him being more of a wise guy. On the first night when Melvin came home, he said to the agents, 'It looks like you missed my laundry basket.' He plunked it at the feet of the lead agent. 'I'll be back later. Hope you'll allow me to sleep here. The building laundry set-up is on the main floor. Box of detergent is a quarter. When you get done here, you can do my laundry, little favor for the inconvenience.' Melvin left a quarter on the counter in the little kitchen and left."

I laughed out loud. "Can't blame him."

⚖

NOW A DARK WINTER HOVERED OVER WASHINGTON. Newspapers, tabloids and TV programs no longer wallowed in Kennedy's death and the Johnson aftermath. Nixon and Watergate, President Ford's pardon of Nixon, a bad economy and a testy Soviet Union sucked the oxygen out of other news. But Melvin or Madeline, or Yegor, and Yegor putting it on *your guys* never left me.

On this Wednesday evening, a familiar scent that did not belong in my walk-up apartment building stairway took me out of those thoughts. The scent got stronger as I unlocked and opened my front door. A couple lights had been turned on, and Bob Seeger's *Night Moves* came at me from my cheap radio.

A tall woman rushed at me, smothered me in a big embrace, pressed her head against mine. It took a couple beats to fully recognize her—Biddie.

The last time I had seen her was on my visit home after graduation in 1973, five years before.

ON THAT DAY IN MAY, BIDDIE LOOKED AT ONLY me across the dining room table, around which five sat—my father next to me, Grandma Ida at the head, Grandpa Yuri, and Biddie across from me.

Biddie wore one of those light blue summer dresses with a flouncy layered skirt, little puffed shoulders and short sleeves to hold up her dress cut low in the front. My half-sister's breasts were like her mother's but younger, more upright. Biddie's hair had the same lushness as her mother's. White socks in slip-on shoes finished it off. On anyone else who looked that good, the whole outfit would have brought up the heat in me. If I hadn't known, I would have guessed her age as somewhere around eighteen, even twenty, not barely fifteen. She had grown up ten years in three and a half.

Grandma Ida made all my favorites. Years later, I still tasted and smelled the pot roast as only she made, the potato chunks and carrots out of the roasting pan smothered in the juices but crispy on the outside, green beans grown in the yard and soaked in melted butter, homemade bread also slathered in locally churned butter, and then blackberry cobbler with whipped cream.

Cutlery clinked on good porcelain plates and leaded glasses, and the five of us breathed as we ate, shifted in chairs that creaked a bit. The others looked my way almost constantly. They all waited for me to talk. The only one who had graduated from a great university with a job in the big city, the future head of what might become of this little family.

Grandpa Yuri broke the quiet. "Frank, your father says you not staying in these parts?"

"I start a week from Monday. Clerk job at the FBI. They'll try to fast track me to become an agent, on account of my Russian. Then training at Quantico, a new training school just for us."

Grandpa Yuri looked at my father. "Yes, that good. A Bureau man." He waited, stuck his fork into a slab of roast on the serving dish and hoisted it to his plate. He leaned forward and poked his fork at me as he talked. "It a crime what the banks do to your father's farm. The banks take all money from crops, then take cropland and orchards and livestock, then house and all rolling stock. The stuff that not work they sell it to the scrap dealer. Maybe, Frank, when you get down there, you make someone to investigate the banks and to stop this crime, yes?"

I glanced to the side at my father. Grandpa Yuri had dragged out *your father's farm* and said *father* as if my father was the biggest farmer in these parts, as if Yuri hated me, had never forgiven my father for what he had done and not done when his daughter died.

Father's eyes remained fixed on his plate of food, his fork and knife lying side by side, signaling he was finished.

I caught Father shifting his head and blinking away the moisture, the anger and helplessness. That's what had happened to many fathers who owned small farms and had to borrow for seed and equipment between crops. I understood them both. Father and Yuri, each in different ways, had the best parts of their lives taken from them by monsters bigger than the biggest farm machines and could never reclaim what they had lost. Only memories and yammering remained for them. And I understood the inevitable shared suffering of getting too close. Maybe it was best not to get too close if I couldn't fix it, and I couldn't fix what had happened to Father and to Yuri.

Ida said, "Hush, Yuri. Don't send Frank off on assignments just yet. Let him stay here as long as he wants and grow into his new work."

"Yes, Grandpa," I began. "It is terrible. Wish I could have helped more from school and all, but I guess what I sent home . . ." A shifting of the head and shoulders from Father stopped me, and I realized the other three at the table didn't know about the money I had sent home every summer. And that saddened me, humiliating my own father right after Yuri piled on. "I'm mighty lucky to have a steady job soon. They'll even pay for my bus fare from here to D.C. But I can't get the money until I get there and put in an expense report."

Biddie said, "I'll come visit you, Frank. I love Washington, all the presidents and monuments and history. Will you have a gun?"

Biddie had never been to Washington, never even to Chicago. She just talked—like a girl. "I don't know. But there's lots of training in the care and use of guns before you get to be an official FBI Agent."

Father, head still down as if saying grace, said, "Aw, it's not so bad round here. I have a job, and that old house was nothing but falling down. You know, Frank, I never told you the barn roof caved in the winter after you were last here. Rottinghaus is getting old and wants me to take over the repair business—buy him out." He chuckled, and the chuckle made him look up and look around the table, a little pride creeping back. "The money's better than farming most years and a lot steadier, and he doesn't want much to buy him out." Father's eyes—redder, deeper, shadowed more deeply than I remembered. "But I miss owning my own place," jabbing a crooked yellow-stained finger at his daughter, "I miss your mother. You can tell her that, if you don't mind, Biddie."

Biddie looked at our father across the table, her expression not saying anything.

"Well, will you tell your mother I miss her?"

"Yes, Father."

"Tell her, please?"

"Yes . . ."

Grandma Ida patted the table with both hands. "Biddie, help me get the table cleared, and you men go sit in the parlor. The Braves game should be on. Who wants coffee?"

We couldn't find a baseball game on the black and white console television set. Daylight would not leave for another hour, yet I had to work at keeping my eyes open, at not yawning rudely. I could sleep on any ground but not in a Greyhound seat when strangers might snag my billfold with all the money I had in life and my one credit card.

Grandma and Grandpa wanted to keep talking, didn't want to turn in. They kept looking at me to respond, or just to look at me, their last connection to their only daughter. I said, "If you all will excuse me, I think I'll take a walk around outside and then turn in. Didn't sleep on the bus here."

"All right then," said Yuri.

"Can I come with you?" said Biddie.

I looked at the three elders, as if for permission. "Sure, sure. But not long. Grandma will need you to help clean up."

Far enough away from the house so none of the others could hear, Biddie said, "Frank, I wish you could stay, maybe get a job in Milwaukee."

I couldn't come up with anything that might make sense to her. The gulf between where I had been the last four years and this tiny outpost on the northern edge of the Midwest was too great, too hard to explain. Like trying to explain to someone who had never run the difference between sitting in a stiff chair and racing on a stadium track.

Biddie said, "Every time Father comes down, every cotton pickin' time, all he does is cry. After Mom left him, it was like he died inside. Now, every time he picks me up, she makes it extra hard on him."

"How's that?"

"She's always got a boyfriend, brings them over when I'm not around. I bet she has Cary—that's her latest, a young guy supposedly named after Cary Grant—over right now. Anyway, when dad comes to pick me up or drop me off, she's always sure to have her latest hanging around. So pathetic." Biddie looked off into the orange light of late evening, out across the road and to the orchards rolling away on the other side. "I made her promise to not bring them home when I'm there—but I can't make her keep that promise."

"You can come back here, can't you?"

"The judge said I can't. Not until I'm eighteen, said a daughter has to be with her mother, not stuck with her dad on a farm. And now Dad doesn't even have that anymore."

"You'll be eighteen soon." I tried to sound upbeat and as if I meant it. "Heck, if it works out, you can come live with me. They say there are always lots of jobs in D.C., as long as you can type fast and take dictation."

"Do you mean it? That would be cool. I type really good—I mean, well. I know the difference." Biddie threw her arms around my neck and pulled herself close.

I froze. Biddie had never been physical with me. As she grew out of babyhood, I was never around the house much, and then I was gone. But the body of a young woman up against me was good, familiar. After a long moment, I eased back. "I do mean it. I can get a place big enough, or we'll find you one close to mine."

"You're the best, always were at everything you did. Hope I can hold out that long."

"What do you mean by that?"

"Aw, I don't know. Boys are crazy around me, and every time Mom's boyfriends see me they look at me in that way . . . like I'm next after they finish with Mom."

I shouldn't have been surprised, but I was. I never thought of Biddie much, and never that way. But what she said was true, had to be true in this age after Woodstock, in this time living with a mother like Hilde.

"Have you told Pop? He can tell the judge, and you can come back here and stay with Pop."

"Dad knows but won't go to the judge. That takes money for his lawyer and Dad never has enough money. He put every penny into the farm and the divorce and pays Mom something every month on account of she's got me. He can't help me more."

"Wow, Biddie. Be careful. You can keep a big old hat pin by your bed."

She slapped me on the shoulder.

"Anyone bothering you now?"

"Nah, well . . . a little bit. Like I said, his name's Cary, says I should call him Uncle Cary every time he comes around. Mom lets him spend the night on weekends . . . and I hear them going at it . . . right through the wall, through my earplugs and pillow. I hate that part."

"I mean it about the hat pin under your pillow while old Uncle Cary's around. Biddie, when we get back to the house, write me out your telephone number. I don't have a phone yet, but let's talk regularly when Hilde's not around. Can we?"

"Sure. That'll help, help a lot."

"And if you ever need anything, I'll be only a phone call away. If I'm lucky, I'll be an FBI Agent one of these days, and you can tell anyone you've got a brother in the FBI. Might be worth a lot. Heck, you can tell them now that you have a brother in the FBI, even if I'm not an agent yet."

Biddie cocked her head. She liked that idea, would tell anyone who hassled her about me. "You're the best brother a girl could have."

This one time I hated that I couldn't stay longer, that I couldn't protect Biddie, though I'd think of some way if it ever came to that.

Chapter Twenty-Three

Angela

Googling Smaltz got me nothing, not a single link to him, to anything about his life.

The hell with Agent Smaltz. Maybe if he hadn't come around all hard and snarly and full of threats to leave it alone, I would have let it be. Besides, if he'd slaughtered Melvin, he was not about to do in another sitting judge. That would send too many hounds searching—at last—and he sure as hell knew that.

But his warnings to leave it alone, the bigness of the thing that I was supposed to leave alone, had taken shape, an ugly and kill-worthy shape. Maybe I should leave it alone. There had been enough killing over that one, most of it long ago in a place or places far away. But dear Melvin, his dying wasn't long ago in a place far away.

From that first Friday morning when Melvin was found dead, I had run theories, played what-if games until I'd run out of what-if scenarios. Sometimes the right answer is the last answer still standing after fatal flaws, key facts that do not fit have kicked down all other possible answers. Only one theory, only one what-if game fit all the facts, left nothing out, accounted for it all.

It came to me with the clarity of a high mountain summer morning, out of that deeper sense that tells us to look away, to cross over to the other sidewalk, to not go where we had intended to go a second before. And I now knew the last theory standing was the one right answer.

Only one solitary event, from the time of the cashier's checks and connected to Washington, D.C., could pull together the science of bullets, transfers of hush money and murders of dark-skinned men in that far-away place, cause a brilliant attorney-judge to make it his life's work, get him shot dead, keep dear Madeline from coming home and leave only her bones for burying, then make FBI agents stay on it a half century later—and make them try to keep a lid on it real tight. Only one answer was that big, as old Smaltz had said, *much bigger than all of us*. Only one answer fit snugly, and that empty PJ file might indeed refer to President Johnson.

But I had to keep quiet. Digging deeper without letting anyone besides Peter know what I was digging for might be the hardest part. If I slipped up . . . there were other ways to get to me, to shove splinters under my fingernails and never pull them out. *Tread carefully, slowly.*

My first lead was easy, safe enough. I'd chase that down on a Saturday or Sunday afternoon. But that easy lead had a sharp, dangerous edge. Melvin had found that lead before I did, maybe long ago, and Melvin's chasing down that lead might have brought on the man who killed him.

⚖

THE WEATHER CAME UP A WARM FALL DAY WITH a mild Santa Ana breeze from the desert then out over the Pacific, the air getting warmer all the way to the beach. Good for a last fling at summer, maybe even warm enough to dive into the ocean.

Everyone loves pretty little girls in little pink and white beach outfits, perfect little feet and hands covered in sand and eyes filled with curiosity. Many adults, if given half an opening, would say something to their mom or dad about how cute the twins were, about how in heaven's name their parents could tell them apart when the stranger couldn't. I hoped I'd find another way to break the ice with the strangers I was looking for.

Calling ahead would have been awkward, maybe dangerous. I wondered if the Burdick house had a landline, if the landline had been tapped. My search had turned up one phone number, but I didn't want to try it cold. Everyone got too many cold calls. The house sat directly across from the wide beach. If no one was home, the afternoon, the sand and water play with the twins and Peter might soften my torment.

From Googling, from eavesdropping on tweets and Facebook pages, it seemed one Phoebe Burdick ruled over this house now, watched over her own five kids and a sometime husband, Douglass, grandson of the Admiral and later CIA big shot. From my searches I could not tell if Doug still lived there, if he and Phoebe were on good terms, or if he stayed away from the social networks and had decreed that Phoebe not talk about him to the whole world.

On this afternoon, the warm wind brought people out of their houses, even some of the filthy rich who out of habit or fear shied away from strangers and riff-raff flopping down on this beach. Maybe I'd find someone in that house, in the front yard or up on the balcony looking out at the ocean.

I motioned Peter to a parking spot three houses down and across the street from the Burdick place. That gave me a good enough look at Admiral Burdick's last home, returned to every day after his morning swims until that day he didn't. The house appeared the same as on the Facebook pictures and Google images, same roof tiles, same white with green trim. Only the trees and bushes had changed, some gone now, others twice the size. County records showed no ownership change from the family trust back when the retired Admiral lived here. A Mercedes sedan and Lexus SUV sat in the driveway.

Alice and Abigail together said, "Daddy, unlock us. Let us out."

"Easy," said Peter. "You know the rule. Mommy or Daddy first to make sure it's safe." Then he was out on the sidewalk, the back door of the Camry wide open, the twins tumbling out and standing by the trunk waiting to get their beach stuff.

Alice interrupted my thoughts. "Mommy, come. What are you looking at? We're ready."

"It's nothing, honey. I just thought I saw someone I might have known a long time ago—down there a couple houses." Half-truths made half-decent lies. I was indeed looking a couple houses down there, at whatever was going on past the cars in the driveway.

"Well come on, Mommy. We can't wait."

"You go with Daddy. Peter, leave me the keys. I'll lock up and find you."

The twins each grabbed buckets, shovels, fins and towels until they couldn't grab anything more and headed down the sidewalk to the opening in the sea wall.

Peter looked where I focused. "Gonna check out that surfer dude, are you?"

"Shush, not so loud. Go after them now. Put sunscreen on everyone. I won't take long."

The surfer dude looked out of an Abercrombie and Fitch ad, sculpted torso with maybe five percent body fat, long blond hair, stubble of beard and lean face. He peeled out of his wetsuit and washed it off under the shower by the open garage door. Something about me, the way I stood looking at him, eagerness in my stance, must have made him stop and stare back. He smiled a smile of expensive dental work and the knowing of his place at the top of the male food chain. "Hi, can I help you?"

"I'm sorry for standing here watching... Maybe you can help me. Is this the Burdick residence?"

He bent over and turned off the hose. "You a real estate sales lady or something?"

"No, no. I work downtown—I'm a judge in Superior Court." That usually got me a minute of undivided attention. It did from this fellow. He pulled up to his full height and threw a beach towel over his bare shoulders.

"I'm Judge Cornwell, but please call me Angela. I'm not here on court business—unless you've got some unpaid tickets—just kidding."

"Ah, hi. Can I help you with something, ah . . ." Respect sounded in his voice, as if he wanted to call me, Your Honor. He had seen the inside of a courtroom a time or two.

"You might be able to help me. Is this the old Burdick house, once owned by Admiral Burdick?"

"Yep. This is the very one. By the way, I'm Doug, named after him. He was my great granddad."

This surfer dude was unlike all the clever, suspicious lawyers, who never gave straight answers and would just as soon fire back a question after someone asked them anything. "So sad, about your great granddad." I gestured to the beach and the water beyond.

"You know about that, huh?"

"Just what I read in the old news accounts. So strange."

"You can say that again. My mom knows a lot more than me. My grandma did, too . . ."

"Do you think I can talk to your mom, if I'm not imposing?"

"Nah, you're not imposing."

"Her name's Phoebe, right?"

"Yeah. But she's not home now."

"Will you tell her Angela Cornwell might call her, if you'll give me her number?"

"Sure. I guess it's all right. Can I tell her what it's about?"

"I'm just someone with a strange connection to your Admiral."

"Sure. Ah . . . why don't I have her call you? I'm not sure I should be giving out our home number just like that."

"I understand." But I didn't want to understand, and didn't know what more to say, except this surfer dude sensed my visit was as serious as any courthouse trip he'd ever been on, and this surfer dude knew how to protect the privacy of his well-to-do family members.

"I doubt she'll want to talk about them. Always gets her riled up, freaked out—the way he died and all. She goes quiet any time anyone mentions him. Tell me your name again?"

"Angela, Angela Cornwell." I put on my court face, tried my court demeanor, friendly but with authority. "When do you expect she'll be back?"

Surfer dude Doug hesitated, deciding how much to reveal. "She and Dad are coming in tonight. They've been away. I'm picking them up at the airport. I'll tell mom you want her to call you."

"Thanks very much."

"What's your name again? Sorry. I'm not good with names."

"Angela Cornwell. Your mom can call directly into my courtroom, and, if she wants to leave her best number, I'll call right back. She can go on the court's website for my number. Or . . . wait here a minute and let me get a card out of my bag in the car. I'll be right back."

"Great."

The surfer studied the card, the raised seal on the front side, then turned it over. There was nothing on the back. "Sure. I'll give her this and tell her you have a strange connection to my great grandparents." He raised the card as if he were raising a glass. "So long then, ah . . . Judge Cornwell."

That little sign-off hit harder than I expected. This surfer dude had all the control, and I doubted any Burdick would call me.

⚖

NO ONE NAMED PHOEBE OR DOUG BURDICK left a message or called, not on Monday, not during the rest of the week. No one asked me anything about Melvin. The rest of my leads to his killing sat there without any useful connections and far harder to probe than the Burdick family a fifteen-minute drive away.

But the residue of all the connections—whatever they were—came at me on Friday evening while the twins were hunkered down in front of the TV, and a vegetable and chicken casserole bubbled in the oven. The connections came in a neatly boxed package, marked with a pre-made stamp that said, "Confidential. To be Opened Only By Addressee."

Peter handed it to me. "Must be court business, I didn't dare open it." I wouldn't have minded if he opened it.

The sender was a post office box I did not recognize, but the physical box looked ordinary enough, lightweight and small. Tape shut it tight. And it wasn't court business, the box too light and boxy, not the kind that held papers or a trial exhibit. No stamps or postage meter slip on this one, only a US Government Eagle franking symbol. No court business had ever come to me in a box like this one. I shook it—too light to contain anything that might explode—and nothing inside shifted around. All the judges I knew worried about such things, talked about how to handle strange packages.

I found a sharp knife to slit the tape. A note sat on top of a plain white box inside the outer cardboard. The note, handwritten on note paper with an FBI crest, said,

Dear Judge Cornwell,

Thank you for talking to me and for the documents you provided us. You will understand the need to keep very confidential the matters we discussed. If you think of any other details about your colleague's untimely passing, please let me know. The number on my card and on this letterhead has access to me day and night. We best not send emails or text messages. I know you will understand.

Thank you.

HHS

I handed the note to Peter.

"Well, what's in the rest of it? Not a light blue Tiffany box, I don't suspect," Peter said. That made us laugh.

I shook the little box inside the bigger box. Something light weight moved inside but not much. Whatever was in there had been packed tightly. "Honey, just to be safe, you go to another room while I open it." I laughed again. We both laughed again. Tension made us laugh too easily. I pulled out the little box and flipped off the top, not secured by tape or anything else.

"Oh, my ever-loving God." I handed the little box to Peter and almost sprinted to the girls' bedroom, to their closets. A small shoe rack sat on the floor of each of their closets, holding neat little shoes in neat little pairs, each pair waiting and shouting out to be picked next. Except Alice's little shoe rack had a gap, like a missing tooth. One little blue sneaker was missing, the sneaker in the box inside the box.

"I'm so mad I can't see straight, think straight," I said to myself.

"Me, too," Peter responded from behind me.

"That Smaltz prick." Tears of rage and fright worked their way to the surface. "If it's just me . . . I can be careful. But the girls . . . they are so tiny and vulnerable and have just started out on this journey."

"Oh, Angela, Smaltz, and whoever is with him, knows if something happened to you, people would start digging—but if something freaky happened to the girls, no one could connect that up."

"And . . . they know that we know."

A new feeling welled up—stone cold defeat. I had not felt it often but hated it every time—the NCAA eight-hundred-meter finals senior year where I took second, Peter getting downsized by what had once been the biggest consumer tech employer in San Diego and now on the verge of pulling out of all its US operations, my mother's dementia and shaking hands.

"I don't see a safe path. You and I might be the last ones who care about

Melvin with a tiny chance to do something. Hell, we are the last ones—and someone's getting away with it."

Peter pulled me to him tighter for a long time. "We must set this aside for now, get the girls fed and to bed. They have a big day tomorrow."

Chapter Twenty-Four

Frank

I'd never seen Biddie wear makeup. The make-up confused me for a second.

She pulled away, and a string of breathless words spilled out. "Oh, Frank. It's so great to see you, to be here. I hope you're not mad. The super let me in after I proved to him you're my brother. Don't worry. I asked if you had company. I would have fixed dinner—but didn't know if you had eaten, what time you'd get home. I tried to call, but the FBI operator always put me on hold so long I ran out of change. Hope you're not mad at me."

As she talked, I spotted a new-looking American Tourister suitcase and large purse leaning against the radiator under the window. A folded heavy winter coat sat on the suitcase.

Biddie's travel-weary face, her prattling on lightened my spirits—a terrific blend of holding a family member right here, a friend, a gorgeous woman with no pressure for more.

"Biddie," I moved back a step, "you look great. Not mad a bit. Glad you're here." I caught the twinge of concern in her eyes. "That sofa over there is convertible, even has clean sheets." I noticed the newspaper on the sofa, folded open to the classified section with a couple pen circles. "I'll pull the table to the wall, and it makes a good bed. Right now, we'll get some grub if you don't mind frozen dinners or pizza. I'm always stocked up in those and am starved too. You can catch me up while we eat. Too late to go out—it being after dark and all. But it isn't that bad if you move like you mean business."

Biddie closed her eyes but couldn't stop tears sliding down her cheeks. Eye liner ran down with them to bright red lips. "I won't stay long, promise. Looks like lots of openings for secretaries and office clerks. I'm a whiz on the IBM Selectric with MAG cards, and I can cover any front desk."

I couldn't stop smiling and holding her hands out in front of me. "I bet you get an offer from everyone you interview. This town never fills all the office staff openings." I thought, *if you're half as smart as I think you are, you'll soon move past that.* "Let me get out of these clothes, and you spread out in here and put on something like you're staying. I'll holler before I come out of my room."

Biddie sighed happily, threw her arms around my neck and squeezed hard. "Oh, Frank, you are wonderful. Thanks a million." She leaned over to my small GE refrigerator, opened it, pulled out a bottled Schlitz beer and held it up. "You know I'm legal now and have been craving one of these. May I?"

"Sure. Open one for me, too."

We caught up over Stouffer's meatloaf with mashed potatoes heated in my microwave.

Biddie said, "I memorized your addresses from every letter and card."

I had not sent her many, three or four a year, and a couple times I'd said in my letters that I'd love to have her move here.

While the dessert pop tarts were heating in my small oven, I said, "How's your mom, and the guys hangin' round her?"

Biddie breathed in. "Some close calls . . . but no harm done. Mom got mad at me for a while when I burned one with a steam iron. He grabbed me from behind while I was ironing and wouldn't back off."

"Whew, I was worried, you know."

"Thanks, Frank. After that, me and mom settled down. She was more careful about who she brought around, tried not to if I was home. She knows Milwaukee's no good for me. Said I should come and live near you."

⚖

THE MORNING CAME UP CLEAR AND COLD. I gave Biddie a pocket full of coins for phone calls, bus fares, and taxi tips, and we headed out together—me to another day in the squad room, she to job interviews.

Before I could hang up my coat and get to my desk, my phone rang, Agent Sam on the other end. Sounded as if he was calling from home, but that was his privilege. "Hey, Frank, glad I caught you early."

"What can I do?"

"Late yesterday I got a call from my buddy at State, the one who first put us onto the missing Mrs. Brookfeld case. He said that Brookfeld resigned, that he's splitting for parts unknown. See what you can find out, would you? Get his new address and phone number. And let me know."

"Sure, I'll get right on it and report back."

Melvin Brookfeld took my call on the first try. "Yes, I wondered if your agent Sam might want an exit interview. Happy to give you one. Shall we say first thing tomorrow morning?"

We agreed to meet again at the reflecting pool, not a bad place if either of us was being watched or followed. We'd have some chance of spotting the overly curious.

Melvin looked more relaxed. The intensity around his mouth, in his eyes, had eased. We found a bench somewhat shielded from the cold breeze in Constitution Gardens and did not notice anyone hanging near us.

I started this time. "Heard what you did to those search hounds at your office and home. Was great. They should have done your laundry."

"That was fun." Melvin grimaced. "And no, they did not do my laundry."

"You look better and sorry I never got to say how sorry I was, I am."

"Thanks. The reason I asked you here relates to my further unburdening."

I waited.

"First thing tomorrow, I'll be leaving for the West Coast—unless you or Sam or other FBI agents want to poke around me some more."

"No, no. I don't know of a thing more we want from you. And . . . sorry for all the crap. But as long as I'm with the Bureau, that file will never close. I promise you that." My promise surprised me, as if someone else had said it for me. I hadn't planned it but now meant it as strongly as any promise I had ever made—to old Buford, to anyone.

After a long pause, Melvin said, "A decent enough law firm with offices in Los Angeles and San Diego has made a nice offer." He raised his eyebrows and voice a little as if surprised. "They are paying the movers and sent me the cost of one-way airfare. But I'll take the bus. Long distances are crossed better slowly, gives the mind a sense of the changing time and climate zones, the passing of the land, the leaving old places behind and arriving at new ones."

Melvin reached into the inside of his coat, "I should give you this. It may be of some use," and pulled out an office envelope, "but I'm not sure you should have it yet."

Christ Almighty, I didn't come out here to get teased like a schoolgirl. "I'll bite. What is it, and why can't I have it?"

Melvin waited. "This holds everything you might need to get after what I'd been working on. I'll give it to you now on two conditions. They are: first, you will not follow up until at least a year from now and, second, you'll write your 302 report with no mention of who gave this to you—that you treat me as your most confidential informant, your super CI, if you will. Once I've left State and am far from here in distance and time, you can do with it what you wish. So long as you never ever connect it to me. Am I clear?"

"Yes, sir, very clear."

"Well, Mr. Maier?"

"Well, what?"

"Do I have your commitment of waiting at least a year and no connection to me?"

I had never been on this terrain. Confidential informants, CIs, were a dime a dozen. Other agents talked of them like they talked about their favorite beer or baseball team. And no one ever asked for a CI to be outed, except in the little report to the direct supervisor or CI coordinator. But no CI had ever imposed these kinds of conditions. A twenty-dollar bill in exchange for a lead satisfied most of the time.

I was too junior to have been allowed to develop the kind of high-level CI other agents bragged about. But I could do this. Sam would not care, had moved on from Melvin and Madeline. Sam probably wouldn't even read my 302 report on this meeting, probably just send it straight to the Madeline Brookfeld kidnapping file. "We'll wait a full year and not connect you in any paperwork, in anything." I paused to let the next sink in. "You, Mr. Brookfeld, will be my very own first Confidential Informant."

Melvin handed me the envelope. "Go ahead, I did not seal it."

I pulled out two letter-sized sheets of paper folded like a letter. Four columns of data stretched down each sheet. The first column displayed a numerical date, the next column a long number, the next column listed a dollar sign and amounts from $100 up to $4000. The last column showed the name of a bank with another number listed next to the bank's name. I felt a bit like that soldier in Napoleon's army who stumbled on the Rosetta Stone. "Looks like check numbers and the issuing bank with its branch number."

"Indeed, Mr. Maier."

"But no information on whose account they came out of or who they were made out to."

"I can answer that last—it's always the same."

I got it. "All of these were made to one Mr. John Q. Blank and made out by Sally J. Cashier."

"Indeed. And every account is a US Government account, I suspect. But I have not been able to confirm it for each of them—not by the time I was chased off, anyway."

"And . . . this is what you were working on, this made them take Madeline from you?" It was the first time I had called Mrs. Brookfeld by her first name—powerful emotions do make you lose your manners. "And there's more, isn't there?"

"Yes, I did get a bit further. But what you have there is the essence of it, though I again suggest you don't follow up on it for a long time, far longer than a year."

I looked around. "Because if they learn anyone is investigating, they'll do to me what they've done to you . . ."

Melvin said very quietly, as if thinking out loud, "I was not the only one chased off."

There are other Madelines. And . . . I bet I know about one. But I saved that question. I started with, "Then why did you give me this?"

"I've thought a lot about everything. I've checked your file, talked to a few people about you, and you are the only one I know who might someday get to the bottom of this, get there without worrying about children or loved ones—or you will know how to protect them better than I protected mine."

This was getting stranger, deeper, beyond my job description. Melvin knew I was supposed to write up a 302 report for every witness interaction and report I had obtained files or documents or something from a new CI. "Are you sure you want to give me this? I must follow procedures. I like my job."

"Agent Maier, I know some about FBI CIs. Every agent has them, it seems, pays them—sometimes hefty sums—and need not disclose most of what's transacted with them. I'm willing to take that risk. And, as I said in our last meeting, I can handle whatever the law might decide to do with me. I can even handle Madeline's killers coming after me. But I can't let them take family members who have no idea, who never asked for any of it. Hence, I must stop, must stop putting this together, get away from it. And . . . maybe in time when the stench of it has faded and the evil doers no longer care or are gone to their own hell, I might continue where I stopped. But . . . not for a very long time."

Many questions—too many—wanted to climb one over the other. I held out the sheet, as if gesturing for Melvin to take them back and leave me out of it. "When and how did you get this list?"

"Agent Maier, one of my great blessings is also a curse. I have a close to photographic memory of everything I've seen, whether good or bad. Once I see something one time, I can recall it in detail. I typed these sheets up yesterday—from memory. But I'm sure the data on them are accurate."

"So . . . you've seen these cashier's checks?"

"Allow me to not answer that—for a spell. You can in time subpoena the banks for them. They'll have them all on microfiche, won't destroy them for years. The checks will be written on accounts whose holders you can track, can interview, can ask why they needed them, and who got them. That's all I should say, still too dangerous for me—and for you."

"I've been reading too, Mr. Brookfeld, can't help it. One of the reasons you want me to have this is my facility with Russian?"

"It's useful, but the main reason is that you are honorable and will figure out the best way. I must be done with it for now. You grew up a farmer, and made your way out of there, have become one of the better young ones, or they wouldn't have put you on Madeline's case. I choose to trust you. Well then, I . . ."

Melvin started to rise, but I motioned him to wait. "One more question before you go, please."

He sat back down but leaned forward. "Sure, ask, but I can't promise I'll answer."

"This thing, this project, this nightmare of yours comes out of the JFK murder, doesn't it? And, part two of this two-part question: these checks are payoffs either to the killers or to those covering it up?"

Melvin sat for a long time, his eyes fixed on things far off. "It's not that simple. If it were, the Warren Commission and all its helpers would have tumbled to it. It does spring out of the JFK assassination. On the direct cause, I believe, the Commission got it all correct. Mr. Oswald fired the shots and acted alone. That's really all I should say—else I'll get worked up again and stay a while longer, and that I shall not do." Melvin stood. "Why don't you sit here a while? We should not be seen together—especially you without Agent Koslowski. You have some thinking to do about how much to put in your 302 about this meeting, how much to tell him. I'll trust you on that."

More questions shouted at me. "Are you saying my Bureau or Sam are in on this?"

"Sam not. Others in the Bureau, sure. Your D.C. Region has over one thousand active FBI agents, and I fear some may be, as you say, in on it."

"Oh, my—excuse me—fucking Christ!" I thought, *you, Melvin, are now the second one who's said my guys were in on Madeline's murder. Shit, shit, shit to the nth power.*

"I must go now. For you there's no hurry—no statute of limitations on murder. I'll keep in touch. We should not shake hands or leave together. Someone might take note, but I've not seen anyone paying us any attention."

Neither had I, and I followed next to him as he tried to walk away from me. "I'm not letting you leave like this. Charles William Thomas, is that it? Begged the Warren Commission to dig deeper about Oswald connections to Cuba and Russia, wrote memos and letters all the way to Secretary of

State Rogers. Was canned, and blew his brains out—suicide official cause of death, but it wasn't, was it? How am I doing?"

Melvin's brilliant mind flinched, didn't answer right away and then responded very slowly, made every word sit in its own chair. "Wait that year, please, and be careful. I am glad I gave you the list, that your mind is as keen as I thought, that you care. Stay in touch, Agent Maier, and stay careful."

This is, indeed, about dead Charles William Thomas—of the fucking State Department where Melvin worked—and some shitty fucking kind of cover up of the worst fucking crime on US soil since the big stone guy sitting over there.

I looked at Melvin leaving, lanky even in a gray topcoat. He headed toward the wading pool and faded into the line of bare trees and the massive Lincoln Memorial. He looked relaxed, as if he had just come from the gym and a hard game of hoops—or had unburdened himself and dumped it on me.

Chapter Twenty-Five

Angela, January 2011

The machines of Justice slow down for the holidays. Sitting jurors get the week off, and new trials don't start until after the New Year. Life returned to an uneasy normalcy. Christmas, the first Christmas when the girls didn't believe in a real Santa Claus, but still wanted to, had been good. Peter and I hosted a college football party. I found more time to run, some runs to my limit.

Normal sleep patterns returned. With every day's passing, the nagging hell of Melvin and Madeline receded a bit more. I was not sure if time passing made those things fade—or if the missing shoe returned in a box had forced me to shunt them aside.

Who said time heals all wounds? Whoever said that didn't say anything about scars and pain, scars that don't fade and pain that flares up with every change in weather. I exchanged holiday cards with Naomi. She had written a note about that "special visit of last October by a special person". The note didn't mention Melvin. Didn't have to—her note was enough to grab me again.

The pain of those who care about unfinished life tasks, about the unfair death of loved ones, about unresolved gruesome deaths, I got a jab of that kind of pain when Doug Burdick, father of the surfer dude, phoned me.

He caught me at the courthouse after the turn of the New Year on a morning when my latest jury was deliberating. I took his call directly. He sounded middle-aged and a man of business—clipped in the way he talked, unemotional, firm. "Hello, Judge, you won't remember, but you talked to my son some months back. You asked him to tell my wife that she should call you."

"Yes, I remember well. Handsome and polite young man."

"You told him you had a connection—a strange connection—to my grandfather. What would that be, if I may ask?"

Over the months of silence from the Burdicks, I had prepared for this call and now felt calm, ready, yet cautious. "It's rather personal. May we talk in person . . . ?"

That made Mr. Burdick pause, but he too seemed ready and cautious. "Yes, we should meet about it. I'm on a new cell phone with a new number, so we can talk now about when and where best to meet."

I caught his concern that someone might be listening. We agreed to meet on a concrete bench tucked into the concrete walkway by the big rocks forming the sea wall a half mile down the street from the Burdick home. Doug and Phoebe Burdick often took walks on that path, Doug said. It would not seem strange to anyone watching for them to leave the house and head out on that path. There weren't many benches along that side of the street. They could share the bench with me and not attract attention.

When I got there, the walkway and the sandy beach on the other side of the rock barrier were empty. A strong wind pushed up the bay and straight at me, but that was good. It would muffle any talking and had kept all but the hardiest off the beach.

A man and woman in matching blue windbreakers came down the concrete walkway. He looked like he came from money in an unassuming way—no jewelry, plain trousers and running shoes, but a The North Face windbreaker and tight haircut for his balding tanned head—like he golfed or sailed, maybe both. Without looking at me, he said, "Hello, Judge, I'm Doug. This is Phoebe."

Phoebe, no make-up on a weathered face, clung to him and raised her eyebrows in greeting. They sat down, leaving a bit of space between them and me. Doug sat closer. Again, looking at her, he said, "Our son told us right away of your visit. We wanted to call you sooner, but then decided to not call at all. But here we are."

The halting way Doug spoke without saying anything, how Phoebe clung to him as if she were ill, displayed all the signs of a conflicted couple. They made me worry about them, about me, about this meeting. To an outsider the three of us might have looked like fugitives, three strangers sharing a bench or planning a run to Mexico.

"Thank you for coming here, for talking to me. I've been checking around and don't see anyone looking at us. Please call me Angela. Judge Brookfeld, Melvin to me, was a dear and kind friend. I believe he might have contacted you, perhaps early last year, about your grandfather."

Mr. Burdick nodded. "Yes, you are right. It was about a year ago. Then we saw he died last summer, couldn't imagine him taking his own life. We've wondered and wondered who we could talk to about all that, about all that leads up to it."

Next small step. "Police or FBI?"

"Thought about it, sure. Done it even, and it scared the hell out of us. We're not sure who we can trust."

Next step, another small one, "And I'm where you are. But I think I can trust you, and please know that you can trust me. I will never tell anyone what you tell me without permission, or unless I'm forced to by law."

Mr. Burdick seemed to understand. He looked at Phoebe. She silently signaled him to go ahead. "A while back, after that visit with Judge Brookfeld, an FBI agent stopped by, told us to report to him right away if anyone wanted information about Granddad. That made sense with Granddad in the CIA. But one thing didn't make sense."

"What's that?"

"Our son. That FBI agent telling us that some mighty mean people are involved, that they rarely tamper with potential witnesses, but they are hell on the loved ones and children of any witness. They'd be hell on our youngsters if we learned too much, hell on children and loved ones, he said. And it bothered us terribly."

I took a deep breath then plowed on. "Did that agent leave any ID?"

"Sure did, his card."

"Let me guess. Retired agent Harlan Smaltz."

"Yes, ma'am."

That made us just sit for a while, look away. I stood and gazed out over the water, then said as if to the wind, "That visit from Melvin, what was he searching for with you that made Smaltz come out with his nasty warning?"

Burdick reached into his windbreaker pocket and pulled out a little rectangular wafer holding a circular battery at one end with two wire leads coming out of the other end. He held it in his lap but where I could see it. "You are so right about everything. As I said, we met your Judge Brookfeld at our house just about this time last year, liked him right away. He wanted to know all about my grandfather, a fine man that one. Judge Brookfeld insisted we talk away from the house. We strolled along this walk. That gave us pause, and we almost didn't go with him. We didn't want any more trouble catching up to us from long ago."

"But you and he did talk about the trouble from long ago?"

Burdick didn't answer directly. "At the end of our meeting, your Judge Brookfeld urged us to sweep for listening devices. We thought that was crazy, frankly." Burdick paused again and looked far off. "But then Agent Smaltz came around and Judge Brookfeld died so peculiarly. Anyway, we hired home tech guys to sweep for listening devices. This was stuck to the underside of a little built-in shelf that holds our landline phone."

Burdick pushed the device toward Phoebe and upward a bit, as if he wanted me to see it more closely but not seem obvious.

"In a million years, we'd have no reason to look on the underside of that shelf. They said there might have been others, but they had been switched out or removed or were now maybe in our cars, that the batteries of these things had to be kept fresh." He looked away again. "That scared us. It's a whole lot to absorb, to be able to sleep at night with the thought that strangers have come into our house and changed batteries on listening devices, all without us ever seeing, hearing a thing." Burdick snorted out a scoffing laugh, a laugh that said he was too strong to let all that bother him, but bother him it did. "We were frightened, and then you came by last Fall. We've thought about selling this great old house and moving to New Zealand."

Me, too.

"Do you think Judge Brookfeld died because of our meeting . . . that someone heard our conversation? Do you think we are being watched now, sitting here?"

A seagull's cry cut in. *You bet someone heard that conversation near your house, or saw you meet with Melvin, or Melvin followed up after he met with you, and his snooping got Mr. Big Shot's attention, and then Melvin got his gun—or someone else did pretending to be him. Damn.*

The gull landed on the sea wall, then another landed. "Don't think so, not being followed. Nothing active is going on, far as I know. Still, no harm in being careful." More gulls circled. Maybe the listening device from Burdick's pocket made the gulls conjure up images of wafers, cookies, flat candy bars. "Yes, someone's been listening at your house, probably for a long time."

Their listening started the chain that led to Melvin dying. Part of me wanted to shut this down right now and run away, grab the girls and Peter, put our house on the market and flee. Here I was, doing just what Melvin had been doing on the way to an early death. But I pressed on. "Mind telling me what you remember about the last years of Admiral Burdick, what you told Melvin about the Admiral?"

Mr. Burdick glanced away and then at his wife, who huddled next to him. Phoebe took the cue. "I should tell you this part. It might take a little, but I'll try." Phoebe spoke as if she were comfortable speaking, making people listen.

"Take however long you like."

"Granddad's wife and I got very close. You see, they lived in our house here. Doug's father was their only son, and we lived around the corner in a little bungalow. It fell on me to help her after Granddad drowned. At first, I checked on her every day, then some nights I'd sleep over with her, then it fell on me to help her more and more right through hospice care." Phoebe cracked a bit, found a tissue and daubed her nose. That did not alarm me. It was cold enough for anyone's nose or eyes to need a tissue.

"I can imagine. Mom's about halfway there."

"Right up to the end, Francie was most lucid about little snippets from her past. She'd say Granddad knew too much, retired sooner than he wanted to, came here to Coronado where, it seems, Admirals come to die. I'd pat her wrist and tell her it was all right and change the subject. But the next day or the day after, she'd tell me the same all over. One time I said, okay tell me what happened that made Granddad quit the Navy too soon. She'd look at me strangely, like a stork wanting to take flight, as if I had accused her of something terrible. She said, no, no, I can't tell you or trouble would come. She'd look at me like a crazy woman imagining things. We all, the whole family, thought she was an old lady suffering infirmities of old age—until one day she let something slip." Phoebe straightened up, paused and glanced around as best she could before turning to me. "How do we know we can trust you, that you are not part of it?"

"Melvin was my best judge friend, maybe my best friend other than my husband. He was a beautiful man." I looked out at the dark clouds and wind-blown water beyond the beach. The gulls had left. "And there is this. My whole professional life has only one true purpose—to provide the best that justice can offer and, as Melvin said, so mothers can tuck their children in at night and feel safe. If we all just forget about Melvin . . . well, I need to know why he died the way he did. And . . . one more thing, they've threatened our little girls."

"Oh, goodness, I'm sorry—and sorry for not trusting you. Anyway, whenever Francie was troubled about something, right to the end, she'd grab any nearby soft item and try to roll it up in opposite directions as if wringing out water from a sponge, maybe as if trying to wring out sins of long ago, wring out whatever troubled her and flush it down. This one time—I can still see it—she grabbed a nice little purple pillow with a genuine Belgian lace coverlet. We still have the pillow in our parlor. She started to wring it out like a cheap sponge, but it wouldn't let her. Thank goodness her hands were not so strong, and she couldn't tear it open. She would have if she could. Then Grandma said,

"'Doug told me one day. Want to hear what he told me? It started with a death in Mexico, then another death in our state department down there, and kept growing and growing, and my Douglas was getting ready to let it all out. Those deaths were murder, and my Douglas knew who did it and why. That's why they drowned my dear Douglas. Easy to do, easy to do to an old man in the water. Send a scuba diver after him and hold him down, hold him down under the water until he stopped moving, stopped fighting, hold him down . . .'

"Grandma Francie said, hold him down over and over again until exhausted, until imagining that she too had drowned."

Phoebe might have wrung out a pillow in the telling if she'd had one. "I told Doug and his parents right away. Mind you, this was before the Internet and Google. We all thought it sad, the product of the fertile fields of a mind sprouting weeds and thought no more of it. Grandma said these things only that one time. I didn't leave it alone completely. You know the old saw, drunks, madmen and children tell the truth. But Grandma either didn't know more or couldn't pull more up. Granddad was in his eighties, and he easily could have had a stroke or heart attack or embolism on any of his daily swims. Our family buried him without an autopsy, too gruesome the thought of that back then. Too late now. A drowned body wouldn't have told us if someone pulled him under."

I suddenly knew what to do next after I bid this conflicted couple goodbye, but I couldn't just run off. "Did Melvin fill in any gaps?"

Doug answered this time. "We asked. He said it's better that he did not, that he wanted to know what we knew about Granddad, his time at the CIA, and the circumstances of his death. Funny, he didn't write anything down. Listened to us very well but took no notes."

"Well, thank you so much. This helps me a lot."

Doug said, "So, do you have enough to go to the authorities?"

I answered honestly. "I'm not sure. Probably not. I have some ideas that might cause some people to take note." I turned away from the wind and hopped down onto the walkway as if to leave. "I think it best if we not leave at the same time. My car is down there and around the corner. You should probably stay here—make it look more like strangers sharing this bench and a friendly chat. Again, thank you so much."

Doug said, "I'm glad to share this load a bit."

Phoebe said, "Oh, yes, me, too. And please call me any time. Sorry to have been so rude ignoring your request."

"It's quite all right. I understand. We three surely understand. So long now. And call me on that cell phone, or on your son's cell phone, if you think of any other specifics."

I left.

I got home before dark. Alice and Abigail ran to greet me, both talking in bubbling talk of all the things they had done with daddy while Mommy was gone, their three-way game of this great new Super Monkey Ball game, their starting a batch of cookies but not wanting to put them into the oven until Mommy came home. I strained to stay in the moment, to not plunge into what I wanted to plunge into, needed to plunge back into. It could wait until after the cookies were done, until after we had gone to our favorite Italian restaurant and put the girls to bed.

And all that evening with my family, I thought of Melvin, of the closer times with him. Now, after my visit with the Burdicks, one truth cycled through me. Johnny Pitts and all his forensics, and gun ownership reports, his checking of alibis, had it wrong. The same solitary question came with that knowing. Did I, Angela, have the time, the knowhow, the money, and the courage to find the truth of it?

After the girls fell asleep, I pulled Peter up to my little work area, to the locked file cabinet with the disk that now held images of every page and file cover taken from Naomi's house. I loaded it into my desktop computer, scrolled to the sub-file that said simply, "photos", and opened the first of four. I wasn't looking for the blood spatters, or the faces of the men. I spotted what I thought should be there, now that I knew what to look for. All the signs in the background were in Spanish. All the cars were old American models; all the clothes fit the time and place. The two photos of the foreign-appearing place sure looked like Mexico City of the 1970s, and the dead men wrapped in each other and bloody sheets sure could have been Mexican or Cuban.

One loose end could be closed without it getting back to Smaltz right away. It was a long shot, but if my little plan worked, it would tie up multiple loose ends. First, I'd charm Detective Johnny Pitts and then put the fear of what he'd missed into him.

CHAPTER TWENTY-SIX

Frank, Winter 1978

Biddie pushed her arm through mine. "Hey, big brother, thought you'd never get here, thought I'd be eating alone."

Biddie's leaning on me, her smell, her sisterly love felt good. Funny how I never could bring on this feeling with lovers, not since Bekkah anyway. Maybe I should have tried dating for a while longer before the sex.

"Sis, if I say I'll be here, I will. Count on it."

On even the hottest or coldest days, we tried to keep our weekly lunch date. The Florida Avenue Grille was our favorite. She had found a job two blocks away, and it was a short cab ride or longer walk for me. We wouldn't meet there for dinner, too many thugs on the streets, and neither of us wanted to spend serious money on restaurants. Instead, once a week she made dinner for us in her little place. She was onto her third local boyfriend, and that made me think Biddie was her mother's daughter. But Biddie introduced me to each one, and I liked that. My handshake, my cold stare, my Bureau status assured that any man who dated Biddie never did anything stupid.

For a full year now, nothing had happened on the bank account and cashier's check data Melvin had left with me. But my need to find Madeline's killer or killers, to track the bank accounts, to identify *your guys* had not faded. How to start it up again without revealing Melvin as my source? Misleading a subject or witness was one thing, but misleading your supervisor was another. If found out, that might get you two strikes on the Bureau's Internal Analysis scale—halfway to a demotion or worse.

Too many strikes and Internal Affairs would start taking a deep look. Once IA started to ride your ass, you'd fill grocery stamp books, clip coupons, and work crossword puzzles 'cause you wouldn't get any real work. If you were unlucky, IA would collect your badge and weapon and send you home until IA was done with you. And if you were unlucky, at the end of it you'd lose your Agent status, get stuck with a clerk's job, or be fired. One flat-out lie to the section leader would get you fired.

While waiting the year that Melvin asked me to wait, a decent enough plan formed. The plan allowed me to use Yegor, have him help me keep Melvin safe and out of this. Besides, Yegor deserved a little trouble for his high and mighty, for his leering thoughts of that yellow dress on a dead lady, for not cooperating. Time for another visit, if Yegor was still at his number and not shipped out to Cuba.

I found Yegor at the same place, and the operator put me right through.

Yegor said, "Ah, my friend, happy to hear you're still around." I wondered what he meant by that, whether he thought I had been shipped to some ice hole. "Sure, we can meet, but I must check my schedule, and how you say, all the things on my plate."

That had to be short for, *gotta check with the Resident head KGB guy here, and the Resident needs time to clear this next meeting with Moscow.*

I was still too much the FNG to develop my own "ticket", my own file to investigate and bring to justice. Next question: what to tell or not to tell Sam? Sam hadn't commented on my plain vanilla 302 Witness Report after that good-bye visit with Melvin a year ago. Sam had probably never read past the opening lines that said Melvin had indeed quit his job at State and was heading to a California law job. Sam was no fool. He would figure out my visit with Yegor and what I wanted to do next led straight to Melvin. But there was a way—a tiny flip in sequence would keep Melvin out of it.

I found Agent Sam and said, "Hey, on an old file, remember that Yegor full-of-himself-Russki?"

"Sure do."

"Well, he wants to meet, says he might have something useful."

"No shit? Well, go ahead, but stay out in the open, let me know when and where and report back right away. I'll go with you on any follow-up."

"Will do all three. Thanks."

Yegor called back the next day, sounded anxious to meet again, at the same deli as our last meeting.

After one more crushing handshake and slap on the shoulder, we took two open seats at the counter. Yegor said, "Hey in these heavy coats and with all this background shouting, our apparatus won't pick up a damn thing—even if I was wired. You, my friend?"

I carried no wire or recorder. A recorder would be hard to turn on and off under Yegor's trained gaze. A wire would have taken so much paperwork, too many approvals. "Nope, not me. If we didn't come across strange, I'd let you pat me down right here."

After we both looked around to see if either of us brought any helpers, after we glanced over the big plastic-coated menus and a waiter had taken orders, Yegor said, "What's up, my friend? You want to know if we're going into that shit hole called Afghanistan, is that it?"

"No, no, not that."

"What then? Why you drag me away from my important work? More on that lemon sherbet honey?"

I've got to go so slow. If Melvin was into what I think he was . . . damn . . . how do the Russkies fit, will they circle back to us, to me? Damn. "I don't know if there's any connection to her, but I believe you now, what you said the last time."

Yegor nodded. "You believe it was your guys?"

"Maybe, and maybe you're shitting me. But let's say I believe you, and I tell you that what you tell me will never get into one of our 302s, will never go up the line unless you give me the okay, what can you tell me besides that it was our guys?"

Yegor sat for a long time in silence, making little designs with the French Fries in the catsup on his plate. "Can't, honest. Wish I could help, but I can't. Highest orders."

"What if, hypothetically only, we already know it was our guys, and we know they were connected to your embassy in Havana, to our state department guys in Mexico City, what can you fill in so we don't go off throwing around false charges? Better for both of us if we don't start putting out bullshit—unless that's what we both want to do."

Yegor lifted his fork. "I take your point. Not good for America to accuse my country of something we did not do. Not good to go off on bad information or, as you say, on a chase for wild geese. But we have our rules, too, our reports and chain of authority. Let me, how you say, get back to you."

We finished eating in silence, paid our separate tabs, and left with not even a handshake. It had not gone well, and I should not have contacted Yegor again, not so soon, not without more. But I had to meet with Yegor to make my next step work. *Damn, patience was not yet my strong suit.*

⚖

AGENT SAM KOSLOWSKI LOOKED UP AT ME with an expression that made me think about getting the hell out of there, regretting what I'd just asked for. Agent Sam's breathing, his expression, his hard hand-slap on his desk all said, *you are positively shitting me, and if you don't come clean I'll sic IA on you and get your ass fired out of here.*

Agent Sam said, "You want search warrants on what?"

"Bank accounts, sir."

"Yeah, I got that. You want them on government bank accounts to ID who the hell is on them, who bought cashier's checks out of them."

"Yes, sir."

"And you want this because you got it from your super-duper-fucking-first-ever fucking CI. Do I have that right? And I'm not supposed to tell anyone the Russkies have all this payment info on our government bank accounts. I'm just supposed to sign off on your request for warrants?"

Sam knew I met with Yegor and figured I'd gotten the checklist from him. Had to keep him there. "Yes, sir. I won't, I can't ask for the warrants if that means giving up my CI and getting him into trouble. I gave him my word."

Sam's face softened. "What did he do? Bang a clerk in every one of these branches . . . without us knowing about it? What do you think? Or did they have one of theirs assigned to each branch? Very slick if that's the way it went down."

I relaxed a bit. This plan might work.

Sam flipped through the sheets—copies now—with bank account data Melvin had given me. "On second thought, must be someone higher up at every one of these damn banks. This shit looks specific enough to get your warrants, and most banks come running when we whistle, what with us being their only protection against big-time fraud. Okay, write up the warrant worksheets for my approval, and I'll send them over to Rasmussen. Only one thing more."

"Sure, what is it?"

"If this goes anywhere, and you get a ticket, keep me in on it so you don't fuck up and make us all look bad, okay?"

"I'll do that, sir, and thanks."

I would have clicked my heels at how this had come out. Yegor never got back to me. That was okay—if my little ruse worked—better actually. Let Sam and anyone think the check data came from Yegor, that he was my super-secret CI. If Yegor couldn't come clean on what he meant by *your guys*, he deserved whatever blew back at him. And I had not lied; I'd never said Yegor had given me the lists of cashier's checks.

Three weeks later Agent Sam called me over to his desk. "Frank, how long you been with us?"

"Going on five years, sir."

"So why the hell do you still behave like an FNG?"

"Sorry, sir. I have no idea what you mean, what I did?"

"Well, for the last couple of days, the SAIC, the one who reports to the big boss, has chewed me out and then crawled up my butt all on account of you."

I didn't know whether to get ready for a big old rat-fucking joke at my expense or a transfer to the Bureau's worst office—say El Paso. If the Special Agent In Charge of the whole D.C. office had chewed out Sam, that was a big deal. "Sorry, sir, for whatever I did."

"You really have no clue, you clueless fuck, do you?"

"No, sir."

"Didn't I tell you on that thing you had the warrants for, to pull me in if you had something real?"

"Yes, sir, you did say that. I didn't think I had much of anything until one or the other of the banks coughed up what we wanted."

"Well, how come when the banks started responding to those warrants, the SAIC has my ass on his desk?"

"I don't know, sir." But I did know, at least had the outlines, and it was big, bigger than anything I had ever done here or even heard about in this or any other squad room.

"Well, how's this for big shit. You, Mr. FNG, and I, and my whole squad are one inch from IA climbing all over us. But, because I bowed down and bent over and told them how dumb you were, we're not all busted. And because I'm three times smarter than you, I gave him up."

Gave who up? Yegor, I hope to hell.

"And that seemed to do it, but stay the hell out of this, and swear on a stack of your Lutheran Bibles to cut all ties to your Russki Yegor. Will you do that?"

"Sorry, sir. Don't know what to say."

"Good. I'm way ahead of you. Your chum Yegor's probably getting dressed down now for meeting with you. Unbeknownst to you, the Russkies have clerks working at most of our big banks, and any clerk has access to all the accounts at the branch. Easy enough to pull the government accounts and look for cashier's checks in high round numbers. You could have told me, don't you think, that Yegor had explained all that to you. And what makes it worse is that there's an active investigation on all those Russki clerks right now—and your warrant just about blew the whole thing sky high."

Wow, what the hell? I couldn't think it through right now, too many angles, too many possibilities. Was Sam throwing me off? Did Sam or higher ups connect the bank account lists to Melvin, but blamed it on Yegor and the Russians for cover?

"Sir, I would have told you right away if my list and the warrants had led to anything solid, anything Russian or that big."

Sam stood up as if to show me the door. "Tell me this one thing. What did you promise Yegor in exchange for this list of checks in US Government accounts?"

Think fast, make it good, stick to the truth. "Nothing, sir. Nothing. I promised Yegor nothing."

"Okay, FNG, I believe you. Even though you have no clue. And we are all over it. From now on you stay out of it. And if you ever go off on your own—well don't."

Chapter Twenty-Seven

Angela

Johnny Pitts hadn't yet retired and seemed pleased to go on my little Easter egg hunt. We decided on the next Saturday, when I had no court duty, and all the gunshop sales people would probably be on duty. Pitts said, "It's a long shot. The one who took the application might not be there and might not remember a damn thing. But I'll help you."

I had never set foot inside a gunshop, never studied the racks where all manner of rifles stood like tightly-clustered soldiers, handgun displays, boxes of ammo stacked like boxes of golf balls or cartons of cigarettes. I had never seen gun buyers when they looked for their next toy. Saturday must be the big shopping day, this place as crowded as my Friday courtroom. The jargon they spoke was new—the numbers they threw around using "aught" instead of zero, the brand names they threw out as if talking about brands of butter. I wondered what Melvin must have thought, must have felt right here—or what the imposter must have felt.

On the way in through the front door, I spotted two security cameras covering all entry points—the front door, the front wall and metal grate over the small windows—but no cameras on the inside, or they were well concealed. That explained Pitts's hesitation the first time we met. Obvious inside cameras might spook customers who didn't want a record of them gleefully holding the biggest automatic rifle. Besides, the gunshop lets in only known customers or decent-looking folks.

Pitts showed his badge, asked for the salesman by name, and every sales clerk in the shop jumped to attention. We got lucky. The particular salesman still worked there, although occupied doing inventory or something.

The salesman took us to a small office away from the crowd and the transactions. He said he remembered Detective Pitts from the last time back at the end of the summer after Judge Brookfeld died, remembered going over the application with him, and Pitts comparing the thumbprint and signature on the application with those of the recently dead judge. One didn't forget about things like that—even in this small warehouse full of guns and ammo. The salesman pulled up a copy on the store's computer, then collected the original from the file room. This store followed the law to the letter and more.

Pitts, his finger by the original signature, turned to me. "This signature look like your Judge Brookfeld's?"

It did look the same as what I remembered from the few times I had seen Melvin sign a batch of orders or the occasional decision. "Yes, I think so."

"Well, Judge, now it's your turn."

I faced the salesman on the other side of the desk. "How far back do your security cameras keep what they catch?"

He shook his head. "I know what you're getting at. Detective Pitts and I already talked about this. Those cameras are set to override old data about every sixty days. We could send the images to a server and save them." He shrugged. "But our paper records last forever. Anyway, in the winter with caps and coats and what not, some days we can't tell one customer from the other on camera. The cameras are useful only for a real break in, mostly useful to deter a break in."

I expected this, that the cameras would not help us identify who came in and out now about a year ago. But I had Plan B. "I understand. Do you remember anything about this applicant, what he looked like, what he wore, said, whether he was nervous, had an accent from not around here, anything?"

The salesman's eyes widened a bit. "Ma'am, usually I'd not be remembering anything. But when this here detective came in, it sorta came back to me. Put two and two together. The name sounded familiar from something else, and I remembered hearing or reading about a dead judge. We don't get many gun applications from people with names like Brookfeld, who turn up dead a short while later. So, yes, elderly chap, nice looking, outdoorsy type, but not beaten up by weather all his life, not like some of the shooters we're used to."

"May I show you some pictures—see if you remember?"

"Sure, whatever you need." He breathed in deeply and exhaled slowly. "I ain't never turning down a detective and a judge."

I pulled out five sheets of letter-sized paper, each with head or waist-up shots of older white men, each of them of a different man. Several courthouse clerks had let me shoot them with my iPhone and hadn't asked why. I laid them side by side on the desk.

The salesman slid his thumb down the length of each one, as if sizing up a target. He stopped at the fourth one and looked up. "That's him, that's our gun applicant. That's your dead judge."

"You sure?" said Pitts.

"As sure as my mama lives in Joplin, Missouri." He pronounced it with an "a" at the end.

I wanted to shout out, to explode, to scream. The salesman had passed over the photo of Judge Melvin Brookfeld and landed squarely on the one of Harlan H. Smaltz—taken on the night Smaltz picked up Melvin's files when we had pretended to photograph him loading the box into the trunk of his car.

Pitts said, "Would you mind if I recorded your ID of him in this little tape recorder I brought out?"

"Don't mind a bit, sir."

I turned on the video function of my iPhone to record every second as Pitts most properly placed numbers on each of the photo shots and once more but slowly walked the gun salesman through the identification of the gun purchaser, asking all the right questions over each of the five photos.

Out in the parking lot, Pitts said, "Very interesting. Let me do some checking, and I'll get back to you soon."

At last, perhaps I had someone in law enforcement, someone with investigators and time and a budget to do this, someone who would reopen the investigation and then change the police report, someone with clout.

⚖

PITTS STAYED SILENT FOR WEEKS, THEN MONTHS, I didn't know what to make of it, worried that he might be in on it, too. I hadn't told him about the shoe returned in a box, about Smaltz's warnings, spoken and written. I hadn't told him my thoughts about where it all started. Maybe I should have. When Pitts and I went out to the gunshop, I had talked as if my interactions with Smaltz were routine business: the FBI collecting up my files, routine meetings at the courthouse and at our home. But I had told Pitts that I didn't trust Smaltz, that something about him didn't make sense. Pitts got it, or so I had thought.

On a Friday evening in March, Pitts called the house. Peter answered and handed me the phone. "May I have a minute? Won't be long," Pitts started.

"Ah, sure." I turned into the house and yelled, "Peter, I'll be just a minute," code for, *make sure the girls do their reading*.

"Wanted to get back to you on our gunshop visit. Must admit you had me going. Well, it turns out that Agent Smaltz went to that gunshop not long after

Judge Brookfeld passed. Had a sit-down with the chap who sold Brookfeld the gun. Eyewitness memory is so unreliable. Our gun-sales guy picked Smaltz because he did remember him, and more recently than when Judge Brookfeld bought his gun. We checked some of Judge Brookfeld's decisions in the courthouse. Near as our best handwriting experts can tell, it's his signature on the gun application, an exact match—and not close to how Smaltz writes."

Through sounds of dishes smashing inside me, through my welling fear, I managed, "Thanks. I've been thinking, too. There had to be another explanation for that gun store clerk picking him out of our little line-up as the gun buyer—and not Judge Brookfeld. And, yes, eyewitness accounts are often astoundingly wrong. Thank you. You didn't have to call here on your Friday evening, could have called me at court."

"Oh, right. I don't mind. Didn't want to disturb you in the middle of court or meet at that Mexican joint again."

"That's so good of you. Anything else, then?"

He hesitated as if he hadn't heard me, or as if he needed to think about how much to tell me. "Ah, glad you asked. I'll be taking retirement next week."

"Really?" Equal parts disappointment and surprise in my voice.

"Time for my old bones to play with the grandkids while I still can."

That was it, wasn't it? Got to you, too. Damn. "Ah, if anything new comes up, who'll have the file?"

"Sure, Judge, I expect you'll get a call from the one who gets the lead on it. Or you can try calling in a couple weeks and get hooked up."

Damn, I knew that. He knew better than to tell me in person, probably afraid I'd see through him, throw something at him. "Well, then, good luck to you. Hope you get that time with the grandkids. I guess that's it then, right?"

"Yes, Judge. Oh, except we checked out Agent Smaltz too. He's totally legit, based in the D.C. region and pulled in on old cases or security checks where he can help."

"Great. Good to know. And thank you."

"Have a good evening, Judge." Pitts hung up.

He'd been scared off, too, but what do I do now?

If Smaltz had met with the gunshop clerk after Melvin died, the clerk would have remembered them both—Melvin and Smaltz—would have talked about both meetings. But he didn't, passed right by Melvin's photo without blinking. Smaltz, and whoever he worked with, had indeed slaughtered Melvin, had drowned Admiral Burdick, had blown the brains out of those two dark-haired men in Mexico City or Havana, and someone had paid them or those with them a lot of money. Johnny Pitt's delay and horse feathers explanation, where did those come from? From his grandkids. From Smaltz threatening them.

I had nothing more to do, nothing more that made sense and wasn't loaded with risk. Time to turn to things I could do.

Chapter Twenty-Eight

Angela

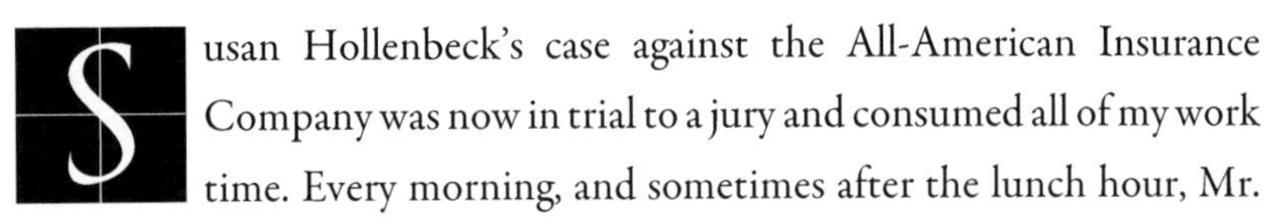

Susan Hollenbeck's case against the All-American Insurance Company was now in trial to a jury and consumed all of my work time. Every morning, and sometimes after the lunch hour, Mr. Montague or another on his team presented one or more new motions to exclude a document, to not let some witness testify, to ask me to allow their own witness not listed at the start of the trial to testify, to prevent an argument from reaching the jury's ears.

Before the jury pool was called up from the first floor, Mr. Montague announced that there was a witness problem.

"You haven't been able to work that out?"

"No, Your Honor. Counsel," meaning young Mr. Lucas, attorney for Susan Hollenbeck, "and I have tried. But counsel tells me he needs an employee of my client to vouch for the emails and other items in the underwriting file to prove his case. Unfortunately, the one or two employees he says he needs are out of our control."

"How is that?"

"Ah, Your Honor, they found other employment months ago."

Standard Trick No. 101: send crucial but unfavorable employee witnesses beyond the reach of a California subpoena, all expenses paid. My anger came not from the trick pulled again, but from Montague's feigned disappointment, disgusting really. I turned to Ms. Hollenbeck's lawyer.

"Mr. Lucas, is that true? You need a witness or two who is familiar with the insurance file, but have not been able to subpoena them, to get them here?"

Young Mr. Lucas waited a few beats, then said, "Your Honor, may I check outside? We asked the two to be here on the first day of trial. Maybe we got lucky—ah, despite them having left their old employment with Mr. Montague's client."

"Certainly, and Mr. Montague, why don't you have a seat?" *I'm not going to let you send them on another vacation before Mr. Lucas gets to talk to them—if they are out there waiting for him.*

Mr. Lucas returned, holding the inner courtroom door open for a young woman and middle-aged man, showed them where to sit, and came up to his table. "Your Honor, there must have been some miscommunication. Mr. Montague had indeed told me of their departure a while back, but we found them, put them under subpoena, and they have both agreed to stand by until called to testify."

After I confirmed their availability when needed to testify, the two strangers left my courtroom.

Montague remained poker-faced. If you didn't know better, his expression, open palms, all said, *wonderful, so glad we worked this out*—when anyone familiar with lawyer games, knew better. In truth, Montague prayed the fired employees were in, say, China. Sometimes, we drag witnesses through the courthouse doors, pry them away from lawyers or bosses trying to hide them.

And with that, the jury panel came up. Twelve of them plus two alternates were picked, and the trial began.

Susan Hollenbeck arrived and departed in a wheelchair maneuvered by her husband, her face pale and puffed up with retained water or chemo, her fingers witch-thin, her head covered by a wig. To anyone who looked closely, Susan could not hide the plastic tube running from an opening in her blouse down to a lower place inside her, but here she was.

Once in a while, she smiled through her pain—a lovely smile that seemed to surprise everyone who noticed. Some days Susan left at the noon recess and did not return. But when she was there, without uttering a sound she made a stronger witness, a stronger exhibit, than all the other witnesses and exhibits presented around her. The Hollenbeck children, already grown, had not yet been allowed in the courtroom because they were expected to testify. They waited out in the hall, waited along with their dad, for their turn to tell their part of the story.

For me it was easier to preside over a jury trial. The jury, not I, would make the important decisions. But any mistake by me in allowing witnesses to talk about things they were not supposed to, in letting the jury see documents the jury was not supposed to, in letting the lawyers shout out about things they were not supposed to, could cause having to run the trial over again. Any new trial wouldn't happen until long after this one, sometimes not until after all the appeals had run up and down the court system over the next half decade. By then Susan Hollenbeck would likely be gone and most of her claim with her. Dead people are, under California law, not entitled to an award for their pain and suffering while they lived. In its wisdom, the California Legislature had passed a law that said no amount of earthly money will ease their pain and suffering in the afterlife.

Mr. Lucas had his act together. The two ex-employees both testified, and both said they had been let go not for performance-based reasons, but for a reduction in force. Their firings, probably because of this very trial, could not easily be challenged. Hard in the teeth of the mortgage meltdown, every insurance company on earth let many thousands of employees go, closed many offices. It remained nicely convenient that these two were among those let go, though afterwards neither had left Southern California. They both said they were aware of Susan Hollenbeck's health scare, that they took it to their boss, who said to accept the risk—but charge a double premium. Yes, Susan had paid that premium every month, month after month, just as required.

But All-American then refused to cover anything related to the current health disaster.

Susan was the last scheduled witness for Mr. Lucas' side of the case, and she would be on the witness stand all day—longer if she needed to take many breaks. The insurance company did not let her take the stand. It had seen enough, had run its bluff and did not want to sit at the poker table when Susan's testimony rolled out. The jury would love her, relate to her, hate the insurance company, and sharpen their verdict pencils.

I thanked the jury. "The case has settled confidentially, but your presence and close attention helped the parties to settle more than you know." Some of the jurors glared at Mr. Montague and those with him. Most smiled when they looked at Mr. Lucas, who stood alone. The insurance company agreed to pay her family for all medical bills past and future, the estimated half million dollars for Mr. Lucas fees and expert costs, plus another $3.5 million—all together likely less than the jury would have awarded but too much to turn down.

In the quiet moments during the trial and before any settlement—while the lawyers talked about problems they could work out and during an afternoon off for a juror's emergency child-coverage needs—I thought about real evidence in that other, bigger case.

Evidence. I had so little, and what I did have—cashier's check receipts, photos, Smaltz at the gun dealer—amounted to nothing worthy, nothing compared to that thorough and final police report, nothing to prove criminal charges beyond a reasonable doubt, murder even. *Damn.*

Should I press a theory that HHS murdered dear Melvin, that HHS was part of a gang who a long time ago misled my country on the Kennedy murder, that the gang drowned Admiral Burdick before he could blow the whistle, that the gang slaughtered others in faraway places? And broadcast my theory to whom? Hold a press conference, storm into Pitts's former cubicle at police headquarters, scream at my presiding Judge McGee or one of my favorite local prosecutors?

Smaltz and some of his older buddies could be witnesses, could fill in the blanks, could confess. But that happened only in movies. I had no clue how to get to him, to make him lay it all out. I had nothing to entice him—or force him. If I had more, a witness and documents, fingerprints of the killer from Melvin's death chambers or on the gun, I'd know what to do. I had met the District Attorney of San Diego County and the United States Attorney for the Southern District of California, each the top prosecutors in their domains. They would each listen to me—if I had anything worth listening to.

I had no FBI internal memos, no recent emails from and to Smaltz, no live witness who had seen or done it, who had been there and could explain it all—and who would be willing to do so. I had nothing that counted in my hallowed system of justice. In my courtroom, the evidence to connect HHS to murder would not hold a single charge, would get me sued for malicious prosecution or defamation, would have them all laughing at me, would have no weight on the scales of Lady Justice, wouldn't even be put on the scales. If I pressed on, California's Judicial Council would investigate me, might even kick me out of my own courthouse.

Every six years California judges must stand for reelection. Usually they are not opposed, but this crusade of mine would not go unnoticed among the many under-employed lawyers. I would draw challengers, and if I lost the election for my judgeship, no self-respecting law firm would hire me. *Damn.*

Time to leave it alone, let it be, to tell Peter we were done with it. At last, that felt so right, but also wrong. I might be able to leave it alone, but Melvin's, the Admiral's, and the other deaths would not leave me alone. They had burrowed in. They would never leave me.

If I did press on, I had sort of figured out how to protect myself from now on. One judge's peculiar death was enough. More than one might trigger a closer look. Numbers and daylight would protect me, the girls and Peter. This wasn't a third world country where big shots slaughtered their enemies and bragged openly about it. Or was it? *Oh, damn.*

After the two trial sides left my courtroom, cleared out the larger exhibits and projectors, I said to Mora and Mrs. Patterson, "That felt right. Our system worked, I'd say."

They both agreed.

"Wonder what's up next," I said.

Before Mrs. Patterson could check the computer screen for the next trial sent to my courtroom by the scheduling computers or the Presiding Judge, the phone rang.

Mrs. Patterson picked it up. "Yes . . . Certainly . . . You caught us at a good time, no trouble at all." Then, "Judge, it's for you. It's a call from the Judicial Council." Mrs. Patterson made a just-bit-into-a-lemon face. "A Mr. Frank Maier asks if you might have a minute."

Chapter Twenty-Nine

Frank, Fall 1981

After Agent Sam chewed me out for the blow-back from my cashier's check scheme, I drew a series of short straws. He gave me tasks I had when I first showed up as an office clerk—listening to tapped Russian phone calls and checking the good parts against the translated transcripts. Now and again, he loaned me to other overloaded squads to help on petty bank robberies and stolen cars crossing state lines. I stayed quiet, didn't complain, volunteered for overtime, and expected to get transferred any day.

Felicity Cates at last brought me back to real work. The case arrived on a late November evening, down from the Special Agent in Charge of the whole Bureau Region. Had the call come in from ordinary schlubs, the FBI screener would give the caller the telephone number of the Washington Metro police, who most times did nothing for at least twenty-four hours. But not this one. Mrs. Marigold Cates traced her lineage back to land holdings and mansions that predated the Civil War. Her husband, Harold, a Virginia Assemblyman, was on the rise in Southern politics. Felicity was their seventeen-year old daughter. Lead agent Sam picked me to assist. I wasn't sure if he had forgiven me, or if I was the first and only single, non-parent agent he could find.

Harold Cates met us after dark at the iron and gold leaf entrance to his estate. Lamps atop the stone pillars on both sides of the gate cast good light.

Harold, in a white button-down shirt, freshly-pressed beige slacks and loafers, came out to the car before Agent Sam pulled to a stop.

Harold started out shouting then notched it down after Sam opened the car window. "Thanks for coming out, officers. Need to talk to you before you see Marigold. She's about lost it with worry. The train wrecks you see comin' and can't get outta the way of are the worst. And Marigold swears she saw this one coming and warned our li'l girl a hundred times."

The big iron gates opened. Harold motioned us through and walked along, showing us where to drive. He kept talking. "Go easy on her. I'm sure our girl's all right, but Marigold fears the worst. Our li'l girl knows how to take care of herself."

The path ended in a big circle with a portico over steps leading up to the main house. After we got out and shook hands, Harold led us up the stairs and through a heavy wooden door.

Marigold—naturally blonde, red-lipped, in a going-out-for-the-evening little black dress and looking not a day over about twenty-eight—and a Negro housemaid awaited us. Marigold rushed into a hug from Harold, then, "Officers, I'm so glad you're here. Harold does not want to talk about it, keeps his stiff upper lip. But I'm frightened out of my skin. Before we start, would either of you like anything? Tea, coffee, soda, something stronger? Viola will get you whatever you all like."

Sam and I both said, "Thank you, no." We sat in two side-by-side cushion chairs indicated by Marigold. We pulled notepads out of briefcases.

Sam said, "Please, tell us whatever comes to mind. We'll fill in as you go."

My role was to take notes for his later 302 Witness reports, at least three of them. Harold, Marigold, and Viola.

Viola silently left the room.

Marigold started. "Felicity's such a strong-headed child, thinks she knows what she wants, what's good for her." She rubbed and rolled her hands together in her lap. "But she doesn't know . . . well, she doesn't know men, men who aren't like my Harold, men who go and do anything, men like that Coach Parker she has such a crush on. Felicity doesn't know he's a vicious beast."

Over the next two hours, Marigold, with a few asides from Harold, told us the rest—or the beginnings—of Felicity's story. Of course, Felicity was a straight-A student, homecoming queen, captain of the football cheerleading squad, and the number-one ranked tennis player for her age group in the whole state of Virginia, with early admission to Duke. But she had a crush on assistant football coach and math teacher, Buddy Ray Parker. Marigold was convinced Parker had kidnapped Felicity, taken her to a cabin in the woods for the weekend, maybe through the Thanksgiving week.

"Call it a woman's intuition. It's never wrong. Might be having his way with her right now as we sit here. Oh, damn, damn, damn." Marigold's voice trembled, "Felicity, wherever you are, stay strong and know we love you, will find you and bring you home."

Sam said so quietly I could barely hear, "Mrs. Cates, you fear the worst. May I ask why?"

"Yes, yes, of course. This is Felicity's fourth year on the cheer squad. In that time, I've, well, gotten to know lots of the girls and their mothers. Only an idiot could miss the things unsaid, the exasperations, about that Buddy Ray beast, that animal. Harold, you remember Barbara Elizabeth, how she got red in the face, started stammering . . . He's taken others before, and no one says or does a single thing—ruined for life if it ever got out."

Harold said, "Marigold, let's stay positive. Felicity could come through that door any minute, maybe call us from a friend's house."

Trouble with Harold's theory was that Felicity had not talked about staying out this late, had not taken any clothes or toiletries, and none of her friends' mothers knew about any overnight plans. Felicity had not acted unusual that morning, had kissed her parents good-bye, and said, "See y'all tonight. Some of us may catch a show after the game, but I'll stop here first. If we lose, I'm thinkin' I'll stay home—maybe bring some friends."

The football game—the second play-off game for Felicity's private school—was long since over. The losing home crowd had dispersed quietly, the visiting winners piled into honking buses and cars, the home team showered, dressed and faded away. But there was no sight or sound of Felicity, now at almost eleven at night. No, neither parent had attended the game, both too busy.

Took my Bureau two days to find Buddy Ray Parker—actually his hunting cabin—a pick-up truck ride on a dirt lumber road in the woods. Title to the place stood in the name of Parker and three others with the same last name. A local cop had seen the APB photo, spotted him in town, followed him not to his hunting cabin but to another nearby cabin in the woods, and called it in. Clever bastard to not use his own family cabin but another one, and I wondered if Buddy Ray called in some of his hunting friends to share the fun.

I was part of the eight-agent team to raid both cabins at the same time. We would have taken more men, called for more help, but that would have taken too long—had to get on this ASAP after the local cop saw him.

My group raided the decoy cabin. We didn't have a search or arrest warrant, not enough time in these "exigent circumstances". Turned out we didn't need a warrant. The front door and all the boarded-over windows were only locked from the outside with heavy wood boards slid into holders—bear-proofed. No cars were anywhere around it, but recent-looking tracks sat in the gravel and dirt parking area out front. Two of us went inside as quietly as the porch floor boards and locking door boards allowed. Two agents stayed outside.

I saw her first. My training stopped me from yelling, from running into a bullet if Buddy Ray had been waiting. Tear stains streaked her dirty face. A nasty dark bruise raised her left cheek. Her hands were tied up over her head to the stout posts of the bunk bed. She was still in her cheer sweater, now dirty and ripped or cut down from the neckline "V". A coarse brown blanket covered her below the waist. Her bare ankles were tied to the opposite bunk posts. She propped up her head as best she could and whispered hoarsely, "Thank the Lord, it's you, whoever you are—it's not him."

"No, I'm not him. You are safe now." I ducked back out the door and yelled, "Someone call for a medic—a female medic—and give me a hand."

Felicity's hands and feet were puffed up and blue. She struggled to stand. I looked away and wanted to wait for a female, but Felicity would not wait, got up as soon as she was free of the ropes, grabbed the blanket and wrapped it around her. She staggered into a small bathroom with a hand-pumped faucet and closed the door. I had noticed an outhouse at the edge of the woods. Splashing water noises mixed with groans and sobs. Through the door, she croaked, "I want my parents. Call mom at home and have her come get me . . . right now. Please do it."

I half motioned, half told my partner to do it, and kept a look-out.

After what seemed a long time, Felicity came out, her lower body and legs still wrapped in the blanket. She did not look directly at me. "Did you guys call Mom? Is she coming to get me?"

I said, "We're working on it. Now let's get you out of here and find out where to meet your parents."

⚖

BUDDY RAY SHOWED UP AT THE CABIN NOT long after Felicity departed and well before nightfall. He unloaded a couple paper bags of groceries—hotdogs and hamburger meat, canned beans and peas, milk, a soda bottle, toothbrushes, toothpaste, a box of tissues, and Kotex. How considerate, how easy to arrest and cuff.

Felicity met the town's only female medic at the local police station.

Except for a few asides, sort of nodding and shaking her head, she refused to cooperate further, to file a complaint, to allow anyone to take body fluid samples or photographs of her clothing or her body. She again begged, crying, to call her parents and have them come to get her as soon as they could. We complied.

Buddy Ray stayed in the local jail overnight. He made bail by the afternoon of the next day. Buddy Ray's lawyer said to the assigned US Attorney, "A lot of shit will come out about the school, its young ladies, and the Cates family if any of y'all touch my client, say the slightest bad thing about him. He has an ironclad defense of consent six ways from Sunday. That Felicity girl got into the car with him. She'd been teasing him for a coon's age, was wanting a little bondage and hard sex. Young women these days are a different breed. The lady part has been lived out of them by the time they're high school seniors, if ya'll know what I mean."

We had it on tape and played it for our case team. The lawyer's exact words.

My team members raised all the obvious questions through gritted teeth. What about the ligatures on Felicity's wrists and ankles, on needing to tie her up and lock her in, on blood in places where there's not supposed to be blood, on no extra clothes?

Sam shook his head. "The family... Felicity... none of them is cooperating... and won't. The father's career would be toast. Momma says she'd just die, and her precious girl ruined for life if any of this got out."

The prosecuting attorney never asked for a preliminary hearing. Buddy Ray was back teaching math after the Thanksgiving break. No one asked why he called for a sub on the Monday, Tuesday and Wednesday of the week, and they all knew it was deer hunting season in these parts.

In my quiet times, my dreams, images of Felicity and Madeline—they could have passed as sisters—blended together. I had been chased off Madeline's case, but not Felicity's. Not completely. Not yet.

Wasn't hard for me to find Buddy Ray a second time. Teachers come and go from the teachers' parking lot, live not far from their school, come and go on the same schedule on the same days of the week. Over the Christmas and New Year's break, Buddy Ray moved to his cabin with a couple other guys.

Buddy Ray's Jeep Wagoneer, nimble and high enough for rough country and big enough to haul a deer on the top or hanging out the back, was easy to see from a ways back. On the night I picked to follow it, its engine sputtered, popped and died on the dirt road in the woods up to the cabin. A couple quarts of kerosene in the gas tank did that every time, and this was the perfect place for the engine to stop. Not likely anyone else would be by anytime soon on this night.

About three in the morning on that crisp, clear night, I, driving my own rented Chevy Nova pickup, pulled in behind the jeep, its engine hood up and Buddy Ray peering over the engine. He appeared smaller than an assistant football coach should—maybe a linebacker after years of lost conditioning. I didn't try to sneak up on him, no need to. "Hey, need a hand, a cable or something?"

Buddy Ray stood up and turned around, shielding his eyes from my brights. "Don't think it's electric. Fuel's not right, near as I can tell."

"Need a lift back to town or someplace else? Hate to leave you out here until morning."

"Sure, thanks. Let me close her up."

I caught him on the right spot, the flat side of the hammer on the left temple, hard enough to bring down a buffalo but not hard enough to crack bone. Buddy Ray had his gloves off and fell face first. Perfect to get the cuffs on and yank the hands behind his back.

"What the fu . . . ?"

I snuffed out Buddy's half scream, half moan with my boot sole on the side of Buddy's face. "Quiet, and I promise I won't kill you now. Got it?"

Buddy Ray got very quiet on the cold dirt road, no sound, no movement.

I grabbed his belt, pulled him to his feet. "Let's take a walk to the confessional. You the confessor, and I'll be your priest. Got it?"

"You asshole, whoever the fuck you are, fuck off . . ."

Another hammer tap shut Buddy Ray down, knocked him to his knees. "You want to die now? Here? I know people who'll melt your rotten carcass in a lye and acid mix. No one will ever know."

Buddy Ray shook his head. I pulled a bandana out of my pocket and wrapped it around his eyes. "Let's take a little walk, get off the road, wouldn't want to get run down."

I turned off both sets of car lights and, by flashlight, yanked and shoved Buddy Ray into the dense growth by the side of the road, far enough in that no one could see us from the road. I could still see and hear anyone who rolled by. No one did.

I got Buddy Ray to tell the truth—or at least a story that sounded true. Felicity was a flirt, wanted to be everyone's friend, flirted with Buddy hard, teased him, touched him every time they walked out of the stadium together, took all his math classes, stayed after class to get his help on problems when she didn't need any help. At least that's what he imagined or lied out. "I gotta tell you, whoever the hell you are, she wasn't askin' for it. She was beggin' me for it. After our last game, I said I'd take her home, and that was that. She loved me tying her up and having my way, moaning the whole time."

"Drivin' that Jeep there, were you?"

"Sure. She said it was cool."

"Did she think it was cool that she couldn't open the passenger door when you took her up here?"

"What the fuck . . . I . . . how did you know about that?"

"Never mind that." I touched Buddy Ray's face with the cold hammer.

During my weeks of following Buddy Ray, I had checked out the Jeep, had seen that the passenger side had no inside handle. "Just remember. I'm your priest. Did she think it was cool to have no door handle? Remember, you must tell the truth here." A cold hammer tap to the back of the head. "Only the truth."

A couple more stupid answers followed by my hammer taps, and the whole truth came out. "Nah, damn it . . . she wanted to get out, and I had to bust her one time to get her to shut up . . . I should a taken her home. But . . . God dammit . . . women like that drive me nuts, and they love it too in the end. She was comin' around, . . . like all the others, with a real man and not them know-nothing, tiny walnut pecker high school boys. None of them boys know what they're doing, how to please a hot one, get her started out right."

I'd heard enough. "Okay, asshole, listen extra good. No later than three days from now, your letter of resignation is on the principal's desk. Within five days, you leave that shitty apartment you call home, and you get the hell out of here, far from here. And if you ever draw a beef from another woman, I will hunt you down. I will broadcast the tape recording I'm making of our little chat, and I'll see you in jail or in your grave. Do you understand me?"

Buddy Ray, tears now streaming and sniffling, bobbing his head up and down hard.

I made him get into the back of his Jeep, face down, and took off the handcuffs. "Count to a hundred, slowly, before you look up." I left without turning on my headlights.

Two weeks into the new year, I called Felicity's school and asked for Mr. Parker about a personal matter. The staff person said, "Ah, Mr. Parker is no longer here. Sorry we don't have a forwarding telephone number. Ah, yes, the address he gave us is in Alabama. Would you like that?"

Chapter Thirty

Angela, September 2011

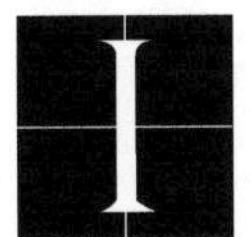 took the call from one Frank Maier. "Hello, this is Judge Cornwell."

"Thank you, Your Honor, for taking my call."

"How can I help you?"

"I'm a freelance private investigator, have done some work for your Judicial Council. I'd like to set up an appointment. I can fly down this week or next."

"May I know why we can't just talk here?"

"I'd rather not." After a pause, the voice of this stranger, an older man, continued, "Never know who might be listening in on this call."

"That important, huh? Is one of my colleagues on the short list for the California Supreme Court?" I knew that wasn't it. Those reference checks came in the mail or on my computer with a simple form to fill out. If I responded on the form with a harsh answer or accusation against the applicant, a live person would follow up with me. I hadn't filled one of those forms out in a long time.

"No, Your Honor. It's not that. But it's important. Very important."

Time to stop being nice. "Look, Mr. Maier, I don't know you. I don't have enough time to do all that I must. If you are on the JC, you know every judge has a big load. I think we're done, Judicial Council or not. You can tell them that and quote me."

"It's about Judge Melvin Zachariah Brookfeld."

The middle name got me. "Okay? That was a while back, the file's closed and done."

No longer a request, more like a command. "I must talk to you about him—and can't on the phone."

I didn't want to talk on the phone either, even a courthouse phone. "Let me pull up my calendar. And . . . can you come here?"

"Certainly."

My calendar was up on my screen. I suggested the following Monday. Maier agreed.

"Do I have a number where I can call you? Wouldn't want you to fly down if I'm tied up."

"Sure, here's my cell number . . ." He rattled off the numbers. "See you on Monday late afternoon. Thank you, Judge. Appreciate it."

The California Commission on Judicial Performance had oversight responsibility for all sitting judges. It could remove the seriously deficient, had done so in recent years—three from my courthouse. The Commission should have followed up on Judge Brookfeld. But why with me, why now, this long after his death?

Judge Brookfeld wouldn't handle any more cases. No point in investigating him to remove him. If his past decisions or rulings were corrupt, his case files would show it. The California Commission on Judicial Performance should start with Sandy and Melvin's research clerks before Sandy. It should start with all the criminal defense lawyers who appeared before him, then their clients—most in jail or dead or on the streets again. Sandy had not told me about any call from the Commission, and he would have if they had called him. Just like Smaltz, the Commission had skipped all the logical places to start checking on Melvin. This Maier fellow was going way out of any sensible order—but maybe he wasn't on Commission business.

I called Sandy with more assignments. He said he'd get right on it, vowing he would work into the night.

I called Peter. Maier had not called or shown up at the house. I called the Burdick number. Phoebe answered, sounding happy to hear from me. No one had recently called her about that old matter. I called Naomi. She too said it was good to hear from me, and no one had called her either.

Late the next day, Sandy Shields came into my courtroom. "Near as I can tell, your Honor, Frank Maier was career FBI, like that Smaltz guy. There's that association of retired FBI agents. A Frank Maier belongs to it, but they wouldn't give me any contact info. Offered to contact him to contact me. I declined that one. I think the same Frank Maier was a stud hockey player at Cornell long time ago. In the Cornell Athletics Hall of Fame—that's big, near as I can tell, especially for hockey. I peg his age at about sixty-two."

"And today?"

"The person at our Judicial Counsel I talked to couldn't confirm he's with them, though they hire investigators. There's not much on him, but he does seem like a real person. If he's a real PI, he's got no website, not on Yelp, must get all his clients by referrals, and mostly on very private matters."

"Thanks, Sandy. Very much. Wish I knew more." At least he called first, didn't just thump on my front door late in the day. Better start than the last one.

⚖

LIKE SMALTZ BEFORE HIM, THIS FRANK MAIER eased to the back of my courtroom and waited quietly for the day's work to end. His build and age matched what Sandy had learned. He too was dressed in a good suit but no tie. He had a strong handshake, though his hands were a lot stronger than he let on, a hockey player's hands. His face, maybe a bit younger than his age, gave nothing away.

I led him back to my chambers and motioned him to take a seat facing my big desk. A boyishness settled into him, the way he looked at me out of smiling eyes, somewhere between reading a funny one-liner and flirting.

"Well then, what can I do for you, Mr. Maier, about our dear Judge Brookfeld?"

"I'll cut to the heart."

"Good." *About time.*

"Not too far back, I got an email from him. It made me go check some things out—"

I felt my frown, my mind spin in the madness of what Maier had just said and interrupted him. "What?" I stood up. "He's been dead and cremated for over a year. What kind of huckster are you? Leave now, or I'll buzz for my bailiff."

Frank held up his hands, palms out, and shook his head. "Sorry, Judge. I should have explained. I did get an email from him. It has an email sender address of this very courthouse. But it's dated last year—sent with that delay feature that's part of all email software these days."

I sat back down. "All right. Tell me more, but it better be good."

"The opening lines—I've memorized them—went, 'I am sending you this and the attachments on a long delay. I would have withdrawn it unless I could not. Circumstances beyond my ability to control must have caused my premature demise, paralysis or some other calamity. Below I explain the likely circumstances.' That's what the opening said. I have a copy here." Maier reached into his inside coat pocket and held a folded sheet of paper.

"When I got it, I checked Google and the other usual places. Melvin Brookfeld didn't take his own life, not in a million years. Attachments he sent me lock it down."

Rising anger, irritation, or the kind of curiosity that a child feels at the mouth of a strange dark cave made me say, "So why are you telling me this? Why now?"

Maier unfolded the sheet of paper and looked at it. "Because Melvin said here, 'A good place to inquire about my demise will be my colleagues in the San Diego Superior Court, especially Judge Angela Cornwell. She'll know as much as anyone about my last day or days, or the circumstances of my disappearance.'"

My curiosity vanished, replaced by the thud of a heavy load falling onto me, onto my back, a load I had almost forgotten, but not. "Wow, he knew it—they might come after him. And . . . I . . . he found stuff that exposes them, and they found out what he found out. And . . . he sent you to me."

"Yes, Judge, all of that."

"May I see that email print-out?"

Maier handed me the sheet.

It read as he had said, dated June 13, 2010. I pulled up that year's calendar on my computer. Sunday. Melvin had come in on a Sunday to finish that email and its attachments. More details. The sender wasn't Melvin, but JSS, John Sandy Shields. Melvin had come in on Sunday so that he could send this from Sandy's computer. Melvin had a notion someone in a high place was tapping into his computers or would grab them after they grabbed him. I said, "But why not while he was alive, why not tell you while you were still at the Bureau—and saved himself?" More questions piled in—this was a good first one.

Frank looked at me for too long. "When we talked on the phone, did I tell you I had been in the Bureau? Don't think I did, Judge, but good you checked me out." The boyish grin again.

This Maier was no fool either, but I pressed on. "You've not answered what I asked you."

"True. Not sure, but I'm guessing back then he thought he needed to find more on his work in progress. Probably didn't have enough when he died."

"More for what?"

"For your kind of place, Judge, for a court with good solid evidence to put bad people away, documents, witnesses." Maier shook his head. "Why am I lecturing you about courtroom worthy evidence?"

"Tell me about the email attachments."

"Sure. One's a directive from J. Edgar to all Bureau region heads, marked top secret, dated three days after Kennedy's assassination and declassified in two thousand seven. Two parts, short and sweet. Part one said no one is to investigate the Soviet Union or the CIA, said it's clear Oswald acted as a lone wolf, a narcissistic crazy. Part two said the Secret Service, FBI, CIA, and Dallas police are forming a joint task force, known as the—"

As Maier talked, I had almost interrupted him to let me see the attachments. Now I could not hold back. "The Dallas Kennedy task force, DKTF."

"How did you know?"

"I'll tell you later, when I can get my head around this. Go on now, what else about the DKTF?"

"Per that Hoover memo, all agents, police, staff, anyone must forward all questions, leads, inquiries to the DK task force members for screening and coordinating all responses."

"What about the other attachments to his email, his, ah, post-mortem email?"

"Photos of a couple guys wrapped in sheets with their brains blown out." Frank hesitated and stared at me, at me nodding to signal I knew all about that. "A cashier's check with a tiny handwritten number on the front. I've been reading around the edges for years—decades—and I knew that little handwritten number by heart."

"On a check?"

"Melvin got his hands on cashier's check copies issued out of government accounts at big banks."

I nodded, as if I knew about this too. My nod made Maier say, "You know about those, huh?"

Still no time for me to reveal a thing. "Go on."

"I figure he got the checks through a buddy at State or in response to a FOIA request. One—for four thousand bucks—had a handwritten number on the front. The number matches a CIA watch list number of those days, matches the Watch List number for . . ." Maier's slow cadence slowed even more, "a Lee Harvey Oswald."

"Oh, my goodness." *Those tiny markings on my copies . . .*

"Yep, the CIA had LHO on its watch list since fifty-nine. We do that for ex-Marines who defect to the Soviet Union. That's what he did. That was his watch list number. The list is Top Secret, intended for eyes only and on a need-to-basis, but Melvin saw and remembered Oswald's number and matched it up with the payment to him of four large. Lawyers at State see things the rest of us don't, aren't allowed to see, ever."

"Holy, Mother of God. You mean we, our own government, paid Oswald?" *That ass Smaltz is right. This is bigger than most.* "I read that the Warren Commission or the FBI did a funds tracing of Oswald's money, and it balanced, with no indication of anything like this." I caught myself but couldn't stop the thinking, the asking, caught how easily all the details came back, how intense and frightened I felt once more.

"Hard to trace funds you don't know about. If the tracers never see the funds go to him and don't see them come out, they won't ever know. Old Lee must have hidden the CIA funds and what he used them on, no paper trail, no bank account, no kept receipts. Cash only for everything in and out would have been a good start for him. He lived like a slob, so he wouldn't have bought anything big or fancy. Could have just given the CIA cash to Maria, and no one would be the wiser unless she made them wiser or put it in her bank all at once. No one would trace it later."

Maria, his wife, an enigma in the history books. I skipped to another topic, needed time to think. "Why you? Why did Melvin send all this to you?"

Maier nodded the nod of an old man bringing up memories of long ago, looked up to his right at the ceiling. "Melvin and I go way back, from maybe before you were born, Judge. I was there when they brought his Madeline's skeleton out of Jug Bay. When he stopped working on this stuff the first time and left D.C., he gave me some keys to what he was doing, left up to me whether to use them but made me promise to keep him out of it and not use the keys he gave me for a long time."

"Too long. You've waited too long. No one who can do anything cares anymore—except maybe you and me and Naomi."

Maier's mouth turned into a snarl, an upper lip curled to the side, as if he were lining up someone unaware to check on the ice, check hard. "Judge, we both know someone else out there still cares, don't we? They still care a whole lot."

That's for sure. "So, you use the keys you say Melvin left you?"

Maier looked down at his big hands, gnarled fingers under well-worn skin that barely seemed to hold in the blood and bones and tendons. "I started to get after it—but I got chicken. I'd never been afraid of doing anything in my whole growing up, in my whole life, even when I knew I'd get into trouble for it if they caught me. But on this one, they scared me off Melvin's case, off Madeline's bones. Not anymore. I'm too old to get scared off by much anymore, not by doing this one last thing even if it's my last. I should tell you, Judge, how I got chicken, got chased off, if you have a few more minutes to listen."

I said, "Sure."

And Frank Maier told me how he got scared off.

Chapter Thirty-One

Frank, Winter 1983

Most times clean slates are good, get to wipe off sins of the past. My clean slate in Atlanta started out great, until it didn't.

The Atlanta Region offices were part of a giant building on the corner of Peachtree and Baker Streets, right next to the Federal Courthouse and United States Attorney. No longer any need to run through a big city for a lawyer to prepare a warrant and then find a judge on short notice while half an FBI squad babysat the location to be searched. I and other agents in my office could move fast here.

The supervisor of the kidnap squad, Chuck Oglethorpe—ChuckO, we called him—was a good guy, assigned cases as they came in to the next available agent. ChuckO gave the more dangerous cases, those with accusations of rape, eye-witnessed child abuse or ransom demands, to the most experienced agents and let them pick their team. All the senior agents tried to pick me to help. I was the only younger agent without a wife and kids, and I made myself available for anything at any time.

No more tedium on Russian phone taps and checking the translated transcripts. No more trailing new Soviet Embassy workers—though I often did think about Melvin and Madeline, about Yegor and *your guys*, wondered if any of *your guys* were posted down here.

ChuckO regularly said to our squad something like, "Remember, word has gotten out that we're better, more discreet than the local cops. And if the parent or spouse says the kid's been taken across state lines, we've got jurisdiction and will check it out. And—if it smells real, we've got to get after it fast. Nothing's worse than finding a body in the woods. We've found too many."

Biddie visited me more than I could take off to run up to D.C. Wasn't that far, and every visit was good. I missed our lunches and weekly dinners and meeting her boyfriends.

Over the last holidays, she married a good guy who worked for a PR firm. The wedding took place at the Marriott across the river in Arlington. One of the best parts of the wedding was that the bride's and groom's sides of the church held about the same number of guests. Biddie had made lots of friends fast. She was a knockout in a long white gown, long white gloves that extended over her elbows, tiny blue flowers in her hair, and barely a touch of makeup.

Pops gave her away, and Hilde came, too. I was surprised at how squat Hilde had become—in just a few years—dowdy, no longer a magnet for every horny loser. Her German accent seemed heavier than the last time. She hugged me like an old aunt might have but didn't say much when I was near. Pops was pleased that Biddie had made it this far, but still sad at himself having to live in a rented flat and with nothing but Social Security payments, odd jobs and a little income from the tractor repair shop to look forward to, enough anyway that he didn't ask me to help pay his way to the wedding. Yuri and Ida had both passed away close in time to each other. What little they had, they left to their church, nothing for their former son-in-law, or their grandson, and that was all good with me.

During an idle spell, I dialed my old boss, Agent Sam, mostly to say hello and that I missed working with him. A second reason I called him was to do a little trolling on my most painful open file.

Sam sounded happy to hear from me. "Hey, my best FNG ever. What the hell you up to?"

"Thought of you and the squad a while back."

"What'd I do?"

"Nah, not business. My half-sister got married, and I ran up for the weekend. Happened too fast for me to stop by, and I know how busy you guys are."

"Ah, you should have. I'm mostly tied to this desk."

"Anything more happen with those checks and old Yegor?"

All joviality gone. "Now you know, Frank, you ain't supposed to go there."

"I won't. Just wondering. Next time I'm up your way, I'll call first."

"Yes, do that. Take care—FNG." Sam hung up before I did.

Information gave me Melvin's California telephone number, and he came to the phone right away. I told him about the check follow-up, the disaster that had been.

Melvin said, "Yes, sometimes the only way to get information is like a silent mosquito—in tiny bites so the victim does not know until later, doesn't know when it happened or which mosquito did it."

"You know I still want—to get after them. Anything else I can do that you can think of, though I hope I'm not stirring things up."

"Yes, time does blur ugly memories, and we tend to remember only the good times of our lives more vividly. Stay careful, Agent Maier."

"I do all the time, sir."

There was a long pause. I almost asked if Melvin was still on the line. Then, "If you must . . . but only if you must . . . as an agent it might be safe for you to ask around about the DK Task Force—that's short for Dallas Kennedy. Someone in it probably knows. Your call on that. Got to go, but let's keep in touch. Let me know. Someday it might be safe to open this up again—even for me."

"Thanks, will do."

Wasn't hard to find the DK Task Force. It seemed like everyone knew someone who knew someone in it. I found an intern who listened and seemed to not want to hide, gave me the when and why of the task force, some of the names in it. She said, "Our task force fields all inquiries about that horrible act and all involved." I waited, and she filled the silence some more. "You know we must respond to the media, any new leads or information, on a uniform basis. We help researchers locate unclassified documents and give background guidance, help them to not put anything out that's false."

"Ah, where might I find any records on Charles William Thomas. Whom should I contact about him?"

"Let me call you back on that. What's your best number?"

Shit. Got to give her my number. She knows who I am and where I work. "Sure. Here it is."

The information person never called back. A few weeks after my call to her, Agent ChuckO stopped at my desk. "Frank, come with me. Now. Do not ask why."

He, almost running, led the way down the hall, two more left turns and into a small interior meeting room. A good-looking young man stood, extending his hand. "I'm Agent Harlan Smaltz. I'll only be a moment, and thanks for coming so promptly."

This Smaltz chap, dressed in the standard blue sports jacket and gray slacks, spoke with confidence but gave off no sense of shared missions, of one Bureau agent talking to another. His black hair was in a Marine cut, and he hardly blinked. This Smaltz chap let out that he was far above us all, that despite his fresh face, he had a mission that had the backing of big shots. "Have a seat, if you like."

ChuckO remained standing. Me, too.

"Agent Maier, I'm here in response to your call to the DK Task Force. But there's more. The bank account list you got from your CI connects to an operation we've been looking at for some time." His stern tone turned unpleasant, as if he'd just as soon strangle me than talk to me. "Your rogue search warrants almost blew the whole thing. You are ordered to stay out of it, never touch it. Your Russian pal has been sent home, and if you ever go near this investigation, you'll have a one-way ticket out of the Bureau. This comes to you from authority higher than me. The joint task force includes us, the CIA, and State's own security. The Task Force's orders come from the highest authority. Do I make myself clear?"

"Yes, sir," I snapped back but wasn't about to knuckle under to this little shit on what he'd spooned out. I asked, "Are you at liberty to provide any info—in case I think of something or need to direct someone to you?"

This Smaltz chap looked down for the first time—not a sign of thought but a sign of wanting to hide as much as he could, to hide what his face might disclose. "We'll contact you if we need anything from you."

Smaltz left, no handshakes this time. ChuckO stayed, sat down and motioned for me to sit. "We can stay here in this room, away from squad stuff, telephone calls."

"Sure."

"Your little curiosity about old stuff and the reaction we got from up north made me and others look at your file."

"Yes, sir." I wanted to say more, ask about what my warrants had stirred and why such a big deal about my call, why this Harlan was so high and mighty, but Chuck O's look kept me quiet.

ChuckO tilted his head down and looked straight at me from under bushy brows—one of those manly no nonsense, no question looks. "You heard him, and you should have. And now, listen to me."

"Ah, sure." *Oh, hell?*

"We do a deep background search on every new recruit. And we like self-starters. We like the guys who don't ask permission every time they need to take a piss. But sometimes that gets our agents into trouble."

"I understand."

"Nah, you don't understand. You only think you do. After I checked your file, I asked some of our field guys to do a bit of deeper checking, with some of the old contacts about you."

I wanted to stay stoic, silent, but a little, "Oh?" slipped out.

"You had an incident at Cornell your freshman year, didn't you?"

Time to dodge. "Ah, I had several. Us hockey guys were always getting challenged. Which one?" I tried to put on a knowing look, as if we had fights all the time off the ice.

"One Willy Buford. The locals couldn't quite connect the dots, couldn't arrest you, and he didn't want to bring charges. But someone put one hell of a beating on him, and all evidence pointed to you."

"He had it coming." My sudden candor surprised me. I must have wanted ChuckO to know what I had done, my pride about it, and I sure as hell didn't want to get investigated, put on the Rubber Gun Squad and then fired.

ChuckO hesitated for a moment. "Glad you owned up. If you hadn't, would have been a strike against you on your IA form, maybe worse."

"Thanks, I guess." I started to get up.

"Not so fast. What was this about you and your stepmother getting sideways?"

Here goes my great career. "She was never my stepmother, just my father's second wife after my mom died."

"But you and she did get sideways?"

"Yeah, she came onto me hard from when I was little. I just acted pricky around her, didn't know how else to get her to back off."

ChuckO grinned. "I think I get that—she says you got way more than pricky."

"No, sir, and you can strap me up on this. I never touched her, never responded to her come ons, never laid a hand on her."

ChuckO nodded. "That's our sum up, too."

"Thank you, sir." I wanted to get up, but I waited for ChuckO to stand first.

"You know that big Cates case you worked on?"

"Sure, never forget that one."

"The subject . . . let me look at my notes . . . got it, Buddy Ray Parker, up and disappeared even though no one brought any charges, any complaint."

"Shit . . . how could anyone know. "That's good, I guess, or did he turn up somewhere else?"

"Do you know anything about where he went, why he left his school where he taught right in the middle of the school year?"

I had a good answer, one I had ready back then. "I can guess, and it's just a guess. Her mother and father ran in circles that had contacts outside the law to fix it that Parker never did that again—and that asshole got too scared to stay around."

ChuckO nodded. "It was something like that, but the father swears up and down he would not do that, didn't know people like that, had not done that to Parker himself and hadn't hired anyone to do it."

I spun in the silence, spun what to say next when ChuckO said, "Did you have anything to do with his disappearance?"

Best to stay silent and act as if I didn't know until I had to tell him more. "You know that case—how it turned out—was a rough one. A couple months later, I did call the school to see if he was still there and up to the same old MO. Got nothing from personnel except he had left with a new address in Alabama."

"Just testing. Glad you told me that 'cause someone did report to us that a stranger called the school about Parker's whereabouts. Had to be you or another agent on that case who made the call." Chuck relaxed for the first time in this meeting. "Seems like Parker's doing the same thing somewhere there in Alabama now—but not for much longer. Get the hell out of here until I find another easy case for you to help on, or your next transfer comes through."

Jolted, I stood but could not leave. "Sir, I didn't put in for another transfer."

ChuckO stood, too, and his face softened. "I put in for you. You need to go where your slate's clean and you'll go with my highest recommendation. It's best for you."

Had to play this straight, show nothing. "Thanks, I guess. Where'd you put me in for?"

"Couple regions. No sense fretting until one of them bites."

"Okay."

"Between you and me, there are assholes everywhere. The only thing you got to do is keep your supers in the loop, don't pull any more of that rogue shit, and be done with whatever the fuck is going on with this Dallas Kennedy Task Force. We are ordered to stay out of it. Got it?"

"Yes, sir."

"Now get the hell out of here."

"Yes, sir."

I left by myself, didn't want to walk back with ChuckO, didn't look back at him. For an instant I thought I felt a bit of what old Buford and Parker must have felt—small, guilty, caught by higher authorities for bad acts that stemmed from my own deep flaws, and wondering where the hell my career, my life, would unfold.

That same day in the dark of late evening, I didn't pay attention to the man standing by the front of my apartment building—some guy out for a walk or quick run across the street to the deli market. The stranger took me out of my thoughts. "Agent Maier, if I can have a moment. I didn't want to concern your squad leader."

Smaltz. I wondered how long he'd been standing here, waiting. "Sure. Want to come up?"

"No. Only take a minute. I wanted to give you this."

That's when I saw the envelope of the kind that holds things so they won't bend in the mail, but it had a plain front with no address or label. I took it.

"Might want to wait to get inside under light before you open it. The people our special ops is rounding up are very, very bad, they are hell on family and relatives of anyone who they think is after them. The members of our task force are mostly single men with no kids. We intercepted this. This is for your eyes only and you must destroy its contents after you look. This is only a sample. If you should ever need another copy, you can contact me directly. My card is in there. Do I make myself clear?"

"Yes, sir."

"If anyone should contact you about these, about Mrs. Brookfeld, about Yegor, please direct them to me or whoever you are sure is part of the DK Task Force. Do not follow up on your own. Do I make myself clear?"

"Yes, sir."

"Good evening, then." Smaltz left.

I had to get more, tried to follow without Smaltz noticing. That not-being-seen part was easy for me in the dark streets with only sporadic car lights, but also easy for Smaltz to fade away into one of the newly opened MARTA stations, or hop on a bus, flag down a cab, or even walk away fast. I lost him.

As soon as I got inside my apartment door, I slit open the heavily-taped edge of the plain envelope and pulled out of it two black and white glossy photos. A paper clip attached Smaltz's card to the top edge.

The first photo showed Biddie entering the front door of her little apartment building in D.C. I knew it well. The other photo was taken up at Biddie, stark naked and from the front, coming out of a bathroom door into her bedroom, and with no idea that a camera lens snake lay on the floor or up through a hole at the bottom of the window looking up at her, someone on the other end clicking away. I didn't recognize the door or the bedroom. *My ever-loving Jesus. That must be her new home with her new husband. Hell and high water.*

I slumped down onto the sofa, the one Biddie had used for almost two weeks while she looked for work and her own place I'd brought with me to Atlanta. I sat doing nothing, letting my rage take me wherever it would. At about midnight, I headed to my 24-hour gym. Time to work out, punch some heavy bags, pump some heavy weights, and imagine the end-point and how to get there and, worst of all, how I had to stay the hell out of it.

I DIDN'T TELL ANGELA ABOUT THE ENDING TO the Felicity Cates case, not the very end. But I told her most everything about my time in Atlanta and my two meetings with old HHS.

Chapter Thirty-Two

Angela, 2011

Maier ended his story with, "I stopped, shut it down, never lifted another phone, another finger on that case—couldn't handle that what they did to Madeline would be what they'd do to Biddie and her two babies."

I could tell him about a little shoe and threats on a surfer dude. Not yet. "Yes, I get it. But now . . ."

"Judge, there's enough in that email and its attachments to raise holy hell, maybe not enough to convict anyone but enough to keep me snooping around a while longer. If you crow about a case, some bad guys will think twice about coming after you." Maier got that impish expression again. "We had some bad, bad cases, never enough to take to trial. Any decent federal judge would toss them on the first defense motion, but plenty good enough for our US Attorney to threaten to file and go public—sometimes got a nice plea deal quick and easy. Big shots can't stand the exposure."

Maier looked down at the desk, his clasped hands. "But these guys don't bluff like penny ante thugs. I lost Biddie a short while back, ah, how do they say it, of natural causes. So, they can't hold that over me, and I hardly know her two kids, my two nephews. One's a Marine, the other works somewhere in Europe, so they're well protected. It's a good time, maybe the last time, the last chance I've got to set things right for Mel and Madeline."

This Maier was real. Almost too real. And committed. "Yes, yes. I'm in the same place you were back then. I've got nothing to push to our local DA or federal prosecutor. They'd all tell me, nice try, honey."

I glanced at the wall clock above and behind Maier. I had been measuring him and whether he was shoveling smoke. I was good at that—first with clients and other lawyers, then with witnesses and lawyers in my courtroom. I got no smell of smoke from this Frank Maier chap. What he said and how he said it all fit. It was getting late, and I wanted to be home to help put the girls to bed. I had work to do for tomorrow, risks to assess.

"Mr. Maier, I must get home. God knows I want to get to the bottom of it, but I'm not sure I can help you, don't really know how."

"Sure. Here's my card . . . I thought I might be down here a while and have rented a furnished place. Call me. You must get home, and I must learn whatever you can tell me."

I took his card—plain white, with Frank's name, email address, a couple telephone numbers under two simple words, "Private Investigator".

⚖

AFTER THE GIRLS WERE TUCKED IN AND QUIET, the dishes done, the court papers for the next day reviewed and organized, I told Peter about Maier. Peter didn't interrupt. At the end, he said, "Melvin pulled us back in, didn't he? Not sure we should thank him."

I checked Maier's card. The email address matched the sent-to address of Melvin's email from more than a year before. One of the two phone numbers matched the one Maier gave me during our first call.

Peter and I pulled up the downloaded file of Naomi's documents, scrolled to the four-thousand-dollar cashier's checks, only a couple. There it was, a tiny set of three numbers and initials so small and faded I could not make them out. One of the initials might have been an L. They sat right below the large printed receipt number. *What else have I missed about this, about this Maier chap?*

Peter and I talked, agonized, most of it in our backyard. Deep in the night at the end, I said, "Back to the only question, the first question. Why can't I leave it alone, wish this Frank Maier chap good luck and be happy he's on it? Why meet him again? Tell him what I know, risk them coming after us?"

Peter reached for me, took me into his arms, against his broad shoulders. We stood there like that for a long time, breathing together until he said, "Let's sleep on it. Your deeper mind will give you the answer. I'll help, and if you believe in such things, Melvin will help us, too. In the meantime, and until this is done one way or the other, I'm with you whatever you decide, whatever we do."

⚖

TOO EARLY IN THE MORNING, I JUMPED OUT of bed. "Love, need to burn off this adrenaline, clear my head about Melvin's new info and now this new guy," code for me going for a run, and he'd get the girls up and off to day camp.

"Be careful out there. Run where there's lots of people. You are very precious."

The usual early dog walkers and chattering middle-aged women and couples greeted or watched me. I had come to know many of them, and we all cheered each other on with friendly glances and hand gestures. Soon I paid no notice to them or my surroundings. The same cleansing began with me only worrying only about where to land my feet on the street and sidewalks, where to speed up, where to hold steady, where to stay wide of cars. My deeper sense kicked in, as it always did, at about three miles, pulled up what troubled it or whatever it wanted to analyze with no interference from . . . well, from me.

The last months had been so nice, though tinged with a bit of guilt. Since my winter meeting with the Burdicks and follow up with Pitts, Melvin hardly jabbed at me. And now he crashed back, maybe carrying enough to bring down those who had slaughtered him, drowned Admiral Burdick, murdered Madeline, and who knew how many others. *What to do? What to do?*, my soles tapped out on the pavement.

Two pelicans stroked their strong wings against the morning air off the Pacific. Peter and I had never made enough to have an ocean view, but anytime we wanted, we ran to great views of the beach and the waves beyond. Early surfers were already out. Down by the bushes and hedges that framed the beach, homeless men and women started to stir. Tick, tick, said my soles. *Shall I call Maier or wait for his call? If I call, what to tell him? I know some things he might not. I might help bring in the killer or killers.*

A red light at a curb made me stop and look both ways. As a sitting judge, I'd decided to not run against any light—and get caught by a cop or future juror.

What to do? The default of every lawyer who didn't know what to do next came to me. I hated that default but knew it was true this time—ask more questions, get more info.

Three blocks from our little house, I eased to a walk, tired but a good tired, a clear-headed tired. I opened and closed the little half gate into our front yard. It always reminded me of those half gates between the courtroom visitors and the area where lawyers sat or stood.

I stopped there for a while, thinking, wondering about Smaltz and whoever else worked with him, what they could do to me and mine, to Frank and maybe others, wondered which side of courage was the right one—get the hell out of here and protect my family, or try to reel them in and gut them. Frank, was he phony or true, could he protect himself, protect me and my family all by himself? Then again, all the forces of protection hadn't helped JFK, MLK, and many others. Maybe Frank and I could pull this off. *Shit, there goes that Ambition thing with a capital A again.*

So far Smaltz had no idea about everything I knew, about Frank with me, what Melvin had given to Frank and now me. I hope he didn't, anyway. Quick surprise often neutralizes power, like a mongoose's quick strike on a cobra's neck. *Help me, Melvin, to do the right thing.*

"Hello, again."

No. It's him . . . maybe darker suit and freshly cut hair. I know who now. What the hell is wrong with me? This must stop. I tried to pretend he wasn't there. I'd walk right past him as he stood in the morning shade on the little brick landing leading into the side entrance to our house.

His deep-set eyes bored in again. I stopped, had to stop. "Don't worry. Those inside can't hear me, and I'll be brief."

My mind stopped too except, *Hell, this must be what it's like under hypnosis or mushrooms.* "Okay, but I'm done by the time I count to ten. One—"

The old man interrupted. "As you finish this, remember two things. First, the only prize cared for by the powerful is power. Those who have sought and held power over others will ever chase power. Take their power away, and they are hollowed out, and they will fall like a hollowed-out tree."

Made sense, had seen it many times, the big-shot syndrome. Smaltz and Maier each held a great deal of power for a long time. "I think I understand that. And the second thing?"

He raised his index finger for emphasis, "Deep-seated preferences cannot be argued about—you cannot argue a man into liking a glass of beer. Remember that when you have to deal with strong-headed men. Talk, argument will not move them. Fear of losing their power will move them, faster than you might expect."

I sighed a sigh of fatigue for this day on too little sleep and all that was to come. I lacked the energy to engage. I'd think about what he said later. "Is that it?"

He looked down, then bowed. "The spirits of Melvin and Madeline will help you."

The old man turned, walked away down by the side of the house through the back yard, stopped at the back hedges along the back alley, waved to me and then was gone.

⚖

FRANK WORE A DIFFERENT SUIT. HE CAME WITH an eagerness that didn't fit my mood. He bounded up the walkway, up to the little landing, and quickly stepped into the house. That email from Melvin—or maybe the looming hunt—had taken hold of him, given him a purpose of the kind he yearned for.

"Thanks for coming here. Beer, coke, iced tea, water?"

"Nothing, thanks."

"Say hello to Peter. He'll be in and out, checking on our girls as we talk. There's nothing he can't know." Peter and Frank shook hands—could have been two big-time coaches, head coach and junior, aware of their bodies, their strength, aware of what they had done, the foes they had beaten badly in past contests, and now both stuck in the present long after their glory days. But they hadn't lost any of their old intensity, of knowing how to find a way to win.

I went into our backyard. "Better we talk out here."

Frank followed me.

When seated, I said, "Mr. Maier, the last time we met, you said you saw Madeline's bones pulled out of Jug Bay. Tell me more, please."

"Call me, Frank," that boyish smile, "even if I can't help calling you judge or Your Honor. Yes. Madeline must have been a stunner, taken right off the D.C. street at the end of her workday. Must have been in a hell of a fight with someone who killed her and dumped the body in water hidden by tall grasses and trees far from any boat ramp or road or popular fishing spot. Two years later, a couple fishermen snagged their lines on her bones. Dental records—we had them from not long after her disappearance—made the match."

I again winced inside that I had made Melvin and Naomi remember, had made them talk about Madeline. "And all your leads turned into nothing, until now maybe?"

Frank sat back. "No, it wasn't that we had nothing. We had leads, some good ones, but orders from up on the Seventh Floor always stopped us, stopped me, or scared me off."

Peter said, "Seventh Floor?"

"Yeah, that's the top floor of Bureau headquarters . . . but maybe the orders came from different places, higher places. And for sure we never had enough to take to any deputy USA."

I knew Frank meant Deputy United States Attorneys attached to whatever cases he put together, or maybe local prosecutors for Melvin's murder, or who knew? I was getting ahead of him. "Harlan Smaltz has been leaving heavy tracks."

Frank stilled, his breathing shallow, eyes not blinking, no part of him moving for a long time, then, "Tell me everything you know about my old pal, Harlan H."

Frank's eyes fixed on me, the concentration of his whole body—another hungry lion stalking—made me shudder a bit. I hoped my shuddering didn't show. "I suspect your old pal knows everything, enough to round up and put away anyone left from the old days, from those dead men, and dear Melvin. The trick will be to pull it out of him, and how do you suppose we can do that?"

Over the afternoon I, and Peter from time to time, told Frank everything from the first frantic calls to clear my courtroom on that Friday morning, to my meetings with Pitts, then Naomi, and Smaltz, with the Burdicks, and the funky line-up for the gunshop clerk. Whatever Frank did, said, how he moved and followed along drew me on, made me trust him. Peter trusted him, too. I sensed that without needing to take Peter aside.

Alice and Abigail respected our quiet tension and peeked out the screen door a couple times but never interrupted. They didn't need to. They were with my every thought. Their safety, I suddenly knew, was the only thing that mattered. The girls ate dinner with us—pizza, antipasto salad, and gelato—in silence, not their bubbly end-of-day chatter when they got to eat with their mom and dad and company. But their eyes stayed wide open, kept cutting at Frank, wondering who he was, what was so important, how he could tie Peter and me up on a day that belonged to them. Peter cleaned up the kitchen and hung out with Frank while I helped the girls to bed.

As I tucked her in, Alice said, "Mommy, why is that man here?"

I couldn't lie. "He's helping find a bad man."

"A bad man from your work in court?"

"In a way. Quiet now. Not to worry about that before sleeping."

Abigail in the other bed said, "The bad man who killed your judge friend?"

I tried to shield my surprise at how she knew, at how she remembered our one bed-time chat from months before. But I shouldn't have been surprised. From a while back, I had learned that children listen far more astutely than adults realize. "It's all good. He's just checking what I know—about my friend."

After the girls were asleep, Frank spun out a plan and then another. Every plan started with me. I was the bait, had to be. If Frank made first contact with Smaltz or a prosecutor, Frank's plan would be DOA. I had to call or email Smaltz, honoring his earnest requests that, if something came up, to let him know right away. Next, I would induce him to come to San Diego again, and then tease him into incriminating himself.

Every version of the plan had to hide Frank Maier's presence in town and conceal that I even knew Frank Maier.

The closer we got to what seemed the best path, the stronger that new feeling welled up in me. I wanted to leave the men, disappear, cuddle up next to my girls, and sleep until morning while also hoping Peter had sent Frank back to wherever he came from never to bother us again. If I let myself be the bait, what came after that, what if . . . Frank said too often, "I'll take care of that . . . won't be a problem."

"Frank, how can I be sure those monsters won't come after my girls?"

Frank didn't answer right away. He knew, and he too had been scared off. "If you help me, you'll have some hard hours, maybe days. If old Harlan comes out to us, I've got ways to find out where he's staying, whether he's working alone, and where he'll be moving."

"Not good enough." And I meant it.

Frank breathed in deeply, looked right at me and then at Peter. "I can promise you this. If you or I get any sense that you or your young ones are in danger, we'll shut it down, call 911, and let it be. And we'll be careful. Judge, you've already built a lot of protection—Pitts and your line-up, your turning over the files to Smaltz, even the little shoe. If anything happens to your girls, there's now a straight line to Smaltz. And he knows it."

"Not good enough." Again, I meant it.

Again, Frank didn't answer right away, then said, "Melvin's last email and attachments have given me a lot to go on, to dig some more, maybe pull a meeting with old Harlan, just the two of us, have it out." He looked at me and shrugged.

I exhaled. "You don't need me."

Frank pursed his lips and nodded. I wasn't sure if it was a nod of agreement or that he understood. He pushed back a bit as if to get up. "One more thing before I go. If Melvin's last email ever comes out and old Harlan is still walking the streets, he and whoever is with him could have a mind to come after me. They'd know I was still ripping off the bandages—they could come after you because Melvin told me to see you."

I glanced at Peter. He suddenly raised his fists to his chest, one of those involuntary movements signaling a need to strike out, to defend me. But he looked at me to respond, and I knew Frank was right. I could not force him to forget Melvin and go have a good life. Frank would not do that. As long as he pushed on, my name would tie in. What I knew and had done already could not go away, ever. And our girls might be no safer if I did nothing more to help Frank from now on.

I stood, paced around our little yard. "I'll call Smaltz. But if he says something that puts him into it—into the killings—let the system, my system, do its justice. Will you promise me that?"

Peter also stood. He wanted to do this my way—or let it go.

Finally, Frank said, "No promises. Can't promise. If he comes out, and we get a record to trap him, can take everything we've got to your favorite prosecutor, sure we'll play it your way. But we can't know what he'll do, what we'll have until he's here." Frank paused. "We won't know we have a case, your kind of case, Judge, until it's in the can, with only the editing on the cutting floor left."

And he was right. I cringed inside about what might happen but saw no other way.

Chapter Thirty-Three

Frank

I never had a better lure than Angela, official or unofficial. If she called any man—from her judge perch or as a woman on the street—the summoned came running. Her dark brown hair lay on her pretty head very professionally, but long enough to swish back and forth when she shook her head. Slim, with a face and curves to turn most male heads, her confident walk, speech, and stare all captivated.

Now and again I wished I were younger, wished I had run into someone like her back when it mattered. Maybe I had but wasn't ready then, maybe Rebekkah was the one if I had chased harder, hadn't been too young and too stupid to know a good partner when she fell into my lap—or I fell into her lap. No time to look back. Time to play the end game of this, the longest, most important game I had ever played.

⚖

ANGELA CALLED ME LATE ON MONDAY AFTER our Saturday strategy sessions. "He picked up the phone at his end, must have seen my number. I had a message all worked out but didn't need it."

"All right, you've got me. Then?"

"I'm not sure what did it. We talked for a good fifteen minutes. He, that murderous thug, asked about my girls right off the bat, then my caseload, the crunching California State budget. I tried to walk that fine line of blind cooperation and still being distraught over Melvin's untimely demise." Angela laughed and changed her voice as she said, "*You know, Mr. Smaltz, after all this time I still can't get over Melvin's untimely demise.* I hated me for it."

"So, is he coming?"

"Yep. Melvin's delayed-send email that I said he sent from the court got him."

That was a nice touch, all true but misleading. Angela had hinted to Smaltz that Melvin's email had come to her from the court computer instead of to me and then copied by me and given to Angela.

She explained more. "Or the J. Edgar Directive, or maybe my noticing the little handwritten number on that one cashier's check and me asking Smaltz if he had any idea about that. Maybe it was that I was ready to take this to my favorite assistant US attorney but wanted to check with Harlan before I did, as if I needed to get permission from Harlan.

"Whatever it was, Smaltz bit hard, promised to check his calendar right away, check available flights and other, as he put it, activities they might have for him in the San Diego Region. Even thanked me for not sending it all in e-mail, ah, per his earlier instructions to call him first."

Smaltz promised to get right back to Angela on when he'd be out and ready to meet. Near the end he said to her, "Would you mind terribly forwarding Judge Brookfeld's email and the attachments by secure courier? We might not need to meet then, after all."

Angela and I had worked through this question many ways. She told Smaltz, "Oh, dear. I'm not comfortable doing that—putting these things out in the ether once more. Besides, it seems clear Melvin didn't want me to forward this to anyone. His email and attachments have that for-your-eyes-only gloss. But . . . under the circumstances and after what you warned me, I'm happy to read them to you in person, to talk to you about them, maybe show them to you if you—before I take them to one of my prosecutors."

Angela finished her recount of the call. "Silence on the other end for a long time, then Smaltz got irritated, made me wait before he said, 'I understand completely. Will be back to you shortly.' Frank, you know what's so obvious now, any high school civics kid could figure it out?"

"Tell me, Judge."

"If Smaltz were really working on Melvin's death in any official capacity, he wouldn't come out here. He could just get a local search warrant, and I'd give him everything I've got."

I shook my head. "Almost. But he doesn't know that you don't have any new documents. He doesn't know that only I have Melvin's delayed email and its attachments. I've not yet given you anything new. Must keep him thinking you've got what he wants. Fear's a great motivator, but it screws up the thinking process something terrible—and you're right. The local region would be all over this and helping the D.C. region—but fear makes him—"

Angela interrupted me. "You know Melvin's favorite Justice said, *Detached reflection cannot be demanded in the presence of an uplifted knife.* Smaltz now sees a knife hovering over his eyeball. We've got to get him, Frank."

I paused for a beat. *Damn, this judge lady could be hard as nails under that pretty veneer.* "And, Judge, he thinks you're holding that knife. Let me know when you have that meeting set so I can work my magic. Did he say where he's coming in from and when?"

"He did, bullshit artist. Said the D.C. office keeps putting him on these contract assignments, something about he's got all this institutional knowledge that they keep wanting to tap into. And he's got a Virginia area code. So, I suspect he's coming in from D.C.—wasn't lying about that."

"Did he say if he was bringing anyone with him?"

"Glad you reminded me. Once or twice Smaltz paused before he said *I*, as if he meant *we* but stopped himself . . . Maybe I should clue in the local cops? Once in a while, they do send someone around to a judge's house, extra patrols and such."

"If they'll do it, great. But most times, don't they need a credible threat first?"

"Yes, afraid you're right. Maybe it's time my girls had a big dog. He knows too much about them, probably knows they are at summer camp in the morning and home after that."

Damn it! Angela and her family were vulnerable to an unannounced blitz. "Angela, if he doesn't call back in a day or two, please think about moving out for a couple of days . . . or offer to house sit one of your friend's big dogs—and let me know."

A sigh on the other end. "Yes, Peter and I have talked about that."

⚖

SOME OF MY CONNECTIONS REMAINED AT THEIR jobs, and they always wanted to help an old buddy and hockey teammate, to laugh again about old times and promised to get together for a brew the next time we were in the same town. In my new line of work, I'd rarely needed to call any of them. But the few times I did, not one turned me down. I guess I had been a good squad member and then pretty good squad leader after all.

The second agent I called was happy to get airline passenger lists covering two days for all flights from Dulles and Reagan airports to San Diego. If I struck out there, I'd ask him to check flights into Los Angeles. And the airlines were happy to provide them. In this time of the Bureau needing to tap into any flight on short notice, the airlines never said to go get a search warrant first for something as benign as a passenger list.

One Harlan H. Smaltz popped up on an American Airlines nonstop from Dulles to San Diego, with a return four days later. I asked my old buddy, "Would you take a look at the other names, see if any take the same two flights?"

"Thought you might ask, Frank. Already done. One Stephen R. Wright takes both flights—at least he's the only peculiar name. The others sound like grandmas or kids. The kicker is they've reserved rental cars from the same counter and are staying at the same US Grant Hotel. And get this. One of the rentals is a panel van. I think that's who you're looking for."

This is getting serious. But I knew it would. "Panel vans spell trouble, says me."

"Yep. Team, I'd say."

I clicked away on my computer. "Thanks. Thanks a lot. I got to find out if they've got local thugs helping, too."

"Frank, want us to notify the San Diego Region and get you some help on this, whatever the hell you're working on?" He laughed. "Which I know you can't tell me. Those two jokers are crossing state lines, and that might give us jurisdiction."

"Thanks, let me think about that and get back to you. I can handle those two if that's all that's coming."

"Be careful and shout out if you want help."

"Will do. Thanks."

The US Grant Hotel was a couple blocks from Angela's courthouse on Broadway. Renting a car when Smaltz came only to talk to Angela, renting a van on top of that, told me all I needed to know. The outer limits of my plan were taking shape. I could let Angela meet with Smaltz at her courthouse or maybe in his hotel lobby, not anywhere else. And I had to stay tight on Stephen R. Wright, or whichever one of them drove the panel truck. That panel truck signaled big trouble. But I had one advantage. They didn't know I knew.

I took a jog up Cowles Mountain, a seventeen-hundred-foot hill not far from downtown San Diego. Had to clear my head so I could protect some good people and destroy the bad ones. Taking in the view from the top of Cowles Mountain, west to Point Loma and the Pacific, east to higher mountains and south to Mexico, I quietly said, "Melvin, you're the smartest man I ever knew. Pour some of that into me over the next few days. I'll need your help to make this one play out as it should."

Smaltz and his buddy wouldn't be on a plane until Thursday, and probably wouldn't want to see Angela until the next day. I had time to set my pieces.

Chapter Thirty-Four

Frank

Smaltz had one of those rental car memberships that allowed him and Wright to go straight to their stall numbers in the car rental parking lot. Anyone could drive into that lot and find the stalls listed on the reservation confirmation. Hours before the two customers landed and looked for their vehicles, their car and van would be waiting all nicely cleaned up. Lots of strangers drove into that parking lot to pick up people returning cars or to reclaim glasses or smartphones left on the counter. The only security guard was at the exit hut, checking rental car contracts. He never bothered strangers in the lot if they looked like they were heading for their rental cars or were leaving after dropping someone off.

No self-respecting PI would be far from a couple of good tracking devices with fresh batteries and magnetic cases. The undercarriage of both the rental car and the panel van had enough metal to clasp onto my little rectangular devices in their magnetic cases. A dab of glue would make sure nothing knocked them off. I'd worry about retrieving them later, or I'd toss the hard drive of the computer I used to monitor them. When done, none of it could be traced to me.

Late on the Thursday Smaltz and Wright landed, Angela called me. "Meeting tomorrow. He said evening would be best for me. He asked if I wouldn't mind coming over to his hotel a couple blocks away—the U.S. Grant."

"That's good. Stay in the lobby area. Don't go outside with him. Don't let him leave with you. Call me as soon as you're away from him."

"I told him a quiet corner of the lobby would be great, maybe dinner after we finished our business." Angela paused. "He jumped on that . . . said he'd make reservations for two."

I had it down well—my Smaltz and Wright plan—but let none of it out. I wanted Angela to think Smaltz was alone, that the girls were safe. Angela could take care of herself in the lobby meeting, so she didn't need me there. Others needed my help.

On Friday morning, I parked at an overlook three blocks above the Cornwell house, from where I could see the streets around their house and both doors. I wore a Padres cap and windbreaker with big pockets and was glad a cool Pacific breeze came through here. Wouldn't look too overdressed, not for an old guy out on his daily drive and walk.

Early in the afternoon, the girls got home from their day camp with Peter. They entered the house through the side door—two excited little girls and a proud papa.

And I waited, worried over my tracking system, that it would work without a glitch. I checked my little laptop a couple of times. It showed both tagged vehicles sitting in what looked like a parking garage at the US Grant Hotel.

At about the time Angela's court closed for the day and she might be getting ready to head over to her Smaltz meeting, my laptop beeped. One of the two vehicles—Wright's van—was on the move.

I dialed the Cornwell home. "Peter, this is Frank."

"Glad you called. I was beginning to worry a bit . . ."

I cut him off. "Listen up. Not much time. A van's coming to your house, will act like he's delivering something or needs to read a meter. Close and lock all your windows and doors. Tell him he's got the wrong house, that whoever he asks for—Angela or the Cornwells or you—moved out of the area a while back. He won't know one way or the other. Make sure the girls stay extra quiet. They'll do that if they know it's important, and it is. Don't let him see you. He doesn't know your voice."

"And then what?"

"I'll take it from there."

"How will you—?"

Had to cut him off again. "Don't worry. I'm looking at your house now and tracking this chap. He won't be expecting me. Got to go now. So do you."

I drove down into a decent intercept position where there were no parking restrictions. Twenty-three minutes later a panel van passed by my car. I ducked down in the passenger seat, my head below the head rest so I'd be hard to spot from behind.

Wow, that son of a bitch, where in the hell did he get flower store decals on both sides so fast? Must have brought them with him. Easy to go anywhere with those, and that explained his short stop on the way. My tracking laptop told me the stop was at a shopping center with a big anchor grocery store and its cheap flower department.

Wright even wore a blue uniform-looking shirt with a florist's decal on the pocket. *Damn, as good a cover as we ever used. Wonder if he had it ready or hustled to get it made.*

Wright's first mistake helped me now. A big arrangement in a big cheap vase with some water took both hands to hold easily and made him pay attention to them at every step—opening the passenger side, hoisting out the flowers from a side shelf restraint, and either setting them down when he closed the van door, or leaving the door open, or maybe kicking it shut. The bottom outside of the right leg pants bulged a bit where I expected it might. He should have brought a dry bouquet. This undercover stuff wasn't his gig.

And the whole fake florist get-up trapped him, stopped him from making too big a fuss about what I had coming at him. He would not want to explain to any nosy neighbor or cop what he was doing out here as a fake flower delivery guy, with fake florist decals on his van, a fake florist uniform, delivering flowers for no occasion. And Wright wouldn't pull the pistol holstered to his right leg unless he absolutely had to—or unless Peter let him step into the house.

"Here, let me help you with those," I said as Wright stood up and tried to kick the van door closed, his hands full. "You new at this flower delivery gig? I know." I fibbed. "As a kid I worked in a flower shop."

Wright, younger than me and as pasty white as any office clerk—staying indoors in East Coast summers will do that—visibly started. "Ah, no problem. I got it." This guy was no field man. He likely looked at computer screens all day and barked orders, out of his element now, insecure.

He, with the overstuffed vase of sunflowers, contrasting red roses, and green lacy things, worked his way to the half-picket fence gate. Whoever put this together was no flower person, either. The arrangement was ugly. I walked along with him. "Careful now. Let me help you through this fence gate, tough to unlatch it with your hands full."

"Damn it, old fellah, I got this. Now bug off."

I opened the half door in the fence, held it open, and let him make it to the front door on his own. Wasn't but ten steps if I needed to stop him from going into the house.

Wright set down the vase on the little front landing and pressed the bell button, pressed it again. I heard Wright say quite loudly, "Delivery here for Angela Cornwell . . . need someone to sign for them . . . really . . . wrong house . . . moved? Are you sure . . . I'll be damned. Sorry to bother you."

Wright leaned a hand against the house wall, thinking, fuming.

I yelled out, "Wrong house?"

Wright sneered at me as if he might give me the middle finger, pulled back the sneer, and started to walk away from the front door.

"Hey, you gonna' take the flowers back to the shop? Can I help you find the right address?"

Wright hesitated, and finally took the flowers back to the van, with me close and ready to help at every step.

I had studied the neighborhood. Short blocks and cul-de-sacs, nice houses not far from the beach looked like they belonged to folks with good jobs or retired with nothing to do except snoop on other neighbors. Up the hill the houses got bigger with big windows taking in the ocean view. And that set my next steps—couldn't let this chump leave, couldn't let him make that first phone call back to Smaltz, but had to do it in a way that wouldn't cause a fright on this quiet street.

Wright didn't want to fuss with the van's back door again. He poured out some of the water and set the flowers into the passenger side, another mistake. He walked around to the driver's side, and I moved up to the passenger door, toggled down its window and held the door open a tiny bit. As he climbed into the front seat, I leaned in. "You new around here? Have kind of a Baltimore accent?"

The sneer again. Wright ignored the question, pulled his seat belt on and around and pressed the ignition button. The van's warning ding-ding sounded, and the dash display lit up with a red icon. That's what happens when the passenger door is ajar. I pulled the passenger door wide open and jumped in fast. This nice big van had plenty of passenger foot room for me and the flowers.

"What—you stupid—get the fuck—"

The last word got stuck on the barrel silencer of my Glock 43 stuffed into Wright's mouth. "Shut up and do what I tell you."

"Fuck you—" Wright mumbled, tried to grab my arm, but with his turning movement restrained by the seat and seatbelt, his grip was nothing. This chump wasn't a fighter, didn't go for my eyes or throat. And I caught another break—all the side windows were tinted, so I only had to worry about anyone seeing us through the windshield. I glanced around. No one yet.

I shoved the barrel in harder. Wright gagged, his eyes got wide, his face red, and he let go of my arm. I pulled Wright's head from the back and jammed the silencer deeper into Wright's mouth.

"If this goes off, it's on you. Got it?"

Wright nodded. I let him pull his head away and his mouth off the barrel silencer. "What do you want . . . if you let me, I'll get my wallet."

"Both hands on the wheel, asshole."

Wright put both hands on the wheel.

"Look out the window like you're leaving the curb and checking traffic, but don't leave yet."

Wright looked out the window, giving me enough time to strap on my seatbelt. "Here's what we're gonna do. You drive. I'll direct. One mistake, one hesitation, and you go straight to hell. I might do you with a gut or chest shot into your lungs first. Understand?"

"I understand."

"Let's go. Drive."

When we were on the freeway with Wright fully occupied driving in the directions I gave him, I said, "Where's your cell phone?"

"In my left shirt pocket."

"Who you gonna call or text about that bad flower delivery?"

"Don't have to call anyone . . ."

I tapped the side of Wright's face with the silencer's end. "I know when you lie. Don't. When are you and your buddy Harlan supposed to talk or text next?"

"Shit, man. Who are you? Okay. Harlan's going to call me, told me not to call him unless there was a problem with my, ah, delivery."

"I know that. I want to know when, asshole." I tapped the side of his head again.

"No time. We set no time."

He was lying. They had to have set a default time. I hit him harder, saying, "When, asshole?"

"After a meeting he's in—unless I call him first. Maybe an hour, maybe two."

I believed that last response. It made sense, and thugs usually fold fast. So damned used to having their way, hurting their victims, they don't know what to do when they're on the receiving end. So far, so good. Peter and the girls were safe for a while longer.

We arrived at my destination, and I waved at the guy in the security booth of the storage yard where I had rented two insulated side-by-side units, the kind start-up bands use until they give up or get good. The guy in the booth barely noticed us, only looked at the storage grounds pass now hanging from the rearview mirror post. I had taken it with me after I rented the two units.

No other cars in our row. My two units were at the end. I kept my cap covering my face and made him turn the van so that it faced the end unit. That way, the aisle cameras could not see our faces.

I handed him a small cloth sack with a drawstring, "Put this over your head and tie the drawstring." He looked at me and hesitated like he'd swallowed a whole frog. "Don't make me put it on you. I'd shoot you first."

I shoved my gun silencer harder into his ribs.

Wright did what I wanted.

"Now sit tight." That sack over his head allowed me to get out of the van on the side away from the last camera and open the gate of the storage unit. The cameras would catch the van, but this vehicle was not tied to me. The cameras would catch the side windows of the van, but not see through them to Wright's sack-covered head.

Once inside, I made Wright remove his sack, ease the van's front into the locker and get out. Three chairs, a card table, duct tape, and a solid new ball peen hammer waited in there for Wright and later for Smaltz.

Close to dark, Smaltz too did what I wanted. He called Wright on cue, and Wright, sounding a little excited, said what I told him to say. We'd practiced before the real call. "Hey, Harlan . . . sorry it didn't go well on your end. Well, I've got it covered. She'll come around real good . . . get on over here. We'll button this one up."

Wright told him to come to a parking lot next to the storage place, that Wright would wait for him in the flower shop van, that Smaltz should hop into the passenger seat. Easy to get Wright to say just what I wanted with my pistol at his back and my hammer lying in front of him. Smaltz had no reasons to doubt that Peter and the girls would be tied up and tucked into the back of the flower delivery van.

When Smaltz arrived at the parking lot, all he got was me, duct tape, and the same hood over his head. He had no idea who I was and that we'd met before until I had them both safe and sound in the storage locker. Not all self-storage units are open twenty-four hours a day for customers. I had made sure this one was.

Chapter Thirty-Five

Angela

Smaltz was waiting, dapper in a suit, tie and matching coat pocket kerchief. He stood up like a gallant gentleman, ready to kiss my hand or cheek if I offered. I didn't. He had selected a little seating group in a corner of the first floor of the two-level lobby—rounded leather chair and large soft sofa away from the foot traffic flow and far from anyone who might overhear.

"So nice to see you again, Judge. I thought we could talk here."

I had been in this grand old hotel many times for client meetings, Bar Association functions, and the occasional celebration. But this was different. I knew too much, and Smaltz's every gesture felt wrong and this place too sumptuous. A hollow warehouse, or behind a garbage dumpster better suited this meeting, but Frank and I and Peter had agreed this get together would take place out in the open, in public, inside the hotel's security perimeter. I said, "Nice to see you, too." We sat down.

"Judge, would you like something to drink—a Perrier, a little bite? They do it properly here."

Time for me to jangle his nerves, make him guess and play what-if games. "Thank you. Nothing for me, but don't let me stop you."

"Very well. Let's get to it. Tell me about that email from Judge Brookfeld. I see you didn't bring it. Ah, I don't expect you stuffed the whole thing into your purse."

I reached into my purse, pulled out my smartphone, ran through a sequence of touches, and set it on the low table between us. "No, I didn't bring that. We need a good record, don't you think, so we don't lose a thing, remember everything?"

Smaltz acted unfazed, smiling. "Good idea. Is it on and working?"

"Sure is. It picks up everything at this distance. It's my only techie gadget."

That graciousness again. "Great. So, tell me about Judge Brookfeld's email, when he wrote it, when he sent it out, who it was sent to, the gist of it and the attachments. We'll worry about what to do with it and any copies later."

This meeting would proceed on my agenda, not his. "Why don't you now, Mr. Smaltz, tell me what has you chasing all over the country for Melvin's files, for his connection to the Burdick family and the drowning of the Admiral, for that gun dealer out in El Cajon, and back to San Diego for this email. What's all that about when any local FBI grunts would be doing all that, would show up at my house search warrant in hand?"

The charm clicked off. Smaltz leaned back against the big leather chair, then pulled himself forward over the table and recorder and stared back at me. "Dearest Judge Cornwell, I'll tell you, but it's still all classified, Top Secret or Eyes-Only. I can't let you record what I'm going to tell you. And if you won't give me a copy of Judge Brookfeld's materials, I'll have a search warrant by tomorrow, and you'll be served right away. I left instructions back at the office, probably already prepared. Might even come by the house with it later."

I could play this game, too. "Then tell me the name of the lawyer you'll use, the judge you'll apply to. Maybe I know her. Let me put it this way, Mister, threaten me once more, and I'm out of here and next you'll deal with a team of San Diego's finest federal prosecutors for slaughtering Judge Brookfeld."

Smaltz remained leaning forward. "Don't you, Judge, threaten me, either." But his jaw and shoulders slackened for an instant. "I'll tell you what I can, but it won't be much. Where would you like to start?"

"What kind of theater glue are you guys using these days to affix a false fingerprint onto your own skin? When I did a little acting, we used Graftobian Spirit Gum—could affix all kinds of things to our faces or hands, and nobody was the wiser. Your forgery kits are slick, too, I'm told. Makes copying anyone's signature easy."

Smaltz laughed loudly, the laugh carrying out away from us. But the laugh was too loud. Frank and I had sized everything up right. The laugh settled down. "Judge Cornwell, we are not nearly as clever as some of the cases you've seen—or maybe you've gotten this from TV. It's plain as the giant chandeliers in this lobby that Melvin took his own life. What else?"

This time Smaltz fought to stay in role, turned back to the charmer. I couldn't tell him about the salesclerk who picked Smaltz out of my little line up, not yet. Maybe this next would shake him some more. "You know that gunshop has security cameras on the entrance—two of them—and hidden cameras on the inside. It stores the images for a whole year—gun business needs good security—sometimes longer. San Diego's finest retrieved those images for the day Melvin signed the application and again when he picked up the gun. He's not on the cameras either day."

Smaltz remained calm. "Well that is a puzzle—how anyone could tell. I've checked that store out, you know. It has a lot of customers. Easy for him to get in and out without those cameras picking him up."

Maybe this would get him, "Tell me about the DK Task Force. Were you part of it? Do I have that right?"

"Yes, you do, Judge. That was a joint task force set up after that terrible time. We had to get control of leads, press inquiries, the thousands of rumors, research junkies, record and react to them all." Smaltz shrugged. "Routine crisis control."

And so it went for another half hour. I asked about Admiral Burdick's drowning—Smaltz admitted he had met with the family, and the Admiral had known all about the DK Task Force, what it did.

I asked about Oswald's financing and all those checks left by Melvin. Smaltz said, "You know it's not uncommon for the CIA to pay confidential informants, even pretend to be working with the informant to trap bigger fish."

At last I was sure I had it right, had the whole picture and all the details in it. Any prosecutor could now try to find real evidence, put together a case, and haul in this arrogant killing prick. Trouble was, I had no evidence, not one witness or document to prove a damn thing about any crime, any courthouse murder, in a real courtroom. I stood up. "Thank you for coming. I must be going now. Tomorrow or the next day, I'll take what I have to my favorite AUSA and let the chips fall."

I reached for my smartphone on the table. Smaltz was quicker. His hand clasped over my hand. "I wouldn't do that. Not yet. Why don't you call your Peter before you leave here? Tell him you're on the way home, that you're not staying to have a nice meal with me, hmm?"

I did. Peter answered. I said, "Hello, honey. We are done here, heading home. It's still light out, so don't worry . . . love you . . . I'll be home soon. "

I turned to leave and said to Smaltz, "Thanks. That was a good suggestion."

Smaltz jumped to his feet and held up his hand. "Wait one moment, please. I need to make a call myself, and maybe I can walk you to your car. Must cancel that reservation over in the restaurant. It's the decent thing to do on a busy evening."

He pulled out his own smartphone and tapped the screen a few times. At the first ring tone sounds, Smaltz walked away, out of my sight and hearing, around a pillar and past the grand staircase.

Time for me to leave. On the way to my car, I tried Frank's number and got him right away. "Can't talk now, but it's all good," he said. "Get on home. Peter has more info." He hung up.

Peter came outside before I could close our garage door. "Hi, Love, I'll walk you in." He told me of the flower delivery that didn't happen. I told him about my Smaltz meeting.

⚖

WE HEARD NOTHING MORE FROM SMALTZ THAT evening, but Maier called ninety minutes after I got home. "Hello, Judge. I must be brief again. Have you got enough for a real case in a real court room?"

Frank must have heard my exasperation, maybe even heard the slump of my shoulders. "No, that prick gave me nothing to take to anyone. And you, where are you? What are you doing?"

"Everything is all right, coming together at my end. You and the girls are safe. Will check back soon."

"Frank, you can't do that to me, to us. Tell us where you are, what you are doing. And let me tell you more about what happened."

"Judge, I can tell you this much right now. Smaltz is with me." He paused and let out a breath. "Under lock and key, as we say. And the flower delivery guy is with him under the same lock and key. Got to go."

"Wait, please. How do I know they are not making you say this and will come back at us in the middle of the night?"

"Now, Judge, you know that's not what's going on. Must really go now. Will check back soon." And Frank hung up.

I did know what he'd said was true, that we could relax for now. The three of us had worked out code words we'd use if things turned bad, if they made any one of us call the other with a gun to our heads. He would say something using *San Diego* or *Ashland* or *Cowles Mountain*. One of those meant take care and stay close to your phone. If we worked all three locations in, that was our code to the person on the other end to call 911.

He had not mentioned any of those, not close.

No more calls came in during the night or the next morning, another normal summer Saturday. No call or visit from anyone on Sunday, either. We fretted about what to do, to think, whether to run, hide, carry on as if nothing had happened, whether to get a big dog. Frank had sounded so calm and confident, Peter and I tried not to worry. But we stayed at home with the curtains and shutters closed and tilted so no one could see in from the outside.

On Sunday late afternoon, Peter and I dared to take the girls to the beach and warm water. Nothing struck us as peculiar. One week passed, and then another.

Chapter Thirty-Six

Angela

At two minutes after nine in the evening on the third Sunday after I last saw Smaltz, the girls already tucked in, my cell phone vibrated with a text message from Maier: Hello, Judge and Peter. Sorry I've been gone a bit. Busy. Please listen to the attached.

The attached was an audio recording. I placed the phone on the kitchen table. Peter and I listened all the way through, saying nothing, barely breathing. After two beats of silence, Frank began.

San Diego, California. I'm at a location that I should not disclose right now. Better you not know. What follows are excerpts from a fuller, longer recording. I'll keep the longer recording in a safe place. This shorter version places the excerpts in a more logical order than the sometimes jumbled original.

A pause, then Frank again.

The other voices are Mr. Harlan H. Smaltz, formerly of the FBI, and Stephen R. Wright of the CIA.

After a short silent pause, Smaltz's voice—though low, slow, as if he were in pain, breathing hard, pausing often, exhausted—came on.

Melvin should have backed off the first time we warned him... warned... him a lot... to stop what he was doing... Nah, one of the guys who knew her and on our DKTF... was gonna follow her home and warn her to her face, bruise her up a bit if... he had to... before Melvin got home... but it was raining like hell... he offered her a ride home... A hard cough, then one more. *We had a safe house out of the city . . . had to get Melvin to back off. One of the guys got careless, didn't watch her in the bathroom. She . . . flattened a metal soap dish by stepping on it, made a sharp and ragged edge . . . broke the mirror with a fist in a towel, came out of there like a wolverine . . . with cutting edges in both hands . . . sliced his face and neck big time. Two guys practically . . . had to kill her to stop . . . turned out they did kill her . . . nobody wanted to . . . okay . . . I was one of the guys in that safe house . . . one of the guys who got rid of her body . . . dumped her in that back water.*

Another DKTF guy gave the Russkies that nav. chart . . . Hard coughing, then . . . *We figured it might come in handy to pin it on them . . . we knew that Russki Kaminev . . . we knew he knew her . . . wanted to do her . . . high and mighty asshole, that one.*

Yeah, before I got recruited for the DKTF . . . I'm hearing about Thomas down in Mexico City. He wouldn't leave it alone either . . . yeah, he took a bullet to the head in his upstairs bedroom . . . don't know if he did it or one of us made him do it.

Damn, too fucking smart Melvin . . . couldn't leave it alone . . . yep, that was me buying Melvin's gun . . . wanted to use it soon as I got it . . . easy to get copies of a couple of his decisions and copy his signature. Easy to pull up his prints and put them on my own thumbs. Your honey judge was right about all that. I called that smartass to get together for old times . . . told him I'd come clean on what really happened to his old lady . . . figured that would get him. You know what? He said for me to keep it to myself, couldn't change it. He wouldn't see me.

Lot easier to get into the courthouse than into his secure condo. Would you believe that? I couldn't wait any longer . . . this shit, that old shit, what happened back then couldn't get out . . . and he was getting close to putting it out . . . he kept sending in FOIA requests, and other stuff was getting declassified . . . I'd followed him to court a couple times and knew he came in real early. Followed him that morning too. Easy to walk into the courthouse ten minutes after him with . . . my card . . . Smaltz laughed . . . that hurts. Got to his chambers not long after he came in, opened his lap top and got settled. Didn't know what I was gonna do until I did it. Smaltz paused, maybe winced. *Bad planning by me.*

He never begged, nothing . . . the way he looked at me, waved at me, what he said will go with me to my grave . . . He said, "Unless you can bring her back, you can leave now." That got to me, that's when I had to shoot him. He said it like he had me . . . and I guess he did have me . . . silencer made a sound like a traffic pop . . . Another pause. *Good thing I've kept in shape. For an old man he moved up and out of his chair quick before I put him down . . . No one in the courthouse gave a damn about that little noise.*

Yeah, the porn on his laptop . . . did it . . . don't make me laugh again . . . if that stupid ass Pitts had checked, he'd have figured it was put on the day that Melvin died. . . . Looked at Mel's docs files for a minute, didn't find shit . . . had to get outta there . . . But if someone had come in on me, would have been easy. Visiting an old friend and found him dead. Old Johnny Pitts is . . . an idiot. Never had to worry about him checking courthouse camera tapes, him biting so hard on suicide. Then, easy to get him off our back, what with his doting on his grandbabies. That's what he liked to call them, didn't want nothing to happen to them. Hah, kids get them every time.

Those dead guys in Cuba . . . others on the DKTF took care of them with the help of our black ops guys. Easy for us to hire goons when we can put them away for life . . . if they don't do what we want. Easy to hire goons in shithole countries.

Your lady judge and her loser hubby . . . intermeddling bitch. Couldn't keep her nice hard ass out of it . . . damn, what I wouldn't have liked to do to her . . . thought my finding that kid shoe in the front yard on my first visit to their house and mailing it to them would back them off . . . I had Melvin taken out, her too. But damn it to hell and back, you showed up . . . Maier, you self-righteous son of a bitch . . .

Another pause, then another voice. Peter whispered, "It's that flower delivery guy."

Old Burdick was going to raise holy hell. He knew about Thomas . . . and the guys in Cuba . . . couldn't let that happen . . . sent some of our black ops guys to hold the old guy under. Afterwards, we bugged the Burdick house . . . and got nothing for years. Then . . . out of nowhere here comes Melvin again . . . damn him. Had to do him ourselves . . . hard as hell to get black ops guys here. Lot easier in other parts long ago.

Angleton wanted to pin it on the Soviets, but the Soviets didn't do it. What? Yeah, Angleton, our head man . . . in those days . . . Russians thought Oswald was a total nut job . . . didn't want him . . . but we're not as picky . . . heck, to get that J. F. K. boy, we'd take anyone. We didn't need to hire Oswald, just had to let him loose, encourage him, keep him in walking-around money. Did it all himself.

Then Smaltz again. *All the old DK guys are out to pasture, dead, gone. We're the last two who are, ah, . . . still . . . still keeping a lid on things.*

Sobbing sounds, then Maier once more.

Smaltz and Wright each carried a pistol in an ankle holster. I returned their pistols to them. I set one bullet for each pistol on a table in front of them. I untied them before I left—except for their feet. They had to untie their own feet from the chairs before they could run after me. That duct tape is a bugger to take off without scissors or a sharp knife.

Left the pistols out of their easy reach. They couldn't get to their pistols, load, aim and shoot me before I left. Pulled my Padres cap snug over my face going back and forth. And they knew I could shoot back a whole lot quicker and easier.

I left them locked up and waited, waited until two shots from where I had stashed them. Two shots but not at the door latch. That told me everything anyone needed to know. I looked in on them, and they are both fully dead. The Bureau's already gotten them out of there, cleaned up, and no one will know.

Please do not worry about anything. You are safe and will never be bothered again by the likes of them. I'm sure of it. If anything new comes up, I know where to find you. Appreciate all you have done very much.

The recording stopped.

Peter and I sat in silence for a long time, stunned, not knowing what to say, what to think, relieved but not, and neither of us knew what to do next.

Chapter Thirty-Seven

Frank

Thanksgiving fell on November 26. I tried the land line for the Cornwell house at nine in the morning. They'd be up but not yet have left for wherever they'd have the feast. Peter answered.

"Hello, Peter. This is Frank Maier."

"Holy effing cow," Peter yelled.

A girl's voice shouted out, "Daddy, you said a bad word."

A dog barked as if it agreed with the girl.

"Hope it's not too early. I figured the girls would have you up. How's my favorite Judge's spouse?"

"He's great! Angela, pick up. It's Frank Maier."

"Well, Frank Maier. As Peter said, how are you, where are you? Can we see you?"

"Heck, I'd love to, but . . . I'm not in your town any longer."

"We tried to find you, but you changed all your numbers. I know you'll never answer this," said Angela sternly, "but I've got to ask. Where did you do what you did, whatever the hell you did?"

Not much sense in holding back from these good folks. "Ah, I took them to a self-storage unit, an insulated one, the kind shitty bands and down-low film makers use."

"Wow. Are we safe? Are you safe? Those places have cameras all over, and you had to rent it in someone's name."

"I know how to spot and dodge them, use gloves and wipe any prints. Wright got himself a van with tinted side windows. I thanked that prick a couple times for doing that. And my cap covered my face from all the up high cameras. When I counsel businesses, I always tell them to put cameras at eye-level, not too high or too low. The name I put on the rental contract . . . you guessed it, Harlan H. Smaltz. I paid for a month in advance, so no one asked for my ID." I laughed softly. "If they had asked, I would have shown them my Smaltz driver's license."

"Mother of Mary, you are a clever one. Turnabout is fair play," said Angela.

Peter chimed in. "Nothing on the news, nothing anywhere?"

"The Bureau's got a tip line. Can call it—and that's what I did on a burner phone." Peter exhaled loudly enough for me to hear. Angela snorted. I talked on, "Once the FBI figured out who the dead guys were, you can bet all the apples in Wisconsin that no local cops, no news hounds, nobody would ever know. You can bet the bodies were shuffled off to next of kin and a nice ceremony held for each one but all very quiet."

They both waited, then Angela said, "Did they really kill themselves, no help from anyone we know?"

"I didn't, not even close. When I left them, they were both alive and kicking. How do we say it—in full control of all their faculties."

"How on this God's good earth did you make them kill each other or whatever they did?"

"Aw, not so hard."

"No, seriously, how did you?"

"Set a card table in there with a couple chairs and left them with a couple decks and a wheel of chips. I figured they might want to cut the cards or play for who got the two bullets. Only fair."

"You son of a bitch," said Peter softly so maybe the twins could not hear.

Angela said, "You weren't afraid they'd get out and come after you?"

"They couldn't get out until I let them out. I latched their storage locker from the outside."

"You clever son of a bitch," said Peter.

"Seemed to me they could use one or two bullets to maybe shoot the latch off or shoot at nothing and hope someone heard. I figured they wouldn't do that."

"Oh?" said Peter and Angela together.

"Too much hate in them for too long. Too much fear in them now for what might hit them after my recording got out. They had only each other left to hate, and only each other to blame for screwing up, for the flower man blowing it and Smaltz getting nothing from you and then running right into my bear trap. That much hate and blame and fear could break only one way."

Angela whispered, "They lost their power and had nothing left," then a bit louder, "That's BS, Frank. Why should I believe that you didn't just shoot them in the head with their own guns? Do to them what they had done to Melvin and the others."

I was ready for that one from Angela. "Judge, you set them up, helped them do what they did."

"What? You're a great slinger, but that's nuts."

"Judge, I moved up your own timeline a couple days, from the next Monday to Saturday. You convinced him."

"I'll bite. What the hell are you talking about?"

"After I'd recorded what I needed, I gave them their pick. They could wait until morning and meet with the prosecutor of your choice, Judge." She gasped at that but let me talk on. "The prosecutor would take their full written confessions. Or . . . I'd send my recording out to their old friends, their families, maybe some news outlets. But I kinda knew what they'd do, was their only way, the two of them together in there."

"Holy mackerel," said Peter.

"Little things can be the most convincing. Before I left them to stew, I took them out to the Porta-Potty, one at a time, like nobody was coming back until morning."

Peter continued, "They had two guns, could shoot whoever came for them."

"Yeah, sure, but one bullet each would be popcorn against the muscle they figured would be on them from the outside—a SWAT team, dogs, maybe a robot, and everything they'd done out there all over the world. No way they'd let all that happen the next morning, not ever."

Angela said, "You clever bastard."

"Judge . . . you're too nice."

Peter asked, "How long did you wait around—after you faked leaving them for the night?"

"Didn't take long, maybe forty minutes for one to kill the other—and then himself." I paused again for them to catch up. I had dropped a lot on them.

Angela said, "Where did you wait all that time, where no camera could spot you waiting and when you took each to the bathroom?"

"Why, yes. I forgot. Old HHS actually rented two units side by side—in case I had to separate them, or wait them out, or needed to call you without them listening or being on camera. Left their rented cars snugged against the units. The boxy van made for a bit more protection from cameras when I helped an old man to a bathroom break, both of us wearing caps and looking down. No one would care about two guys on a pee break. Took them one at a time, and they each cooperated so nice. Didn't want to foul their locker right then."

"My goodness. Did you have to . . . that way?" said Angela.

"With what I had to put them through to get them to talk, no prosecutor would touch them. Coerced confessions. Hell, the President would probably order them left alone. In the best interests of the nation to not prosecute them, he'd say."

"Frank, you might be right," said Angela slowly.

Peter said, "Can you tell us what you used to get them to talk?"

Angela said, "Peter, shame on you. What difference does it make now?"

Peter said, "Honey, it's a guy thing. Frank, don't tell us if you don't want to."

No use holding back. "From when I was little, I liked the feel of hand tools. Hammers are best."

Peter said, "Damn, you're a hard man."

Angela said, "Frank, who's got a lot of hate?"

"No other way. Peter, did you tell Angela about the flower delivery?"

Angela said softly, probably again so the twins couldn't hear, "Yes, he did, right away. I tremble now at the thought of Wright here in our house with the girls and his pistol to their heads."

I said, "Not hate. Just doing a job, finishing it, long time coming."

Angela said, "I guess there was no other way." She paused. "If someone comes calling with a proper warrant, we'll turn over what you sent us."

"I'd bet all the chips I left on that table that no one will come calling for my recording. No one wants it to get out, not ever."

Angela said, "Wait, I've got it. An old classmate works at the Kennedy Library. Researchers will have a field day—and one Frank Maier will spawn many Ph.D. dissertations, will go on the interview circuit, write a book."

Peter laughed.

I laughed until I had to hold my cell phone away from my face.

Angela said—at last, "How did you think of all that? Is that how the Bureau operates?"

My answer came easily, the true answer. "Nah, most in the Bureau don't operate like that—no fun in them. Anyway, I just kept thinking, what if I were half as smart as Melvin, what would I do now, this moment, what's his next move?"

Angela said, anger in her voice, "Damn it, Frank. Stop, he never would have let you do what you did to those two."

"Angela. Sorry, I mean, Judge. You didn't know him back then after we found Madeline's bones. He would have let me do any damn thing."

Peter said, "How did you get them both out to the storage place?"

"Caught Wright off guard by your house. Once I had him tucked away, hands tied with duct tape, feet taped to a chair in the sound proof storage unit, Smaltz rushed to him like a moth to a flame."

Angela whispered, "Detached reflection cannot be demanded in the presence of an uplifted knife."

"Judge, you said that a little while back. It's a good one for what white-hot panic does to you."

Angela paused, and I had nothing to fill the silence. Then she said, "In the end, we all did it for Melvin."

Peter said, "For Melvin and Madeline."

I said, "Here's to them, wherever they are."

Angela said, "They're with Oliver, of that I'm sure."

Peter asked, "Honey, who is Oliver?"

Angela laughed a happy laugh. "I'll tell you when we're alone and have some quiet time."

I thought, *I'm clueless about that one, but no need to crowd them.* "So long then, Judge, Peter. Give the girls a hug for me. We did this for them, too. Enjoy your Thanksgiving."

⚖

MY INSTINCTS HELD TRUE. THE BUREAU MIGHT have ordered up all the storage units camera feeds, might have figured out that the two dead men had a visitor, that the visitor set up the card game and knew about the murder-suicide, maybe even helped it along. But nothing ever came back around to me. Maybe whoever looked at it figured it all out, knew what I knew, knew I didn't kill them, just bruised them a bit, and they didn't dare open it up. Just too ugly.

I never worked on another case as a PI. I had been frugal, and the Bureau's retirement package is among the best. I bought a farm in upstate New York within a short drive of Cornell.

I, finally, did check on Rebekkah, found her, her long white hair, her smart face, especially with glasses. In the summer of 2012, she moved in with me. Her children and grandchildren all approved. I regale them with stories, mostly made up, of field work in the Bureau. Rebekkah's ex had long before lost touch with her family. He was a controlling brute and no longer cared to know them, be around them, when he couldn't control them anymore.

Every Thanksgiving, I call the Cornwells. I think they like our chats, always ask me to stop by if I'm in town, but I've never been back to San Diego.

Peter has gone to school for a Master's in Science and a teaching credential. He'll have those by the time the girls are too far along in school, and his schedule will match theirs.

At the end of 2013, Judge Angela Cornwell was invited by the Governor to apply for a position on the California Court of Appeal, and soon after by the senior Senator from California to apply for a Federal Judgeship. She declined both invitations. She asked the Presiding Judge to assign her the heavy criminal cases no other judge wanted, the kind Melvin had shepherded through the system called Justice.

Author Note to Readers

Immediately after the JFK assassination, both J. Edgar Hoover and President Lyndon B. Johnson ordered the FBI to not investigate for any Soviet involvement or CIA treachery. Both felt the United States must not become embroiled in accusations against the Soviet Union or its own agencies, and that Oswald must be portrayed as a psychotic loser acting alone.

Charles William Thomas, a career diplomat in the US State Department, died suddenly on April 12, 1971. News reports assigned the cause to a single gunshot to the right temple while he sat or lay in the upstairs bedroom of his home.

Thomas had been posted to the US Embassy in Mexico City. After the JFK assassination, he urged his superiors to open an independent investigation into Oswald's ties to Cuba and the Soviet Union, to the FBI's or CIA's advance knowledge of Oswald. Thomas wrote to both the CIA Mexico City Station Chief, Winston Scott, and then to the Secretary of State, William Rogers, urging a further investigation into the Oswald, CIA, and Soviet connections.

No one followed up. Instead, Thomas's superiors failed to promote him the next time he was up. The foreign service has an up or out policy. Those who are passed over for promotion are expected to resign. The Thomas firing occurred six days after he sent off his last memo.

Thomas kept up his contacts with some of those associated with Oswald, but he never developed what he hoped to gain or find. In his last years, Thomas was forced to work as a domestic for a wealthy family. For a detailed account with sources, see Shenon, P., *A Cruel and Shocking Act* (Henry Holt and Company, 2013).

Lee Harvey Oswald had been on the CIA's top secret "for eyes only" watch list from 1959 forward, one of only three hundred ever placed on the list up to that point.

I know of no Dallas Kennedy Task Force by that or any other name. Frank, the other named FBI agents, as well as all San Diego Superior Court judges portrayed, are fictitious. The statue of Justice outside the Aspen Courthouse is real, no blindfold and fully chromed.

The San Diego Superior Court complex has seen major upgrades. The fourth downtown main Superior Court was completed in 1961, a long low-rise building that spanned several blocks with traffic underpasses. Internal passages tied it to the jail. Old timers did speak of it as a high rise lying on its side. A newer courthouse and District Attorney office building, called The Hall of Justice, was finished in 1996, but the old courthouse remained in use. An internal passageway tied the new Hall of Justice to the old courthouse. In 2018 a third and even newer Superior Court was finished. Court reporters and transcription machines have been replaced by audio recording equipment. But law agency personnel can still enter without being screened for metal objects. Hallway cameras are now everywhere.

Many law enforcement agencies have lengthy procedures that must be followed before firing any line officer. During investigations for serious offenses, the transgressor is placed on the Rubber Gun Squad, a euphemism for busy work or no work at all and only allowed to carry "rubber guns" to fool the public.

San Diego, 2022

Acknowledgments

Special thanks to The Society of Former Special Agents. That organization circulated my need for help about FBI operations in Washington, D.C., in the 1970s. Soon after, several retired agents from that time and place volunteered to help me get the details right. Retired Special Agents Harold Gossett and Dennis Rasmussen responded to my questions on many aspects ranging from types of desks used and how files were kept, to dealings with Confidential Informants. Thanks to retired Chief Detective Joe Richardson. He set me straight on police procedures at one important crime scene. I did not cover every crime-related detail of this story with these professionals, so any errors that remain are solely mine, not theirs.

AUTHOR BIO

Raised on three continents by a single mother, G.J. Berger started his professional life as a naval architect/marine engineer soon followed by law school. He became a lawyer in San Diego and has shepherded many cases through the state and federal court systems. G.J.'s two prior novels, *Four Nails* and *South of Burnt Rocks–West of the Moon,* have received numerous honors and awards. His writing has received praise from Publishers Weekly, Kirkus Reviews, and Huffington Post. G.J. lives in San Diego with his English professor wife. Hence, any grammar errors are intentional. They travel to their two sons and grandsons as often as the kids will have them and enjoy scouting out locations that might yield new material and interesting characters for GJ's writing journey.

Made in the USA
Middletown, DE
24 April 2024

53451024R00179